C000054567

The Teller
Volume 2

John Clegg

Grosvenor House
Publishing Limited

The right of John Clegg to be identified as the author of this
work has been asserted in accordance with Section 78
of the Copyright, Designs and Patents Act 1988

The book cover is copyright to John Clegg

This book is published by
Grosvenor House Publishing Ltd
Link House
140 The Broadway, Tolworth, Surrey, KT6 7HT.
www.grosvenorhousepublishing.co.uk

This book is a work of fiction. Any resemblance to
people or events, past or present, is purely coincidental.

A CIP record for this book
is available from the British Library

ISBN 978-1-80381-475-9
eBook ISBN 978-1-80381-476-6

The front cover image of the Stretton Hills, as described
on page 349 and that on the back cover, showing Oswestry hill fort,
were supplied by a Shropshire based photographer,
Alexandra Preston. (Studio details available on the internet)

Dedication

Hannah and John-Joe

About the Author

Any reading the introductory material in the first book, were probably left wondering, why with such a love of history, I chose instead to read humanities?

Basically, I was young, London was absolutely rocking and I couldn't wait to escape from a small town on the Welsh Marches. The University of Surrey offered a place via the clearing scheme and I jumped at the chance. It was before the Guildford campus had been completed and so, as strange as it sounds, Surrey University was at the time, in Battersea.

Back in those days, although I had 3 good A level passes and 8 O levels, the latter didn't include a foreign language, a requirement stipulated by all universities offering a course in history. I was busy cramming for this when London called.

And as they say, 'The rest is history.'

I didn't burden the first book with this amount of detail, there was enough to explain as it was, but slipping it in now, clears that little matter up.

Preface

As promised, the Teller returns to the Iron Age hill fort (Old Oswestry) to relate more details of Vanya's life, plus how the original inhabitants of area between the present-day rivers Severn and Dee, coped with the incursion of those descending from the western hills, not only the first wave of liberators, but others driven out by the worsening weather at the end of the Bronze Age.

Acknowledgements

Darren Broome for giving an insight into the mysteries of iron working. Adrian Cottrell, who although not Welsh, passed on words he'd learnt to help with the story and also Colm O Cinnseala, who is Irish, speaks it fluently and passed on a few key words I needed.

Apologies to both the Welsh and Irish as I've tweaked those words, partly to simulate how they change over time, but also to enable English speakers to pronounce them.

Introduction

As with the first volume of the Teller, this book deals with everyday struggles of surviving in the late Bronze Age, made all the harder by two tribes now occupying the same small realm. As with most tribal, or even national histories, what compelled them to venture beyond home territory was the desperate need for food and raw materials. In this case, wheat, barley and iron.

The Teller again relates all in a slightly tongue in cheek manner, with a few sparks of humour thrown in.

Contents

Prologue

As promised, I'm returning to relate more about the life of Vanya. This time I took the easier route, being conveyed up the Habren river as far as Amwythig. I called in quickly to hire a horse, but managed to slip away before being forced to accept hospitality in exchange for the usual. I know it's my calling, but sometimes, I have to admit, maybe it's age, but I just don't feel like it. Just not in the mood. I'll make up for it when I return the horse.

But anyway, it's just as well I left when I did, for there came such a surge from the mountains, it would not only have made my fording of the river impossible, they tell me it even washed an upstream ferry away. I took the long way round, but even so, had to wait for the waters to subside, costing me two days.

As usual, I feel nervous, especially as the first part of the tale has a fair amount of everyday detail; how two potentially hostile tribes struggled for survival in the same patch of territory and although bloodshed seemed imminent, eventually managed to negotiate a system fair to all.

The wildest of those in the hill fort up yonder, would probably prefer it, if they had actually hacked lumps out of one another, but they will have to accept disappointment, for the basic background to the tale, even though not action packed, has to be explained otherwise none of the rest makes sense. I must try to think of a way of livening it up a bit, mind you, or it could mean an early exit, or a meeting with the water trough. What happens later in the tale should placate those of a more violent disposition.

That's strange, the whole bastion looks different. So many people swarming over the lower slopes. Grand works must be underway. It's quite amazing. At least half the community must be up there toiling away.

Oh here they come. My little welcomers. It really gladdens the heart to see such joy on their faces.

Part 1

Chapter One

"The Teller's coming!" a small boy gasped. He had beaten his two friends up the long slope of the entryway, sprinting up the path, a brown straight line between the palisaded defences bristling atop the steep earth banking either side. He gulped enough air to shout again and eyes wild, face shining with sweat, he pointed down the valley. People stopped what they were doing and families emerged from dark interiors. Their thatched dwellings, virtually filling the bastion's interior, were dotted about like massive burgeoning shaggy mushrooms and storerooms on their support posts had a jaunty look as if thoroughly pleased at having managed to sprout on what little ground remained.

Slowly a crowd gathered at the main east gate and the three boys raced back down the well-worn track to re-join their comrades escorting the Teller to his destination. Workers dotted on the mid-sections of the ringed defences stopped and stared. Some held iron picks, a few shouldered their iron-tipped wooden shovels, but the majority of men wielded trusty antler picks. Moving earth in the wicker baskets seemed to be a job for women and children. They all downed tools and descended like ghosts swelling the ranks of the young ones following the Teller's horse as it plodded, head low, slowly ascending the narrow killing zone, its palisaded sides now crowned by watching faces.

The Teller was mildly surprised at the all the attention. Recognising the ruddy faced official waiting to greet him, he slid wearily from his horse not wanting to appear vaunted in his presence. The man offered a hand and beamed a practiced smile, not at him directly, but at an imagined distraction, just above eye level away in the middle distance.

As he was led through the throng, all watched intently, silently peeling back to form a funnel. The sound of hooves' dull plod on soft mossed turf receded as the horse was led away to food, water and stabling in the lee of the palisade and the Teller, hurrying a few steps, caught up with the official, briskly leading the way towards the main hall. When attempting to explain, bad weather had delayed him, the man had merely returned an impenetrable stare. Even details of the Habren ferry being swept away, had made no impact. With the hall entrance looming ahead, he decided, 'Best keep a still tongue.'

Inside, with eyes gradually adjusting, came the slow realisation of the true enormity of the dining board. He had heard tell of it, apparently split from a forest giant and eying its girth dominating the whole width of the hall, he was filled with awe. Above, were the dark bulging shapes of hams, hung to cure along the length of a central beam and even higher, almost lost in the dimness, dangled looping strings of sausages and flitches of bacon. Central as always, a small fire had been lit, crackling expectantly, ready for the pile of logs to be heaved on later.

A small trestle table, near the hearth, was laden with bowls and wooden platters in precarious stacks. From an adjacent rack hung flesh-forks, ladles, skewers, chains and hooks, their crusty blackening contrasting with the rosy glints reflecting off wicked blades dangling in readiness.

Now used to the gloom, the Teller spotted an opening, far side and guessed that to be where the aroma of roasting meat drifted from. It reminded him, he'd not eaten since sunrise.

"We thought it would please you to be seated here." *The voice gave him a start.*

I am truly honoured.

"Well of course. You wouldn't have expected anything less would you?"

4

Before he could answer, that it wasn't quite his way to be living in such high expectation of preferment, the man swept past him. A servant had appeared in the main doorway and was obviously now of greater interest than his reply.

In truth he hadn't known what to expect. On his previous visit he had felt apprehensive as to how his style of delivery would be received, but had sensed on that final eve of the telling, it and the tale itself had in fact been quite well appreciated. He felt quite overawed now, however, on seeing he had been raised in status, not merely offered food as had happened previously, but deemed worthy of a place at the chieftain's dining board. He silently beseeched the spirits to grant him the gift of words powerful enough to warrant it.

He was led across the central rise of the fort's interior, all eyes following their progress to a strange shaped dwelling. It comprised of two circular huts joined by a central ridged roof. Below overhanging thatch there were the usual gullies to channel rainwater away, but where the central deluge would spout, was a water butt, mellowed at its leading edge by much usage and above the glisten of mud below, dark green moss gave way to a lighter hue, that blended in pleasantly with the pale riven front. It had been fashioned from a hollowed trunk, having a transom type board either end as would a boat. Eying it warily, the Teller wondered, 'Was its generous girth there to accept those unfortunates who failed to meet the chieftain's expectations?'

He couldn't remember seeing it, or the strange double hut on his previous visit and glancing around, noticed many other things had changed, but his attention was sharply brought back to the entrance as knuckles on the sounding board, rapped an urgent order for those within to ready themselves. The two ducked under the protruding thatched porch and proceeded into the gloom.

The couple had obviously been expecting him and both shot to their feet, smiled and gave hint of a welcoming bow. The woman,

5

removing an apron, briskly patted to straighten the front of her skirt and her man spread an arm of invitation to approach the fire, the heart of the house. At this point, having observed all was in order, the official reminding the Teller, as one would a forgetful child, they were to meet again later, gave all a hearty farewell and headed towards the doorway. There was a discernible sense of relief as the three watched his departure, ducking back out to become fleetingly silhouetted against the sunlight.

The Teller was led through the passageway into the adjoining hut and shown the section, curtained off for his exclusive use. His host, looking a little nervous, anxious to please, said he hoped everything would be found adequate and with a hint of a bow, retired. It was only now, the Teller thought he vaguely remembered the man, but seeing so many people on his travels, he couldn't be sure.

Against one curve of the wall stood a wooden bench, top burnished by nothing more than honest toil and dangling above, tools hung, neatly arrayed on a rack. There was a sharp pungency of cured leather and the hides hanging from beams led the Teller to surmise, the man of the house made his living by fashioning shoes. This was later confirmed, the man working in tandem with his eldest son, but apparently, the rest of his surviving children had moved on and now lived in various locations dotted about the valley.

Drawing the curtain aside the Teller was mildly surprised to see all his belongings had arrived before him, neatly stacked by the wooden cot, awaiting snug beneath the curve of thatch. A bowl of water had been placed on a shelf and refreshing himself, he resisted the impulse to groan with relief as the liquid cooled his face. A cloth for drying had been left folded on the bed. The coverings, turned back in welcome, had that tight-straightened, neat look that only women seem able to manage. A wave of relief surged through him. Over the ensuing few days, he had no need to worry about where exactly he was to rest his head. It was good to be back.

He re-joined his hosts by the fire. The man apologised for not having drawn his attention to a detail of huge importance. The Teller was led back to be shown a section of the daubed wattle that could be opened by raising the locking bars; an escape route in the event of something always feared in a building such as this; the thatch catching fire.

They returned to the hearth where a tasty bowl of hot pottage, slab of bread and horn beaker of sorrel barley-water had been put on offer. The liquid's sour hint cut through his thirst and the food itself was surprisingly commendable. A stool had been made available and from where he sat it soon became obvious many eyes were watching from the doorway. There were muffled sniggers then outright laughter as one child, who had obviously been pushed, struggled to reverse his forward motion, being keen to regain concealment. The shoemaker shouted, but the shrieks of delight mingled with the merest zest of fear, suggested the man was quite a genial soul.

"I'll try and make sure that doesn't happen again syr," *he said returning to his squatting posture.*

They're just children. They mean no harm. And please, there's no need to call me, syr.

"Very well, syr. I'll do as bid." *The man's eyes suddenly widened and a troubled look darkened his brow.*

The Teller turned to see a tall slender figure, enrobed in light grey linen, who on meeting his gaze gave slight glint of fellowship and his ethereal air on approaching the hearth, bestowed an almost spiritual aura. All rose in greeting, but rather than stepping forward as did their guest, the hosts seemed more intent on shrinking into the gloom, as if keen to appear as inconspicuous as possible. The fact that the stranger's white locks were constrained by the simplest of tight bronze circlets, identified him as the Seer. Being bearded made his blue glint of eye seem all the sharper.

Then came the thorny question, 'Had he met this worthy gentleman on a previous visit?' Logically he must have done, but as said, he encountered that many, from all strata on his travels, it was hard to say. Eying the man, he reasoned, 'Surely, one such as this would be remembered.' He could hardly ask, however. Slightly amused by the inner shudder, at imagining the look of affrontery at a previous meeting having been forgotten, he decided it best to say nothing and wait for a clue.

His mental debate was interrupted by, "I trust you have been made comfortable. Ah pottage I detect." *He glanced at the shoemaker's wife,* "Highly spoken of, I hear."

The lady gave a nervous smile and bob of appreciation.

Turning to the Teller, "I thought you might appreciate a tour of the fortress to witness the grand programme being undertaken."

The Teller thanked his hosts and left for an amble around the walls. It had been obvious on arrival, that the already substantial fortifications were being added to. A two-ring defence would soon be four. It was all very grand, but did beg the question, Why is the chieftain going to all this trouble when the existing banks and palisades are that impressive only a fool would command his forces to attack them?

The Seer smiled and answered, "I can trust you to be discrete?"

His enquiring gaze received an assuring nod.

"Well the answer to your question is threefold. Firstly, the work is being undertaken because there is the manpower and wealth to do it and secondly it is being done so hopefully, it won't be needed.

You look puzzled. I'll explain. You see, on completion, when the mighty defences are looked upon with awe, which believe me they will be, no aspiring chieftain will dare pit his forces against them."

On the verge of saying, 'I thought that was what I just said,' the Teller felt it wiser to keep a still tongue. Then on wandering further he remembered, You said earlier, the answer was threefold.

The Seer stopped, turned and with a conspiratorial squeeze of his arm said, "Now this is where I need your discretion." *He lowered his voice,* "I must admit, I shouldn't say it, but this massive undertaking is mainly a form of display, a personal statement of might and power. You have probably noticed similar works being carried out at other locations? Well this is intended to be bigger and better than every one of them."

Without really thinking; his jocular reply of, "What? Don't tell me he's going to all this trouble, just so he can say, 'Look at mine it's bigger than yours,'" *had escaped his lips. The words were out there, with no way of sucking them back in. The ensuing silence was intense and he felt the same horror as if having just stepped off a cliff edge.*

After some consideration, the holy man asked, "Are you saying what I think you're saying? Do you forget who you're talking to? You shock me! You deride our chieftain, your host! A mightier man the sun has yet to shine upon! Have you lost all sense of propriety?"

A long pause followed. This was not a good start to his visit. A deep colour and a feeling of panic were on the rise. Breaking the silence, faint noises of life carrying on as normal drifted on the breeze and at that precise moment he would have given anything to have been part of it.

Eventually, however, the Seer's glare softened, his eyes twinkled and he said, "But basically, yes you are right." The Teller thought he even detected the man chuckling softly to himself and with a brief glance aloft, gave a silent prayer of thanks to the spirits. Also, at this point came the certainty; no, they hadn't met previously. The empathy felt was a first-time experience, an instant bond not easily forgotten, but he still reproached himself for not guarding his tongue. He might not be so lucky a second time.

To gain a better view of the workings, they followed the walkway, in fact the fighting step, rear of the palisade that guarded one side of the entryway. Way below, using earth from the excavated ditches, two extra ramparts were being heaped up.. Between the original outer palisade and the first of the two new ramparts was a strange row of scooped-out hollows. The Teller resisted the impulse to enquire as to their purpose, thinking it best for now to maintain a low profile and let time heal his indiscretion.

They returned to the fort's interior, skirted the stone walled dwelling immediately to the south of the entryway and explored down the pathway, a twin to the one just ascended. More figures could be seen toiling on the new defences and between them and where they stood were five deep pits strung out in a row. Two men were hammering posts into the depths of the first.

What are those hollows for, *asked the Teller no longer able to hide his curiosity*; water?

"No not for water."

Yes, now I look again, that would make the water as available to your attackers as it would be for those being besieged. So, are they building work huts?

10

The Seer smiled and called down, "Our honoured guest asks, are you building work huts?"

The men paused, looked up and one cheerily replied, "Huts yes, but not exactly for working in."

Not for living in surely. Who would want to live down there?

"Them what don't have no choice," *came the reply.*

He doesn't mean prisoners, surely? *said the Teller.*

"Well in a way yes." *The Seer called down,* "Tell us. Who are you making such home comforts for?"

"Mister pig," *came the answer accompanied by a laugh.*

"But there's no way in or out!"

"Yes there is." *The man was clearly enjoying himself* and *went on to explain,* "We puts 'em in when they're little grunters and pulls 'em back out when thaim big porkers. Soon after first frosts."

"Surely that's difficult. Dangerous in fact."

"Not once the spikers have finished with 'em." *By way of demonstration, he put a clenched fist atop his colleague's head and made as if to hit it with his hammer.*

The Seer explained that sows would give birth to litters in sties soon to be built in the hollows, opposite side of the entryway and the young castrated boars and their sisters, surplus to breeding requirements, would be kept and fed in the deep pits below. Come winter, once dispatched, they'd be hauled up and butchered inside the confines of the fortress. A feast day to look forward to. It was calculated there would be enough cured meat, at each year end, to last through to spring.

The Teller shook his head and said, I must be truthful. If you had given me until the end of day, I would never have guessed pigs to be the answer. Water, work huts, some sort of shrine maybe, but nothing as mundane as pigs. But what happens in the event of a siege?

The Seer answered with a slicing motion across his throat. They continued their walk.

As they approached the main east gate, the Seer asked, "May I enquire what tale you will be treating us to this evening?"

Yes of course. It's actually nothing more than a continuation of what happened to Erdikun and his family.

"You say, nothing more than just a continuation. I find them a most remarkable family. Their talents seemed to spring out, as if from nowhere. I have to admit I spent many a long year studying to gain the knowledge I have now. Some of my students will never achieve the standard required to be acclaimed as, 'one who knows,' yet Mardikun, seemingly with no formal training, had enough innate ability to be regarded as a Seer even to the point of being able to predict the darkening of sun and moon. I find that incredible."

The Teller, realising this was what their little tour of the fortress had really been about said, I know it seems unbelievable, but such people do occasionally appear as if from another world. Don't ask me to explain how or why, all I am relating is the tale as it was passed down to me. I have complete faith in the details being true, otherwise I wouldn't relate it.

The Seer shaking his head sadly, said, "What a waste. What a sheer stupid waste. To tell you the truth, your description of his end, his murder, upset me for days after you left. It even gives rise to anger now, almost as if it happened only yesterday. What would I give to meet the likes of Mardikun?"

The two parted company and the Teller returned to his quarters, spending the rest of the afternoon on the bed that had looked so inviting earlier. It was the ideal place to relax and compose his thoughts for the coming evening.

The meal served later in the Great Hall was clearly in his honour and to his relief, was not a precursor to the grand affair he'd heard in full swing, on the inaugural night of his previous visit. The central hearth, with much bustle and urgency, was now being put to full use. Pots of various vegetables and relishes, sat black amongst the embers and above, merrily steaming, was the massive tribal cauldron. Surrounding the hearth, on their spits and spikes, looking disturbingly like roasting babies, glistened small plump carcases of various birds.

Broth was served in wooden bowls, but the cuts of pork and venison were eaten off slabs of bread as were the small roast birds that were seized with such relish. Salt to accompany the fare was passed down from a splendid bronze pot sitting in pride of place, centre board, before the chieftain.

The Teller, sitting straight-backed, glanced either side at the men eating. They slouched and with elbows firmly rooted to the dining board, attacked hand-held food with repeated bobs of head, resembling some sort of automatic contrivance that had had its timing broken. Beer was drunk in copious quantities, but not by the Teller, always mindful of the need to keep his wits about him. He also declined the tempting confectionaries that arrived to be handed round on wooden platters.

Those squatting around the room received broth, bread and beer, nothing more. The two royal hounds in fact were treated as if more vaunted, being thrown the odd tasty scrap, plus of course gristle and juicy bones. No swordplay followed; no trials of strength or girls dancing, but the official who had greeted earlier, arose from the vaunted place on the chieftain's right, to give a short speech of welcome. It was obviously a task, oft performed, for on completion, came a confident smile in expectation of vocal support and he was not disappointed. Quite a roar in fact. One, even greater, followed the Teller's short vote of thanks, leaving a rather rigid smile on the official's face.

Hearing instructions for his platform to be hauled in, the Teller stood and asked, Considering it's such a beautiful evening would it be in order for me to commence the tale from the fighting step of the palisade?

This would allow the likely inclusion of women and children, meaning the tale could flower a little and move on from relating the mere procession of cattle raids, battles and gore so relished by his warrior audience. He preferred to describe, actual lives of their ancestors, tales handed down to him from long ago.

The chieftain smiled, nodded his ascent and they all filed out, following in order of rank to where the sinking sun shafting between the houses, threw shadows as if from giants sloping their way down towards the east gate.

Chapter Two

All settled in a half circle, below where the Teller sat on the fighting step of the palisade, his nonchalant air disguising how he really felt. A bench was provided for the chieftain, his lady and main dignitaries, but the rest either sat on the grass or if a grown man or wishing to appear as such, crouched into a comfortable squat. The Teller waited for the women to settle their children, before standing to thank them all for such a heart-warming welcome and added, I am quite humbled. *He then raised his arms aloft as done on the previous visit and implored,* Bring me magic. The magic of words. Grant me the magic of words to paint pictures in the minds of these good people.

Now if you cast your thoughts back, *he began,* you might remember that Erdikun had led the Y-Dewis horde down from western hills to do battle against the tyrant, Gardarm. Their mood had been merciless following the murder of Erdi's brother, Mardikun. Gardarm, had at last received a fitting end and his corpse burnt, for the ashes to be cast into dark, bottomless waters lest any part of him should remain to taint the valley. What was left of his Seer was gathered up and unceremoniously given the same treatment.

The wild Y-Dewis were first welcomed as liberators and given shelter in the hamlets and outlying farmsteads scattered across the territory, but as you can imagine this only suited until the inevitable tensions began to creep in. There was a major difficulty of course, for other than sign language, they had no language in common. There were also differences in customs, beliefs, styles of dress and even some everyday things you don't normally stop to think about. The people of these rolling hills and valleys were grateful for their liberation, but began to make noises to the effect, could the Y-Dewis now kindly return from whence they came? They couldn't feed them forever and come the onset of winter, all feared the likely prospect of starvation. These warrior incomers, so wildly cheerful and powerful now took on a menacing guise, not helped by their passion for beer.

With the heat of alcohol coursing through the system heightening desires, no woman felt safe. None ventured out unless accompanied by a strong protector or hunting dog. Hanner Bara, previously only mentioned in dark mutterings by the female sisterhood, suddenly took on iconic status, for she was a ready outlet for unwanted male attention and in fact, came to be jokingly regarded as a most valuable first line of defence. We all know the lengths men are prepared to go to for the hint of female company, well here was a woman not only happy to disport herself for their pleasure, but in fact for a small consideration, willing to offer her very body as a receptacle for their desires.

There was a collective gasp from below, followed by low laughter from the men and shocked open mouthed, 'Did you hear what he just said?' *looks exchanged in the female section. An attractive lady, recognised from his previous visit, returned the Teller a narrow-eyed look as if in judgement, but within was a gleam of suppressed mirth.*

A gentle palms-down motion, brought calm and they settled for him to continue. Even their hunting dogs, with their wolf-guard collars bristling vicious spikes, proved menacing. If these weren't bad enough to evoke dark mutterings and avowals of imminent action, there were the goats. The odd goat was obviously kept by the locals for its milk, but the Y-Dewis brought herds of the things, down from the mountains, eating everything in sight. To cap it all the Skreela as the Y-Dewis were referred to when out of earshot, even commandeered a prime plot to sow some strange crop they weren't willing to share knowledge of. A crop you could neither eat nor turn into linen. Seeds were scattered from pods and as the plants flourished, blooming yellow, the locals, under threat of a beating, were ordered away from the very piece of land that had once been their own.

The Skreela chieftain, his family and tribal elders settled themselves on a spread of the most fertile land. It lay to the north of the fortress and had been tended for the exclusive benefit of the previous rulers by the wretches in thrall to them. A brook ran nearby, easing fear of drought and those who had slaved for the old regime now slaved for the new. The incomers had no tradition of living in hillforts and so other than having the one now in their possession, cleared of corpses and debris in readiness for ceremonies, tribal meetings and the regular market, for the most time it was left unoccupied. They did of course maintain the defences, appreciating having such a readymade refuge, plus they scoured the interior for Gardarm's legendary bronze hoard, but try as they might, found no sign of it.

Where we sit now, *said the Teller*, was virtually abandoned. Oh, I forgot. They did find one unexpected item of interest when clearing the place, but I'll tell you the details later. *He was also itching to add, the Y-Dewis, sensibly, had an aversion to living in a place with no immediate source of water, but didn't dare; remembering the warning he'd been given by the ruddy faced official, on his previous visit.*

First, you need to know about 'the fear.' It had always been rumoured that the Skreela boiled the corpses of their dearly departed and ate the remains, but an even greater cause for horror spread like a monstrous panic across the valley. Nobody knows how these things start, but once they do, they fly like a contagion with no regard to plausibility. What if these incomers had brought the silent death with them? You will have all been told, that back in the dim mists of time, our ancestors settled here from far-off-lands beyond the sea. We came as farmers and were welcomed. We brought new ways but also respected the traditions and beliefs of those who dwelt here at the time. We even, it is said, revered and embellished their monuments, the circle stones.

Then the silent death swept the land. The very people who had made us so welcome started to die, right before our very eyes. Nobody knew the reason why. Whatever it happened to be, the killer blight didn't seem to affect us, just those native to these shores. They say for every two full hands of people, *the Teller, closing both raised palms to leave just one forefinger erect, continued,* only one survived at most. In some valleys all lay bloated and rotting, in others, a handful of those still clinging to life, emerged like the walking dead. The silent reaper had struck them also, but for some mysterious reason had not killed them. So, the fear was, did these Skreela now bring a new form of silent death with them?

Yes, I know what you're thinking, it's irrational. The two tribes had already been inter-trading for generations; they met four times a year at the Feasting Site and on occasions even intermarried. So why would they suddenly be disease carriers? But the people were frightened and a frightened people are apt to believe anything. Panic was probably fired by the realisation they had ousted one lot of rulers, only to allow in a wild tribe that had the frightening potential to be even worse. As said, terrified folk tend not to think rationally and are ripe for being swept along on the strangest flights of fantasy. A few rose above those fears and suspicions, Erdi of course being one, but generally a sense of hysteria lurked ready to be sparked into acts of violence.

With now belonging to neither side, Erdi and his family felt caught up in the centre of all this. He had initially been welcomed back a hero, but soon sensed the mood changing. Nobody was yet saying it to his face, but he could tell when folks fell silent at his approach, he had been the subject of discussion, with the implication being, all the problems had stemmed from him. Which in a way of course they had, but were they now suggesting, life had been better under the old regime? Better under the insane, Gardarm? Yes, he and Mardi had brought the knowledge of iron back with them from the south, but that knowledge would have eventually crept in anyway. Stopping it would have been like trying to hold back the tide or the spread of the silent death they all feared of late.

He and Vanya still felt extremely raw after the loss of Mardi and were drawn ever closer as a result. Their mother, Mara initially had her mind taken off the tragedy as she and Inga were fully occupied tending the wounded, not least the item of interest I referred to earlier, found when clearing the fort's interior. Inga's zeal was sharpened by the fact the work gave blessed relief of time away from her husband Dommed, who had become withdrawn of late. He hardly said a word, but when he did, his utterances were laced with bitterness.

Penda, who had always been the ruling voice of their small community was still actually there in person, but almost as if afflicted by the same doom-laden sickness invading his neighbour, was absent in spirit. Something had changed in the man and he often glowered alone beset by black moods he refused to talk about. At first, he seemed strangely oblivious to the loss of his youngest son, then one day, reality suddenly hit; Mardi would never be coming back.

His hatred towards the former overlords seemed to transform into a loathing of all in power. To him, they were all the same. Then when told his family no longer had exclusive fishing rights, awarded way back in the time of old Tollan's first arrival in the valley, he seemed to go into rapid decline.

The Y-Dewis chieftain had declared, the fish belonged to everyone and despite Dowid, Erdi's uncle if you remember, vehemently reasoning against it, the ruling stood. Dowid had argued, that without proper management there would soon be no fish left to fish, but it had fallen on deaf ears. He didn't heap blame on Erdi, the one indirectly responsible for their massive change of circumstances, he wasn't the type, but did say he couldn't see the point of battling on. With the future being so uncertain and with his son Yanker now living with the tribe that ruled from Y-Pentwr, he declared, he and his family might as well move east to join him.

Mara, absolutely distraught at this decision, implored her sister-in-law to reason with her husband, but to no avail. Erdi did his best to coax his uncle to reconsider, reminding him of hunting trips; their little encounters regarding fish over at Five Pools and down on the Habren, but even with those memories drifting back, it brought naught but a faint smile. He was asked, 'Had he forgotten how they had laughed? How their sides had ached at the hilarity of their first attempt at capturing young boar?'

"Yes, fond memories," he had answered, "but those days are over now. You've got new lords to bow to and I can't see much good coming from it. Maybe they will rise you high, you who have lived amongst them, inciting them to topple that madman, but will they really favour you? What sort of leader rewards one who has brought such good fortune to his tribe, by taking away his family's established rights? Did the man not realise, those who manage the pools are none other than your father and uncle?"

Erdi of course, had also been stunned by the injustice and replied with no great conviction, "When he made that particular pronouncement, I'm not sure he realised he was punishing the very one who had helped him most. That's another reason why I need you here. I feel isolated. Your support would help right wrongs such as this. They have to understand our ways of working here. I'm worried, Dowid. If we don't sort out a system soon there's bound to be more bloodshed."

"Look Erdi, no man could have tried harder to reason with them. Yet where did it get me? They just stared back, blank faced and I was given the beggar's farewell. Couldn't even get to see the main man himself."

"With you here Dowid, a voice of authority and common sense, I could assemble a group to apply pressure when needed. If enough of us stood together they would have to listen."

20

His uncle's mind was made up, however. He and his family were soon to leave and that was that.

At this point Dommed happened to make a gloom laden appearance. Dowid eying him, turned to Erdi and gave a look of, 'Need I say more?'

Their intended destination, the bastion that became known to the locals as, Y-Pentwr, was not the title its actual occupants used. Y-Pentwr was a cymry term which when translated meant, the pile or heap. It referred to a prominent hill that rose abruptly from flatlands southeast of Habren Ford. As you know people often have irreverent terms for their neighbours as regards such things as eating preferences and sometimes even have jokes about them being hilariously stupid and so when their neighbours began assuming elevated notions, based largely on their lofty location, someone came up with the name, The Heap and it stuck. Although taken for granted now, nobody would have guessed back then, that the seat of power for all surrounding territories including your own, would be located there. Also the name Y-Pentwr, as I said, a cymry term, is a good illustration of how the two languages, even at that early stage, had begun to intermingle, eventually becoming one.

Going back to domestic troubles besetting Erdi, they didn't end with his father's black moods and his uncle's imminent departure. If you remember, the third family there was dominated by Dommed, who was not only now a changed man, but openly hostile. When not in Dommed's presence, his wife Inga and daughter Talia were like their old selves, but as soon as he appeared, their manner changed completely, for basically, they were petrified of him. To add to the prickly atmosphere, Penda and Dommed were barely on speaking terms. Their once close community was fast resembling a garment coming apart at the seams.

He felt extremely worried about the strain this was putting on his wife, Gwendolin. Basically, apart from Erdi's family, all those settled west of Elsa's ridge were strangers to her. From her brief time living amongst them, she knew the Y-Dewis better than these who supposedly, were her own people. At first, some of her old Y-Dewis friends came calling, but Penda soon put a stop to that. Although lonely, she found her own company preferable to being drawn into family friction, but the feeling of isolation had turned her into a wraith-like figure and that beautiful light no longer glowed in her eyes. She knew Erdi was valiantly shielding her from the worst of his fears regarding inter-tribal wrangles, but stories leaked back and she never dared venture alone beyond the palisade walls.

Those fears and tensions seemed to blow in on the wind and the threat of violence lurked just below the surface of all tribal interactions. It would only take one small incident for it to erupt. Erupt and shower fire and destruction like those legendary mountains in far off lands. Then the blame would be laid at her husband's door.

Erdi also worried for his son, Deri. He was still only tiny, but somehow had caught the mood of the place. His tottering approaches to his grandfather had received nothing but growls and one day, looking up with a worried look, he'd asked his father, "Why Dommed not like me?" The tiny lad, who should have been out playing in the sunshine, instead wore a look of constant worry and followed his mother about like a new-born lamb. A number of times when returning for something forgotten, she'd almost tripped over him and then had had to chide herself for the angry outburst at him always being underfoot.

Then grandma Vana went missing. They looked for her everywhere. Night was descending fast and the mood was becoming desperate. Clouds were billowing up in the west and they gave little for her chance of survival without shelter. It was Vanya, who on impulse, walked up to the ancient cairn and found her. The cairn was a relic of the old religion, but their family still made use of it. The remains of Tollan and Mardi had been interred within. Also, all those tiny mites 'that had not managed to stick,' as the saying went, in an attempt to put a brave face on infant mortality.

At first when drawn towards a shape lying in the grass below the mound, it seemed too minute to be a body. It looked no more significant than a discarded item of clothing. But it was in fact Vana. She gently touched the old lady's cheek expecting her to stir, but the skin was cold, almost clammy to the touch. Vanya, spotting the tiny wooden box her grandma still clutched, managed to, very gently, prise it free. On sliding the lid, she saw it still held a lock of Mardi's hair. The first of his curls Mara had clipped off as a keepsake. Then, those being happier times, Penda had whittled the box to contain it.

Vana was cremated and her bone fragments placed in a funerary urn. This was interred alongside the ashes of her late husband. It felt as if their once charmed community was now blighted.

When after what was considered a respectful period following such a death, Dowid and Morga announced they were finally departing. An immovable sense of futility and emptiness descended. All were tearful, but there was no last change of heart, their minds were made up. Erdi asked, to please give his cousin Yanker his best wishes and to say he was desperate for his help. Watching them leave he felt completely isolated and wondered what he had unleashed. They hadn't said it, but their leaving was a direct result of what he had set in motion.

Then into this mood of desolation rode prince Bonheddig and the reason for his visit didn't lift their spirits any. He was of course pleased to see Vanya, which was mutual, but after her initial thrill at his unexpected arrival, came the slow realisation, something had changed. With Erdi's status now raised to that of, honorary warrior, she was now deemed a worthy match for the young prince, but she could just sense, something was not right.

With him having two elder brothers he was not expected to rise to the title of Y- Dewis leader, thus was spared the obligation of a royal marriage. These were usually arranged as contracts between tribes, rarely becoming love matches, but regarding his marital intentions, although not requiring a contract, there were still certain prerequisites to be met and he carried the burden of one of them with him that day.

This is what Vanya had sensed all along. She knew something had changed. It didn't seem right at all. Pulsing with apprehension, she listened as Erdi translated parts not fully understood, but the conversation had just gone round and round to nowhere in particular. She guessed the ramble was to soften the blow of what was to come. Or perhaps the prince was too nervous to deliver that blow. Finally, plucking up courage and with heart pounding, she dared ask, "Alright, you'd better tell me. What's the matter?"

Heddi, with colour slowly deepening, attempted to pick through the logic and somehow dress up the reason for having been sent.

"You've been sent!" said Vanya with alarm. "You didn't just come here to see me, you were sent?"

Unfortunately, although the tribal elders had been highly entertained by the story of her miraculous rescue from the ends of the earth, the details of the saga now raised certain prickly questions and before endorsing her fitness to partner a prince of their realm, they wanted answers. They requested, she present herself and explain what exactly had gone on when in the clutches of the Tinners.

By this time Penda and Mara had appeared and were listening. Also Dommed hovered, sniffing a chance to add to the family's woes.

Vanya, affronted and stunned to the point all colour draining from her face, felt her mind reeling in confusion. Over time she had found a way of shutting out the horror of her ordeal, but now here was the very man she hoped to marry, digging it all up again.

Heddi felt ashamed at having to ask, but said the task had been forced on him by his father, Gwenithen, bolstered by insistence from tribal elders and his two elder brothers. You know the sort of adviser, *said the Teller*. They say in that weaselly way, "You don't think we enjoy doing this do you? We are only thinking of you. Of the integrity of the tribe." Also, the two princes weren't exactly enamoured by the fact their young brother was about to marry a girl of natural beauty, while they were expected to suffer a lifetime of misery, each bound to a woman they would never have picked, if given the choice.

Heddi looked aghast at the impact his request had made. It had hit like a body blow and couldn't have been worse, had he loudly proclaimed, she was not worthy of him. With the nightmare reeling once more in Vanya's mind, her eyes stared wildly and feeling entirely helpless, she was unable to prevent the returning trauma from burgeoning into an uncontrollable fit of shaking. Mara, her stern look blazing fire, flicked a sign of dismissal in the princes' direction. No respect for rank or status, he was to leave and be quick about it! She tenderly enfolded her daughter and led her back inside the house.

When Dommed, with a finger pointing meaningfully at his nether regions, chose this moment to sneer, "Huh! No need to ask what went on down in those southern parts!" Penda went for him with a knife and if Erdi hadn't been quick off the mark, would have buried it deep into the man's guts. He managed to pull them apart and with voice shaking, uttered, "Say one more word and I'll knife you myself!"

At this Dommed glared, but thought better of putting it to the test. Their once happy community had fallen apart. Erdi felt he could now no longer look on his neighbour without a loathing rising from deep within. What had changed the man so drastically? Or had this bile, now so obvious, always been there without him realising. Perhaps an insane jealousy had always lurked beneath the surface and until recently he'd managed to mask it.

Erdi went inside to comfort his sister and then wandered around to the barn to sit in the gloom and think.

Chapter Three

Now, *said the Teller*, that's got all that stuff out of the way and I bet you have that itch of wonder, wanting to know what that item of interest was. The one they found when clearing the fort. Clearing all the dead and debris. Well to do that I'll have to take you back to the day after it fell to the invading forces. This is way before Dowid and family had left, by the way.

Remember this was back in those early days of delirium. The hated regime had just been toppled and not much thought was given to the question of, 'where shall we go from here?' Men of both tribes worked together sweating out the previous night's beer and cider. It had been quite a celebration. The huts damaged during the battle had been completely laid waste in a drunken frenzy. Now all needed clearing up. Serviceable timber was stacked for future use and the debris was added to a huge pyre heaped on the Arrow Field below the fortress.

Women, as they do, continued tidying after the men had considered the job finished. They also assembled neat piles, stacking weapons and missiles, found strewn across the battle ground. If you remember, Mara and Dommed's wife, Inga, were amongst those attempting to bring order to the chaos. The corpses were stripped of anything useful and carted down by the men to be flung into the furnace. It was rumoured that a small number still clung to life, but this was mercifully snuffed before they too were swung up into the flames. The old order was going up in smoke and the sweet smell of burning flesh wafted up as a reminder to Erdi, that he alone now shouldered the responsibility for his people.

Those in power, those normally turned to in times of trouble, had been wiped out and apart from himself and Trader, not one of the tribal elders spoke the Y-Dewis' language. Even if in command of

26

such, none had had any previous direct dealings with the incomers or anyone else above village level for that matter and so in those early days were unlikely to have made a scrap of difference. Thus the reason for Erdi's haste, on hearing a commotion from over by one of the storage pits.

At last we're getting to it, *said the Teller with a grin.* A wounded man had been hauled from the depths and those doing the hauling were keen to add him to the inferno. The warrior was barely conscious and looked close unto death. Even though bloodied and filthy Erdi recognised the man and ordered those encircling to move back and give him air. He had no real authority other than the power of his demeanour, yet after an uneasy pause, they did as instructed. For the moment, it brought a stay of execution.

"We've been ordered to spare no-one," a ferocious looking Y-Dewis warrior said at last, looking anxious to get on with the task.

Erdi gently pushed grey hair back from the prone man's face. Yes, it was the crusty old officer who had fairly judged the slingshot competition years before and had also, so nearly intercepted them on the Habren.

Erdi looking up, reasoned, "Believe me, this is a good man,"

The crowd suddenly parted and the Y-Dewis chieftain, Gwenithen himself, stood with arms folded, surveying the scene.

Erdi repeated, "Believe me. Believe me, Sire this is a good man. Has there not been enough killing?"

After a long pause the mighty Gwenithen replied, "A commendation coming from the likes of you, I trust. Take him out of the sun and let the women tend his wounds. If he survives and can walk, he then has two days without let or hindrance to be from these valleys." Thus said, he left, returning to his carousing with a few chosen colleagues.

On Erdi's instruction, a section of wattle was brought over from a mound of debris and the old warrior gently laid upon it. Once safely in a hut's cool interior, he dared leave to go in search of his mother, hoping the magic of a woman's touch might save the man.

Mara didn't need asking twice and dropping everything, strode over, dress rustling, to see if she could assist. While she and Inga, carefully peeled back clothing to assess the damage, Erdi was dispatched to fetch her medicine basket.

Having made use of one of the fleetest Y-Dewis' ponies, he was relieved to see on his return, the man still clung to life. His plight had attracted a third helper, a Y-Dewis woman. How fast the mood to slaughter can turn to one of compassion. She looked as concerned as Mara, regarding the old warrior's plight, which was fairly understandable, for as sweat poured from reddening flesh, his eyes stared wide, as if in horror of being cooked from within.

Speed was of the essence. The basket's contents were rummaged through and they managed to force an infusion of willow bitter-bark into him. There were other medicinal preparations available extracted from plants such as yarrow, ivy, vervain, blackthorn and elder, but in the short-term, cooling waters seemed the best remedy to calm the fever.

The new addition to the ladies' of mercy, was introduced as Brialla. She was quite tiny, but had a proud, confident air and despite her lack of stature had a glare and tongue, sharp enough when riled, to put the mightiest man in his place. Erdi recognised her and remembered her ability to do exactly that from his time up in Y-Dewis territory. The glow of red when the sun caught her auburn hair should have been warning enough. He couldn't remember details of her man, other than he was of warrior class, plus there was vague recollection of a brother, close to or maybe even one of the ruling-elite. He had a feeling the old warrior, in the care of these three, now had a fighting chance of recovery. Even if the man had been fully conscious, he could not have imagined what he had helped set in motion. Erdi left them to it.

While all remaining wreckage was being dismantled, for stacking or burning, he took the trouble to survey the storage facilities. What he saw gave cause for both shock and worry. A number of the pits had been neglected, with their contents barely fit to feed to the pigs and on examining what they called 'the dry stores,' raised up on their wooden supports, he found at least half had been left to rot and were basically no more use, than for adding to the pyre billowing plumes of smoke below.

Those so recently revered and exalted, those who had impressed, as if in full control and beyond reproach, in reality had been criminally complacent and neglectful. Pomposity and exclusion of those likely to see the truth had masked the fact they had forsaken the most fundamental of their responsibilities; upkeep of facilities essential for survival. Bronze had been exacted in tribute from the people and for what? For something Erdi himself could have organised better, for nothing more than enough food to keep his family. Proof of how rotten the system had become was evident right there before him. Basically, he and the rest of the tribe had been made fools of. He gave a post a vicious kick with an instep. It was black, sodden with decay and the blow sent the small store lurching, to rest at a drunken angle. If all were to survive through to spring, a massive task lay ahead.

As regards the three ladies' administrations to the sick warrior, when the news spread, Y-Dewis warriors and local men carrying scars from the recent battle found their way to their door. Wounds were cleaned and dressed and the whole enterprise became quite a talking point. Mara and Inga had no mother tongue in common with Brialla, but experience they'd all gleaned from raising children, provided common language enough, plus mutual respect.

On the third day of receiving their tender care, the old warrior's shoulders were carefully raised, for him to be offered a little broth as if to an infant. It was about this time the door darkened and Mara looking round saw Brialla's brother for the first time.

Her heart did something it shouldn't have, considering she was a married woman and she'd tucked in a loose lock of hair, hardly realising she'd done it. Brialla, eyes narrowing, hadn't missed the giveaway sign and shaking her head gently, smiled to herself.

In those first heady days, almost to the point of it seeming unhealthy, Erdi noticed the two tribes appeared as if joined as one. It was fired by the drug of triumph and kept alive by drunken celebrations, but he knew it couldn't last. Such moods soon evaporate.

When at last it became obvious the crops planted would not yield nearly enough to see them all through winter, then there would be trouble. For that reason, the full knowledge of his discovery regarding grain reserves he thought, best kept to the chosen few. As the men worked like brothers, he watched, knowing once the daily grind of life returned, it only required one incident to spark off conflict and mayhem. It wasn't hard to imagine the scenario; a warrior's drunken fumbling of another man's wife; goats consuming spring wheat; the stealing of sheep for a Y-Dewis feast day; an incomer claiming more land than allotted; a clash regarding revered customs; mounted Y-Dewis youths flattening crops in a wild game of chase, ----- the list of possibilities seemed endless. The whole thing could erupt like an abscess.

He sought out a Y-Dewis advisor, hoping to impress upon him the need to act immediately, rather than when forced to. The man knew him of course, but that didn't explain his strange amiability and compliance. He nodded in agreement to such an extent Erdi wondered if he'd actually understood a single word. It was only at the suggestion, that maybe a curtailing of Gwenithen's celebrations might now be in order, that it became obvious he had. The change from sublime grin to thunderous frown was instant. He was clearly drunk, however.

Erdi had the feeling of being the only sane man in the contagion of madness. Somehow a meeting had to be arranged between the tribes. If things were left to drift without basic rules set in place, they were inviting disaster.

Realising the subtle approach was getting him nowhere, he ignored the man's protestations and as he had done once before up on the Feasting Site, pressed on to see the chieftain himself. Feeling emboldened by the fact circumstances warranted it, he marched into the midst of the celebrations, to be met by instant silence.

The revellers stared open mouthed and couldn't have looked more astounded had he jumped in amongst them, wild-eyed, stark-naked. Gwenithen peering at him, as if waiting for two fuzzy outlines to become one, suddenly roared out that Erdi should join them in a drink. This could hardly be refused under the circumstances and he found himself feted for his audacity.

He of course accepted the invite, for what else could he do, but wore a most uneasy smile, for rather than putting an end to the revelry, he now found himself in the thick of it.

Once things had calmed a little, he took courage and asked a nearby worthy, 'Would it be possible to put a suggestion to Lord Gwenithen?' The chieftain cocked an ear as Erdi's request was passed on and all watched in amazement as he, ranking no higher than warrior remember, was enthusiastically invited, not only to join the great man, but to actually sit beside him.

Eventually, having had need to put the same argument three different ways, Erdi, when finally managing to penetrate the chieftain's befuddlement, was amazed at the success, for Gwenithen not only beamed understanding, he actually gave enthusiastic support for a meeting to be held to discuss tribal issues.

He left holding mixed feelings. Yes, Gwenithen had agreed to the meeting, but there was no guarantee he'd remember on waking, nor have had his mind changed by jealous advisors. As Erdi had sat up there with the great man, their lowering looks had not gone unnoticed. In Y-Dewis territory, having useful knowledge of a land they coveted, he'd been welcomed amongst them. They found his humble manner, his limited knowledge of tribal customs and ways of doing things, charming and amusing. Down here in his own territory, however, Erdi knew he would be viewed as a threat.

He was therefore mildly surprised, when next day confirmation was given, the proposed gathering was definitely to go ahead, being timed for the evening of the following day. Erdi and Dowid represented their family. Even though his departure was imminent, Dowid had thought it was the least he could do for his nephew. Dommed wanted nothing to do with it and Penda glowered alone at home in his dark unapproachable mood. "What's the point? They're all the same," he kept saying.

Trader reluctantly turned up, politics not being high on his list of interests and strangely, his wife Gwedyll, who of course had a foot in each camp, chose to stand alongside Mara and Inga rather than amongst her own people. Many others from the home tribe attended, even two that certainly hadn't wished to; Blade's parents, dragged there on account of them having been complicit in Mardi's murder. It was Blade's father, in fact, who had rushed to the fort with news of Tollan's death and the likelihood of Mardi attending the funeral.

Donda, their daughter, hovered, watching nervously from a distance and the small innocent at her side, staring with mouth half open, looked horrified by the question he dare not ask.

The meeting was not at all what Erdi had had in mind. He had envisaged a meaningful discussion for the mutual benefit of both tribes, but what materialized was not much more than a list of proclamations with him appearing entirely complicit with each of them.

Firstly, Gwenithen gave thanks for the assistance given in wiping out the tyrant and all those upholding his regime. This was a good start and Erdi felt quite comfortable translating and let's be honest, even slightly elevated, for the chieftain, almost with a look of deference, remained silent as he passed on what had been said. He kept it simple, not having sufficient command of cymry to understand every word of the high blown rhetoric enriching the original version.

As he listened to the second point, however, he began to feel thoroughly ill at ease. A plan would be drawn up to initiate the settling of Gwenithen's people. Relating this brought a definite stir from the crowd. Then when the chieftain thanked his new subjects for being prepared to put up with the few hardships this was likely to cause, Erdi, translating the words, felt completely traitorous and watched horrified as the mixture of worry and anger rippled through his people.

On the third point, regarding the grand tour of the whole territory, undertaken to assess possibilities for land clearance and drainage, he felt a strange out of body experience, as if observing himself doing the translating, a person he hardly recognised. That person proclaimed, 'a record will be made of existing resources, the population will be counted, (a thing never done before) and other details will be gathered, necessary for the plan of settlement.'

He now actually began to fear for his safety and awaited the fourth pronouncement with trepidation. With relief, he realised it was in fact, benign; thus the telling of, 'Once the interior of the fort has been entirely cleared of wreckage and all made good, the local market will be allowed to re-commence,' was accompanied by the feeling, he was now at last re-entering his own body and that the mood around was softening slightly.

Then came the announcement of the fate of the warrior Gwenithen had spared, lone survivor of the garrison. They were told, that if the man survived, once able to do so, he had freedom to leave and any attempt to hinder his progress would be punishable by expulsion from the realm. If not beyond the bounds within the two days allotted, however, the man would be put to death.

As the severity of this last pronouncement sank in, Blade's parents were hauled up for judgement. Three witnesses stated the case against them and their new lord, on lending an ear to Erdi's translation, conferred with his Seer, before passing the entire matter over for the holy man's judgement.

A tremor passed through the Y-Dewis ranks. They knew what to expect. All were in dread of the living death. As expected, the Seer, who alone had the power to intervene between spirit world and mere mortals, raised his arms and as the pair quaked before him, made the following declaration. 'From that moment forward, they would be denied all access to his powers. They would be without his protection, outcasts and must face the potential horrors of the spirit world alone. Any found helping to ease their plight would share their fate. From that very moment they were barred from their own smallholding. They were non-people.'

Jeering followed their stumbling departure. Supporting each other, they swayed from sight as if their very bones were turning to liquid.

Erdi, when living amongst the Y-Dewis, had been told of this sentence feared above all else. Some had been known to sicken and die following its pronouncement. He was stunned to see the effect it had had on two of his own people and with him having translated, it gave a slight sense of retribution on behalf of his dead brother.

He mentioned to an official, there was a daughter to consider, who in his opinion was blameless. The man conferred with the chieftain and Donda was summoned. Looking upon the young woman, they judged her to be of the right stock, good for breeding. She was told she could either join her parents, who would surely now be forced to leave as beggars, or remain for her to be allotted a suitable partner. Even though the family land was to be re-allocated, she would not be left without shelter. She and the child would be bound into the care of a fighting man, if such a man were to prove willing. A few necks craned to get a better look at her.

Before the grand tour got under way, another thing of note happened. It came about as a result of Erdi visiting the old warrior, anxious to know his state of recovery. The man was still weak from his ordeal, but well enough to struggle into a sitting position. Eying his visitor sternly, he said, "When I saw you disappearing into that flood back on the Habren, I honestly thought that would be the last I'd see of you. Far from it. On you go, on down to the ends of the earth and come back with your sister, we thought we'd never catch sight of again. For a quiet lad you seem to go to extraordinary lengths to do the unexpected. Even when it comes to the fate of an old warhorse like me. They tell me all are finished, done for."

Erdi nodded.

"You couldn't just let me go quietly along with the rest of them, could you? Oh no, you decide it's me alone that's to be saved! Knew I could never trust you!" Suddenly reaching out, he pulled Erdi into an embrace, hoping the glisten of tears would not be noticed.

When he had calmed a little, he said, "Look there's something important you should know."

"Where Gardarm hid his bronze?"

He shook his head. "No, listen. I think I'm the only one left alive who knows where Prince Aram lies buried."

He declined to give details as to how the prince had met his end, only saying he'd had no part in it. Erdi listened carefully to the directions given. He needed to, because as you know, it doesn't take much forest to become lost in, let alone lose a body in.

The following day, guided by the man's instructions and helped by one of the hounds, Erdi found the grave. It had been little more than a hurried scraping which had allowed wolves, lynx and ravens to make off with much of the lower carcass. The late prince had been highly respected by the Y-Dewis leaders and on being told his grave had been located, a work party was dispatched.

They were instructed to follow the same protocol they would have done, had Aram been one of their own. The Seer arrived to make a humble plea for his soul. It was felt, there might yet be time to harness that mysterious essence, the tribe revered. Aram was to be given the same passage into the next world as if he had been one of the Y-Dewis royal line. The power of the man's spirit would therefore always be poised in readiness. There to answer the call, in time of need.

On being told all was in order and that a suitable tree had been chosen, the Seer gave his blessing and a prayer of thanks to the spirits for its provision. It was felled and then hollowed to such a degree, the trimmed sides stood barely the width of an axe haft in thickness and the structure, long and trim, gave no hint of the craggy look it had once had. Using wooden boards wedged into grooves, rendered watertight by moss and tallow, the ends were sealed. Aram's remains were placed inside, the top was covered for obvious reasons and the wooden container was hauled up to where a spring issued from the hillside. Here, it was filled with water and a fire lit. Heated stones were immersed to boil the water and a cover placed to keep all simmering.

Erdi was present to witness the strange ritual. A pit had been dug near the source of the stream and accompanied by chanting, Aram's skeletal remains apart from skull and upper arm bones were reverently interred and a libation made of the boiled waters and rags of stewed flesh.

With hindsight It would have been wise to have had some of his people in attendance, on account of strange rites such as these being mangled and misconstrued on the retelling, mushrooming into a fabulous unsettling rumour when spreading across the valley. Eventually that rumour becomes accepted as truth, for the people to avow, "Yes! The Y-Dewis do boil and eat the remains of their dead. A friend of mine has a friend who has seen them doing it!"

Aram's skull and the two arm bones were wrapped and borne in reverence, to the fortress for the final cleaning and loving application of wax. The incantations accompanying this meticulous process sent a chill down Erdi's spine. A small shrine, dedicated to the prince was constructed and his bones interred.

Meanwhile, whilst still pliable, courtesy of the boiling water it had contained, the hollowed trunk that had aided the revered man's entry to the nether world, had the last semblance of its curves straightened, with all held rigid by two thin oak braces wedged across its width. Once the ends had been re-boarded and sealed, what had so recently been a tree trunk now stood as a long, pale, straight-sided trough and was taken down to the meadows to be used as such. It was rumoured that cattle availing of its liquid during pregnancy gave birth to the finest of calves.

The old warrior, now fit enough to leave, was allowed to pay his last respects at Prince Aram's shrine and Erdi, accompanying him to the base of the fortress, was given, not emotional thanks, but a penetrating look and nod of respect. The Y-Dewis had gifted two day's provisions and Erdi was greatly relieved to hear the man had managed to walk safely beyond their southern boundary before time allotted had elapsed.

Following this came the grand tour.

Chapter Four

Erdi had vainly hoped for the tour to be a subtle affair, but as it turned out vain was more apt when applied in its other sense. The old chieftain's coach was drawn out of storage, the Y-Dewis wore their finest attire, horns proclaimed their advance and banners displayed their effulgence. Where it would have been wise to blend in and show a little humility to the people whose land they now needed for survival, they instead paraded as overlords. Worse than that, thrust into the vanguard, absolutely essential as an interpreter and guide, was Erdi. This should have been a job for a prince or high ranking official. These had all been turned to ashes. Failing that it was a job for a village elder, but they had declined and worse, Erdi sensed they viewed his isolation with a great deal of interest.

In desperation he had turned to Penda, not expecting much success, but potentially it had a double benefit; endorsement of his actions from at least one tribal elder and hopefully restoration of Penda's self-esteem.

"You brought them. You stick with them!" his father had said, before turning his back. With him having been one of the most avid, regarding the felling of Gardarm's regime, this seemed particularly unjust and left Erdi feeling completely betrayed and abandoned. His father hardly seemed recognisable, to the point it was frightening to witness.

Dowid who, if you remember at this point had not yet made his departure east, told Erdi, considering he would not be around to see the outcome, there was little point him becoming more involved than he already had been. Normally, he assured him, he would have gladly helped. Erdi did actually believe him.

There was no point trying to involve Dommed. Erdi wasn't prepared to give him the satisfaction of refusing, plus the chance to sneer something like, "Thought I'd see you choke in the end. You've bitten more than you can swallow, young upstart!"

Trader said he'd be glad to help in other ways, but please, he wanted nothing to do with politics.

So, feeling completely isolated and traitorous, Erdi accompanied his new masters on a tour of his homeland. He expected resentful looks and having been so far let down by all, wasn't let down in that respect.

Riders went ahead to warn relevant villages they were to receive honoured guests. The fact they had been chosen as hosts warmed the mood somewhat, but Erdi still suffered muttered comments such as, "Am I supposed to bow to you now, Erdi?" or, "I'm surprised you consider our humble abode worthy of your presence."

They visited all four corners of the realm, west towards the hills; north as far as Nant Crag; east above the marshes where the river Preye rises; over Elsa's ridge to Five Pools; south as far as the burgeoning settlement of Amwythig on the Habren; west as far as the Nwy – Habren confluence, before returning back north to the fort. Two days were spent exploring each section and those they descended upon, initially honoured at having been chosen as hosts, were thoroughly glad to see the back of them once their capacity to consume food and alcohol had been fully realised.

Land with potential for clearing or draining was recognised and the whole tribe had had the full might of their new masters impressed upon them, but above that, little was actually achieved. By the time the tour was complete, what exactly had been seen and precisely where, had become completely muddled. Conversations at times became quite heated, with contradictions flying as to where certain features lay. Even Erdi, who of course knew the territory, was shouted down. Then when daring to broach the subject regarding fishing rights by asking, 'In view of what he was doing for them, would it be in order to have them restored to his family?' Gwenithen had simply stared back in amazement. Conferring with his officials, he was told, "Yes it was Erdi's family who had had the rights revoked." This brought on such a fit of laughter, the man looked in danger of choking. When he had regained his breath, Erdi was told other rewards would make up for the loss.

'Yes, easy words,' he thought. 'Try telling that to my father.' When finally asking permission to be excused, he returned home in a mood of quiet despair and with an abiding memory, summing up the whole futility of the mission, haunting his mind. It was the Y-Dewis' insistence on using the coach. He had tried to impress upon them, taking it on such a trip would be nigh impossible, but it had been like trying to reason with overexcited children. After the main trail north gave out, they spent more time trying to make headway than was spent on the reason for being there. In the end sense prevailed and the coach was sent back.

It didn't stop them thoroughly enjoying themselves, mind you and the plan to record in detail all they encountered was completely forgotten. When Erdi had tried cutting through the revelry to point this out, he had been told, 'Just join in. Enjoy yourself. Stop acting like an old woman!'

He had landed himself in a desperate spot. How was he to enjoy himself with his own people eying so darkly? In Y-Dewis territory he had been respected and looked upon as an esteemed advisor. His knowledge of Gardarm's regime and fortress' layout had been invaluable. Here, however, although honoured with the rank of warrior and deemed worthy to bear a sword, it was in fact an empty distinction. He could feel himself being shut out; no longer invited to take part in day-to-day decision making. What was worse; those now excluding him were the very ones he'd have to reason with when attempting to gain a fair deal for his own people.

The Y-Dewis elders were probably highly amused at the way he'd been so easily pushed aside and given a sword to play with.

While he'd been touring the territory a rather strange thing had happened back in his own hamlet. When Mara had at last returned from her medical duties, what she had dreaded turned out to be not quite as bad as expected. The huge shadow of woe seemed to shrink once she plucked up courage to face it. She had dreaded the thought of home, with Mardi now gone forever, for rather than the cheery mood the little sanctuary had once evoked, it now brought a feeling of depression. The company of Inga and the bright little spark, Brialla had taken her mind off it. Helping the old warrior and the wounded had given a new purpose to life, but return she must and was actually pleasantly surprised at how bright and fresh Vanya and Gwendolin had made the place look. There were even flowers to welcome her home. Then to her amazement men started appearing at their door. They bore small gifts, things for the pot. They were the warriors she had helped. Her spirits were lifted as were those of Inga and Brialla. Helping the old warrior had opened up this opportunity and they decided, if required, they would happily do more of the same. As she glowed, Penda's mood darkened ever deeper.

Erdi returned to the normal round of chores, but with little relish. As he worked, he tried to untangle the problems swirling round inside his head. It wasn't his way to be obtrusive, but there seemed to be no other solution. If disaster were to be averted, he would have to force himself to take on that unwanted lead role. No-one seemed willing or able to help him.

Then his son appeared and asked, in his infant way, what was the matter? Erdi didn't answer in words. He simply picked him up, hugging and holding him close, hoping he'd not see his shiny blink of eye.

Then, late one afternoon Vanya appeared. He had been that deep in thought she had almost startled him. She was carrying a piece of hide stretched over a frame of four wooden laths, that formed a flat shape, tight as a drum. Its length was slightly greater than its width, a shape as yet, without a name. She asked him what he thought of it? Her latest venture. Using black, white and shades of ochre she had dabbed quite a striking pattern and Erdi told her it was strangely distinctive.

"But can you see what it is?"

"An interesting pattern."

"No. You're too close. Hold it further away."

He held it at arms-length. Suddenly his eyes widened, realising he was looking at a painting of a bear's head. Turning he said, "That's brilliant."

"You do mean it. You're not just saying it to be kind."

Something so simple had managed to lift his mood. He asked how she had achieved it?

Vanya told him, that first she sketched rough detail with charcoal and then added the colour. She would then let it lie and often, when going back to it, would find to her horror certain details, once thought complete, now cried out for further embellishment or even completely re-doing. The process could go on for days, before finally satisfied the creation was finished.

Looking rather shocked, he replied, "Vanya, that's exactly how I dream up stories!" She had put into words what his mind did without him realising. He continued as if thinking aloud, "The basic idea is usually quite simple just like your charcoal sketch. It's getting the detail right, filling in all the colour and making it real, that's what takes the time."

He found their conversation enlivening, exhilarating in fact and before he knew it, was telling her details of the ludicrous tour and

42

the plan he'd really had in mind. Then, he detailed the snags blocking the way to a solution. She basically knew the problems he faced, but thought it would probably do him good to open up, pour them forth. The sun was almost down by the time he'd finished and feeling some of the weight had lifted from his shoulders he thanked her.

"But I didn't do anything, Erdi."

"Yes you did. You listened. Actually getting the problems out of my head and into words seemed to somehow untangle them."

"You could do with a bit of poor Elsa's magic," she said laughing.

Was this why she had the dream? That very night Vanya dreamt of a lynx. It was quite a labyrinthine dream, trailing her through misty forests, but the gist of it was this: the lynx could talk and had said it came with a warning. It told her, 'When storms blow up from the south, put your trust in wolves.'

Erdi laughed when she told him. "A talking lynx? Was it male or female? I wouldn't believe a word a male lynx told me."

Vanya didn't laugh. Instead she grabbed his arm. "Erdi, I've just realised whose voice it was. It was Elsa's."

Erdi's smile froze. "Vanya! I've been that weighed down with the loss of Mardi and worries about the Y-Dewis flooding the place I'd clean forgotten about poor Elsa. Why don't we get her out of that ghastly place? Let's try dragging those waters. We could pull her up into the light. Her spirit will thank us. It's the least we can do."

"What? Actually go there? You know the warnings. Dire threats. Considering the supposed fate of those even daring to approach the pool, there's no telling what evils might be dredged up by actually fishing its waters."

"But that was a warning given by those now gone. Elsa wouldn't have feared its powers." Erdi laughed as he added, "In fact the main proclaimers of those warnings now lie at the bottom of it. At least, their ashes do."

"Oh, I don't know, Erdi. It's inviting danger. Demons could follow us home. Evil could stalk us and the family for life."

"I'll just have to do it on my own then." He didn't feel as confident as his words sounded.

The next day it rained, but that did give Erdi chance to prepare the net. Vanya helped. They folded it to form a bag and sewed the sides together. The mouth was held open by two staves, snake-tongued both ends by simple knife cuts and held in place by twine. To ensure it would sink they attached loom whorls.

"Make sure you tie those tight," said Mara looking on. "Don't want you losing them. What are you fishing for, anyway?"

They didn't dare tell her. It would have caused such alarm, she would have tried to put a stop to it.

The whorls were made from a strange soft metal excavated from mines located a good three days south. On refining the ore, a small amount of silver was often extracted as a side product. The base metal ingots were sent for trading down the pretty Temesa river, then north or south on the Habren. Erdi had been shown the mouth of the Temesa by Garner, south of where they'd been ambushed in the Habren Gorge. The metal bars, although extremely heavy, could be easily heated for pouring when molten, into moulds. It was particularly useful for weighting fishing nets and lines, but for the fishing of Elsa's remains, loom whorls came easier to hand that day.

The rain eventually stopped and when sure no-one was watching, for it wasn't the time of year to be snipping holly, Vanya cut enough to make three bunches from the trees standing either side of the path leading north from their hamlet. It was at this point a strange feeling surged and on returning with the prickly load, she told her brother she'd had a sudden change of heart and would accompany him to the Black Pool. Needless to say, he was mightily relieved.

With next day set fair they managed to gather a few provisions, without having to explain the reason for taking them. The holly, tied to Erdi's spear shaft, was slung across a shoulder and the net was carried between them along the trail leading to the black waters.

It was a pool lying to the north east and because of its evil associations, was rarely visited. Unless forced to venture near in pursuit of a stray animal, the locals stayed well away. The fens surrounding were treacherous and the pool itself, legend had it, was bottomless. Realm of the dark and evil. A punishment for challenging a Seer's accepted wisdom in this world, was to spend an eternity of torture in the next, meted out by the spirits that dwelt there.

On a mound where stood a holy grove, the distant waters on a sunny day could be seen to glisten, and like a syren's call, seem irresistibly inviting. But on a still night, watched by those huddled in terror, the souls of the condemned could be been seen hovering like ghastly spectres above the marshes.

On approaching the pool, they saw that a narrow wooden walkway barely visible beneath the tall grasses, wound off into the unknown.

Erdi led the way, his confidence boosted by the fact they were on a mission for good. In places, the structure, when lurching alarmingly under their weight, elicited gasps of fear and an instinctive need to cling to one another. Edging further, they both muttered, "Help us Elsa" and even had there been an audience, would not have feared ridicule for doing so.

On reaching the pool, they saw that the two end boards extending precariously out over the water were held by nothing more than bindings to the walkway. Vanya undid the sprigs of holly, passed them forward and Erdi cast them on to the black waters. They didn't sink. That was a good sign. They would hopefully ward off evil.

Erdi had always imagined two men at the pool's edge, flinging a poor condemned soul to sink to the depths, but now realised they couldn't have done, as there wasn't the room. The bodies must have been dragged along the walkway, weighted with stone and then simply heaved or booted off the end. So not even given a dramatic entry to an eternity of torture. Completely ignominious in fact. As yet, he doubted, anyone would have attempted the task they were about to and the arrangement of end boards didn't look in any way designed for the purpose.

Vanya stood back to give Erdi room to swing the net. It splashed and sank. Eventually the tethering rope went slack and floated snakelike on the surface, proving the pool wasn't in fact bottomless. He edged to the very end of the planking, that bowed precariously under his weight.

"Careful, Erdi! Mind you don't slip!"

Gently testing its springiness, knowing it would frighten her, he half-turned and muttered meaningfully, "Vanya,------ if something from down there suddenly yanks this rope---------- run!"

"Don't Erdi! I'm scared enough already."

The net had snagged something and he carefully eased it back in. A shining black shape resembling horns of a devil quivered above the surface.

"Ah! What is it? Let the rope go, Erdi!"

He was on the point of doing just that, when he realised it was only ancient branches he'd dragged up. They were disentangled from the net and flung aside so not to become caught a second time. It took a number of attempts before Erdi was able to say with confidence, "We've got her! This time it's Elsa." He didn't know why. He just somehow knew it was.

He drew the net in and as it angled its way up, something dark caught within could be seen rising through the brown soup of surface liquid. A cool breeze rippled the pool. Reeds silvered and swayed as if some invisible sprite had weaved amongst them. Erdi jumped at Vanya's firm grip on his arm.

Both peered. They had snagged a body, but it was only partly netted. Erdi tentatively pulling in with one hand, forced his spear shaft against whatever it was, with the other, trying to retain it in the net. Almost within grasp, the sodden weight when clear of water caused a disintegration and a large portion of their catch, exuding large wobbly bubbles, disappeared to be reclaimed by the murky depths. What remained was pulled alongside the walkway and the whole thing hauled up from the reeds. As water oozed from the rotten fabric, they stared in awed silence.

Finally Vanya whispered, "How will we know if it's Elsa?"

"It is, Vanya. That's Mardi's jerkin. She was wearing it when the hounds took her."

They carried the net between them to solid ground. Gently prising apart what resembled blackened fish skin, they found, rib, spine and arm bones, the latter still trapped in the sleeves. Lifting the soggy mess to investigate beneath, they both recoiled and gasped at the sight of Elsa's skull, picked clean by eels.

Both then sat and pondered. How were they to lay the revered lady to rest? They abandoned any notion of dredging for the rest of the corpse. They already had where heart and spirit would have resided and deemed that sufficient to free her from evil. They decided on traditional cremation, but her skull would be spared the flames, to be enshrined hopefully, in the same manner as the Y-Dewis had honoured Aram, thus giving her a double chance of salvation.

They built a small funeral pyre and reverently laid Elsa's remains upon it. Along with the skull, one rib bone was kept back. Sharing a smile of satisfaction at Elsa's spirit being liberated heavenwards by the plumes of smoke, they returned home warmed by an inner glow.

Late next day they returned to the ashes, still smouldering, but cool enough around the edges to rake for surviving bones. These were fragmented to be placed inside the small funerary urn. Finally, when the centre of the pyre was raked over, the exposure to air brought the fire softly crackling back to life, its smoke causing eyes to water.

"Stop it Elsa!" said Vanya laughing, "We're trying to help."

When satisfied they had all her remains, they walked up to where a spring oozed forth on the western slope of Elsa's ridge. It was the source of the brook Erdi and Yanker had had to steel themselves to cross when up there exploring so many years before. The ground was soft and using an antler pick and hands to scrape the earth, a small pit was quickly dug. Elsa's urn was placed within and the hole covered over. The location of the grave was disguised using a spread of leaf litter and they stood silently holding hands, each lost in their own particular memory of the revered earth mother. Finally, after laughing at the fact they both blinked back tears, they turned for home.

Now they needed Heddi's help. On his next visit to see Vanya, one prior to the visit that had caused such family anguish, he was told the story of Elsa and her magical powers. Enshrined, she would ward off evil and guard against hostile incursions in a manner even more powerful, than that of Prince Aram.

Heddi, gazing on Elsa's skull with awe, proffered fingertips, but on touching, they jerked back as if shocked by some strange force.

He needed no more convincing and left to entreat with his father, Gwenithen the mighty, that Elsa should be given the same veneration as had been offered Prince Aram.

They were fortunate. Not only did the chieftain immediately warm to the idea, he also thought it politically wise to honour the memory of a lady who had meant so much to his new people. A shrine was built alongside that of the late prince and Elsa's skull, having received the obligatory cleaning and waxing was lovingly placed within, accompanied by spine chilling incantations ringing out across the valley.

So, *said the Teller*. Elsa had been rescued from an eternity spent in the clutches of evil. The news did eventually leak out that her ashes had been interred at the site still known today as Elsa's Well and people journeyed there to partake of the waters. One man claimed he had dragged himself to the venerated spot, virtually a cripple and though not claiming he'd somersaulted back down, he did tell awestruck listeners, "After drinking the water I couldn't believe it. I was able to stand up straight. First time I'd been able to do that in years." Soon other tales of wonderous cures spread amongst the people and as of course you know, to this very day, those carrying ailments still travel from far and wide in order to partake of the curing waters of Elsa's Well.

Now I hope this doesn't confuse you, said the Teller, but I will now take you a little further forward in time to where we left Erdi, head in hands and deeply fearful. It was that day, Prince Heddi's visit had so upset Vanya. If you remember he was wrestling with the problem of how the swarm of incomers could be settled in his home valley, without that very attempt leading to bloodshed and starvation. Also, he needed a way of convincing the Y-Dewis elders of his sister's honour, without the questioning of it, returning her to the more dead than alive state he had witnessed following her rescue. And yes, Dowid and his family have now finally departed. *The Teller laughed at his own mischief of muddling the tale.* Sorry to jump about like this.

Continuing with a roguish grin, saying, I'll behave myself from now on, *he glanced in the direction of the lady he'd made eye contact with earlier. She wore a playful expression of disbelief. He always felt incredibly nervous when setting out on the telling, but could now sense he was getting into his stride.*

Chapter Five

Erdi was deeply troubled, *said the Teller*. He had his head in hands sitting alone in the gloom. Somehow a balance needed to be struck between his own people and the Y-Dewis. It was an easy thing to say, but with the former sullen and the latter still in a state of oblivion following their victory, as much as he sat there thinking, no hint of an idea presented itself. Also, there was a pressing need for more grain. He could imagine fights breaking out over what supplies they had.

Favoured communities such as the Salters often produced a surplus, but what could be traded in exchange for it? People still clung to their small caches of bronze hardly able to believe its value had fallen so low, with some even cherishing the belief that given enough time its former worth would return; their secret little hoards usually being in the form of axe-heads and bars, but as the playful saying went;

> 'What once would have procured the pregnant ewe,
> Would now not deliver the lamb to you.'

It did still have some value, however, but he doubted there was enough to trade for the huge amount of grain required. After Trader's legendary deal for the salt, belief in the metal's value had slumped and so had the trading of it, meaning the only disposable holdings of bronze lay in those secret hoards squirrelled away before 'the great collapse', as it was referred to. He banged his forehead gently with a fist asking, 'What's happened to Gardarm's bronze? There must be a mountain of it. Where did he hide it?' Even his old warrior friend hadn't known the answer to that one.

51

Vanya appeared; she had guessed right and was relieved to find her brother in one of his favoured pondering spots. She was still reeling from the shock of Prince Heddi's visit, finding it hard to believe, that the man she loved had basically visited for no other reason than to ask for proof of her virtue. She was in great need of solace and seeing her brother alone in the gloom, sat down beside him.

He told her he was surprised at Prince Heddi and that it had seemed completely out of character, coming to his intended bride with what was basically an insult. It was in fact, a betrayal. There was no other way of putting it.

"He's probably regretting it now," she replied.

Erdi then revealed his intention to ride over and demand to see Gwenithen, the mighty man himself. He'd ask whether he was aware of the damage he was doing by insulting the very family that had brought his people such benefit? Then having avowed this, he poured out his own troubles. She had heard every last detail of it all before of course, but being a loving sister, she let him continue.

On completion, thankful she had again listened, he simply stared into space, not expecting an answer.

"Erdi, get the people to bring us their bronze. We can turn it into something others will be glad to trade their grain for. How many axe heads can one family need? Make them into something else. If Mardi were here, he'd soon be casting brooches, entwining torques and hammering out bronze cauldrons."

Erdi, giving his sister a vigorous shake, said, "That's brilliant!"

"Where are you going?" she called out after his disappearing figure.

"I'm off to see Trader," he shouted back.

On the one hand she was of course pleased, but on the other, felt a little bereft, for any idea of challenging the chieftain on her behalf, now seemed to have been blown clear away by the sheer impact of her idea.

Trader was somewhere out on the property, but rather than go in search and with the added attraction of having Gwedyll there to talk to, Erdi decided to wait. He regaled her with the details of how, with Vanya's help, he'd dragged Elsa's remains, up from the depths. She had heard tell of their exploits, but still shuddered at the very thought of venturing near those dreaded waters.

In the ensuing silence, Gwedyll's puzzlement grew, for having sensed something important was troubling him, she now wondered why he was holding back. Of course, he would have liked nothing better than to have had the opportunity to share his fears regarding the Y-Dewis now dominating their territory, but with her being sister to the actual leader of them, it was not an easy matter to tackle. He need not have worried, however, for once he did broach the subject, she actually became the more vehement of the two.

"When I grew up amongst them, Erdi, I considered the values we held and the way we behaved to be perfectly normal, but having spent years here I'm now shocked at the contrast. Up in the hills my people's tendency for certain wild ways seemed to blend in, but down here, now they're living among us, it seems to clash to the point I have to admit I feel a little embarrassed, for in certain respects they actually look quite primitive. The way my brother behaves at times, laughing, joking, then suddenly strutting about with such ludicrous self-importance---. Well to be honest, I sometimes wonder if we had the same parents!"

She was as fearful as Erdi regarding the likelihood of trouble breaking out. He explained the idea that had been forming in his head and the frustration of not being able to implement it. It involved recording in detail, doing it properly this time, what lay in their territory and noting which areas could be cleared for settling, but with not having the required authority to put the plan into practice it would just remain a potentially good idea. Also, if not backed by his own village elders, putting pressure on Gwenithen to take action, things were likely to muddle along until the right of might became law. He said he would need at least two assistants for the initial expedition and a total of eight to run the scheme once finished.

While undertaking this there was also the question of how to keep himself. No small matter, for he could hardly expect his own family to support him. His father would probably view it as a fool's mission, not only poking his nose into other people's business, but worse, doing it for the sole benefit of those who should return to the hills from whence they came. Dommed would likely sneer, that Erdi was simply attempting to burnish his own self-importance and would certainly resent him not being there to shoulder responsibilities, doing his share of the daily grind. He also anticipated a good deal of resentment coming from all quarters once the reason for his investigation was fully realised. Their attitude already was, 'Why should help be given to settle these people when the simple answer stared you in the face? Tell them to get back up into the hills!'

He was also concerned about the effect all this was having on his wife. She found the atmosphere, now Dowid and Morga had moved east, almost unbearable. Dowid had always made her laugh and Morga had seemed like an elder sister. Now she faced the daily diet of negativity and bitterness from Penda and Dommed.

Gwedyll, patiently listening, letting all pour forth, obviously knew of Dowid's departure, but was genuinely surprised and saddened to hear how difficult Penda and Dommed had become. Erdi said the atmosphere was that bad he was seriously thinking of moving out himself. It was dragging both him and Gwendolin down and he felt guilty that she had to endure more of it than he did. He was also concerned for his son. It was not natural for one so young to be constantly wearing such a worried look.

She reassured him saying, "Children are tougher than you think, Erdi"

A pause followed and then Gwedyll suddenly realised, no mention had been made of Vanya.

Erdi simply gave an airy reply to her question, hoping his evasion would go unnoticed. He was too embarrassed to go into detail regarding the upset Prince Bonheddig's recent visit had caused. After all he was her nephew.

A few of you have probably noticed, *said the Teller with a grin,* giving birth to and raising sons gives certain women an unfair advantage when it comes to dealing with men. They seem to sense when part of a story is being held back and from the look on Gwedyll's face, Erdi knew she was homing in like a hawk.

"Erdi?"

"Yes?" He guessed what was coming and was right.

"There's something you're not telling me."

He tried keeping a straight face, but feeling like a child being questioned by his mother, couldn't prevent a sheepish grin spreading.

"Come on, you might as well tell me. I'm bound to find out in the end."

He reddened slightly.

"Out with it, Erdi!"

He was left with no choice other than to tell her exactly what had happened. She was furious. Not with him------ with her nephew.

"You can't blame him totally." Imagining the pressure, the young prince must have been under, Erdi offered words in his defence. "Yes initially, I was surprised at him, but now I think about it, he would have been left with little choice. Your brother, Gwenithen and tribal elders would have insisted on his course of action. They are bound to want answers regarding the purity of a girl wedded into the royal line and are not likely to condone the marriage until they get them."

"We'll see about that!" she said and was sufficiently angered to have taken immediate action, had not Trader, at that very moment returned.

He was told the details and although looking grave, Erdi knew from past dealings, his friend was unlikely to advocate a head on approach.

Finally, he said, "Alright, so the lad's made a mistake, but which of us hasn't? There's nothing to be gained from charging in there kicking up a fuss. It's obvious that Gwenithen will want reassurance on the matter. The fact she didn't return pregnant would have been proof enough for me. But Gwenithen? He's bound to want clear answers to blunt questions. But surely, there has to be a way of getting those answers without shaming and upsetting the girl."

A long silence followed.

I do have to apologise here, *said the Teller*. As you've probably gathered, Trader was quite forthright in his opinions regarding such matters as ruling councils and holy men, but when I relate the following, which believe me, is essential in attempting to portray a fundamental part of the man's character, it should in no way be construed as a veiled insult aimed at the most learned and revered Seers of today.

The Teller giving a slight wince, said, If you'll allow me, I'll continue.

"**Look Gwed,**" said Trader at last, "that Seer of yours seems a fair-minded old booby!----------"

Abrupt laughter greeted this, with even the Seer's face breaking into a smile.

The *Teller said*, Well I did warn you.

Trader continued, "Not that I have much time for their dark mutterings as you know, but what if just you and the Seer spoke to Vanya? Your brother would trust his holiness to report back with the truth and Vanya wouldn't have to face the ignominy of her honour being probed by a wizened bunch of old hill farmers.

Gwedyll laughed and said, "He's not my seer," but she did agree it was a good solution. Then added, "I'll still have a word with that Heddi, mind you."

"Well that's your privilege, but I bet he already knows he's done wrong. First though let's get the main business out of the way. You can always give Heddi one of your lashings once it's all sorted out. Come to think of it, you'll need to be there anyway, Erdi doesn't know enough cymry to deal with a matter this delicate. You'll need to be there to translate. And like I said, you'll need to do the same for Vanya. Even though she's managed to pick up the language fairly quickly, she still can't really be expected to know what the old goat's asking her."

Gwedyll left them to go about her business and taking a deep breath, Erdi said, "Trader, I'm afraid I need your help on other matters."

His friend frowned. "Very well, but let me splash my face and get these boots off first." He called out, "Gwed? Is there any beer left?"

She returned and by plonking down the jug and two beakers let him know his way of giving an instruction had not been quite as subtle as imagined.

57

They spoke long into the night. Trader was told how difficult the atmosphere had become at home and clearly understood, his young friend's frustration at seeing trouble brewing between the two peoples and being unable to do a single thing about it. Trader let Erdi pour forth his problems, only interrupting when not clear on certain points. He did raise an eyebrow when told of the plan to record all landholdings in the valley, knowing from experience how folk resent having their assets and ways of doing things looked into. He gave a vigorous nod of approval regarding Vanya's idea for enhancing the bronze and shook his head in shared disbelief, at the baffling mystery of Gardarm's missing hoard.

When the full extent of the problems had been laid bare, he and Erdi began to discuss possible solutions. Erdi could already feel a weight beginning to lift off him. Firstly, Trader agreed information was needed for peacefully settling the incomers. Someone would have to locate potential sites. Strict boundaries would need stipulating. This was not like the normal expansion of a local population; it was a mass incursion and if the incomers were allowed to go crashing and thrashing out new slabs of territory without heeding local needs, there was one certain outcome, bloodshed. He didn't envy Erdi's task of digging out the information, mind you, not when you consider he was viewed as the one responsible for bringing the Y-Dewis into the territory in the first place. They seemed to have conveniently forgotten, exactly why it had been done. People have such short memories.

He suggested Gwedyll help in the initial phase. That of putting the idea to Gwenithen, for after all, the chieftain was her brother. Also, as Erdi would be doing a service to both tribes, Trader thought it not unreasonable, considering he had been awarded the honorary title of Y-Dewis warrior, that he should ask to be maintained as such. Erdi looked doubtful. 'Easy for him to say, but it wouldn't be Trader doing the asking.'

On discussing Vanya's idea of transforming remaining bronze into tradeable objects, Trader shook his head and laughed, "You have to admit, she's a clever little thing."

They decided, the people could be credited with amounts brought for smelting, then rewarded with the equivalent in grain or other foodstuffs when the goods were successfully traded. There was plenty of room available on Trader's property to set up a large enough workshop and all they then required, would be men sufficiently skilled to man it. Of course, in view of them organising and bringing the venture to fruition, a small consideration would need to be retained, but the people would surely not begrudge them that.

Gardarm's lost hoard was puzzled over. There had been no sign of it inside the fortress and he couldn't have had a secret pit dug out in the forest for the mere act of doing so and accessing it would have soon revealed its whereabouts. Things like that don't go unnoticed. If it still existed it had to be hidden somewhere where regular journeys to top-up or avail of the contents, wouldn't have aroused curiosity. Also, such a place would need some sort of security; an entryway that could be blocked or a lid that could be locked. The crazier their notions, the more they laughed, but also the more baffling the mystery became.

"Talking of hoards," said Trader, suddenly grabbing Erdi's arm. "No mention of that gold for salt deal! As far as those old hill farmers are concerned and anyone else for that matter, the gold has gone. Slipped through m'fingers." Twiddling them, he laughed.

"All that slips through your fingers, Trader, are things let go to fool the unwary into thinking they're getting the better of you."

Trader wagged an admonishing finger, but wore the faintest trace of a smile.

They both agreed that Vanya's little problem had to be resolved before any of the other pressing needs were tackled. In view of the likely upset and the way things were back at home, Trader suggested she would be best moving in with them for a while. He knew Gwedyll would love the idea. He had one last thing to add before they finally turned in, "I know things look black Erdi, but there is one small grain of comfort."

"What's that?"

"At least it's not raining every day."

"You're right Trader. This must be the best weather we've had for as long as I can remember."

Erdi slept well that night.

The following day, he and Gwedyll set out for the burgeoning settlement just south of the old fort. Having laid claim to the lands immediately north of that prominent hill, Gwenethin had moved his centre of power to where a small brook provided fresh water and the fortress mound to the north, blocked the worst of the winter winds. Having spent their lives up in draughty fastnesses, he and his people were very mindful of such detail.

He and Gwedyll were immediately recognised and escorted between the houses, some old, some new and others in mid-construction. All eyes were on them as they headed for a meeting with the great man himself. They waited outside the largest of the new dwellings. The vast roof was thatched with a shaggy dome of hay which would later be replaced by neatly clipped straw once the wheat harvest was in. The hay would then be used as fodder. Their arrival was announced. On demand, Erdi relinquished his sword to a guard and they were ushered inside. Gwenethin smiled and rose to greet in a most informal manner. He was fortunately in one of his calm moods. They gave a solemn, respectful bow of head and once having received the inviting sweep of an arm to do so, both sat.

The chieftain wore everyday apparel, but at his waist, from a girdle of striking blue, hung a sword, its pommel glinting silver, its sheath, gold-bronze in hue. Around his neck was the gold torque

Gardarm had once prized so greatly. He looked comfortable in his new home, relaxed; stately.

Erdi wondered, 'which is the real Gwenithen?'--- This calm man looking so at home?--- Gwenithen the playful who had found the subject of lost fishing rights so hilarious?--- Gwenithen the pompous? ---Gwenithen the insecure? Or was the true Gwenithen the raging warrior who had swept down from the hills and shown such relish in devising Gardarm's mode of execution? And this man of many moods now ruled them. Success or failure of a plan depended on which frame of mind you caught him in. It was a sobering realisation.

Erdi looked beyond the chieftain and as his eyes became accustomed, suddenly realised what hung arrayed behind the royal chair. A display of trophies, mostly from the previous regime; gold tipped spear, bronze shield, massive bronze sword and he was amused to see dangling, the flint hand axe Trader had had dealings with. Midst it all hung the revered bronze cauldron that had once been such an item of contention.

Gwedyll, on occasions, had flashed anger and fire at her brother with a fair degree of success, but today was certainly not the time for such an approach. Charm, tact and feminine guile were called for. If Gwenethin felt in anyway pushed as regards altering the approach to gain details of Vanya's ordeal, he would be sorely angered, dig his heels in and she would get nowhere.

After the usual exchange of pleasantries, Gwedyll divulged her reason for being there. She then turned to Erdi and said, that she respected the fact it was his sister they were discussing, but could he now please leave them to talk on the matter alone?

Erdi was glad to oblige. Anything to obtain the desired result. If Gwenethin were to sense the slightest loss of esteem with Erdi as witness, then the cause would be doomed. He retrieved his sword and wandered the small village, his smile at watching the women working and children playing, masking the fact that inside, he was gripped by a tight knot of tension.

Youngsters were building a dam and squeals of alarm accompanied a desperate search for more mud as the pressure of the widening waters breached and washed a section downstream. It reminded him of his young days. The stream with its chuckling falls and swirling pools looked like the perfect hideaway for sticklebacks and crayfish.

The repeated ring of metal being struck drew him to a hut on the edge of the settlement. A small raised open hearth of clay, glowed deep red, its contents pulsating in rhythm with the pump of twin bellows, worked by a figure crouched in the murk. Another, he recognised as the iron master, glistened with sweat as he brought down his might on an iron bar. He looked up and smiled, the whites of his eyes contrasting with the smeared black of face. His attention was drawn to Erdi's sword and noticing the enquiring look, Erdi happily unsheathed and handed it over for inspection.

The previous owner of the weapon had been amongst the dead, cremated the day after the battle for the fortress. With Prince Gardarm having banned the use of iron with a passion that had driven him to insanity, the sword was of course of bronze, not steel. The man looked along it, turned it this way and that, shrugged and handed it back, as Erdi had done, hilt first.

"What do you think?" Erdi asked in cymry.

A slow grin spread. "If ever you want a proper one, come and see me."

"What is that you're forging?"

He was normally unwilling to pass on any information regarding his dark arts, but with Erdi being the revered Mardikun's brother, he divulged he was forging a spear point. What looked like a single bar was in fact three welded by heat and hammering. A bar that had been left to harden in the furnace ran central to two outer bars of softer un-heat-treated iron, rather like putting a long thin strip of crispy bacon between two equally long thin strips of bread. Not that anyone had yet thought of doing such a thing.

This was fascinating, especially when not required to become involved in the heat and filth of the process. Erdi checking outside to make sure Gwedyll was not waiting, returned to watch as the bar was extended by the heat-welding on of a further short length. This was of the softer metal. After successfully hammering the two sections into one, the bar was rotated for the added portion to be forced deep into the glowing charcoal. The rhythm of the bellows intensified and the heart of the hearth began to spit sparks. Using tongs, the iron master clasped the protruding bar end, to examine the extent of the glow on the other. Not satisfied, he returned it to the furnace, its intensity increasing in response to the renewed urgency of the bellows. When withdrawn for the second time, its colour graduated from black through deep red, to light red then white hot at the very end. This portion when hammered, began to flatten out. Repeated heating and hammering on the stone anvil produced an emerging flattened, flared shape. It was heated and flattened further until he was fully satisfied with its thickness and profile. After another visit to the bowels of the furnace, that same end portion was hammered against a bronze horn jammed into the end of the anvil and gradually with yet more heating and hammering a socket was formed.

Erdi had wondered why a metal horn should be protruding from the flat stone anvil and on inspection found it was held rigid by that same soft metal they used for fishing weights. He surmised this had been melted and poured into the void around the slender bronze shaft of the horn, so once cool, it locked it in place. The bellows-man paused and wiped his brow with a filthy rag. He was absolutely running with sweat.

Using tongs to hold the socket; what was to become the business end of the burgeoning spear was thrust into the heart of the furnace and the bellows, sounding like floppy ill-fitting boots, went to work again. When white hot, the slowly evolving weapon was withdrawn and held on the anvil, but with hammer fully raised, the man paused and stared at the broad entryway.

It was Gwedyll, calmly waiting in complete contrast to the sweat and hammering in the fervid gloom and borne on the breeze, gently wafting hair and gown, came the faint, fresh aroma of sweet perfume.

Erdi thanked the man and hurried outside. He apologised for having gone missing, but a slight shake of head implied, 'no matter.' Her face gave no hint of success or failure.

At Erdi's questioning she said, "I'll tell you, but be patient. Let's fetch the horses first." Apparently, a child had told her where to find him.

As they rode south, she said she couldn't be certain, but the fact her brother hadn't dismissed the matter out of hand meant there was a fair chance of success. It would be discussed with his advisors and a message sent. She turned to Erdi, puffed a look of relief and smiled.

"It's the best I could do, Erdi. Pushing too hard would have got us nowhere."

Back at his home, Erdi and Gwendolin tried to impress upon Vanya that even though they had gone to this trouble, no-one was forcing her to face the dreaded examination. It was basically an insult and wouldn't it be better if Prince Bonheddigg was told to look elsewhere for a bride? Vanya shook her head. She was determined to go through with it, saying she had nothing to hide.

Vanya would possibly have been of a different opinion if asked to advise a course of action to another, rather than herself, but as we know, love can have a blinding effect, furnishing a strange ability on those directly involved, that enables justification for actions they would not normally recommend.

It was two days later that Erdi received the message; the Seer wished to see Vanya regarding a certain enquiry. Despite Penda growling, "I'm surprised you still want the man!" she put on her best gown, braided her hair and they rode to collect Gwedyll

At first sight of Vanya, she gave a piteous look and hugging her said, "You look lovely. We should be going to your wedding not to this interrogation."

As before, Erdi was asked to wait outside and with Gwedyll alongside as interpreter, Vanya entered the building indicated, ready to offer herself for the Seer's cross-examination.

The wait outside seemed endless and Erdi was beginning to attract strange looks. To take his mind off the worry, he wandered over to the iron master's hut. The man gave a welcoming smile and stooping, pulled something from a pile of metal. It was the completed spear point, ready for socketing onto a shaft. Erdi found it hard to imagine how such a gleaming blade had been fashioned from such uninspiring lump of metal. The socket now had a hole for nailing it ready for action.

The iron master said, "I shouldn't be telling you all my secrets, but the hole is punched using this." He held up a tool from the stack of those leaning against the anvil. The business end was a man's foot in length, slender as an antler pick, with a round, flat head for receiving the hammer's impact and a sharp end for delivering the power of the blow. The handle was simply an iron rod entwining itself and the waisted portion of the tool. He passed it for inspection. Erdi took it reluctantly, feeling no inspiration to grip it as one would a well-balanced knife or polished axe handle. The punching end was not round as he had expected, but slightly elongated.

The man noticing his puzzled look, explained that that particular tool preceded the use of a second, looking exactly the same, but for the fact it had a completely circular punch-end. The reason, he said, was not to tear the-----he used a cymry word Erdi didn't understand.

He took him over and pointed to a wooden shelf. This made no sense at all. The man smiled and with a filthy finger nail pointed out the lines in the wood just visible in the gloom.

"You mean the grain."

The man nodded, as one would to a co-conspirator.

"You mean, iron has a grain through it, just like wood?"

The man, putting a finger to his lips, smiled. "It was your brother who first made us aware of this." He held up the first punch again. "By using this, it tears as little of the grain as possible. Cutting across it weakens the metal. The second punch simply forces the opening wider. Shouldn't be revealing all this, but it's hard not to, considering it was your brother who first brought us the knowledge." Giving Erdi a sideways look, "And you don't look the type to be setting up in opposition." He had obviously noticed him unable to resist the desire to remove the punch handle's rust and grime by rubbing fingers and thumb together, then wiping his palm on the back of his leggings.

"Is the hole punched when the metal's hot or cold?"

"Hot," he said. "Done on the peeg." Pointing to the bronze protrusion on the anvil, he made opening and closing movements with his fingers.

"Oh, you mean beak." Erdi gave a bird-like whistle and the man laughed and nodded.

He thanked the iron master and went back outside to wait.

The sun had started to dip to the east by the time the ladies finally reappeared, his sister looking almost unrecognisable, bowed and cradled in an arm of comfort. She had obviously been crying. It seemed a long ride back to Trader's. Vanya looked pale and washed out and her hair, that had been so radiant earlier, now hung lank. Once home, Gwedyll bustled about preparing food and giving Erdi, pottage with bread, insisted Vanya try force some down. Erdi eyed her efforts in dismay. She needed help for her hands shook that much the contents of the bowl dribbled down onto her blouse.

Erdi was of course, desperate for answers, but following a look flashed from Gwedyll, the questions remained unasked on his lips. Vanya was laid down to rest and Erdi followed Gwedyll outside, where at sufficient distance, keeping her voice low, she explained what had gone on.

She said the Seer had been surprisingly understanding and had often paused, asking Vanya to take her time. He realised his probing was opening old wounds. Vanya's account had been quite without emotion until describing what had happened, once they had all been ferried over the Habren. She told the Seer that one particular girl, one of the two captured from somewhere along the western coast, didn't seem to mind what they wanted from her. For this she was favoured during the day, often given a horse to ride and received extra food when they stopped at night. She seemed to enjoy the flattery and elevated status.

It was when describing how they came for her and her friend that the Seer could see Vanya was beginning to break down. She said her friend, who was roughly her age, had warned, they were almost certain to be picked on. She had noticed their looks and now cursed what had once been a reason for pride, appearing older than her years. The girl wasn't giving in without a fight, mind you. 'She would kick them where it hurt most!' She was the one Vanya had learnt her few words of cymry from.

That night they somehow managed to fight them off. The men, half-drunk and weary from the day's travel gave up and went for an easier option. The next night, however, they flung Vanya aside and dragged her friend away. The sound of the brutes like a pack of dogs and her screams and cries of anger and pain, still haunt Vanya's sleep to the present day.

"And Vanya?" Erdi dreaded the answer.

Gwedyll shook her head. "It was a miracle. Maybe they thought her too young. Maybe Elsa's spirit was looking after her. She has a strong independent manner that men can sense, but that's only likely to deter the faint hearted, not animals like them. Whatever the reason, by some miracle Vanya has come out of this with just her mind scarred. Made infinitely worse of course when forced to flee and leave her friend behind. The telling of that was when she finally broke down completely and the Seer announced, he had heard enough. It's strange, but I think she carries a huge burden of guilt at being spared."

A few days later they were requested to visit the chieftain himself. He welcomed them and they were offered food. Young prince Heddi was there, pale faced in the gloom. No mention was made of Vanya's ordeal, but the simple fact of having been invited to dine alongside the chieftain was sufficient message to all, Vanya's honour had been upheld.

As they left, Heddi rushed out in pursuit. His hands actually shook and he looked like he'd not slept for nights. He begged Vanya for forgiveness, saying he was not worthy of her.

"Leave her alone! You've done enough damage," Gwedyll scolded and then added, "In fact come with me!" She marched him down to the small stream and berated him with a finger wagging of such ferocity, he flinched and blinked as if actually being struck. Like many women, Gwedyll was a splendid sight in full cry.

Erdi had not seen anything quite like it since his mother had flown at Dowid years before. He had been bending by the fire and without thinking had let one go. It had started as a deep growl but rose to a crescendo that ended abruptly with one arm raised and a bolt-upright foot stamp.

Mara had looked up in disbelief. Creeping round the fire she had launched into such a thrashing with her spoon he'd had to run for the door. "You dirty devil!" She yelled after him. "How dare you! I've just finished cleaning in here!"

So, *said the Teller, letting the laughter subside*, with Vanya's little problem dealt with, Erdi's way was clear to tackle the land issue.

Chapter Six

Erdi already had a plan in mind, but in the initial stages needed the help of two able assistants. He asked Gwen if she thought Tam, one of her cousins, would be willing to join him? He was a bright lad who he'd met on his excursions over to Five Pools.

"Anything that gets him out of daily chores," she'd answered and so Erdi rode over Elsa's Ridge to ask him in person. It wasn't Tam who needed persuading, however, it was his family. Not only did they not want the boy tainted by the same stigma that Erdi now bore, they were also obviously reluctant to lose a useful pair of hands. Erdi pointed out the spring planting had been completed and gave his word he'd have Tam back well before harvest time. Also, what they were doing would hopefully be for everyone's benefit. This brought some doubtful looks, but after being told a sizeable reward could be expected for such work, they went into deep discussion and finally agreed to let Tam go. To avoid having to repeat the journey he asked for loan of one of their pigeons telling them, when it returned and had a ring of twine attached, it meant Tam was needed. No twine meant he wasn't. In fact, it meant his attempt to win Gwenithen over to his idea had failed.

He next went in search of the forest folk. He needed the skills of his mushroom trading friend, skills taught to all male members of that wandering clan from the moment they could walk. The man listened to Erdi's plan and would have dropped everything that instant to join him, but was told to wait until the borrowed pigeon returned with its message.

Following this he set himself the task of tracking down the two bronze masters he'd become acquainted with, whilst being held at Gardarm's pleasure, in the fort. Those who had befriended Mardi to the point of letting him in on their secrets. The pair had had the

70

sense to absent themselves from duty on hearing of the imminence of the Y-Dewis assault on the fortress and so Erdi assumed they'd still be alive. He just now hoped they hadn't fled the territory for he needed their expertise turning bronze axes into items of equal usefulness, but of greater variety. On finally locating the pair he had little problem in persuading them. In fact, both were ready to go the moment he suggested it and were happy to transport their tools and whatever else was required down to Trader's abode. It was obvious, they were elated at being needed again, made even better by the fact, for the first time ever there was no toil and grime required to produce the bronze, it was already there waiting for them to complete the glory side of their trade.

While this had been going on, so had quite a number of other things. Vanya moved in with Trader and Gwedyll as arranged; Mara's new friend Brialla and her family had been given the house and land, Blade's parents had formerly owned; some of the Y-Dewis were allocated land vacated by those who had fled on hearing of the massacre of their men, the day the fortress fell; Donda was allocated to a widower, admittedly a fair bit older, but not faint of heart and Stench now found his charcoal in high demand even though he himself wasn't. Mara's distress at Vanya leaving was alleviated by the knowledge, her daughter would be moving to a happier atmosphere away from her gloom laden father and the surly Dommed, plus with Brialla now living just a short walk away, she could now escape the awful atmosphere herself.

Whenever able, Dommed's wife Inga joined them. The three now regularly foraged for the medicinal plants that were keenly sought after when put on offer up at the market. Some of their best customers were men. Strange really when you think about it, *the Teller said with a laugh.* Why would three attractive ladies, excitedly chatting together like young girls, find their bunches of leaves so sought after by men?

When out on their searches they took Brialla's massive hunting dog, Bled. No man would dare trouble them with Bled on guard.

As they went about what seemed like pleasure rather than work, their chatter and laughter rang through the woods and their hounds seemed to share the enjoyment, sniffing this way and that and chasing squirrels. They never ever caught one, but no amount of failure seemed to diminish their ardour. The three began to develop an instinct as to where certain medicinal roots and plants were likely to grow and always probed ahead with spears before bending to dig or cut. The snakes chanced upon weren't deadly, unless the person bitten happened to be ailing at the time, but there again, none of them wanted to nurse a badly swollen hand.

The more successful their enterprise, the gloomier Dommed and Penda became. The latter would have been gloomier still had he known why his wife made herself look so presentable for supposedly just a scramble through the woods and Brialla's brother was also mindful of his appearance when hearing Mara's visit was imminent. Mara knew she shouldn't be feeling like she did, but couldn't help it. There was something about the man that, when anticipating the walk up to Brialla's house, sent her spirits souring. It was just innocent talk, but it made her pulse race and left her quite breathless.

Erdi now had a clear plan in mind, but before putting it to the Y-Dewis elders he thought it best to try it out on Trader, Gwedyll and his sister. He rode over early one morning to ensure catching them all in. He didn't exactly gabble out his ideas, but there again, became pretty animated in his explanation and on completion looked expectantly from one to the other anticipating enthusiastic support. There was silence.

At last Vanya said, "I agree with everything you suggest, especially the idea of not going to Gwenithen directly--------------- but it won't work."

"Of course it will. It has to."

"Not the way you're proposing to go about it."

"Why not? I don't understand."

"It's like this," began Vanya, as if talking to a beginner. "You've let your enthusiasm blind you to the likely outcome, when from out of nowhere, an outsider turns up to tell elders of another tribe, how to do their job."

Gwedyll nodded in agreement.

"They were once only too glad to have my help and I'm not really doing that, I'm----------"

"Yes you are," interrupted his sister. "Now listen! It's like this. You don't go to them with the plan. You go to them with the problem. With a few hints and a bit of coaxing, you let them come up with the plan. A plan identical to the one you've just told us. They then take **their** plan to Gwenethin and with his approval you carry out your ideas with the full backing of the Y-Dewis elders. Do it the other way round and you'll either be met with stubborn resistance or if vaguely successful, bitter resentment."

Erdi looked at her open mouthed. He turned his gaze to Gwedyll who had a hint of a smile, then back to his sister and said slowly as if a light had shone inside his head for the first time, "This is how you do it!"

"Do what exactly, Erdi?" asked Vanya sweetly.

"Get your own way."

"Well what a thing to say!" said Gwedyll with mock horror.

"Even though I know that's the way they work," said Trader, laughing, "I still can't spot it coming. She gets me every time."

Taking Vanya's advice, Erdi put his problems to the Y-Dewis elders and throwing himself on their mercy, asked if they could help. It worked like a charm. By the next day he had permission to roam the territory on their behalf, seeking out possible places to settle Y-Dewis families. All provisions needed for the trip would be supplied and one of the slaves who had been on cleaning and cooking duties since the demise of the eel stealers, was gifted Penda in his absence. That didn't lift his father's mood any, but at least the work would get done.

Erdi asked Vanya if she could make him four of the hide-covered frames she used for her paintings and he released the two pigeons, each with twine attached to a leg. His plan was at last underway.

Whilst awaiting the arrival of his two assistants he assembled the supplies needed. A pack horse was put at his disposal to carry them. Erdi had his pony, but the other two would travel on foot. None of their territory lay much more than a day's walk from the growing settlement south of the fort and so the expedition was not expected to be arduous. It would be undertaken in four stages and at their conclusion he'd hopefully return with the solution of where to settle those Y-Dewis, not already hacking out pieces of unoccupied territory. Time was of the essence; already, tempers had flared over water rights and the roaming of Y-Dewis' flocks, but regarding the latter, there was one completely unexpected benefit. The nibbled spring wheat, when eventually harvested, gave a better yield than that left untouched.

Not having so far to travel, the forest dweller was first to arrive. Erdi realised he didn't know the man's name. On being told, he didn't even attempt to get his tongue around it and instead told him, from now on he would be called, Madarch. This was accepted with a shrug, as the man had no idea what the cymry word meant.

It was at this point divine providence came to Erdi's aid, for as someone might later put in much finer words, it's a bad blow that brings absolutely **no** benefit. Sensing an easy target after the fall of the old regime, a band of renegade Bleddi warriors swept down from their fastness. Houses were burnt and they would have made off with livestock had not the Y-Dewis warriors swarmed forth like angry hornets to drive them back up into the western hills. Consequently, the short-sighted attitude of Erdi's kinsmen did a complete about turn, with people realising, without these incomers, they were at the mercy of any war party taking a notion to attack. Incursions into their homeland would give easy chance for plunder and glory. Yes, they would receive mention in battle poems, but as the vanquished, rather than the victors. Each area was now keen to have a contingent of wild Skreela, as they were still sometimes called, living close by.

Erdi's little expedition had of course been delayed somewhat, but what a change in attitude from the folks he encountered. As he, Tam and Madarch travelled north, he explained what he hoped to achieve.

Following the main trail leading to Nant Crag stream, the small party then headed west, being well received and thankfully, even given shelter without having to produce Gwenithen's seal of approval. Its pattern had been pressed into a wax tablet and bestowed in case of need to requisition food or accommodation. Not wanting to flaunt this high honour, Erdi treated it as a last resort.

The following morning, they reached the border defined by the Dwy river, flowing in from the western hills. A fire was lit and Madarch was left to keep it smoking. Erdi and Tam then returned due east in as straight a line as they could manage. At times they had to hack their way through, and at others simply follow convenient paths and animal trails. At regular intervals Erdi climbed the tallest of nearby trees to check on their location in relation to the sun and the fire still smoking behind. At times, rising ground saved him the effort, but then Tam had to be sent to summon Madarch forward for the process to start over again. All dwellings and crops encountered were recorded by drawing charcoal symbols on one of the hide-covered frames, Vanya had provided. She had even sewn together a large, flat leather satchel to keep them dry.

At the end of each day, having put his tracking skills to full effect, Madarch had no problem locating them and was never empty handed. Grinning as he approached, the fruits of his hunting and gathering would be held up in triumph. Day by day, they worked across the first of the four sections Erdi had mapped out in his mind, moving east to west one day and west to east the next, starting a little further south each morning. Not only was everything recorded, but the people were counted. Operations were sometimes of course hampered by the weather and when heavily overcast or raining he concentrated on gleaning local knowledge to check the accuracy of what he'd recorded. Needing to know how far each homestead or village was from certain known reference points and from each other, he asked questions like, "How many spans of the sun would it take you to walk to Nant Crag stream or to the nearest point on the Dwy river? What's the extent of this patch of swamp? Where does that trail lead?"

Some were glad to assist, others not so and as always there was the odd one, born plain contrary.

"T'all dependers," he called them. There was one man in particular, he recalled, who seemed to hold a deep resentment, obviously viewing him as a young upstart, expecting simple answers to questions, as if there might be no complications or vagaries involved.

"I wonder if you could help me? I'm checking on some information I've gathered. Rather than having to walk there myself, I was hoping you could tell me, how many spans of the sun it would take to walk from here to the bridge that crosses Nant Crag stream?" ----Simple enough on the face of it.

"T'all depends. On a fine day it don't seem that far, but if it's raining_____"

"Well let's assume it's a fine day?"

"T'all depends."

"On what exactly?"

"Some mornings it's a struggle to even get up from m'bed let alone walk to Nant Crag."

"Well alright. Let's assume you're feeling fine and the sun's shining. How long then?"

There was a long pause. "T'all depends."

"Depends on what?"

"Well. Depends on which way you go. There's two trails what lead to Nant Crag."

"I'm assuming you'd take the shortest."

A flicker of triumph crossed the man's face. "T'all depends on the weather. If there's been heavy rain, the shortest route gets fearsome boggy and then the longest trail's the shortest."

"Alright!" Resisting the temptation to retort, "Didn't you mean, quickest?" Erdi through gritted teeth, made another effort. "Let's suppose it's a bright morning, you're not feeling the least bit stiff, it hasn't rained for days and so you take the shortest route to Nant Crag. How long would it take then?"

The man just stood there with his brain churning.

"Well?"

"T'all depends."

"What this time?"

"T'all depends on what you're going there for. If you've a basket of wheat strapped to your back, it takes a mite bit longer than if you're lugging nothing."

Erdi drew a deep breath and being very careful not to lose his temper or leave anything out, asked, "If it's a fine day and you yourself are feeling particularly nimble, and being in the middle of a dry spell you decide to walk to Nant Crag taking the shortest route, carrying nothing whatsoever, going at a steady pace and not stopping, how long would it take?"

He stood there struggling, but this time knew he was beaten. Reluctantly he murmured, "Wouldn't take much longer than one span I spose." Then added with relief, "Provided there's a fair wind in favour, mind."

"Thank you. You've been most helpful."

Much of the time on their travels they were fed, but sometimes had to fend for themselves and even though both Erdi and Tam had spent a large part of their lives hunting and foraging, in Madarch they had a master. He always passed spare moments, when on fire duty, tracking down food, but if put to it as a main task, he was amazing. He never failed and would turn up with items such as fungi, hare, hedgehog, squirrel, fish, snake and numerous varieties of edible roots and plants. He taught Erdi the art of tickling trout. He'd heard about it, but had never seen it done. No-one was likely to starve in Madarch's company.

He did draw some strange looks, mind you, being one of the forest-folk. They were generally viewed with suspicion; looked down upon and Madarch didn't help matters by being ever reluctant to make friends with water. Erdi had sort of got used to him, but on a hot day, would find himself recoiling from the pungency. This fact made his hunting prowess all the more mystifying.

Tam one day, wafting away the odour, frowned and said, "Move downwind a bit Madarch. I'm surprised you don't put the woods themselves to flight. How is it you're so good at catching stuff?"

"Just talks to 'em," came the reply.

At the very start of the trip, one man, nodding in the direction of the swarthy youth had asked, "I can understand why you're trying to get an idea of what's in the country hereabouts, but why do you need the help of a thing like **that**?"

Erdi answered, "When you're out hunting, how well would you do without hawk or hound?" That silenced the man and Erdi hadn't realised at the time, just how apt his words would turn out to be. It was the first time, by the way, he had ever tasted snake and their knife sheaths, once bound by the cured reptile skins, were more greatly admired than the steel blades they contained. Madarch had busied himself with this along with various other forest skills and to Erdi's surprise, almost to the point of being slightly annoying, seemed to have an instinct as to where certain villages lay in relation to others. When pointing out mistakes on Erdi's plan, he was invariably right. It was more than simply knowledge gained from his people's wanderings, it was a strange innate gift, just as a hound somehow knows its way home.

Everyone they met was informed of the enterprise of transforming bronze into tradeable objects. Trader was well known and so there was no explanation required as regards where to find him. Some seemed unmoved by the opportunity, but others could see the sense of it and looked keen to take advantage. He knew that once the increased value of the goods was appreciated, everyone would want to take part.

As Erdi moved from one section of the territory to another, eventually covering all four, there were certain other developments, some quite minor, but one of particular significance.

The Teller advised his audience, It would be as well to take note of this, for reasons that will become clear later.

Firstly, the widows of slain warriors, those who had not fled the moment they heard the fort had fallen, now not only had Y-Dewis families settled in with them, they were informed these very guests were to be considered the new owners of the house and surrounding land. The dispossessed had the choice of living with the new decree or moving out. You can imagine the devastating impact it had. First they lose their cherished husbands and then everything else of value in their lives.

The men mentioned would have been of the farmer-warrior class rather than the warrior elite who had occupied the fort. As mentioned on my last visit, there was not the same threat of being raided that you people face today. In times of trouble, they packed themselves into their worthy redoubt, but in everyday living were spread out across the countryside. The fort, apart from the market, had only been somewhere to go if pleading a case, or if summoned. It had been the preserve of the chieftain, his family, his warrior guard plus the Seer and his acolytes.

Returning to the plight of those poor bereaving, dispossessed ladies, some now found themselves, objects of particular interest. Strange how these things work isn't it. Unattached Y-Dewis men of various ages found themselves drawn to certain doors and I'm not suggesting these were love matches, but the opportunities such suitors offered came as a welcome alternative to the plight the ladies found themselves in, thus those chosen, found it more agreeable to take up with their admirers than to remain in servitude. Succour was provided in exchange for their skills, whether innate, or learnt at their mother's knee, plus each had another certain something to offer. Once land had been allocated, the newly joined couples set up home in a contract of survival. So, along with the intermingling of the tribes, gradually came intermingling of languages and customs to match.

Now you have all heard tales of people being in such a state of desperation they trade their own children into slavery. I know it's hard to believe, but at the point of starvation a certain logic takes

80

on an urgency. Following such a course of action ensures not only the survival of their child, all be it as a slave, but also of the rest of the family courtesy of the food gained from the deal. Surely better than them all starving together. But generally, the instinct to defend the family to the point of death was as strong amongst these people as it is in you. I'm mentioning this because of what follows.

One day when Vanya was up in the market with Gwedyll, a Y-Dewis woman approached, asking if she happened to be the one known as Vanya? She apologised for enquiring, but the story had reached her, of her miraculous escape from the clutches of the slavers. The edginess Gwedyll felt, at the woman's manner, was not helped by her sudden grasping of a sleeve, pulling Vanya closer. She wore such a look of agony and sadness, Gwedyll was concerned the woman might be demented. She was actually on the point of intervening, but paused on hearing the woman ask, 'Had there been a Y-Dewis girl captured and enslaved along with her?'

Vanya nodded and a feeling of dread arose at what she sensed was coming.

"Was the girl's name Rowena?"

Vanya looking horrified, whispered, "Yes."

"Rowena is my daughter."

"I'm so sorry. Rowena was my friend. She fought them. She helped save me."

"Is my daughter still alive?"

Vanya blinking back tears, nodded in affirmation.

"Rowena lives." The woman, her face streaming with tears, squeezed Vanya's shoulders and whispered, "Thank you."

Vanya and Gwedyll stood in shocked silence as the bowed figure slipped away into the crowd. Even if her daughter was now a slave, it was better than her being dead.

A little later Vanya said, "Gwedyll, I've never told anyone this before, but I think it could have been advice Rowena gave me that stopped them. They never came for me a second time."

"What happened? What did she say?"

"Before we crossed the wide river, she warned me. She said they would probably tire of that girl who seemed so pleased with herself. Apparently, men like them enjoy a struggle. They would look upon us as a challenge. Then Rowena told me I might be lucky on account of looking so young. You won't tell anyone this will you?"

Gwedyll vowed silence. Yet as always, the word must have leaked out, *said the Teller*, otherwise how would I be able to tell you what was divulged? *He put a conspiratorial finger to lips and said,* You have to imagine this is Vanya talking. *He altered his voice slightly,* "Rowena asked whether I had the look of a woman yet. Down there. You know where I mean. I said yes, I had started to, but it was not exactly obvious. She told me to pull them out. She said, doing that could save me. 'But won't it hurt?' I asked her. 'Not half as much as they will,' she said."

"So you did it?"

"Yes and when they saw, that first night they attacked us, they never bothered me again."

"I'm surprised those brutes let a thing like that stop them."

"Well so am I. But I can't think of any other reason. Then of course the closer we got to Tredarn, the safer things became. They hardly wanted me arriving covered in cuts and bruises. I didn't tell the Seer any of what I've just told you. Didn't see why I should have to."

Now going on to another point, *said the Teller*, while Erdi was taken up with surveying the country and passing on the message regarding the bronze opportunity, it became evident to the Y-Dewis elders that although iron was a marked improvement on bronze when fashioned into tools and weaponry, the drawback was, there was simply not enough of it. As far as could be ascertained, all the easily obtainable ore had been exhausted and there was urgent need for a new source. To make matters worse, their southerly warlike foe seemed to have found ample supplies and were making much of the advantage gained, by launching cattle raids. In fact, news had come in from Bleddi traders, a fresh incursion was heading their way, that very moment, down the Habren.

The decision was made to send an intercepting force and drive the raiders back up into the hills. Gwenithen called on a number of veteran troops and put them in charge of the young volunteers eager to be part of the action. He then pondered on who should lead the expedition. His youngest son, Bonheddig almost ran to be first there and pleaded with his father to be appointed leader. He viewed such a worthy undertaking as his chance of gaining redemption. His willingness to risk his life could restore a feeling of self-respect. He would be worthy of Vanya once again and to the fury of his two elder brothers, the chieftain granted his wish.

As a safety precaution he asked the old warrior, Taweler to accompany him. Tawaler was known as Tawy by those close to him, including a certain Brialla who happened to be his sister. Mara had tried not to show concern when told of his call to arms. To do so would have alerted Brialla to her depth of feeling towards him. Like all involved in such entanglements of the heart, Mara thought no-one would have noticed what she herself would have picked up in an instant, if having been an observer rather than a participant.

The first section of the journey took the column close to Trader's abode and there beside the trail awaited a pretty maiden. The column halted. She reached up and to the envy of all, the young prince was handed the gift of an amulet dangling on a thread of fine red yarn.

"Wear it next to your heart it will keep you safe."

That very heart soared like a bird. The young lady watched the warriors ride from sight and after a short prayer to the spirits, turned to walk the short distance back to Trader's.

When Erdi finally completed his task of information gathering, he had four large sketches of the territory drawn on the framed hides, Vanya had provided. When placed together for examination, Madarch helped with certain adjustments and Erdi at last felt the project to be complete. To his knowledge, such a task had never been undertaken before and there was no word to describe what now lay before him. There was the word map, for scratchings in the dirt depicting trails and rivers, but his version also had symbols denoting villages, forests, fens and hills and the word map didn't seem adequate. He called it a 'bird's view.' He retained the services of Tam and Madarch and they accompanied him down to Trader's. Erdi wanted the wise man's opinion before approaching Gwenithen himself.

Trader, looking at what Erdi called his bird's view, pushed his cap back and said, "Erdi, I must admit, I'm mighty impressed." He of course knew how to reach most of the settlements shown, but hadn't known exactly how they all lay in relation to one another. Erdi told him, 'nor had he.' He also admitted, there had been plenty of features he'd needed to scratch off and relocate as more details became evident, plus the fact the whole undertaking would have been near impossible had he not been aided by the undreamt-of abilities possessed by Madarch. He seemed to have knowledge of certain regions, even though never having visited them before, as if viewing from the sky.

Even so, he knew what he'd drawn was far from perfect, but it was better than nothing. He pointed out the places favourable for clearance and settlement and those that could be drained. He also said, better use could be made of existing land. He'd found evidence of great wastage. The old method of exhausting the soil and moving on was still in practice. It had to be impressed on Gwenithen that in order for so many extra tribal members to be sustained, this had to stop. But on the beneficial side, he had discovered certain families combined their resources. They teamed their oxen for spring ploughing regardless of who owned the animals or the land. It was a far better method than that preceding, where many families struggled on with just a single animal.

Trader, yet again, suggested Gwedyll should act as translator. Erdi knew enough cymry to get by, but something as complex as this had to be explained by a true native speaker. An audience was granted and Erdi laid the 'bird's view' before the great man, who was fortunately in one of his calm, stately moods. His full council was present and all were stunned into silence.

As he had done with Trader, helped by Gwedyll translating the tricky bits, Erdi pointed out what had been discovered and places for possible settlement. He offered himself and his two assistants as guides to settle families into areas suggested and there was not a single murmur of dissent. He informed Gwenithen that many more families could be settled on existing farmland if a stop was put to the wastefulness of exhausting one patch of land before moving on to another. With so many now in need of that land, the old system was no longer sustainable. Gwenithen was also informed of the efficiency of sharing oxen.

The chieftain later sent out the decree that anyone exhausting the ground they currently relied upon, would be denied access to any further. Midden contents were to be spread to fertilise the soil and from now on fields were to be left fallow every third year. Also, families were instructed to use oxen in pairs to improve efficiency. The animals would work for everyone, even those who had none. No longer would men need to scratch furrows with antler picks or drag a plough themselves.

Whilst on his travels, Erdi had discovered how inexact some of the land boundaries were and how no-one seemed to have the final say in passing judgement. Some feuds had gone on for generations. He discussed the problem with the Y- Dewis elders in the manner Vanya would have advocated and once again, it worked like a charm. The idea of four Y- Dewis administrators each having local advisors reporting to them, seemed to be the solution that popped up from out of nowhere. While this system was being set up, Erdi would still be required to give his advice and judgement. Not a job he relished, but at least his time would be rewarded by payment in kind, which was not only fair, but theoretically, also acted as a deterrent to having his time wasted. He would view the problem, set the fee and if one of the contesting parties didn't agree, he'd deny them his services. Simple as that and the matter would be referred back to the area administrator.

Once the scheme was running, Erdi found it best to discuss all findings with this man before any subject of contention was taken to Gwenithen for final judgement. On being informed, that certain landowners were being particularly difficult, Gwenithen had a certain man he could turn to. The person in question was surprisingly muted for one of such vast girth and had quite a genial countenance and reasonable manner. Erdi of course knew the man from his time with the Y-Dewis, but had no clue as to what he actually said when sent to quietly intervene. After the man and his translator had slipped in to reason with the obdurate, however, Erdi always found the original surly mood of non-compliance, no longer evident. The man's name was Arthur, but the Y' Dewis called him Arth for short.

As things began to fall into place, Gwenithen began to look on the young Erdi as if only now seeing him properly for the first time. Having discussed all with his advisors, he was one day summoned to be told that a small plot of land had been bestowed on him. It lay to south of the main settlement not far from Trader's expanse of land and a house would be constructed for his family to move into. He wasn't at that point party to another decision that had been made. His mood might not have been quite so light if he had been.

Have to tell you this bit, *said the Teller*. One morning Mara, up and about, even before the birds had begun their chorus, was washing and readying herself for the day's duties. Although still but a dim light, if anyone had happened to have been stirring at the time, it would have been obvious from her expression, she was in a state of puzzlement and shock. Looking over to reassure herself that Penda still slept, she slipped outside hoping to spot Inga, anxious to tell her what she had dreamt.

When Mara did eventually find the chance to grab her attention, she still wore a troubled look and on checking to see that Dommed and Penda were well out of earshot, said, "I need to talk to you."

"What is it? What's so important?" hissed Inga.

"I had a strange dream, Inga. Come with me, I'll tell you." She led her out beyond the palisade before daring to say, "I dreamt I was in bed with a strange thing."

"What sort of strange thing?"

"Well I didn't know what it was to begin with, but it turned out to be a horse."

There was an involuntary squeak of laughter and removing the hand she'd clamped to her mouth in shock, Inga said, "You're joking!"

"No, I'm telling you, it was a horse. But then----wait, this is the strangest bit; the dream changed and I wasn't in bed with a horse at all. It was Tawy, Brialla's brother!"

This time Inga couldn't hold back and with sides aching with laughter, held on to Mara for support.

"Luckily I hadn't woken Penda. He didn't see me wash myself. You know where I mean."

"What?" Inga almost shrieked the word, as she gripped Mara's arm.

Mara added with a look of concern, "Well. It made me feel **quite** funny."

"I bet it did! Whatever had you been eating?" She then managed to gasp, with tears of laughter streaming. "Can I have some?"

Of course, the men in the Teller's audience always loved a hint of bawdiness and even the women laughed. One lady in particular looked up at him and smiled.

Meanwhile Erdi, beset with official duties made all the harder by having to release Tam back to his family as promised, asked himself, 'How exactly did I end up in this position?' Every day he was expected to deal with petty complaints regarding boundaries, encroachment, sheep wandering, goats devastating, setting of traps on another's land (in fact poaching), pollution of streams and even on one occasion having to investigate when one family complained, they'd had the 'evil eye' cast on them by a neighbour. He passed that one over to the Seer.

When laying out new settlements he found the easiest solution was to surround single dwellings with a circle of land roughly two sling shots across, these days referred to as 500 paces. The land immediately surrounding the dwelling was used for crops and beyond that for grazing. Where circles inevitably left voids, that land was shared between adjoining neighbours.

In the new hamlets, the surrounding land was held in common, but of course in the early days their time was almost completely taken up with felling trees and clearing land. There was game to be had in the forest, but Erdi was concerned it would not be enough to sustain them through winter. When the Y-Dewis elders were asked about this, they seemed evasive and unwilling to see it as a problem. He could sense they weren't telling him something and his unease increased the closer they came to harvest time.

88

One day when up in the market talking to Trader, they heard news regarding the recent punitive expedition to the south. A lone rider had returned at pace to inform Gwenithen that Heddi's force had triumphed. They hadn't managed to draw the Gwy into battle, but had succeeded in doing what they'd set out to do, drive them from the Habren valley. There were casualties, however. Tawy, the wise old warrior actually directing the campaign, was amongst the injured. The news brought quite a stir. Locals felt quite a surge of pride regarding the fighting prowess of the tribe that had descended on them and now referred to them as **our** warriors.

As Erdi and Trader discussed this news, their conversation was stopped by the sight of a couple approaching. The man, wearing a serious look, said, "Excuse me."

Erdi didn't like the sound of that one bit and braced himself.

"I wonder if you could advise me on something?"

Erdi giving an inward sigh, waited.

"I've got a patch of ground a neighbour wants. There's no need to trouble yourself looking at it."

'In other words, he wants my advice for nothing,' Erdi thought.

"It's normal size. Just a strip a pair of oxen could easy manage in a day. Just wondered what would be a fair trade for it?"

Erdi said, "See those hills over yonder."

The man nodded.

"Well I own a strip of land in a valley just beyond. Can you tell me what that's worth?"

The man looked quite enraged. "How can you expect me to know that? I'd have to look at it first!"

89

His wife nudged him gently. "I think he's trying to tell you something, dear."

When they had gone Trader, looking at his young friend, said, "This job's changing you, Erdi. Try not to lose track of who you are."

Coming from such a close friend, this was deeply worrying. He replied, "I wonder who I am myself some days. I don't want to do this for very much longer."

Then came the shattering pronouncement. The year's harvest was to be shared equally with the Y-Dewis, to help see them through the winter. This was what they had been holding back from telling him. Erdi had recorded all the likely crop yields and had dutifully passed this information on to Gwenithen. Erdi's people were justifiably worried and incensed. He was branded a traitor. The house he'd been gifted stood as proof of his collusion and he was almost frightened to leave it. There was even talk of burning it to the ground. Gwendolin was petrified and suggested they ought to be given armed protection, but Erdi reasoned, that doing so would only confirm the suspicion of him being party to the ruling. He had turned his family into outcasts. There was still Trader and family to turn to and of course his resourceful helper who said, "Now you know how I feel."

Erdi looking at him, smiled and wondered, 'After all that's happened so far in my life, how has it come down to having little more than you for consolation?'

Madarch was a strange man. He couldn't exactly be trusted to tell the truth and if people were careless enough to leave things lying around, he felt it his right to help himself. This even included their women if willing and not put off by the smell of him, but to Erdi, he seemed strangely loyal. Gwen had found him amusing and just so long as he didn't wander into the house uninvited, didn't mind him being there. When helping set up his sleeping quarters in the stable, she'd muttered to Erdi, "I bet it's better than he's used to." Followed by, "Can't you get him to wash more often?"

It was actually the man's ingenuous nature that helped answer a conundrum, but more of that shortly. First, I have to tell you of Gwedyll's sudden arrival one morning. It was obviously a matter of great import for her horse looked hard ridden and she was without escort. Reining in and alighting gracefully all in one movement, betraying her Y-Dewis origins, she told them the latest news.

The expeditionary force had re-crossed the Habren that morning and she and Vanya had been there on the track to greet them. The men were dirty, tired and dishevelled, but at the sight of Vanya, Heddi had simply glowed. He had leapt from his horse and would have swept her up into his arms had he not been so filthy from battle and travel. Tawy had a shoulder injury, but was still able to ride, two men were slumped on their mounts, another had a bandaged head wound, but all things considered, she said, they looked in a cheery mood.

Now do you remember me telling you of a matter of some significance? *asked the Teller*. I mentioned it way back when giving details of Erdi's map making. It had happened on the campaign these men were returning from. As if the skirmishing to drive the Gwy out of the Habren valley had not been significant enough, there was something else of import, something the small force had stumbled upon. The implications weren't that obvious at the time, but they happened to have intercepted two of Gardarm's former guard down on the Habren. On being recognised from the style of shields and weaponry, they were asked how they'd managed to escape the massacre. Apparently, they hadn't been in the fort at the time, but on other duties. This scrap of news brought back by the returning heroes was passed on two days later by Trader. Erdi happened to be down there seeing how, what they called, 'the bronze solution' was going, but before he could ask, "What other duties had the men been on?" their conversation had been interrupted by a fresh load of bars and axe-heads arriving.

The value was ascertained, agreed on and the amount inscribed on identical clay tablets. The contributor made his mark on each and received refreshment while they were hardened in the fire. On departure he was given one to keep, sufficiently cooled of course and its twin was put into one of four boxes, all according to which part of the territory he was from. One box for each of the areas Erdi had mapped out. While Trader had been dealing with the man, Erdi, still impatient to know, 'what other duties?' took the opportunity to examine the items already produced. There were arrow heads, brooches, horns, buckles, hooks, polished round discs for ladies to view dim reflections, plus gleaming atop the pile, were three fine torques. He wondered who the proud wearers of the latter would be?

Once alone again, he was at last able to ask Trader, "So what happened to the warriors they intercepted. What other duties had they been on?"

He shrugged and said he didn't know.

"What? After me standing here all this time, waiting!" He decided to waste no more of it and go directly to find out. Victory celebrations would by now, almost certainly have run their course and he hoped Prince Heddi would be sober enough to receive him.

He was nursing a hangover, but otherwise in fair spirits. Erdi allowed the prince to regale him with the campaign saga and when just about to embellish the tale further, he interrupted with, "What happened to those two warriors you apprehended?"

Heddi said that they had simply questioned them and let them go on their way. They had no reason to do anything else. Time had long passed for meting out punishment.

Erdi then asked, 'what duties had the men been on?'

92

They had apparently been guarding the old copper mine. You know the one. The Ogof mine, lying less than a morning's walk south of here, deep in that hill overlooking the Nwy river.

Satisfied, but slightly disappointed, Erdi returned home. He was relating the latest news to Gwendolin, busy hanging out the washing, when Madarch wandered within earshot. Erdi's look of annoyance at his impertinence was either not interpreted or more likely ignored. This turned out to be quite fortuitous in fact, for Madarch went on to ask, almost as a child would, "Why were they guarding the copper mine?"

Erdi returned him a blank stare.

"Who against? They say the mining stopped when Gardarm went mad. So what were they there for? Even I wouldn't think of stealing a hole in the ground."

His words had the impact like a slap from an ox-blade shovel. "Come on, get your things!"

"Why? Where are we going?" His swarthy friend looked bewildered.

"Down to the copper mine."

With that the Teller gave a shudder. It's turning a bit nippy, *he said.* Thank you all for listening. Spirits willing, I will continue with the tale tomorrow evening. *To a rousing applause, he climbed down from the palisade and headed between the houses towards his temporary home. It had been a long day. He was looking forward to seeing that bed again.*

Part 2

Chapter Seven

The Teller awoke early the following morning and lay quietly composed, staring up at the thatch while listening to birdsong. He always found it the ideal time for working out the order of the tale and the colouring in of the details, ready for the coming evening. He smiled at the memory of the previous rendering. At one point, the way he had moved the story back and forth in time had almost brought on a headache, but going back over it, felt fairly certain he hadn't lost the thread at any time. However, he decided it would be best to have a word before embarking on the next part of the saga.

On being given bread and crispy pork by his hostess, he thanked her and said he felt guilty eating what must have been a treasured reserve of meat. They certainly would not have had such a grand start to the day themselves. Replying, 'it was her pleasure,' she had absolutely glowed, giving him the impression, that having him as a guest was probably the envy of others. Wandering over to the door he caught a fleeting glimpse of a lady passing by. Taking a sip of hot nettle brew, he stepped outside. He had not seen her face, but instinctively knew who it was. His pulse quickened. The lady who had smiled at him the previous night was collecting water from a small pool behind the house. Water from the roofs of three houses drained into it and a small platform allowed enough depth to fill a container without getting feet wet.

"She wants you to go and talk to her." *The low utterance from behind almost made him jump.*

"What gives you that idea?" *he asked his hostess. With the initial nervousness of the previous day now gone, she replied as she would to one of her sons, not with words, just a look of tried patience.*

"I wouldn't know what to say to her."

The woman stared back in disbelief. "What!" she hissed not wanting her voice to carry. "You the Teller lost for words!"

He didn't bother to explain the stomach-churning dread, experienced every time he was confronted by an audience, nor the countless times he had asked himself why he put himself through it, but watching his hostess's narrowing of eyes, then look of genuine concern, he felt a certain degree of compulsion and when an impatient flick of head urged him not to miss the opportunity, he felt sufficiently bolstered to take a deep breath and approach the pool.

The lady, dipping the goatskin sack, on hearing his approach, looked slightly startled and as nervous as he felt. They needn't have worried, however, for conversation flowed as easily as the water running over the lip of the bag she hauled from the pool. He relieved her of the burden and they made their way back between the houses.

She slipped in brief details of work she now undertook, necessitated by her man's sad passing and he managed to convey the fact, no little lady was waiting anxious for his return, without it sounding like he was labouring the point. The self-chiding for not pressing on with her work must have been repeated at least three times, yet still the conversation flowed until with face suddenly clouding, she said, "Oh no, Ryth!"

The Teller, on looking round, saw the ruddy faced official approaching. The one who had re-awakened misgivings when officially ushering him into the fortress. A huge grin shone to accompany an over-exuberant greeting and looking thoroughly pleased with himself, he stood between them, completely breaking the mood. After a few embarrassing moments, with the conversation now meaningless, the lady thanked the Teller for kindly carrying her burden home and after a nod of self-dismissal in Ryth's direction, disappeared inside.

Completely unabashed, he asked in his grand manner, if all was well, "Are they looking after you properly?" *and realising he'd achieved what he'd set out to do, gave a hearty farewell and strode off.*

"So how was Megan?" *the Teller was asked on his return.*

The question gave him a pleasant jolt. 'At my age,' *he thought,* 'like a youth welcoming the chance to talk about a pretty young girl he'd just met.' *Then smiling to himself, he realised he'd done exactly as Erdi had, as related in the tale told on his first visit. He'd been that carried away with the flow of conversation, he'd forgotten to ask the lady her name.*

"That Ryth shows an unhealthy interest for a married man," *came a voice from over by the hearth.*

That evening the telling was held in the Grand Hall and the Teller sweeping in to applause, took the small dais. He was pleased to see, that once again, it was a mixed audience.

Now before I begin, I must inform you that **yes**, Dowid and family have now at last departed for Y-Pentwr.

There was a cheer, plus laughter.

I must apologise, *said the Teller,* but that first part of the tale has a lot of dry stuff in it. It has to be told, however, otherwise nothing sounds plausible. You can't just announce a tribe of people arrive and everyone gets along like they've all arrived at a family gathering. It has to be explained, it was not quite that easy. But as said, some of it's a bit dry so I danced it about a bit. Nearly lost the track myself at one point, *he said with a grin.* Brought on quite a headache.

More laughter.

It will be more straightforward from now on. Now where was I? Ah yes, the mine. You all know where it is, for the ancient Ogof, lying in the midst of your sister hill fort is still going strong to this day. Back then, with copper revered and jealously guarded, the so-called Seer had been at work telling tales of horror and giving out dire warnings of entanglement in a world of monstrous demons, certain to befall those who dared enter the Ogof without his blessing. A ceremony was held each year. The miners were assembled to receive the shield, a protection conferred on them by the Seer's magical words of wonder, enabling work to be carried out in the monster's lair free from its malignant forces.

When one poor soul had had the misfortune of a tunnel collapse completely burying him, his family had not only the loss to bear, but also the stigma, for it was said, the man must have brought it on himself. No-one was exactly sure what he had done to deserve such a fate, but it must have been heinous beyond all imagination to have cracked his shield of protection. Otherwise, how had the evil forces managed to crush him?

You laugh. I know it sounds unbelievable now, but these were less sophisticated times. The Seer we have in our company today is a learned man, respected by all, but back in Gardarm's time, his Seer was basically no more than a tool to use against the people. If you questioned the code of belief, then you basically questioned everything that governed the harmony of the world and as explained on my last visit, the whole structure of that system was based on the value of bronze. Control the alchemy of its creation and you controlled the people.

You probably think them naïve, but I wonder how many of you would manage if suddenly dropped into their world. You in these grand bastions take for granted your improved wheat crops, larger cattle and stronger horses.

So, hoping to enter this world of hidden malignancy, we have Erdi and his strange companion, Madarch. They arrived at the mining village to be greeted with, "What, you back again already?" It hadn't been that long since there on mapping duties.

It was an attractive location perched safely back from the flood-line, just up from a ford across the Nwy river. As you know, the prominent hill with copper mine entombed, looms above all and a short walk west brings you to where the pretty Tant river runs into the Nwy. No doubt we have all been amazed at the extent river windings can change over quite a short period of time, but just as now, those combined waters, were not long in their flow eastwards before swelling the mighty Habren, coursing up from the south.

Erdi remembered that spot well, for it was there he had feared he'd met his end as the surging waters had inundated the flatlands across on that southern bank. He wandered alone towards the river. The treacherous marshes with their whispering reeds visible to the southeast stood as a poignant reminder. If they had been drawn towards the Ogof hill that day, they would have all been lost. He felt a sudden pang in his heart for his brother. How they'd laughed once realising they had escaped to higher ground. 'Mardi,' he said quietly to himself, 'you've no idea how much I miss you.'

The sudden appearance of Madarch jolted him back to the present and the need to face a task he wasn't relishing, entering the labyrinth. He had made up his mind, they weren't putting a single foot inside, before a miner had been persuaded to guide them underground.

"We are not entering without one," he said to his companion.

There were tales of people wandering in never to be seen again. It was said that on a quiet night, their ghostly voices could be heard echoing from deep underground. Whether truth or myth,

Erdi wasn't risking entry without a guide. After some persuasion and the offer of a half peg of peas, one of the men agreed. Erdi asked him for an additional horn lantern.

It was a steep climb up to the mine entrance and the view, when pausing for breath, was spectacular. Dark along the skyline stood the range of hills Erdi had found so enigmatic when little more than a child, viewing them for the first time, off Elsa's ridge. To the east stood the prominent escarpment, home to the Ridge People and far down to the southeast, Y-Pentwr rose from the flatlands.

A small palisade still surrounded the mine entrance and within its confines were three recently abandoned huts. The miners had used two as temporary shelter prior to the fall Gardarm and the third had been the guard's hut.

They struck flint to spark tinder into sufficient flame to light the candles and with lanterns held out, ducked inside what was a surprisingly wide opening. Any comfort gleaned by that, however, was soon dashed by the sinuous passages narrowing to such an extent, in places progress could only be gained by crawling. Erdi shuddered to think of a lifetime spent working in such conditions. In one awkward section, having passed a confusing number of tight passages leading off in both directions, they had to ease themselves to a lower level and then shuffle along bent low, almost on all-fours to avoid painful contact with the spiteful rocks above. The slightest contact hurt as if cracked with an iron bar. Erdi cursed and groaned, as yet again he tried rubbing away the pain, then a memory struck and he started to laugh.

"What's so funny?" their guide called back.

"Take too long to explain," he replied. The tale Trader had told the four Bleddi traders had sprung to mind. The one luring them into a deal they'd been so pleased with. He'd even been taken in by the notion himself. 'Horses in a copper mine! That Trader!' He started to laugh again.

They came across an opening to a further gallery winding off like a monstrous throat down into the depths and their guide explained it just led to abandoned workings. They eventually arrived at the workface still charred from its final firing.

"So what did you expect to discover?" the miner asked.

"I'm not sure exactly, but there's obviously nothing here. When was this last worked?"

"Many moons back."

"Did you ever actually deliver the ore to the fortress?"

"No, we just got it out from here and the worst of the waste was smashed off and dumped in old workings. Gardarm had his own people doin' the carting away for 'im. Sometimes we dragged it out into the open, other times they come in 'ere and fetched it out."

"How did they manage that? They'd have got lost, surely."

"No. We'd lug it part way for 'em and it was always the same three. They got to know the two main drags."

"Drags?"

"Yeh, the upper and the lower."

"Seems a strange way of carrying on. Would have made more sense to have hauled the whole lot out, ready for loading."

"Not up to us to ask the reasons why."

"What about that other tunnel we just passed? It looks quite wide. Where does that lead?"

"It's cursed," was blurted with such severity, it elicited the faintest of gassy rasps from Madarch.

"Munner go down there," the miner insisted. "I told you, it leads off down into them old finished workings. Winding tunnels what worms into the hill. People that's been known to creep down there, they dunner come back. Down there be ghosts and demons. The Seer, he come round special-like, warning us."

As the man's voice echoed, his eyes shone wide in the lamplight.

Hearing a timorous moan, Erdi wondered how his companion had been able to pack such meaning into a sound so indistinct, but managing to remain calm, said to their escort, "That Seer is with us no longer."

"But his curse is! Munner go down there!"

"Would you wait for us?" Ignoring his colleague's horrified look and shake of head, he continued, "We'd like to take a quick look."

Their guide uttered with alarm, "I ain't going down there, but if you'm mad enough to, then it's up to you."

Returning to the yawning shaft, Erdi mouthing a prayer to the spirits, ventured inside followed by the reluctant Madarch.

"Don't go abandoning us," Erdi's voice rang back.

Like the main opening, the shaft wasn't long in constricting and with dust and small stones spilling alarmingly from the low roof, they edged their way through tight crevices. Then to their amazement, found themselves in a wide, high domed chamber and Erdi holding up the lantern, realised what was blocking further progress. Shimmering the colour of dull gold, was a massive pile of bronze axe-heads.

Madarch gasped and Erdi muttered, "Gardarm's hoard."

In a flash, his strange companion was on the heap, picking up handfuls and letting them clatter back down onto the pile. He then began furiously ramming axe-heads inside his jerkin.

Erdi, ripping at the garment to release the contents said, "They're not ours. They belong to the people." Grabbing him by the scruff he muttered, "And not one word!" He had to drag him away as one would a child, desperate for that one last dip of a foot in a muddy puddle.

"So what happened?" asked the miner. "I heard shouting."

"I'm not going down there again," said Erdi. "You were right the place is cursed."

They hurried to Trader with the news and returned next day with a pair of oxcarts. By organising Delt and the workers into an underground chain their basketed booty was passed, stage by stage, out into the mine's main gallery. From there it was carried for loading onto the carts. It took most of the day and the weight was such, both animals and vehicles literally groaned with the strain of hauling it off the hill to trundle slowly along the main trail home. Trader inspected it on arrival.

Pushing his cap back to reveal the white streak of untanned forehead and giving his temple a thoughtful scratch, he said, "They're all top quality. Looks like he only kept the best for himself."

"They've all got the right ring to them. It seems a shame to melt them down," added Erdi.

"Well even if we do, there's only so many buckles and what have you, I can get rid of. Better to store them and have a good think."

"There has to be some way of trading them for grain. After all bronze does still have a value." Then a thought occurred. "It would be a good idea to tell Delt and the boys, not a word to anyone."

Trader returning a patient look, raised an eyebrow.

"Sorry," said Erdi. "Of course. You've already told him." Then remembering his laughter in the mine, he said, "Trader?"

"Yes,--- I'm listening."

"Have you ever been down a copper mine?"

"You're joking!"

"I thought not. That tale you told the Bleddi, to lure them into a deal on those ponies---------" He watched as a broad grin spread across his friend's face.

"People love a story, Erdi. It's all part of the art of trading. They love to hear things like, the incredible luck you had in chancing upon the very thing they've been looking for. You need a good memory mind you. Sometimes they enjoy the tale that much, next time you meet, they ask you to repeat it. Then there's some folk who just enjoy the search for something and can't believe, the day you confront them with the very thing they've been looking for, is the very day they should be making their minds up. They think, 'What if, in two days-time, I stumble upon a better version?' They need to be told someone else is thinking about it, otherwise they can dither for a lifetime. And another thing, never give them a choice. Just show them the one item. If they've got two to think about you might as well forget it. Little tricks, little tales, it's all part of the job, Erdi. When your father was trading smoked eel up in the market, I bet you heard him say, "Save enough of that for the Seer." Folk then think, 'If it's good enough for the Seer, then it's good enough for me. Hey, I'll have some of that!'"

"No, he didn't actually."

Trader returning a look of despair, muttered to himself, "No, don't suppose he did."

At this point Gwedyll and Vanya joined them. Looking upon the axe hoard, their faces glowed with astonishment.

"Not long ago this would have traded for a kingdom," Gwedyll said. "How did you know where to look?"

"It was just something Madarch happened to say."

Giving him a dig in the ribs, she muttered in cymry, "Why d'you call him by that name? Does he know?"

Erdi shook his head and frowning, a silent, 'Shh' shaped on his lips.

"Madarch!" she said, shaking her head and laughing.

The man in question, beginning to suspect something, wore a puzzled look and as regards Erdi's request, to ride down with a half peg of peas for the miner who had helped them, he would of course do it, but wasn't in the best of moods.

When he'd gone, Vanya said, "He really is a strange one, Erdi. He sometimes has a look of darkness about him. Are you sure you can trust him?"

"Not entirely, but at certain things he does, he's gifted. You wouldn't find better. You can never entirely trust a dog not to bite you and yet we still use them. In fact, we probably wouldn't be standing here looking at this bronze hoard if it hadn't been for him."

"Mmm," she said still not convinced. Then after a moment's thought, asked, "How did you know which tunnel to explore. They say that hill's as riddled as wormed wood."

"It was a word the miner used. He referred to the shafts as drags. In that opening we'd passed, I remembered seeing what looked like fairly recent drag marks, the sort laden baskets make."

"Well, who's a brother bright-boots, then? Anyway, now you've found it, maybe you can help me find something else."

"And what might that be, sister?"

"Elsa's house. I bet no-one's been there since her last day alive. There must be all sorts of secrets and things still in there. She would hardly mind."

"If her spirit wants us to find it, we will. If it doesn't, then we could be crashing about there for days. She cast a magic ring around it."

Vanya gave a dubious look.

"Alright, don't believe me, but if Yanker happened to be here, he'd tell you the same. It's what she told us when we were up there years ago. When Mardi and I did manage to stumble across it, that morning we set out to find you, we had the smoke to guide us. No chance of that now."

There followed a spell of rain, but once things had dried up, Erdi and Vanya set out on horseback, with enough provisions for the day, heading east towards Elsa's ridge. The trail took them within sight of their old home, but Erdi decided to stay well clear, not wanting to be delayed. They followed the main path up through the woods and occasionally, on the far horizon the misty blue of the southern hills could be glimpsed through gaps between the trees.

Nearing the ridge-crest, Erdi paused. It all looked different.

"It's amazing how quickly things change," he said. "It was a miracle we found it that morning. That first morning, I told you about, when we set out with Wolf, a free man at last. We were approaching from over there somewhere," he said pointing west. "Maybe we would have been better forcing our way up through the tangle, as we did that day, rather than taking the easier trail."

On reaching more open ground, a shiver of wind rustling the trees ahead sent a tingling chill up Erdi's spine. He paused for a moment, staring at the green barrier, trying to remember where they had emerged from, on that previous occasion. Suddenly, it all swayed as if something extremely large had just passed through and at that point, the terrain seemed to change slightly, with everything now looking sharper, clearer.

"Come on," he said. "It's this way."

As they picked their way between the trunks and shrubs, he felt that hint of familiarity, almost as if the foliage itself was whispering, endorsing the sense of the right decision having been made. Keeping their mounts at a slow walk, they carefully threaded and in places, lay flat to the mane as low branches scraped along their backs. Erdi's raised hand brought a halt. Instincts told him they were close.

"That's it. It's coming back to me. I think we've found it."

Continuing a little further down the remains of a path, he stopped and pointed, "There it is. In the bank beneath that massive ash tree."

"I can't see any sign of a house," said Vanya peering.

They dismounted, let the horses graze and Erdi carefully pulled back the entrance cover. Both crept inside.

Clothes hung from pegs and still there, exactly as he remembered, were dried leaves, baskets and bleached animal skulls. He almost imagined Elsa in the doorway, saying "Well! I didn't expect visitors today."

As their eyes became accustomed to the gloom, however, they could see the cobwebs and layer of dust, that not only evoked sadness, but gave the impression they had opened a cold ancient tomb and both feeling like trespassers, found themselves whispering. Vanya, unhooking Elsa's gown from where it hung against the wall, was amazed, that even though the whole place had a slight whiff of decaying wood, the garment still held a trace of the revered lady's perfume. She didn't know what she would do with it, but with it evoking such sadness, knew she couldn't just leave it there.

That's how the small wattle door in the wall came to her notice. On opening it they saw a log, hewn roughly square, had been jammed into the earth bank beyond. Pulling it free, revealed a small stone chamber and inside was a hide-bound bundle.

"Look what I've found, Erdi." Carefully easing it out, she passed it to her brother. He held it while she cleared a place to lay it down. Vanya, unknotting the binding sinew. carefully opened the folds of soft leather. Inside was a thick wad of layered linen. When the uppermost piece was peeled back it revealed three pressed leaves, each from a different plant. The other layers held similar, but intriguingly, some also had dried fungi, bark and root slivers included.

"I think it's a record of all her remedies," whispered Vanya. "And this must be, how you extract their magic and apply them." On the upper side of each covering sheet, were strange symbols, neither could understand. "I bet if poor Mardi were here, he'd know what they meant."

Then, looking round, she gave a shiver and asked, "What was this place like, last time you were here?"

"Quite warm and cosy."

"Now Elsa's magic has gone, everything's fast returning to the forest."

Seeing Vanya shudder and pull her cloak tight, Erdi said, "Perhaps we ought to leave all well alone. Like a tribute."

"No. I know, these are her secrets, but I'm certain she'd want us to save them." Vanya laid the gown flat, carefully placed the re-bound find within and folding the garment around, tied it tight with the belt cord.

On their way back they did take the time to call at their old home. Penda was out, fortunately, but Mara was there to be shown their treasure. It was decided, that in view of her recent work, she should be its guardian. Their mother, looking stunned, as if all her feast days had come at once, gave each a hug of gratitude.

Meanwhile to the immediate northwest, Donda's old warrior, daily hacked and cleared the area he and his young beauty had been allotted to settle in. He went at it with the vigour of a man half his age, for hardly daring to believe his luck, couldn't do enough for his young bride. His eagerness to spoil, however, was clearly evident in her burgeoning figure.

When Erdi had chanced upon Donda one day up in the market, he had hardly recognised her. At first he'd surmised her to be pregnant, but a family friend who happened to be there, thought this hilarious and told him, "No, what you are looking at is the new Donda."

Now I know you might find this strange, *said the Teller*, but even though a lady's breasts are one of nature's blessings provided for the obvious reason and are on show daily when infants are fed, strangely there are some men who look upon them with a sense of excitement. The mere glimpse down a lady's front can cause arousal. Apparently, Donda's man can be included amongst this rare group and you couldn't have found a happier individual as a consequence.

Donda had in fact swollen in this region to such an extent, she would have put a mature milk-cow to shame. Fortunately, her man didn't seem to mind the fact, that along with this glorious bounty, there came an awful lot more of Donda in every region. She carried it well mind you, kept it tidy, sailing along like a swan on a calm lake. It was only when she smiled that it became evident the original Donda was still inside there somewhere.

The way nature seems to take its natural course, the way the lure of the unfamiliar seems irresistible, was clearly evident in courtships all across their territory. Even the poor slave girl, the old chieftain had procured up at the Feasting Site, found herself included in the mix. The gnarled warrior who had offered to take her in, had looked a bit old and past it and most assumed he'd merely needed a cook, cleaner and washerwoman;------ but those who care to take a casual interest in such matters were rewarded by something astonishing. They noticed an unmistakeable swell in the young woman's belly, made all the more pronounced by its contrast with her skinny frame and the old man walking beside her, now had quite a spring his step.

Also, it was whispered, Vanya's friend Talia had a Y-Dewis admirer. He was a young warrior and had often been seen calling there. Vanya was thrilled to hear this, but not the question a supposed caring soul had then put to her.

"Are you happy with the amount of time your mother spends with her friend Brialla?"

"Of course. Why shouldn't I be?"

"I know Brialla's brother was injured in battle and your mother seems to have at her fingertips, the magic of curing, but I was just asking, that's all."

Vanya shrugged the insinuation aside as nonsense, but later, when alone, she did pause and wonder.

Then Grik the Fish came calling. He was early this year and in addition to his normal salted sticks of winter fish, he also had herring and mackerel, both smoked or salted. The smoked varieties were delicious, but needed eating almost immediately as he warned they wouldn't keep forever.

He had set out on his normal route, but had had the strange feeling he'd arrived in the wrong territory. Everything seemed different. Even his old friend Penda was a changed man. Mara gave directions to Erdi's new abode and on reaching it, he experienced for the first time that welcoming feeling, that intangible something that silently invites a weary body to tarry awhile. It was Gwendolin's first meeting with the man, but his cheeriness and relaxed manner soon brought a smile, if but wary, before in no time at all, they were conversing like old friends. Erdi trusted his wife, but he wasn't too sure about Grik the Fish.

When it came time to discuss business, Erdi realising he no longer had access to smoked eel or cured venison, always the basic components for their deals with Grik, settled on the solution of asking Trader to negotiate on his behalf, with the idea of compensating him later.

Grik obviously knew Trader well, he was one of his regulars, but he now required a little more of the man. He was in fact now dependant on him to take the stash of salt off his hands, because Penda, for the first time ever, had turned down the chance.

Along the trail, Erdi had told him how his sudden recollection of the false bottom in his fish cart had solved the riddle of the missing sword. Grik had listened, but the story hadn't made the impact you'd have thought it would. With his mind obviously elsewhere, he'd in fact, seemed more interested in enquiring about success or failure of Trader's recent dealings. Erdi of course, being unwilling to divulge such information, surmised he'd probably been attempting to arm himself before coming negotiations.

On arrival and seeing Gwedyll eyeing them from the doorway, Grik called out a hearty welcome. She stood arms loosely folded and after a long, measured look, just returned him a nod. Her puzzled frown in Erdi's direction seemed to ask, 'What are you doing with him?'

Trader looked pleased to see him and soon the two got down to business. Erdi had told his friend the modest amount required, for it to be included in the deal and as they haggled it slowly became evident, Trader was negotiating a far better trade than his father had ever managed. Then nearing its completion, his friend, suddenly sat bolt upright, obviously remembering something. Disappearing for a few moments, he returned with a bronze axe-head. "Finest quality," he said. "Don't suppose you'd be interested? There are one or two more where this came from. Go on feel it. You won't find better."

Grik, turning it over in his hand, lightly tossed it to gauge the weight. "Fine axe, Trader. A year back I would have welcomed such a deal, but not now. I managed to move all my bronze on before the great collapse."

"Pity," said Trader, "but never mind."

"How much of this stuff have you got?"

"Enough. Why do you ask?"

"I might know where you can trade them."

"Well I have to admit, that could be useful. But if you know that, why don't you do the deal yourself?"

"No, too much trouble. I've enough to do without crossing those waters. Besides they're not the easiest folk to deal with."

"I think he means Wolf's people," said Erdi.

Trader didn't answer. He knew exactly who Grik meant. Instead he asked, "Why would those wild scoundrels still be wanting a trade in bronze?"

"The metal still holds sway there, Trader. Bronze still rules. But don't expect an easy deal."

"Oh I know, they can be a tough bunch."

"People get fooled by their manner. Laughing, joking, but underneath, you couldn't find a harder lot to deal with. I see more of them than you would, being way down here. I remember one man thought he could best them." Grik started laughing. "They had him in tears. I'm not joking. A full-grown man reduced to tears of rage and frustration."

The deal was concluded. Grik was given a bed for the night and went on his way the following morning.

Erdi, arriving at Trader's not long after his departure asked, "So are we off across the salt waters?"

"We?" said Trader with a smile. "There's no 'we,' regarding this, Erdi. I thought it might be a little job you could handle."

"It requires a man of your experience."

"No, Erdi. I've already enough to do moving all these buckles and bits. That's going to keep me busy for the next moon or so. Anyway, it will make a change. Get you out from beneath everyone else's problems. You said you'd had enough of it."

Erdi could see he meant it and his expression of glum resignation had Trader shaking with that much laughter, he was unable to prevent a wry smile spreading. Sighing, he said, "I'd better go and sort out a plan then, Trader."

He decided to do as he normally did when confronted by a massive problem. He returned home and after managing to impress on Gwendolin, nothing serious was the matter, went back outside to find a quiet place to sit and think.

She brought him a beaker of hot nettle brew. "Here, this might help." Then, halfway back to the house she turned and called cheerily, "That Grik's a bright soul. Don't think I'd want to be left alone with him mind you."

Erdi, smiling as he blew the hot liquid, settled himself under the tree and thought, 'Gwen's instincts didn't let her down.' Now he needed to think. If he could make a list of the problems involved, then there might be a chance of solving them.

The biggest obstacle was obtaining Gwenithen's blessing for the venture. Not easy when unable to reveal what lay at the heart of the plot. Assuming this were to be granted, he would then need time to ensure all land issues were for the most part, problem free and that no rancorous disagreements loomed. He couldn't leave without doing that. Next came the question of who to take with him. Harvest time would soon be upon them and families wouldn't contemplate a child abandoning its duties, let alone a grown man. Taking Y-Dewis warriors along would be out of the question, for if Gwenithen had any idea of what he and Trader now had in their possession, he might simply demand they hand it over. Next came the actual hauling of the bronze to the Dwy river. He didn't consider that a huge worry, as long as they weren't stopped along the way. Trader had the wherewithal to achieve that. But then came the problem of the boat. Travelling north on the Dwy could be tackled somehow, but what about the sea crossing? Only a fool would attempt that unless accompanied by at least one experienced man. Then came the thorniest problem of the lot, how was he to explain his intentions to Gwendolin? He would be actually abandoning her at the most perilous time. She needed him now more than ever. In view of recent hostile feelings towards them, there would be no alternative other than asking Trader to give her and Deri shelter while he was away.

Poor Gwen, she'd had a lot to put up with and in fact, he decided there and then, if trouble looked imminent, he'd not be going anywhere. His family came first. Then just when he thought he'd listed all the potential hazards and worries, another thought struck him. As if all were not impossible enough, there was absolutely no guarantee the tribes across the water would be willing to trade. Who was to say they had enough surplus wheat to do so? Plus, how was he to haul the cargo back without saltwater ruining it? 'So, all in all,' he muttered to himself, 'not a lot to worry about.'

A vague idea had started to formulate, however, but he needed Trader's opinion as to its chance of success. He was beginning to get that inkling, a notion of how to 'clear the path,' so to speak. Open the way to solving the other problems. He needed Gwenithen's blessing for his plan, but somehow had to avoid divulging the fact, a sizeable bronze hoard was at the heart of it. An answer seemed to glimmer, start to take shape, only to drift away again like mist.

The next day he returned to Trader's and after general talk about bronze and wheat explained, "Before I do anything, I somehow have to persuade Gwenithen to condone the mission. Without achieving that there's no point cudgelling my brains, trying to solve the other problems."

"Yes, I can see that Erdi, but it's a bit tricky, because---------"

"I know. If I tell him about the hoard, he'll probably say it's his by right, "Hand it over!" My notion of avoiding this, is to tell him, not that we have the bronze, but that I might have chanced upon a clue as to where it lies hidden. I'd tell him, it would involve absenting myself for a while."

Whenever Trader pushed his cap back to scratch his temple, Erdi knew enough to stay silent and let him think. "No, Erdi. That sounds messy, limp. You'll find yourself up a blind valley doing that. He'll demand you tell him what you've already found out and probably insist one of his men tags along. Just to help you search of course. Best not to mention the bronze at all. Why not simply say you've heard where grain might be obtained and you need a few days to try and arrange a trade."

"A few days?"

"When you get back, just tell him it took slightly longer than you'd imagined. It will hardly trouble the man if you're returning

117

triumphant. No problem hauling the bronze to the river by the way. I'll get Delt to do that. Oh, and another thing, Gwen and the boy better move down here until you get back. Who are you taking with you, Lightfingers?"

"What? has he stolen from you?"

"No, but I wouldn't trust the little reeker!"

"Yes, I know he's a bit odd and slightly on the whiffy side. He definitely wouldn't be my first choice, but I'll have to use him. There's no-one else available. I don't suppose Delt-----?"

Trader's solemn shake of head meant there was no point finishing the sentence. Instead, as a thought suddenly struck him, he asked, "How am I supposed to explain the miraculous arrival of a mound of wheat? Tell Gwenithen I waved a magic wand?"

"You worry too much, Erdi. You'll think of something."

Erdi had a right to worry, for even when at last confident he'd rehearsed sufficiently to dare approach Gwenithen, he'd been beset by an unforeseen barrier. First an advisor had demanded he state the reason for his visit. It would be discussed and he would then be informed whether it was even worth troubling the great man.

When eventually deemed worthy of an audience, he was ushered in and on finding the chieftain in one of his playful moods, immediately had that sinking feeling. He preferred the stern face of authority, not the look of amusement, the look of supressed mirth that suggested he could well be his lordship's next plaything. As he explained his intended mission, Gwenithen's grin grew that broad, Erdi began to wonder if the man had discovered his secret and was enjoying seeing him blunder into a trap of his own making?

The plea was followed by silence and then a gaze so severe in its piercing, Erdi could feel sweat creep a cool trail down the small of his back. The stern countenance finally melted for the look of merriment to shine once more, "So, Erdikun wishes to travel." He turned to his adviser and said "I cannot see that as a problem, can you?"

The man shook his head, "No my Lord."

Erdi, wearing an uncertain smile, thought, 'This doesn't seem real. There's something not quite right here.'

"Yes, Erdikun can travel. We are in need of such in fact. Tell him," he instructed.

His adviser, pulling himself to full height, said in a manner that lofty, you'd have thought even his master would have found his demeanour repellent, "You are to proceed to our brothers in the east and request that Lady Rhosyn kindly honour us with her presence. Lord Gwenithen requires confirmation that the good lady renounces all claims to sovereignty here."

"If it should please my Lord, I don't think Lady--------"

"That will be all! Report back here before you set out." Erdi was dismissed.

He returned home in a most dismal mood to make preparations for the journey. Gwendolin, managing to hide the fact she was inwardly thrilled he'd not now be disappearing off into the unknown, did manage to lift his mood slightly, with not entirely unconvincing words of consolation, but it was his son smiling up at him, that gave the greatest comfort. Picking him up, he said, "Deri, Deri, what **are** we going to do?" His problems hadn't disappeared, but he now felt he could cope and suddenly an understanding dawned. Remembering Trader's uplift of mood in a similar situation years before, he thought to himself, 'Sometimes you have to experience before you can fully understand. The family matters most, everything else is incidental.'

Early the following morning he reported for duty and was handed two small gifts to bear, the blue linen wrapping denoting they were intended for those of highest rank. One was for the Y- Pentwr chieftain, the other for Lady Rhosyn. Then, as he was leaving, almost as an afterthought, the official tossed this small gem of information, "Lord Gwenithen has granted your request regarding a trade mission and once this immediate task has been successfully undertaken, you are free to relinquish your duties and travel."

Erdi was obviously amazed and with heart lightened, immediately rode home with the news. He was that carried away by the sudden change of fortune, it took a while to understand why Gwendolin's smile had a tearful glint. He reassured her, "Don't look so worried. It's not as if I'm off across the seas immediately. This little task will only take two days at most."

Madarch was reminded, that under no circumstances was he to leave the house unguarded and Erdi set out south, briefly calling in to share the incredible news with Trader. He also requested possession, of one of the three bronze torques. It would be put to good use, for he had an idea forming. Before leaving, he told him of the high-handed manner of Gwenithen's official.

"Erdi, even amongst a bunch of hairy hill clingers, you'll always find at least one who thinks, **his** doesn't stink."

He took the trail down towards the Habren, then the well-worn track, following the river to Habren Ford. His official seal brought a slightly surprised look from the owner of the hostelry there, but he was waved down towards the ferry without charge. Cutting across to Amwythig ford, he headed southeast to the prominent hill they called Y-Pentwr. Light was fading to gloom and drawn by the fire-glow pulsating off the clouds above the fortress, he gave his horse a good dig, for he relished seeing his cousin Yanker again.

The climb was steep and entering by way of the southern gate, he dismounted, showed his official seal to the guards and asked where his cousin and Lady Rhosyn could be found? Their eagerness to comply left him slightly bemused, for only now did he realise, recent duties must have conferred a certain air of authority.

Yanker's face had a look of sheer disbelief when first catching sight of him and grabbing Erdi in a bear hug, literally lifted him off his feet. Lady Rhosyn embraced him warmly and both of course wanted to know the reason for his visit. He managed to delay having to answer by telling Yanker, it was a matter of urgency, could an audience be sought with the chieftain, Lord Haraul, immediately? In the short term, the presentation of Gwenithen's gift, outweighed all other matters.

Walking towards the great hall, Erdi tugged his cousin's sleeve. "Yanker, I couldn't ask you in front of Rhosyn, but I need your help. I need you to come on a trip with me."

Yanker, avidly listening, began to feel a thrill rising, similar to that experienced before a hunt. He replied he would do anything that gave him a break from his daily duties. He had been awarded the honour managing a section of his lordship's estates, which sounded grand, but in reality, involved petty day to day problems, upsets, misconstruing of his instructions and in some cases blatant reluctance to work. Erdi told him, he knew exactly how he felt. They had to break off their hurried exchanges, however, having reached the door of the Great Hall. The reason for their visit was given and after a short wait, they were ushered in.

Both bowed respectfully and Erdi was asked to approach. He said, "My Lord Gwenethin sends his utmost respects and felicitations." Going down on one knee, he held out the gift. "He has asked me to present to you Sire, this humble gift."

He rose and retreating backwards, re-joined his cousin.

Haraul's dark craggy features were lightened by a smile. He wore no sign of rank other than the deep-red cloak wrapped loose and yet power exuded from his calm demeanour. He handed the package to an aid, not once taking his eyes off Erdi. It was returned opened. Within, was a bronze-hilted steel dagger in an agate studded sheath, which was held up for all to admire. Drawn free and turned this way and that, the blade flashed in the firelight.

"Please tell your Lord Gwenithen, it pleases me."

"I will, Sire. Would it please your lordship to receive my own personal gift?"

The chieftain looking puzzled, beckoned with a gentle move of fingers. Erdi approached and knelt. Looking up he said, "I also have a request to make."

The man's eyes narrowed and a sigh indicated, 'Very well, get on with it.'

"Would your Lordship allow my cousin, here with us now, to accompany me on a mission, circumstances have thrust upon me? It could have the benefit of opening up new trade connections, potentially, of great benefit to both our tribes."

The chieftain of course wanted more details and on being furnished with such, said he would consider the matter. He put out a hand to receive the gift offered up.

Parting the loose wrapping brought an instant look of amusement and joy, almost as if a child again. He held up the torque for his assistant's appreciation.

"It is my sad regret it is only bronze and not of gold."

"No matter, young rascal. It amuses me and as fine as gold may be, bronze is by far the better shield 'gainst a sword cut. I shall wear it with pride."

With that, both supplicants backed towards the door and slipped out into the night.

"Where did you get all that, felicitations and would it please your Lordship stuff from?" Yanker asked laughing. "Would it please your Lordship," he repeated with a note of derision.

"I don't know. Just seemed to pick it up."

"I know I've had to learn the bowing and kneeling, but I didn't think it came into your line of work."

"I've a lot to tell you cousin."

Dowid, Morga and the rest of the family were there waiting when they got back. All exchanged stories of recent happenings and it ended up being quite a night. It still left Erdi's main reason for being there unexplained, however. Deciding not to spoil the magic, the joy of all meeting up again, he put off telling them until the morning and a new word was oft heard as ale mugs clinked, "Flishitations," accompanied by the odd jibe from Yanker, such as, "Would it please our esteemed guest to partake in further quaffing?"

Rhosyn was first up the following morning and Erdi walked over to where she sat, cradling her daughter with one hand and stirring the contents of a pot with the other. It was strange to see a royal princess in such a role, but the lady looked truly content. Her daughter glanced up and Erdi gasped, instantly recognising the look of Vanya in her eyes. Although only distantly related, there was no mistaking it, the exact same look was there. She was beautiful.

"So, Erdi," said Rhosyn. "You still haven't told us."

"I'm the bearer of a message I'm embarrassed to relay."

Rhosyn, with gaze firmly fixed on that being stirred, listened to what Gwenethin required.

Erdi apologised again, saying how he hated himself for being the bearer of such a request. She told him not to worry and in a rather faraway voice, still slowly stirring, told him, she hadn't the slightest notion of assuming any vestige of power. In fact, she was glad to be away from it all and was actually staggered at Gwenethin needing reassurance.

Yanker joined them and when told of the request, burst out laughing. He said they would have no qualms about renouncing any claim to power, especially in view of not realising they had any. They would of course need to request a short leave of absence, but apart from that there shouldn't be a problem.

As it happens, they were summoned again anyway. More details were needed regarding their proposed trip across salt waters. By mid-morning it was reported back, Haraul was satisfied and permission for Yanker to act as representative in a possible trade deal had been granted. The man had been highly tickled by Gwenethin's request to meet with Rhosyn and had apparently mused, "Do I detect a hint of insecurity? Does the crown sit a mite too large for its new wearer?"

Here in Y-Pentwr, *said the Teller*, Yanker was not known by his nickname but by his birth name, Dowin, but I won't confuse the issue other than to point it out.

On receiving the news, Erdi bid Yanker and his family farewell and set out for home. His cousin and Rhosyn were to follow close behind on the morrow. The sun was setting by the time he reported the details of his mission to a court official. Luckily, with there being no need to see Gwenethin himself, he was free to return home.

Erdi was not witness to Lady Rhosyn's meeting with Gwenethin. It was considered important enough to be convened in the Great Hall of the fort, tidied up and a fire lit for the day. He could well imagine it, with the one demanding renouncement of title looking high-handed and uneasy and the renouncer of that title appearing as if born to it.

Before leaving, both Lady Rhosyn and his cousin paid their respects at the shrines venerating Prince Aram and Elsa and then continued on to Erdi's house. They stayed that night and left early the following morning. Gwendolin had at first been nervous at entertaining such a vaunted lady in their humble abode, but Rhosyn, chatting unassumingly, as done on their previous meeting, soon put the hostess at her ease.

Erdi continued with his duties around the territory, talking through the latest problems and advising each pair of officials how best to deal with them. He had of late, sensed their confidence growing and was now certain they had sufficient knowledge to handle future issues unaided. Most Y-Dewis families had been successfully settled and the major land muddles had been resolved. There would always be fresh disputes, but thankfully they would not be his concern from hereon. He gave all a hint as to why he'd soon not be there to help, but avoided discussing details.

He was now free to gather supplies for his venture. Regarding food and warm clothing, he erred on the side of caution, especially as this time they wouldn't be carrying any of it. First the cart and then the boat would be the bearers. While awaiting Yanker's return, he busied himself procuring last-minute odds and ends such as hefty sewing needles, fishing line and hooks, plus he tried to glean as much advice as possible from his friend, Trader. He could feel excitement building and dearly hoped Gwendolin hadn't sensed it. Some hope!

At Trader's, he made no pretence at having sufficient skill needed for negotiating a tricky deal with foreign merchants and in fact did the exact opposite, admitting the bald truth, he'd not the slightest idea.

"Now Erdi," said his friend, "I'm not going to try and fool you into thinking, that what lies ahead will be easy. Far from it, but here are a few things you have to remember. A few things I can tell you that might help. When you first arrive on those foreign shores, there's a chance they'll overwhelm you with hospitality. Don't let that lull you into a false sense of security. Avoid telling them exactly why you're there and certainly don't let them know the amount of bronze you have, unless asked to officially declare it. There's bound to be some sort of charge for trading there. Oh, and stay off the tanglefoot as much as possible. First chance you get, visit a market. You will need fresh food by then anyway. Ask the trading rate of any grain you see and failing that, the livestock; it will give you an idea of what your haul is worth. You can afford to be a bit generous when it comes down to the actual dealing, but you don't want to appear like a complete fool. Once you think you've worked out the going rate for grain, you can move on to the tricky bit and actually admit, that's exactly what you're after. Not a few handfuls, but boatloads of the stuff.

Believe me they will gaze upon you, Erdi, with great relish. They will look at a man far from home, a man nervous of returning empty handed, as a wolf would eye a tasty lamb. You can almost guarantee the price will be too high. Be prepared for a show of anger when you point this out.

He could well rage as if insulted to the point of requiring satisfaction by battle. I say 'he,' for there's likely to be a main man in charge. It's not always the case, but usually there's one all the big deals go through. He will then try offering alternatives. Again, there could be anger when you refuse. He'll try and wear you down. Could take days. The man will be keen to rid himself of certain things, hoping you'll be that worried about returning empty handed you'll be glad to take them. What would seem completely out of the question at commencement could start to look like an attractive alternative after days of getting nowhere. But stay strong Erdi. Thank the man for his time and tell him it's all been a marvellous experience. You watch him change then. There's nothing like dangling a tasty morsel, then suddenly whipping it away again. Tell him the experience has been that wonderful, you'd like one thing, a token to take home in memory of the venture. Flatter the man. Tell him you've met some tough customers in your time, but he beats the lot of them. Tell him he's the true master. Ask if you can have a deal on one of his hunting dogs, or something of the sort, just to take home as a reminder of his genius. Hopefully, it will convince him the deal is slipping away."

"And if that doesn't work?" asked Erdi.

"Then I'm afraid to say you're well and truly ------------------." He paused and smiling said, "Then Erdi, I'm afraid to say if that doesn't jolt him into dealing the way you'd hoped, you'll be coming home empty handed. Let's just say you **do** manage to sort out some sort of deal, how do you intend to haul it back?"

I was planning to take enough bronze to reward the Erin for doing it. The year's moving on and we can't still be ferrying it with winter storms blowing in." Shaking his head in disbelief he continued, "Trader, when you hear of voyagers from far off lands arriving with goods to trade, it all sounds so exotic, romantic and easy. I never imagined any of this."

"It's a tough world, Erdi. You still have that seal, don't you? The one, head mountain-man gave you?"

"Yes, I always carry it."

"Good that should be enough."

"Enough for what?"

"Enough to ensure they don't just take the whole lot off you. They'd know their merchants to these shores would be in jeopardy themselves if they did that. Don't look so worried."

Erdi couldn't help it. He knew he was far too inexperienced to undertake such a mission, but circumstances left him no choice. At least he'd have his cousin Yanker with him. He also had possession of the two remaining bronze torques. He'd sensed there might be a need for them and Trader had had no qualms about adding them to the load, especially considering what his young friend was about to undertake.

Chapter Eight

In the dimness of an early morning, the sound of a cart creaked through the mist. Realising Gwendolin was on the verge of tears, Erdi and Yanker did their best to suppress their excitement. Trader would be collecting her and Deri later that morning. She had everything packed and their house was to be temporarily abandoned. The last of the voyager's items, such as baking stone, leather capes, water, fresh food for the day and good-luck amulets, were put under the hay on the cart. Erdi gave his wife and Deri one last hug and kiss and they departed.

Tightly gripping his mother's skirt and watching her sadly waving, Deri did likewise with a look of confusion spreading. Gwendolin, comforting by a gentle kiss on his forehead, straightened and briskly wiping away tears, forced a smile. That last view of them tore Erdi's heart apart.

He had questioned the use of hay to conceal the bronze, thinking it would look strange carting such a mundane load so far. Trader had answered, "To folk born in the area it would, but what do those mountain men know?"

Having estimated the amount of bronze needed, he had roughly half the hoard on the cart. The small party included Madarch and all four walked beside the pair of oxen. Erdi had hoped Trader would have had a last-minute change of heart, allowing Delt to accompany them for the whole trip, rather than just up to the Dwy, but it wasn't to be.

They followed a trail that wound up through the woods, thus avoiding the main settlement south of the fort. Erdi caught a glimpse of the old bastion. It was strange to see it without columns of smoke rising. In places the going was tough and all had to help heave, putting their backs into the slow turn of wheels, but when eventually re-joining the main northern track, the cart groaning along, did accomplish walking pace. On the most severe downward slopes, the break was applied and chucks regularly jammed to prevent the whole load running away, flattening their compliant beasts of burden.

On crossing Nant Crag stream, the sound of wheels ponderously drumming the boards of the bridge, emphasized the stark reality, home territory was behind them and ahead lay the unknown. There was no-one there to check their load. All that had stopped after the great collapse.

The sun had just started its descent to western hills when they at last gazed down on a broad bend of the Dwy river. They continued to the settlement lying just beyond the Feasting Site and to the curiosity of all began pitching off hay to retrieve their belongings and sacks of bronze beneath. Erdi tried to tempt the headman into a deal for the hay, but was told, unless prepared to virtually give it away, he wouldn't be interested.

Delt said, not to worry, for those now abiding near Nant Crag stream, would almost certainly need winter fodder, so he'd have no trouble trading it on.

Feeling quite out on a limb, they watched, as their last connection with home, made preparations to depart. Having refused the villager's offer of shelter for the night, Delt seemed completely unperturbed at the prospect of a night spent beneath the cart. Then for some reason, having wished them good luck, he asked the unsettling question, "Are you sure about all this, Erdi?" Without waiting for a reply, he turned and with a sad shake of head, led the oxen away, "Get on! Hup! Walk on."

That same day Trader had a word in the ear of a 'carrion crow'. The man was told not to breathe a word, but Erdi had left that very day on a secret mission in an attempt to solve the grain issue for the coming winter. Within a few days the whole territory knew. It was probably what saved Erdi's house from being looted and torched.

The three travellers were made welcome by villagers, keen to hear the latest news and of course, details of their quest. The headman said, there would be no problem transporting them as far as the sea, but asked, "What then?" They might not find a trader willing to ferry them over the salt waters to Erin.

"We'll just have to trade for a boat or have them make us one," said Erdi. The words sounded hollow even to him.

The headman studying his guest's face, sensed an opportunity. "Might it not be better to take the wherewithal with you? We have some wonderful stands of timber nearby and I'm willing to do a trade for one of our best oaks. We could hollow the trunk enough for it to float you up to the estuary. There they can give it a trim and render it seaworthy. That's their speciality. We just do river craft. If you find there is in fact a boat available and yours is surplus to requirements, then simply trade it on. No-one ever gets stuck with a boat fashioned from these trees." A wave of hand indicated a nearby lofty stand of oak and ash.

"Straight trunks. Fine girth. No twists or knots. No-one ever gets stuck with one of those." The man's assurance came with an almost disconcerting show of confidence. "We'll soon have you a boat to be proud of."

Erdi had deep misgivings, but there was no doubt they'd be in need of a boat at some point and so decided to take his advice.

The next day the sounds of chopping echoed through the woods. Upon ceasing, there followed a long whining creak as if something was heading up rather than down, until the earth-shuddering crash told different. Once branches had been severed and dragged clear, their trunk lay ready for its new life. Wedges were hammered in to split off the top section leaving a long flat surface running the whole length. The piece removed was roughly two hand spans from top curve to the splitting point. They then went to work hacking bark from the sides. The toughest part lay ahead, chopping and adzing out the middle. It was slow, hard work with one team of six resting while the other six vigorously hacked.

Erdi suggested using fire, but the headman said, from his experience, fire made little impact on freshly felled timber. So they persevered with steel, that almost seemed to bounce off the unyielding wood. The chopping was concentrated on a number of separate spots and at last greater progress was made when steel wedges were driven in to split off the bridging sections.

"Thought we were meant to be going to Erin. Not stuck here chopping wood," said Yanker.

"It's taking longer than I thought," Erdi replied. He really was beginning to get that, 'Wish I hadn't started this,' feeling, but now they had in fact started there was no option other than to carry on.

"Rhosyn probably thinks I'm cruising along the coast by now," said Yanker. "Not stuck here getting blisters."

It's always the same, *said the Teller*, it's those first steps of anything you do that are the hardest. Once they had cut a deep channel down the centre, however, they were able hammer chisel cuts along either side and split along the grain, speeding up the work. It took another two full days before the shape of a boat began to emerge. It was rolled for the remaining bark to be split off the underside, again using wedges.

A further morning was spent attempting to make it look a little more boat-like, before their ragged looking effort was log-rolled to the river for loading and paddling up to the coast. The Dwy had an amazing number of loops and winds, but there was nothing to impede progress, not even the sentry post at Gwal, staring gaunt on its mound, for apart from jackdaws clattering skyward as they passed, it was completely abandoned.

It was dusk by the time they reached a large settlement dominating a huge loop of the river. Light from a roaring fire shimmered deep red in the water and smoke billowed out to the west. Gulls wheeled, delaying lazy return to roost, knowing it was fish cleaning time. Nets hung drying and boats tugged at their moorings as if heeding the call of the sea. People quietly emerged from the houses to watch their arrival. Then the laughter broke out. Some were doubled up.

Their craft, meeting the bank with a jolt and judder, added to the mirth. With their line taken and boat secured, Erdi stepped ashore followed by Madarch.

"Well we've certainly made an impact," said Yanker, taking it steady, climbing over the load and walking along the length of the rocking hull, with arms out for balance. He alighted, managing to remain dry shod, to join the others on the bank.

The headman approached and with face still red from laughter asked pointing, "What exactly do you call **that**?"

"It's our boat," said Erdi, slightly wounded and thinking, 'I can't see what's so funny. It's not bad for a first attempt.' He pointed back upstream, "We launched it up by the Feasting Site. They told us you had men here skilled enough to finish it."

"They did, did they? Think you'll find skilled men don't take kindly to finishing what somebody else has started." He wandered over to take a closer look. "You'd have saved yourself a lot of time and effort if you'd have split out the heart both ends and dropped transoms in."

"I did suggest that, but they said it wasn't their way of doing things."

The man replied with just a thoughtful, "Mmm."

"Would your men be able to finish it?"

"You'd be better doing a deal for one of ours. We've nothing this length, but surely just the three of you don't need to struggle with a thing this massive. What's it for anyway?"

"Travelling west."

"How far west exactly?"

Erdi braced himself, knowing what was coming, "Erin."

"**Erin?**" That set them off laughing again. "Look, you'd better come inside. We can discuss things in there."

As they followed, Yanker taking a backward look, thought, 'It's not **that** bad surely.'

Erdi, catching up with the headman, asked with a hint of urgency, "You mean you can finish it?"

"We'll see."

Inside they were given bread plus fish, still steaming on their baking stakes. They'd seen them jabbed around the fire outside. Yanker suddenly drawing back from Madarch, rasped, "Don't eat it like that! That's disgusting!"

Their swarthy companion looking up slightly puzzled, a fish tail dangling from side of mouth, mumbled, "I did always eat like this." He wondered, 'Why is Yanker constantly picking on me?' He was beginning to wish he hadn't left home and if truth be known, had felt a bit put out the moment Erdi's cocksure cousin had become part of things.

On being asked by the headman, how exactly did he expect the finished boat to look, Erdi told him of the steaming and bending of a trunk he'd seen the Y-Dewis working on for Prince Aram's parting ceremony and said he'd been hoping for something similar.

The headman's raising of eyebrows and nod of appreciation, led Erdi to surmise, 'So I'm not as clueless as you first thought.'

"If you're going to open her out like that and take her on to those wild waters, she'll need to be rigged to stop her rolling. Where's the top section you split off?" the headman asked.

"They told us we didn't need it."

This was greeted with a look of incredulity. Then with a resigned sigh he explained what was meant by rigging. "This is your boat." He brandished one of the roasting stakes before laying it on the hearth. A slender piece of kindling was placed alongside and two twigs were carefully balanced to bridge the gap between. Pointing to the kindling he said, "This one here's your rigger. It'll keep her stable. You won't be in need of it going downriver, but it's vital you assemble and attach it before putting to sea. That section they said you didn't need, would have been perfect. Never mind. Can't be helped."

Erdi felt a weight lifting off him. Their boat was to be finished. After answering a few questions typical of those asked travellers, they were allowed an early night. All three slept like babies.

The next day they watched as the team went to work. You could just sense from their quiet unhurried efficiency, these were masters. The hull, unloaded and hauled up onto level banking, soon began to take on a trim look and temporary transoms were wedged in for the steaming.

When they finally began to ease out the sides to take the curved braces, Erdi asked, "How do you know how far you can force it apart?"

"She sort-of tells you," came the reply.

Towards the end of the second day, the lines of their craft had taken on an elegant look, sweeping in a graceful curve from open-mouthed prow to the blunter aft end. Here a transom was given its final trim before hammer blows on a length of shielding wood, drove it home. The channel to receive it had been packed with sealant and where its upper section overlapped the hull, yew wood withies bound it in place. The oak wedges tapped in to tighten the bindings, brought satisfying, rising notes of security.

"What about the front bit?" Erdi asked.

"The prow?" the man replied. "Here comes the best part. Finished it yet?" he called across to a workmate. The man had been chopping and adzing a block of wood. Picking it up, he struggled over with it. The thing looked a bit of a hefty lump to Erdi's eye, but he kept a still tongue and watched. It was offered up to the prow and scanned from the top and each side. The workbench was carried over and once trimmed further, the block was offered up again. A number of attempts were needed before it slid into the grooves prepared for it. Light taps with the hammer sent it fully home. Satisfied, they struggled, but did manage to prise it out again. Moss and tallow sealant was forced into the channel, running inside the prow's curve, cut to take the chiselled ring standing proud at the sheer end of the block and once aligned, it was driven into place as had been the stern board. Yew wood withies again bound the overlapping top bar of the transom to the hull sides. "Always check these wedges," said the master of the team as each sharp tap of his hammer tightened the bindings.

"When you're fashioning things like boards and transoms, how do you know how much to trim off?" Erdi asked. He'd not seen him once attempt to measure lengths or widths.

"People often ask that. You just seem to get an eye for it. Don't even have to think about it. See that length of wood yonder?" he said pointing. "Put your finger on the boat there."

Erdi placed a finger as instructed.

"No, a bit further towards the prow. Bit more. Bit more. Stop!" He picked up the stave and placing one end below Erdi's finger, wedged the other into the far side for it to span the hull. It fitted perfectly. "Not everyone can do that, mind," he said cheerily. Gentle taps with the side of his fist freed the piece of wood again. "Reckon it's part practice, part something you're born with."

Erdi had no doubts regarding that, but did have reservations about what now protruded proud of hull. "What about that piece?" he pointed to what looked like a drinker's nose, protruding from the prow. The man, returning an arched look, simply said "Watch," and started to trim the block. Soon its lines began to follow those of the boat. When finished, they flowed in to such an extent, it looked like it and the hull had been fashioned all from one piece.

The following day, the last of the trimming and shaping was done and the men went to work with sanding-cloths, giving the whole boat a smooth finish. Two holes were drilled in the upper prow to take mooring ropes; mooring pins were fitted, as were seats, including two narrow box seats fore and aft. While this had been going on, two others had been working on the rigger.

Once Erdi had been shown how to attach it, the finished boat, was launched and once re-loaded, would be ready for departure. At the point of being slid into the water the headman had said "By rights she should be left to dry awhile, but I doubt you have time for that." Blessing the hull with a libation of ale, he asked Erdi to name her and without hesitation he'd called out, "Gwendolin."

The boat, apart from being essential to their mission was a pleasure to look upon; a beauty to behold. The sight of her swaying light on the current, lifted Erdi's spirits and gave a sense of optimism. There still remained a vexing question, however. He had already asked if one of the villagers, a man of the sea, would be willing to sail with them and as yet had received no answer.

Two men approached the riverbank carrying a large flattish lump of sandstone. It had a groove chiselled around its girth. "You might need one of these." It was carefully placed, for securing and Erdi lowered it down into the hull. All helped with re-loading the cargo and once safely aboard, it was firmly wedged to prevent movement.

The meal that evening, started in a fairly muted fashion, but warmed up to end like a small celebration. The villagers had quite taken to these naïve travellers and were keen to give them all the advice they possibly could. They were also keen to know of course, more details of what had happened back in southern territory. They had already heard vague stories of slaughter and invasion, but now wanted to hear yet again, a first-hand account from one who'd lived in the midst of it. Plus, there was the question, did the Y-Dewis really eat the boiled flesh of their dearly departed?

Erdi, without having gone into too much disturbing detail on previous evenings, had hoped he'd satisfied curiosities, but no, seemingly they couldn't get enough of it, probing for more graphic descriptions of the gory bits. In the end, with a sigh, he gave a full, no sling unslung, account of his brother's death, the merciless, barbaric slaughter inside the fort, the Seer being dismembered and how Gardarm's screams could have cut steel. Looking around at faces frozen in silence, he thought, 'Well you did ask for it!'

All then seemed quite muted as information was passed on regarding traders from the Erin Isle. The headman confided, they could be a bit wild, which Erdi already knew of course, but were basically good people. He also assured, there was nothing to fear as regards having their cargo stolen, provided they didn't meet with freelancers along the way and once in safe waters they would be looked after and boat taken care of. They would be treated with the same respect, the Erin were when trading here on home shores.

Erdi then asked the man if he knew of one referred to as Grik the Fish?

"Yes, we know him alright," piped up one of the ladies present and general laughter broke out. It was strange she should have been the one to answer, for perched up beside her, looking thoroughly at home, was Madarch. On first accepting her invite, the first whiff of his exclusive aroma assaulting her nostrils had prompted a severe hand wafting, but once over the initial shock, she seemed quite taken with his company. Erdi's brow furrowed in puzzlement.

More beer flowed and Erdi noticed Yanker had become deeply ensconced, talking to a small group nearby, which was all very well, but there was still a major problem to be resolved. They couldn't contemplate crossing those waters of renowned danger without a man of suitable experience to accompany and guide them.

Erdi grabbed the headman's attention once again and this time became quite insistent, asking did such a man actually exist? He gave an assurance, that if he did, the man could expect a generous reward.

At last, with a sigh of relief, he heard the bang on wood for silence, followed by an order ringing out.

A bent figure shuffled from the gloom.

Erdi's heart sank. The old salt had that just about to go over look and what remained of his hair was wispy white.

"This is Cronk," said the headman. "He's been with us quite a number of years now, haven't you Cronk?"

The man nodded and when he grinned his few remaining teeth stood out like yellowed stumps of an ancient fence.

"Now I know he looks a bit weather beaten----------------"

"Weather beaten?" muttered Erdi. The man's skin, the colour of tanned leather, had deep lines, like parched ravines and his watery blue eyes had a disconcertingly vague look.

The headman continued, "I bet Cronk has lost count of the number of times he's sailed to Erin, haven't you Cronk?"

"Bet he's lost track of a lot more than that," muttered Yanker.

"Also," said the headman, "he can communicate in their strange tongue. Apparently, it's not too different from his own."

"Hello Cronk," said Erdi warily. Seemed a strange name to be calling a man. Sort of name that could invite a punch. "Are you able to leave with us in the morning?"

"First light," he replied and then for some inexplicable reason, started to cackle. He made his way back into the gloom, but before disappearing far side of the fire, half turned and with white of eyes just visible, repeated, "First light!"

The ensuing silence was broken by Erdi asking, "How exactly, did he get a name like Cronk?"

"He just turned up out of nowhere one day, gabbling a language none of us could understand. He knew the basics of sign language, however and we asked him where he was from? Along with his hand-signs, came this strange cronk word and with it making us laugh, that's what we called him. Turns out he's from that island lying to the northwest and in those parts, cronk means hill. I know he looks a bit bent and shaky, but he's a tough old bird."

Erdi glanced across at Yanker. He shouldn't have, for the dubious look and suppressed mirth glinting set them both off. Erdi had to disguise his laughter as a bout of coughing. The headman, slapping him on the back, called for his beaker to be re-filled. "There. Wash it down with this," he urged.

When finally settling up for all the work, Erdi was pleasantly surprised. These people had done an infinitely better job for not much more bronze than that given to the initial owners of the tree.

Chapter Nine

The headman and other swathed figures, emerging like shadows, came to see them shove off into the gloom of the following morning. Erdi felt as if they had arrived paddling an ugly duck, but were now gliding away aboard a graceful swan. The river flowed fairly straight and they were pulled along by the receding tidal waters. In the improving light they entered a widening funnel, leading into a broad stretch, that snaked its way through a vast spread of calm water, where in places, breaching sand offered glistening humps for birds to flock onto. The distant shore lying to the northeast was flatland and to the far southwest, stood the hills that on a clear day could be seen from home.

"Must work! Must work! Not get stuck." Urged Cronk, digging his paddle deep.

As they headed northwest, the channel narrowed and in places the bottom became clear. Flatfish shadowing the seabed settled soft mid clouds of sand. Birds swooped in to strut and feed on the emerging sandbars, until a sudden notion took them to flock and accompanied by a chorus of high-pitched pips and squeals, they silvered the air.

Erdi felt the pleasant sensation of the sun's warmth on his back and scanning ahead perceived that a thin glisten, almost hurting the eyes, was all that separated, shimmering sea and sands from the broad sweep of sky. He later managed to decipher from their navigator, that boats following the wrong channel when attempting to gain deep water, often ran aground and became stranded. Which left the only option of sitting and waiting to be lifted by the next tide, but of course, then came the battle against the power of incoming water. When the boat at last rolled up on the crests, to sweep down into troughs their wizened mariner called down the boat, "We safe now."

"We not," Madarch shouted back from the prow. "I can't swim."

Erdi recalling his own first taste of the sea, shouted against the wind, "Don't worry, we won't let you drown."

"Maybe not drown, but we could dip him for a bit. Get the stink off him," Yanker called back.

"Enough. I don't want you two falling out." Erdi had noticed with some concern, the friction between them building.

"It's alright for you. It's not you sitting behind him!" Yanker's last remark caused the boat to suddenly lurch shore-wards. An alarmed Cronk called from the stern, "Madarch, take steady! All keep same speed. All keep same speed," he urged. "Like we all one. That's better."

He steered them around a headland where the chill of the full sea breeze hit them and the boat rode the water almost as if relishing release from a lifetime standing as a forest sentinel. Erdi called down to Madrach, "Have you checked those wedges?"

"Course I did. They tight," came the sullen reply.

Cronk steered them towards the sands, ridged and glistening in endless lines rippling out to the west and they set to work attaching the rig, pulling the boat inshore each time it was lifted by the incoming tide. The wind was fresh and the water gripped their legs like chilled iron fetters. When all was secure, they put to sea again.

Steady paddling continued until middle day and by giving instructions from the stern, Cronk steered them inshore towards the broad sweep of sands. Following the shoreline, more precise commands, had them nosing into a narrow river mouth that eventually opened out into a long thin basin silently filling and lifting dark swathes of wrack as it crept towards the tidemark.

They paddled inshore, dumped the stone anchor on the mud, and uncoiling a rope for retrieval of their craft, disembarked to pick their way across the ooze, towards the inviting grassed banking.

"Here we rest," said Cronk.

Erdi carried the string of mackerel he'd caught and they soon had a driftwood fire crackling. It was not long before the aroma of fish cooking had stomachs doing what they always do when empty. Dough was laid on their baking stone and they had salt to season the feast.

Later, their boat, now riding at anchor, was pulled in for Erdi to load the skin of fresh water he'd carried from upriver. He'd found that the distant houses, their reflections looking so charming and inviting, were in fact abandoned and derelict.

From that same direction, four men slowly walking in step towards them had a hide-bound boat borne aloft, as if sharing an oversized hat. Each having a paddle belt-tucked, they shared the burden of fishing net, shoulder draped. Suddenly appearing and blinking in the sunlight, the leader of the party looked clearly puzzled by the amusement engendered.

Erdi asked in cymry, did he know what had happened to those who had once lived in the village? With this obviously not penetrating, he reverted to sign language.

This brought the reply of overlapped wrists and jerk of thumb west, 'slavers had taken them.'

Once the man had ducked back into position, the strange assemblage with eight legs, continued to the inlet's neck, where effortless launching and boarding from the banking, was followed by light, deft dips that took the craft gliding out towards open water.

Yanker gave a tug on the painter for their boat Gwendolin to ready herself for a muddy assault and once the anchor had been lumped back aboard, as best they could manage, the four attempted to do likewise.

With the weather having freshened further, there was urgent need to work their way out to sea, beyond each roller's inclination, to sweep them broad-side, in onto the sand.

Erdi again trailed his line for fish, but had no luck until finally, under the reddening sun, saw the line go taut and pulling in the catch, had a mackerel on every hook. With them flapping and slapping in the bottom of the boat, he untangled the feathered lures, slung the line out again and with it immediately digging deep into his forefinger, hauled in another catch from the shoal. Food now secured, they headed in towards the sands and with their boat beached, low and dark against the mid-tide sunset, they busied themselves setting up camp.

Erdi and Cronk searched for driftwood and Yanker, gutting fish down on the shoreline was joined by Madarch. Erdi saw his cousin suddenly recoil in disbelief, vigorously waft a hand and relocate slightly upwind. The cleaned fish strung from the gills, were delivered to where Erdi was having problems lighting the fire. He noticed Madarch had a troubled look.

To prevent the kindling from taking flight and go bowling enflamed down the beach, they erected a windbreak. Dry white driftwood was carefully placed and ragged flames began to rage, driven by gusts, still somehow evading their barrier. At first chance Erdi asked his cousin what had happened down on the shoreline.

"Erdi, I've had the stink of him in my nostrils all day. Like rotting fish in rancid butter. Smells worse than Stench! Don't see why I should still have to suffer it ashore. Can't you get him to wash?"

"I've tried, but he says he doesn't like water."

"He might have a sudden meeting with it if this carries on."

In the cool of the following morning, before the tide took chance to strand them, all clambered aboard and by levering hard with the paddles, felt the relief of that first gentle lift. They worked their way west looking tiny against the backdrop of hills and were in fact, in the whole spread of the bay, the only thing to crawl into the shadow of the headland that jutted out to sea. On Cronk's instructions they steered a course, labouring beneath overshadowing cliffs and by late morning had reached a river inlet on the far side. Their boat rode in on the tide and they paddled leisurely across a broad basin towards a settlement on the far shoreline.

Small fishing craft littered the mud, some tilted, some upturned and on spotting larger boats being loaded on the shore opposite, Cronk gave a loud cackle and cried out, "We in time. We in time."

Erdi was amazed to see that the cargo being stowed had been transported along the narrow trail from the headland, strapped to tiny ponies. They were almost certainly the same horses Trader had handled in the deal with the Bleddi warriors.

With the boat moored, they clambered ashore and Cronk walked purposefully to where the hide covered craft were being loaded. The confident way he stood talking to the crew members, as if all having met before somewhere, seemed amazing. Their trip had taken years off the man.

He returned and with face fissures crinkling into a smile, he said, "They leave tomorrow. We go with them. We safer all together." The men, as he had suspected, were from Erin, trading for copper.

145

They re-embarked and one swift dip of the paddles had them gliding across to the opposite bank where the small settlement stood. Inside the palisade, children immediately stopped their game to stare. One small boy ran into the nearest hut and a family emerged, but with Erdi's greeting in cymry hitting a blank wall of silence, he again reverted to sign language. An instruction was given and the child was sent scampering to a neighbour's house. More people emerged and a young man approached, who thankfully spoke cymry.

They were made welcome and Erdi sent Madarch back to the boat for their basket of fish. The gift brought rather fixed smiles and after being advised it would be best kept for their journey, they were led outside to witness dark shapes, seething to devour tossed food scraps, within a massive stone-walled holding pool, refreshed twice daily by the tide.

The conversation took its usual course with the villagers keen to know where they were from and where they were going. One of the men having witnessed their arrival, asked to be shown the boat. One by one, every man in the place arose from squatting posture and walked to where it sat at anchor. Erdi hauled her inshore for inspection. Peering in and around, viewing from every angle, all were full of admiration.

Erdi was told their cargo would be safe, they had guards on watch at night and he'd managed to evade their enquiries as to what they were actually hauling. Trader had advised him, "Folk might appear friendly, but only tell them what you really need to."

Later, he asked about the small ponies and was surprised by the merriment it engendered. His new companion was keen to share the joke. Apparently, a trader had turned up leading them in a string, looking as if he'd just invented the wheel. The poor fool had become entangled in a deal with some Bleddi warriors, who had assured him the horses were perfect for hauling copper out of the mines. Erdi patiently waited for laughter to subside, keen to hear more details.

At last the man continued, "Some of the tunnels winding inside that hill are so narrow a man can't even get through. They send their children in to fetch the ore out!" His final words were delivered on yet another burst of laughter. Once calm again, he explained, of course they had still done a deal for the ponies, but not at the inflated notion the trader had had in mind. They were, after all, broken-in for duty and being sturdier than they looked, were ideal for hauling ore to the furnaces and refined copper down to the shore.

On imagining the horse trader's meeting with reality, plus recollection of Trader's words, 'Some deals can turn out a bit disappointing,' a whistful smile spread. Erdi then told the man it wasn't the first time he'd seen the animals, but originally there had only been five.

"There must be double that now," came the cheery reply.

The following morning the boat was hauled in for boarding and they joined the strange assembly readying to head out to sea. The four large skin-hulled craft were manned, plus each carried sheeted cargo amidships. Flanking either side, attached in the same manner as their own rigged construction, were cargo boats. The gaps between the manned and cargo vessels left enough room for paddling and the latter had contents covered by hides secured to side pegs. Any waves breaking over would simply pour off as if from a duck's back.

Erdi had noticed the previous evening, that ore stacked ready for the beach kilns had been crushed. Apparently, it was done in the mine and the waste tipped into worked-out tunnels. Ideally, he'd have liked to have walked up there to take a look, but by the time the meal had been consumed and conversation had ceased there had only been time to re-cross the river to examine the boats and their meagre looking cargos. His companion told him, "I know it doesn't look much, but pure copper is that heavy it needs spreading evenly and wedging tight. Any movement, would put the boats in danger of sinking. Believe me, its value once offloaded in Erin makes all their efforts worthwhile."

He didn't bother to inform the man, he already knew this. It might have given hint as to what gave their own boat that rather down at hull look.

He was also told that the narrow galleries riddling the hill where the treasured ore was mined, went deep enough to swallow an army. They even dropped to lower levels and anyone foolish enough to enter unescorted was likely to become lost, never to see daylight again. The whole headland was in fact a honeycomb of tunnels.

So, the following morning, once each helmsman had signalled all was ready, the paddles were given that first lusty dip. The ebbing tide helped the small fleet out to sea, but on open water progress was slow as the men from Erin, held back by their weighty loads, strived to make headway. Repeatedly, Cronk called for downing of paddles, to give them chance to catch up and each time they sat waiting, the current they worked against bobbed them gently north. To the west, was the dramatic sweep of mountains ranging south for as far as the eye could see, while ahead lay flat land, with the hump of an island standing offshore. They headed for this.

By the time the sun had freed itself from the mountains, they had successfully negotiated the dangerous straits separating those offshore flatlands, in fact the massive island of Ynys Isel, from the coast. Cronk informed; had they left any later that morning, they would have been at the mercy of the waters surging south into the channel.

They passed under the cliffs of the small offshore island, marvelling at the blizzard of seabirds wheeling and screaming above. Some bobbed as if enjoying riding the waves and where others roosted high on crags, they resembled small drifts of snow.

Madarch, spotting a dark hump out to sea, pointed and asked was it a whale? Erdi having seen its like on his previous salt-water trips, told him, no, although certainly the size of a whale, it was in fact a huge fish, completely harmless unless you happened to collide with it.

The boats, crawling across a bay's broad expanse, took until middle-day to reach a sandy cove, where with relief, all aboard were able to rest and take first nourishment of the day. They had brought creels of fish and all joined in the work of gutting and the search for firewood.

Erdi, on seeing one of the Erin traders checking the baskets and noticing his look of concern regarding food stocks, told him not to worry, as he was sure they could catch more.

Cronk translated this and also, what was then said by Yanker.

"If we run out of fish, we can always heave Madarch, overboard. There'll be enough dead floating on the surface to keep us going for days!"

Madarch's personal perfume had not gone unnoticed and everyone burst out laughing, even Erdi. The man in question glowered at Yanker with deep resentment burning.

Having rested, they continued westward and by late afternoon, finally rounded the head of the island, to pull into a small rocky bay at full tide. Their boats were paddled to nose into the arc of seaweed, their first touch sending up swarms of small flies. All set about the usual tasks and the remaining fish were cooked, some for the evening meal and the rest to be eaten cold, during the crossing. Their loads were checked and weapons put ready. Erdi went in search along the shore, selecting stones, perfect for slingshot.

Before settling down for the night, Madarch asked, "Why we go so slow today. Why we wait for others?"

"Would you rather cross to Erin alone, have the cargo stolen and maybe get your throat cut?" Yanker retorted.

Madarch, with resentment boiling inside, felt he could say or do nothing right anymore.

Erdi asked Cronk if it was those same raiders that made beautiful locations, such as their present haven, uninhabitable?

The man nodding, said most lived in villages safely tucked away inland and their houses tended to have walls of stone rather than those of daubed wattle. He then advised all to get plenty of rest, for with departure being before sun-up and Erin being as far distant as the entire journey already travelled, it would be hard work all day without rest.

Ahead lay wild, dangerous waters. He warned, many boats had foundered under heavy weather, suddenly blowing in. It was at this point, like a fist of ice gripping his heart, he felt the jolt that all through life had accompanied serious misgivings. He hardly dared listen as Cronk repeated what incredible luck they'd had meeting the copper traders, before then blithely explaining he'd never been further west than this before.

Seeing Erd's look of alarm, he reasoned, "Not from Ynys Isel anyway." He had only ever negotiated the much shorter crossing further north, from his homeland to Erin. He tried to reassure by saying, it was still the same sea they would be voyaging over, it was just that at this particular point, there was a lot more of it. Erdi's confidence in the man was restored slightly, when he explained, he'd been watching the tides and had worked out, that first light next morning, not only coincided with high tide to aid their departure, it also gave all spans of the sun to reach Erin.

It allowed an overnight beaching of the boats without fear of stranding. The alternative, riding at anchor, would have left them at the mercy of the sea and rocks, if a wilful night wind happened to tug at their moorings. He said an early start was vital. Even then it was likely they'd be enduring a night on open water, but at least they should have the comfort of Erin being in sight.

Before bedding themselves down, Erdi repeated instructions he'd been trying to instil all journey. On no account were they to divulge the real reason for journeying to Erin. That would immediately inflate the value of grain. They were not to mention the size of the hoard they carried and also when the inevitable happened and they were asked for news of home, they were to avoid telling the truth. If the traders of Erin realised that in the central lands of home, a bronze axe-head was now worth little more than a fired cooking pot, their mission would be sunk. They had heard it all before, but Erdi was well aware of how tongues can be loosened by too much ale.

There was barely enough light to aid safe passage turn of tide next morning, but all eased out without mishap. Ahead lay a vast expanse of open water and somewhere in the distance beyond, lay Erin.

The day turned into one of near flat calm, which was of course fortunate except the thin mists that tend to accompany such conditions gave the impression, no matter how hard they strained, they weren't actually getting anywhere. The mountains behind were no longer visible and ahead lay a featureless expanse of gently swelling water. In order not to leave the others too far distant in their wake, Cronk suggested two should paddle while two rested. They laboured on well past middle day with still no glimpse of land ahead.

Yanker, asking no-one in particular, "Are we certain there's actually land out there?"

Cronk told him, that from his home island to the north, mountains were often visible, both to the east and west and in crisp autumn air it was even possible to see the mountains they'd just left behind. He'd almost sounded homesick when adding, "Some days, I did feel like I could reach out and touch, long finger of land pointing down from the north."

As the sun reddened, the air cleared and as if having suddenly popped up like magic, dead ahead stood a clear blue thread of the Erin mountains. They cheered as did the crews struggling behind. Cronk gave the instruction to wait, for he needed to confer. His instincts proved right; they had drifted a little too far south and so set a new course accordingly. The fleet master cheerily announced, that for the first time ever, they might have the luck of making the westerly crossing in a single day. It's usually best not to divulge such things, however, for as if listening, the wind immediately freshened, aiding from the south, but the spray now splattering up from the prow, soaked them to the skin.

"Are those wedges still tight, Madarch?" Erdi called out.

"No need keep asking I tell you when they not!" came the irritated reply. "Remember, it's me can't swim."

The distant glow of fires burning ashore, seemed to mock, as drenched and cold, they laboured landwards through the cool evening air. Then Erdi spotted it, riding and bucking against the wind, a boat approaching from the northwest. It wasn't fishing or just passing, it was definitely on a course to intercept.

"We got trouble," shouted Cronk.

They had entered a wide bay and those welcoming fires, that had seemed so tantalisingly close, now looked horribly distant, flickering in the gloom. As the boat neared, Erdi counted ten warriors. Closer still, he could see their craft was a clumsy version of their own. If it weren't for the cargo boats, they could have outrun the threat, but no-one voiced such a notion. The prow was a flat board bludgeoning the waves, sending plumes of spray to splatter white spots on the dark rolling water. The crew, with wild hair and long beards streaming ghostly in the fading light, reminded Erdi of his first sight of Wolf.

Their leader stood as they neared, bend of knees helping his upright stance in the swell. He called out a command.

He was answered. There followed further exchanges and then Cronk translating told them, "The man wants our boat and cargo."

If refused, the hide-bound craft would be speared and sent to the depths. Hand over the boat and all could carry on their way unharmed.

Knowing the theft of their boat would just be a foretaste of what was to follow; their massacre or a lifetime in slavery, Erdi and Yanker made ready with slingshot. With each lift of the waves, the raider's craft reared closer. Their paddles, exchanged so efficiently for axes and spears, hinted at an oft performed routine.

The earie silence mocking tensions aboard, prow nosing prow like some waterborne end of day ritual greeting, was broken by their leader's rasped instruction.

Madarch, perched in the prow, visibly flinched at the ferocity.

"He demands, you throw him a line," Cronk translated.

Pulling himself to a wobbly half standing position, he wailed. "Tell him I can't swim!"

Cronk obliged and the warrior, now close enough for burnt turf and sweat aroma to assault nostrils, leant forward, holding out a massive hand ready to grasp the line.

Seeing Madarch visibly quivering, Erdi shouted, "No! Don't give him the rope. Let Yanker forward!"

Madarch, suddenly rising to full height, rammed his paddle handle into the raiders mouth with such ferocity, spat teeth arrowed into the water. Recoiling, the man stared horrified, his hairy blood-ringed maw gaping wide in disbelief. The following impact of paddle blade jabbed hard to throat, sent him tumbling backwards, where thrashing like a gaffed shark, he gagged and fought for air atop a melee of struggling warriors.

Forcing the erstwhile weapon against the raider's prow, Madarch disengaged the two craft, while his comrades, raking the raiders with slingshot, brought yelps and muffled cries of rage. All four, then paddled in mad desperation to gain safety beyond javelin range, leaving the copper traders to struggle along behind.

Nearing shore, there was barely light to see safe passage, but guided by the glow of fires from Baile Atha Cliath and praying there were no rocks, they entered the river mouth, to steer their boat up to a wharf on the northern shore. Limbs still shaking, made it a long, hard haul up the ladder onto the dock. Tide was now almost fully out. Peering beyond the port beacon's glow, out into the blackness, searching for a sign of the other boats, they at last saw dark shapes limping low in the murk. Cronk called out and on receiving the reply, passed on the message, none had perished.

They were all absolutely exhausted, but Erdi warned against flopping down on the dock, saying, "Do that and you'll struggle to get back up again." Knowing all were now safe, he approached Madarch and smelly or not, reached out to give him a warm embrace of gratitude.

The young hero, scowling, forcefully pushed him away.

Erdi, eying his friend, asked completely puzzled, "What's the matter Madarch? I was trying to thank you for saving the boat. In fact, probably saving our lives. You were incredible. Whatever possessed you?"

Madarch, with tears of rage glinting, spat, "It's that Yanker! You, me alright before he came!"

154

Chapter Ten

Meanwhile, said the Teller, back home, the news of Erdi's mission had had a calming effect on tensions. His own people realised that a man willing to put his life at risk attempting to secure them grain for winter, would hardly have been the man complicit in the plan to rob them of it.

As far as Gwenithen was concerned, he had been led to believe the venture was purely to open-up the possibility of future trade for wheat and barley, not to actually sail home laden with the stuff.

It was during Erdi's absence that the reason for the new strange crop became evident and why the Y-Dewis held it in such high esteem. Its flowers had bloomed yellow and when these died, the leaves were harvested, pods picked and the stalks left for the goats to eat. From the leaves the Y-Dewis extracted the precious blue dye, woad. Only the elite were entitled to don clothes of the colour and only warriors could legally daub skin with it. Flouting these rules carried a severe penalty and to be 'raised to the blue' was considered the highest honour.

The plant was not native, but had been brought from far-off shores. The Y-Dewis avowed it had been brought back by Y-Thlewioo, the legendary navigator from one of his voyages, but Trader, practical as ever, reasoned, the plant had more than likely arrived as part of a trade deal down in Tinner country. From there it would not have been a vast step to have traded it up the coast. "Nothing but a glorified weed!" he'd added.

There was of course speculation as to how Erdi's travels might be faring, plus speculation regarding Mara's concern for the injured old warhorse, Tawy, Brialla's brother. They acknowledged the man had received a nasty wound in battle and Mara had of late been acclaimed as a miracle worker with her care and medicines, but she seemed to be spending more time with the warrior than with her own husband.

This of course wasn't strictly true, *said the Teller*, but you know how people like to exaggerate and relish such gossip. If anything, Mara spent more time with her new friend Brialla than with anyone. Inga regularly joined them foraging for medicinal plants and was often with them when up at the market. The three had probably had more laughs in the short time since first teaming up, than in a good many years previous.

Brialla was quite a forthright little thing and had a habit of asking the sort of questions that cross people's minds, but they never pluck up courage to actually ask. One day, chatting and laughing, whilst conducting business up in the market, Brialla, stopping to think, asked, "Mara? You know the one they call Hanner Bara?"

"Not personally, but I know who you mean."

"She's had just the one child, right?"

Mara said, "Yes. Why do you ask?" Knowing Brialla, she braced herself.

"Considering her line of business, do you think she uses the pebble or the gum?"

"Brialla!" Mara ducking slightly, looked around to see if anyone had heard. "You can't say that here!"

"Well, we've all done it at times, otherwise the brutes would have us pregnant until we died from it."

The Teller said, it was in fact the women, in those early days, who intermingled more than their menfolk. The children did of course. They always tend to. But the women were constantly on watch for

156

things like hairstyles or ways of dressing that could enhance their looks. Y-Dewis women, tended not to use facial colouring, but on seeing the effect berry lip-stain; tincture mix of copper, lead and ashes around the eyes; red ochre and beeswax cheek colouring, had on the men, they certainly did. In return, their habit of wearing tight plaid leggings beneath dresses in the colder weather, was copied throughout the territory.

Of course, on the subject of intermingling, as said before, the obvious happened. Young men of both tribes, rather than being drawn to their own kind, had an eye on what they considered the strange and exotic and betrothals began to be announced, Talia's being one of them. The joining with her young Y-Dewis warrior was to be the following spring.

Mara wondered if Brialla was as forthright in her own cymry language as she was when exchanging banter with her and Inga. Certain words such as love, handsome, beautiful seemed easier to say in Brialla's tongue than in her own and swear words didn't seem the least bit shocking in cymry. What Brialla came out with one day, however, would have made jaws drop whatever the tongue spoken.

There were quite a few early arrivals, men mostly, watching them setting up the stall and Brialla, turning to Inga had asked, "Did you have any problem getting free of the house this morning?"

Inga replied, "He's getting terrible. Some days I hardly recognise him as the man I first fell for. He gets these headaches. I find rubbing the back of his neck helps. Without that, I'd have had no chance of getting free today. In fact, I'd expected to hear at any moment that gloomy voice of his, 'Inga, I need Growler today,' knowing that without his protection, I'd be trapped at home."

"Mine's the same," said Brialla. "Right as sunshine one day, like an angry bull the next." She confided with a giggle, "I wash his feet in warm water. That usually works."

"Dommed likes the honey cake I make. That normally softens his mood."

Brialla beaming, said, "Honeyed fruit! Thought it was just me that had to resort to that sort of thing."

On account of a few men starting to take an interest, she lowered her voice and confided, "He's one of those men who likes these." Then, wriggling her upper body closer, "For me they're just a nuisance. Get in the way."

For such a slight woman, she did require a surprising amount of cloth to cover that region, *said the Teller.*

Inga gave a squeak of laughter and said, "Don't tell anyone, but when the children are out, I sometimes pretend I've not noticed my robe isn't done-up properly."

"But Inga, that's asking for trouble," Brialla chided and then said quite brightly, "Do you swallow, or spit it out?"

Men standing open mouthed, stared wondering if they'd heard her right.

There was a collective gasp from the Teller's audience, pierced by a few female shrieks of laughter. One woman said in quite a deep voice, "Well!".

A man muttered, "No point in asking her then!"

More laughter.

The Teller, putting a finger to lips, appealed for quiet. There are certain things I shouldn't say------ but it's life though, isn't it? Now let me get back to Erdi.

With Cronk's help they located the Port Master, not happy at being roused so close to middle night, but on seeing Gwenithen's official seal and receiving required dues, he informed them, they were now entitled to trade and receive protection while within the confines of the settlement.

"Now will ye let a man get some rest!" was said as they departed, followed by groans of protest as the copper traders descended on him.

The latter, when eventually leading them through the settlement, to edge along the narrows, feeling their way through the blackness, maintaining an unbelievable babble, they repeatedly gave Madarch, congratulatory backslaps and avowals of absolute amazement. Cronk later explained, not only were they stunned by one so unlikely triumphing over the most feared man in those parts, they had also been stunned by the fact they had made the journey in just a single day. Journeying east, not laden down with copper and with the westerlies helping, they had often managed the crossing between first light and dusk, but never before when travelling westwards. Flat calm and constant need to catch the faster boat, they considered to be the reasons.

The following morning, like an excited contagion, news of their encounter spread through the entire settlement and naturally, people were curious to see the man who had felled the mighty Tuafola with nothing more than a boat paddle. Their surprise, however, verging almost on disappointment, was embodied by the hero being naught but a wiry, unassuming, dark-skinned young man, it wasn't advisable to stand next to once the sun was up. He was eyed by some in wonder, mixed with a certain degree of admiration, while others, youths mainly, saw potential profit in challenging him. There was not much to him, yet beating the man who'd triumphed over the feared Tuafola would surely be seen as cast-bronze proof of manhood.

On that same first morning, apart from agreeing a deal regarding their accommodation, Erdi's most pressing task had been to determine the value of their cargo. In most stories you hear related, *said the Teller*, the answer to such a problem is simple. We'd probably be told, the hero just happened to wander through a convenient market to take note of the rate, goods such as grain and bread, traded at. But this isn't just a story, it's what actually happened and there was no convenient market available. Not for days, anyway and Erdi didn't have days to waste. Cronk had warned, if the easterlies started blowing into the bay, they would struggle to work their way out from the harbour, let alone out to sea. In view of this he asked Cronk to enquire about something, that thanks to Trader's exploits, he'd learnt the value of, sheep.

Again, it wasn't that simple. As Trader had predicted, all major deals went through one man and this man was called Un Farqune. When asking those they chanced upon, what rate local sheep traded at, they were given suspicious looks by most and the few that didn't hurry on their way, referred them back to Un Farqune. So, there was no other option than to seek him out.

Cronk stopped the next man they met. They were on the banks of what the locals called the Ruirthech, that ran fast and strong through the settlement. With the hint of a smirk, the man told them, Un Farqune would not be a hard man to find, but added "You'll be needing to cross the abhainn."

Erdi had learnt enough from his friend Wolf to know abhainn meant river, which in turn probably meant, the flow dividing north Baile-Atha-Cliath from the southern settlement would be known as, the abhainn Ruirthech.

The drifting aroma of turf smouldering, rekindled memories of time spent with his friend, particularly the happy occasion down on the lefels where Erdi had witnessed children creeping up whilst he'd been trying to fish. What seemed incidental at the time, had since grown into one of those cherished memories. He mused at the fact, you can't predict or choose abiding memories, they just seem to settle in the mind as a piece of nostalgia, usually being recollections of simple happenings, rather than of events that had huge expectations at the time.

Following the man's directions, they continued along the river and crossed by way of an ingenious bridge fabricated from honeysuckle rope and broad wattle walkway, held up from the water by three hide covered craft. These imprisoned boats were sheeted over to prevent infill of rainwater and their movement, undulating and juddering in the flow gave the impression, they were quivering to be off downstream. Entry to the palisade was barred by two guards whose spears crossed with a forbidding click as they approached. Erdi showed his official seal, Cronk stated their business and they were told to wait. The details of the seal would have meant nothing, but possession of it did.

Eventually a warrior returned, instructing them to accompany him. The huts they were led amongst, were built on quite a grand scale, making the one they waited in, seem unsettlingly like the storeroom it actually was. Erdi was of course nervous, wondering what this mysterious Un Farqune would look like. Would he be a wily wizard, seeping up before him, or maybe towering mightily, as if cleaved from an ancient windswept crag.

When an unassuming looking man, in ordinary working attire, entered, Erdi imagined him to be nothing more than a messenger, but when he said, two from 'across' had been asking after him, it became obvious this was the man himself, which of course, immediately raised hopes of success. In fact, it cheered him no end, for surely, he'd not have much trouble dealing with one such as this.

At Erdi's prompting, Cronk explained, his young warrior friend was on a trade mission for the Y-Dewis chieftain, Gwenithen, and with no knowledge of the language spoken on these shores, had invited him along as translator. Erdi's offer of Gwenithen's seal was brushed aside as if of no relevance but then, when the gift of one of the torques was offered, the man on examining it, said with a look of amusement sparkling, "How very thoughtful."

As Cronk translated, Erdi felt a sudden awareness. He'd just received one of his warnings. The jab in his guts, that was always accompanied by, what he described as a ringing sound in his head. It was one of those instinctive feelings, he knew from experience, could only be ignored at peril. It caused him to take a long hard look at the man, the man portraying himself as no more than a simple trader and as he did so, the realisation slowly grew, there was a hidden force within, a power pulsating behind that calm demeanour.

Then came the prickly feeling, the feeling that always intensified the further he strayed from a position of safety. A position now, so far behind him, it was way back in the east, beyond the sea where the sun had risen that morning. His sense of isolation, being a complete beginner, daring to venture into unknown territory against a hardened veteran, made the task ahead seem all the more daunting.

Before entering into any deal, he needed to establish the going rate of a commodity, simply to use as a comparison, rather than to actually buy any of it. Once appraised, he could then easily work out the value of their bronze and thus, the likely going rate of grain. But first he had to establish that vital figure to give him something to work with. The trouble was, the more he looked at Un Farqune, the more it became obvious, he didn't look like the type to forgive having his time wasted.

Erdi took courage, however, what else could he do? He asked the Erin trader, what would twenty sheep cost him in bronze? The man simply stared back, his face giving no hint of inner feelings. Cronk was asked to repeat the question. The man sighed and replied, "It would be depending on which sheep you happened to be talking about. They're not all the same you know. It's not like snapping out peas from a pod."

Erdi had been right. There was more to this man than met the eye. His feeling of discomfiture was heightened further on hearing, "How exactly do you propose to be getting twenty full grown sheep, of a lively disposition, back home across those waters?"

In a lame attempt at making his enquiry seem realistic Erdi replied, "I'm sure the traders we crossed with would haul them back if the reward were to be generous enough."

The intensity and duration of the disbelieving stare became that uncomfortable, Erdi felt the rising impulse to blurt out, "Look I'm sorry! I know I look like a complete fool, but I can't reveal yet what I've really come here for. This is all just a ruse to find out what my bronze is worth!"

The taciturn Un Farqune, looking at the foreigner, wondered, 'had he found a lucrative idiot or just a complete waste of time?' He decided to give the stranger the benefit of the doubt and off they trundled, aboard a horse-drawn cart, to view sheep.

Erdi found himself being drawn ever deeper, feeling more unease with every bend in the trail, every stream they crossed and low hill surmounted. The rolling country had large patches swathed with wheat and adding colour to the scene, were whole communities busy scything and gathering crops. Many stopped work and waved as they passed.

Less fertile land, bristling with patches of dark marsh grass, was dotted with grazing herds, sheep included. Erdi, keen to have his problem resolved, enquired about the latter, but was told, 'No, he wasn't to waste time looking at those. He was only to be shown the best.'

He could feel pressure mounting and sense of dread growing, but at last on being presented with the sight of suitable sheep, he asked how much in bronze axe-heads, twenty would be?

"That's not the way we conduct business in these parts," said Un Farqune. "Do you want to insult the man? Refuse his hospitality?"

All this of course, Cronk was translating, but I won't labour the point.

Erdi explained, time was of the essence and he didn't have a single moment to spare. Could the man make one exception and tell him, without becoming embroiled in ceremony, what he wanted for the sheep?

The man's shocked indignation, then heated outpouring, emphasised by arm-waving, foot stamps and curses of utter derision, finally abated and the answer was sullenly given like a pulled tooth.

Erdi needed to steel himself. He was now of course expected to state his offer, the start of protracted negotiations, but instead, he took a deep breath and said, "I'll think about it." Even he cringed at the words.

Un Farqune didn't lose his temper, as Trader had predicted might happen, it wasn't his way. He did ask Cronk to enquire, mind you, "Was he dealing with a man or a woman?"

The ride back to the settlement was extremely long and silent, but at least Erdi was now armed with the knowledge of what a top-class ewe was worth locally and therefore, by comparison, how much grain he could expect for his bronze. The bartering rates between major items, provided there'd not been drought or flood, were usually roughly the same. Obviously certain things caused quirks in the market, but he wasn't letting that be an issue. The bronze he had was worth significantly more here, than on the other side of the Erin Sea and that was good enough for him. He had a basis to work with, hopefully concealing the fact he was a complete beginner.

Back in the settlement, Erdi again braced himself and drawing a deep breath, informed Un Farqune he was also in need of wheat and barley.

With patience looking sorely tried, the man asked with a steely smile, "Now look! Is it to be wheat or sheep you're wantin'?"

Erdi told him the amount of grain required. The profile of the heap could be imagined and that profile, believe me, was significant. Almost as if a tiny invisible shaft had struck a section of Un Farqune's brain, the barely detectable jolt on impact led to a slow spread of smile as thoughts formulated.

He finally said, "Such a large amount of grain will not be possible." He did, however happen to have, a splendid selection of furs and hides. Erdi replied, he had no need for hides. At home they had hides aplenty. Un Farqune wasn't to be put off by this, however, becoming quite insistent in fact and with an arm clamped around Erdi's shoulder, he steered him to, "Come look at the fine hides. It can't hurt to be taking a look, now can it?" And fine indeed they were. Erdi stood there, completely confused, totally out of his depth and that prickly anxious feeling had now become a full-blown sweat.

Un Farqune, at last beginning to sense an opportunity opening, smiled and in the next attempt to part the visitor from his bronze, he sweetened the deal by adding a little grain. Then the deal offered, was laced with the inclusion of hunting dogs. If that weren't bad enough, Erdi groaned inwardly as the chance of slaves was added to the mix. The man wouldn't take no for an answer and he was taken to examine the poor creatures, leather collared and bronze chained together. The raising of heads, all haunted by a sad look of hope, was accompanied by the dull sound of dragged metal.

"But these look like your-own people," said Erdi.

"No, not my people. These come from the wild lands beyond the Abhayn Yontach."

By the end of day, Erdi was worn out, completely drained and apart from agreeing to a few hides and the meagre offering of grain, had got precisely nowhere. Un Farqune was now in full possession of how much bronze was on offer and wasn't letting the man go without getting his hands on it. He could have easily pressured the landowners around Baile Atha Cliath to surrender enough of their crops for the deal, but there were other things he preferred to send on their way across the water.

The negotiations ground on all through the following day, leaving Erdi thinking, perhaps taking some of the other options could be better than returning empty handed. Then he remembered Trader's words, to stay strong. He wished he had his friend there with him. He was way out of his depth, but Trader would have known how to deal with the man. His presence alone would have brought him to order.

Then came the news, the copper traders were soon to be away, back across the water. It was their last chance before autumn storms made the crossing too dangerous. It left but two days to rescue the situation and it was just as well Erdi had only heard the broad version of their intentions. There was enough pressure building as it was.

Meanwhile Yanker had been asked to enquire about their friend Wolf, but of course this was slightly tricky on account of Wolf not being his real name. His attempts drew either a shrug accompanied by shake of head or a look of incredulity. 'Was he not aware of how big Erin was?'

Meanwhile, all trace of Madarch had been lost. He'd been whisked away as if a celebrity. The smell of him hadn't entirely deterred and amazingly he'd even attracted female attention. On the second day Yanker decided, a determined effort best be made to seek him out.

Drawn by the roars of "Brane! Brane! Brane!" almost lifting the thatch off one of the drinking halls, he was horrified by what greeted him as he entered. Red faced youths were pushing Madarch back and forth between them, like a child's toy.

Yanker, drawing his sword, strode amongst them and grabbing the biggest and burliest by the scruff, growled in his face, "Leave him be!" Words weren't entirely understood, but actions were and his decisiveness even had an immediate sobering effect on Madarch, who was then astounded to hear, "Come on Maddy, time to go!" Turning to the brawny youth he'd whitened his knuckles on, Yanker snarled, "**We** might make fun of him," and with sword offered for emphasis, "but **you** don't! Come on Maddy let's get out of here."

End of that second day, Erdi had his spirits lifted by the sight of Madarch bounding into their temporary residence, blurting, "Erdi! Yanker, he teach me how to swim!" The young man's face beamed all the brighter for being a good two shades lighter.

On hearing Yanker describe the scene he'd witnessed, Cronk, making use of a local word, meaning lout, said the youths sounded like a bunch of 'bodachs.'

"Hey, I like that word," said Yanker laughing. "I'm taking that one home with me." As is usual when adopted into another tongue, the word was given a personal twist and Yanker proclaimed with a laugh, "You lot are nothing but a bunch of budducks!"

Then Madarch, his face a picture of concern said, "They shout, 'brane, brane,' when they push me. What is brane mean?"

Yanker, with a friendly nudge, answered, "Don't think they were referring to anything between your ears, Maddy."

"It means, smelly," said Cronk.

With a serious look and a sniff under arm, Madarch said, "Erdi, I need different clothes. These ones stinky."

"Don't take it like that, Maddy," said Yanker. "What a thing to say. You're not that stinky!" The following theatrical bout of wafting, wheezing, fighting for air and squinting as if his eyes were running, even brought a laugh from their swarthy forest dweller.

Erdi told his cousin, "Take one of the axe-heads and see if you can get him fitted with something. There's bound to be a woman hereabouts, handy with needle and thread. She'll probably faint when you show her the axe-head, but can't be helped, we've no bronze of lesser value."

"Won't be all she'll faint from," was muttered from behind a hand, as Yanker now had no wish to offend his new friend.

The woman as it happens, following payment on completion of the job, had had to scuttle round to neighbours for the loan of bits and bars of bronze to make up the gulf of difference. Over the course of years of struggle, she had never had possession of a complete axe-head, in her life.

Madarch, having already been cleansed by the waters of the Ruirthech, returned in his fresh attire, looking like a new man. The woman had even combed his hair for him, saying, "Ta' buachaill glan deas ann," which Cronk later translated as, "There's a nice clean boy."

On the third day of negotiations and still making no real headway, just as Trader had predicted, Erdi's will had started to buckle and the offer of pelts and hunting dogs began to look like a far brighter option than returning with nothing. He felt a burgeoning compulsion to do some sort of deal, for his hoard, worth the equivalent of silver here, would immediately return to the value of dull bronze, if hauled back home. The sheer quality of the skins and dogs on offer, even though these wouldn't solve the looming food crisis back home, would enhance the value, possibly three-fold and he tried justifying such weakening, with the thought, 'Isn't this what trading's supposed to be all about?'

Un Farqune, being fully aware, lack of time was piling on the pressure, could sense his young adversary was on the point of cracking.

"Stay strong," Trader had emphasised and Erdi thought, "He'll never let me forget it if I don't."

So, late morning, he decided on a massive gamble. Shaking inside, he took courage and dared to do exactly as his friend had recommended. He complimented Un Farqune on being the toughest negotiator he'd ever encountered and told him there was no alternative other than to return home well and truly beaten. He'd arrived with heady notions of dealing for grain, but it wasn't to be. Un Farqune had won. He did, however, ask to be allowed to trade for something of interest to take home, an item of bronze maybe, something typical to Erin, just to keep as a memento. He added, "I came here with wild notions of trading for wheat, but I have to hand it to you, you've completely outclassed me."

Then he waited, heart thumping.

Un Farqune eying him narrowly, sighed and said, "Very well, give me an idea of how much you were expecting again?"

The final deal, the one that mattered above all others, actually took no time at all. The few hides Erdi had felt forced to agree to in order to keep negotiations open, apart from their obvious trade value, were in fact essential, used for covering the grain.

While the loads were trundled down to the dock, he went in search of the copper traders to negotiate a fair reward for handling the cargo, as far as the mouth of the Dwy, a good two days on from their intended destination, plus they would of course need rewarding for time it would take to return to the copper mine.

Loading continued all through the following day, as one after another, wagons lumbered in with grain from surrounding farms.

It was only at this point that Erdi became aware of how close to failure he'd actually come. Departure wasn't to be the following morning, but that very night. The fleet master explained, they were leaving on the turn of tide and sailing out to a fishing village on the southern promontory of the bay. There would be just enough light remaining to safely accomplish this.

The plan had a double benefit; first, a dark hour departure would reduce the likelihood of another meeting with the raiders and second, they could continue at first light, unhindered by the tidal power sweeping into the bay. So yes, it was true they were leaving Erin in the morning, but were actually setting out from the Baile Atha Cliath that night.

All was loaded and battened down including that stowed mid-ships on their good boat Gwendolin. Unexpectedly, Un Farqune appeared to witness departure. He told both Erdi and Yanker to assure their respective chieftains, he warmly welcomed future trade. Erdi was then presented with a pair of bronze blobs dangling from sinew. They did have a semblance of a neck and cast ring-decoration just below the loop for hanging, but other than that, were in fact, no more than bronze blobs.

Un Farqune asked him to bend forward to receive them. "You requested a memento. Something typical of these shores."

Cronk translated and added, "He says you're a true man and to wear them with pride."

Erdi examining them, looked rather puzzled, but did manage a fairly convincing, "I am truly grateful."

Un Farqune made a slight adjustment saying, "There. They should never be worn hanging completely level."

"Yes, but what are they?"

A smile slowly broke, like sun from cloud, "You're a man. Have a guess."

It brought a roar of laughter.

Erdi then said, "All our time here, and strangely I've never once seen the chieftain."

Un Farqune, still in his trading attire, clicked his fingers. An attendant appeared, engulfing him in a magnificent wolf's-fur coat; a heavy gold torque was placed around his neck and a bronze, gem studded crown was planted on his head. He said quietly, "You're looking at him."

Erdi couldn't help it, his eyes widened in wonder and he felt a squirm of embarrassment on remembering his gift of the bronze torque and how paltry it now seemed. Acceptance of it, however, in view of the might of the king now standing before him, seemed all the more gracious and that hint of amusement he'd noticed, all the more understandable.

Madarch was beckoned. Cronk was translating remember, "You young man, have rid me of a particularly troublesome thorn in the side." (Tua Fola had apparently joined his ancestors, the final blow from the paddle having crushed his windpipe.)

Madarch became the proud wearer of a bronze cloak-pin, cast in the shape of a paddle. There in the fading light, standing silent on the dock now barely higher than the brimming river, the assembled throng watched the graceful craft slip into the flow.

They had caught the turn of tide and journeyed out on the ebbing waters to the southern edge of the bay without hindrance or mishap. The night was spent camped ashore and the moment burgeoning light made it possible to spot hazards ahead, elated by the success of their venture, they shoved off from the coast of Erin.

It was shortly before low water and spurred on by the west wind and the call of home, they made land in the fading light of evening. From there, they worked in stages around the coast not only avoiding the pull from the tidal race between Ynys Isel and the mainland, but by not entering either estuary harbour used on the outward journey, avoided unnecessary delays on their return. There would have been no chance of departure without first regaling all with their story, then would have come the inevitable wait for the in-creep of waters. The tides that had assisted them on the outward journey, Cronk informed them, would have hindered on their return and relishing thoughts of home, they camped, on the sands of the coast. The tide favoured again, when it swept them into the broad Dwy estuary and then on up the river itself.

The copper traders were thanked and rewarded and transport was arranged to float the cargo upriver to the village near the Feasting Site. Cronk, gazing at the generous splay of axe-heads awarded, simply glowed from the gratitude heaped upon him.

He thanked them, saying he had never expected to be included on such a mission at his time of life.

Erdi said, it had done wonders, knocking at least ten years off him and he was to remember, "You are always welcome if ever venturing south."

At the village near the Feasting Site, temporary storage was arranged for the imminent arrival of the grain being shipped upriver. Their own cargo was left for collection stored aboard the boat.

The headman asked Erdi, "What happened to that boat, we made?"

"We found a fool and swapped it for this one," Yanker chipped in before he could reply.

The jibe obviously missed its mark for the man said, "Told you, you'd never get stuck with a boat fashioned from **these** woods."

The good boat Gwendolin, safely tied to her moorings, was given a pat of thanks and on borrowed horses, the three headed home. They had been away less than a whole moon, had successfully carried out their mission and **still** had one axe-head left. One of the riders had a bronze torque enhancing the colour of his swarthy skin.

The Teller thanked them all and left to resounding applause. He had rushed the last section slightly, but had felt that painful pressure building, the one that brings on the desire for a firm crossing of the legs. Too much barley water!

Part 3

Chapter Eleven

The following morning the Teller was standing by the fire when a small figure entered the hut. She paused and then ran up in a flurry and smacked him on the leg. "You killed Mardi!" *she said almost in tears.*

I didn't, princess. I was just telling the story. *With a forefinger, he gently raised her chin.* I'm sorry if I upset you.

You didn't have to make him die! Make Mardi come back!"

"Manda, come here," *came a voice from the doorway.* "I'm sorry is she bothering you?" *It was Megan, the lady he had been talking to the previous day.*

Don't worry, she's no bother. It's just the part of the tale regarding Mardi, it really upset her. Is she yours?

"Goodness me, no! She's my grandchild."

The Teller, slightly surprised at his sense of relief, scooped up the small bundle and delivered her to waiting arms. The infant shot him a parting scowl, before burying her face in her grandmother's bosom. Her dangling legs were deep tanned and had the residue of baby fat that invited a squeeze. The Teller smiled to himself as he watched the lady, gracefully sway her body in through the low opening of her house opposite.

The fact the child would have been too young to have understood the tale told on his previous visit and yet somehow knew about the fate of Mardi, suggested simplified versions of certain sections had probably been retold at night-time gatherings around the hearth. The realisation gave him a certain degree of satisfaction.

That evening he arrived in the grand hall to the usual applause and begin, And so, we have the heroes' return. Erdi was desperate to see his wife and son again and in order to avoid the settlement south of the fort, he suggested they take the forest trail home. With now being so close to home, the last thing he wanted, was to become snagged by a tangle with officialdom. Gwenithen could wait. His desire to see his family was that strong, the ache that bad, it had started to feel as if part of his innards had been cut away.

His heart sank. They were on what was in fact a little used trail and yet directly ahead were two fully armed Y-Dewis warriors, woad daubed for action, out on patrol. These of course knew Erdi was returning from what had been described dismissively as a foraging mission and as you would expect, were keen to probe, but other than telling them, everything had gone as well as he'd hoped and that all would be reported to Gwenithen later, he had the sense to impart no further details. Then the bronze torque was spotted.

"What right has that man to wear such a sign of distinction?"

"I gave it him. What of it?"

"Only my lord Gwenithen can award this. It must be removed."

Once Yanker became party to what had been said, he retorted, "Play at soldiers if you like,--- we've got better things to do!"

Of course, the warrior wouldn't have understood the words, but didn't miss the derisory tone, prompting a kneeing of his mount, with the intention of snatching the offending article from Madarch's neck.

The metallic rasp as Yanker's sword flashed, brought stunned disbelief. No civilian had ever dared such audacity.

Lesser mortals, on seeing that thunderous glare from a trained killer, would have been deterred, but not our ever-plucky Yanker, *laughed the Teller*. He was that incensed; jabbing for emphasis, he snarled, "Don't you touch him,------- unless of course, you intend it to be your----- **last!**" The final jab even unsettled the man's horse.

Erdi riding between them, called for Yanker to put up his weapon and warned the warrior to back off. Brandishing Gwenithen's official seal, he said, "I'll be reporting all to our lord and master."

"Don't be surprised to find he already knows," said the man wheeling his horse away.

Erdi, watching them canter down the track, and feeling quite shocked by the encounter, asked his cousin, "Are you trying to get us all killed?"

At Trader's place, there was a clamour of greeting and tears of joy. Erdi, his whiskers not having had a scrape of steel since leaving Erin, apologised to Gwendolin for looking so dishevelled.

"You look fine to me," she replied, hugging him and burying her face in his chest. As he leant to scoop up his son, she said, "There I told you, your Da would be coming home." Her former pale, wan look was now but a distant memory, for the glow, rekindled the moment they had escaped Penda's gloom to set up home together, now shone, restored to full radiance. Erdi, gazing longingly, pulled her close and with all three in a loving squeeze gave a silent, 'Thank you,' to the spirits that had somehow contrived to provide him with such a wonderful wife and son.

Vanya gave her brother a warm hug, Yanker received the same, but the momentary pause when eying Madarch, was merely in jest, for she said "And you. Come on." His receiving of similar treatment, brought a hesitant smile.

"My! You smell sweeter!" she said laughing.

Gwedyll, smiling at the scene, suddenly froze in horror. She had spotted the torque. "Why's he wearing that? Erdi don't you realise, that could get him into serious trouble!"

"Why he didn't steal it? I thought all that bronze worship ended when Gardarm fell."

"Oh no, Erdi. That will be taken very seriously by my people. It's not the material, but what it represents. He'd better hide it before somebody sees it."

"Someone already has."

Gwedyll, looking skyward, gave a sigh of exasperation.

"Never mind torques," said Trader cutting in. "Did you manage it? Did you do the deal?"

Erdi nodded, "It should all be arriving at the feasting site within two days." He told him the amount their bronze had procured.

For a moment he looked absolutely astonished, then on recovery said, "Good man!" whacking him a slap on the back, hearty enough to have knocked a loose tooth out. He then added, "You had better report to the King of the Mountains before he sends someone looking for you."

"They're not going anywhere without food and drink first," said Gwedyll.

All three eventually rode to present themselves to Gwenithen. Madarch, of course, had removed the torque.

Two officials, who had obviously been expecting them, led the way to one of the huts. With horse tack dangling from every post and beam, it was obviously a store and the strong smell of animal sweat accompanying the general lowly look of the place, brought an ominous feel. Here, Erdi was asked what his mission had accomplished and he gave a brief account of what had been achieved. He knew these to be a particularly joyless pair of individuals, but now got the impression, they'd lately been honing this unfortunate characteristic to a point of perfection.

On conferring, one said. "So, let me see if I have understood correctly. Are we to report to Lord Gwenithen, that you didn't leave the territory in a bid to find a source of grain, you in fact left with sufficient undeclared resources to actually procure the grain."

Erdi slowly shook his head in denial, but mumbled, "Well yes, I suppose we did."

Had he confided with a nudge, "And I've just pissed in Gwenithen's beer," they could not have looked more horrified and instructing them to wait, dashed from the hut as if in a race to be first back with the news.

With shadows creeping longer, the three lounged in a seemingly endless wait, having to endure children peering and sniggering at what was obviously a subject of undying interest.

Eventually at the sound of rapid footsteps, they scattered and the weary wanderers scrambled upright. Bustling in, with a smug radiance of privilege glowing, one of the officials, haughtily relayed; 'Erdi's sword, plus the torque unlawfully bequeathed, should be surrendered instantly!'

Hearing the instructions translated, Madarch retreated, looking most unwilling, but on Erdi's insistence, reluctantly fished inside his jerkin and held it out. Gwenithen had no jurisdiction over Yanker's sword, but the manner in which it was put, made it clear, he wasn't left with much choice.

They were to remain, with one empty pot between them for the necessary and were told not to venture so much as one step beyond the hut door. There was one crumb of comfort, soon food would be provided. Two guards then arrived to plant themselves outside the door, which of course confirmed the fact, they were prisoners.

Sustenance came as promised, even though only bread and water, followed shortly by the arrival of a third official. The same man who had been so high-handed when relating Gwenithen's instructions regarding Lady Rhosyn. Now, he couldn't have been friendlier and talked as if they might have been merely boys caught poaching. He found it all highly entertaining, his eyes widening in wonder when told of the paddle incident and then he'd laughed and clapped, as would a long-lost friend, when informed of the amount of grain procured.

"But where did you discover such a huge hoard of bronze to make this amazing trade?"

Erdi, not fooled by the man's smiles, simply said, "It came from the people."

"I'm not sure I understand."

"It was the people's bronze. The deal was done and instead of bronze we now have grain. Grain to help all through winter. I don't know any other way of putting it. Their generosity will help see both communities safely through the worst weather. Spirits willing."

"Left up to me I'd consider you heroes," said the official as he turned to leave. "But I'm afraid, all I can do is report back with what you have just told me. Then it's completely out of my hands. My master, Lord Gwenithen, will decide your fate."

None of them of course, cared for the sound of that final word. Evening had descended by the time the guards entered and escorted them to where the mighty man held court. They were stopped at the door by one of the dreary pair and Erdi was told, that on entry he was to approach the chieftain to relate in detail, all that had happened on their venture. Yanker and Madarch were told to enter and a spot was indicated for them to squeeze into, amongst the shadows.

Erdi approached the hearth. Gwenithen was enthroned, not at all in a playful mood and beside him stood the official who had acted as if Erdi's new best friend earlier.

"Bow to your lord," he growled, as if Erdi would not have done so anyway. When daring to look up beyond the glow of firelight, he saw there was not just a single row of warriors glowering, as first perceived, the room was actually crammed with very serious looking faces, including those of the elder princes, obviously keen to carry out deeds of very serious intent.

Although bearing the pressure of such animosity, completely alone, a feeling of defiance built within and at this very point, the sound of Mardi's voice entered his head. "Just tell the story Erdi. I want to hear the story." It was almost as if his young brother had asked for a retelling of a Zak and Big Hendy legend. I know it sounds strange, but the notion of his brother's spirit being there, brought forth a surge of strength and determination, fired to a self-belief by anger simmering within. Looking about and glaring at any willing to catch his eye, he decided to no longer feel cowed by such vaunted company.

"You may explain yourself," he was told.

He began, "Thank you my lord, for allowing me this opportunity," bringing a rustle of interest from around the room. Those words of course, disguised true feelings, for he could feel his old sense of independence and rebelliousness returning. Considering what they'd achieved, all three had been treated appallingly and the sense of injustice gave him strength to relate, not just a string of details as if in self-justification, but what had actually happened, as a saga; something to be proud of, just as I'm telling you now.

He told the tale long into the night. His words brought laughter, gasps of wonder and cheers. He finally said that grain for all would be arriving soon for collection at the Feasting Site and he apologised to Gwenithen for having had the temerity to award his friend the bronze torque, his sense of propriety having been momentarily blinded by the man's unbelievable act of bravery.

Silence ensued, followed by Gwenithen muttering something to the official on his right.

The man called out, "Can the three of you retire once more?" and they were led back to their place of confinement.

"Well you certainly told them," said Yanker. "You looked like your old self. I knew which bit you were on, from their reaction." He had picked up a number of words of the invader's language, but as yet, could not fully converse in cymry.

On finally being led back into the main hall, all three were instructed to halt. Each gave a respectful bend of knee to their Lord Gwenithen and with heads bowed, waited. The room was that charged with expectancy, even the fire seemed quenched by the pressure.

Erdi was summoned and kneeling before his chieftain, tensed at the ominous rasp of metal. He heard a collective gasp. The blade had been raised. The commotion behind him, was Yanker being restrained. Then came the lightest of touches of metal on his head, accompanied by Gwenithen booming, "Kervod!"

Erdi arose.

On being handed the sword harness, the official with obvious distaste, furnished it for the scabbard to hang down Erdi's back and unable to bridle true feelings, then snarled the order to bow for the sheathing. Both scabbard and strapping were bound in fine blue fabric. As Gwenithen slid the sword home there was a thatch-lifting cheer. Erdi had been raised to the blue.

On demand, Yanker stepped forward. His sword was returned, not in its original scabbard, but one adorned with bronze. When handed over, the official said through gritted teeth, "My Lord apologises for his impertinence, but believes your weapon deserves greater distinction."

Then Madarch was beckoned. Erdi on seeing Gwenithen's look, as if completely undecided what to do with the man, realised a playful mood could well be imminent. Madarch was ordered to bow. He stood there looking confused until the instruction was translated. He bowed and the bronze torque was reinstated around his neck. Never before had such an award been given to one considered so low.

Finally, Erdi was summoned once more. Gwenithen declared, "Our new young lord will require a title. He shall be known as Lord of Goll Deyrnas." This was greeted by an eruption of laughter. Erdi had been right, Gwenithen's playful mood had indeed burst to the fore, but as yet, had no clue what had been so funny.

It was sometime later that all became clear, Gwedyll explaining that Goll Deyrnas was a fertile land of legend, lost to the sea. She also informed him of how close he had come to an outcome, completely opposite to the one enjoyed. When her brother had first heard of what he considered, Erdi's impertinence and deceit in undertaking his venture without fully informing him of the details, his reaction had been one of severe anger. His advisors, especially his righthand man and two elder princes, had advocated he be stripped of his sword. Given time to calm, however and prompted by the opportune intervention from a rather worried Prince Heddi, he saw advantage in taking the diplomatic approach. His thinking went, 'If his new people witnessed one of their own being raised to the highest honour, would that not help unite the tribes?' Also, if he had revoked the man's warrior status, it followed; Vanya would no longer be eligible as a royal bride. It would have broken Heddi's heart. 'After all,' he thought, 'what Erdi had done had in fact benefited all, even though he had taken a rather dubious route to success.' So, completely ignoring council's advice, Gwenithen had decided to honour the man, but couldn't resist adding the final touch, the title. After all, what better gift for a man whose family had been stripped of their traditional fishing rights, than to name him lord of a huge spread of sea.

Following the ceremony, for in fact, that was what it was, the first to approach and congratulate Erdi, was the crusty warrior whose intervention had saved them, that day when the Gwy had thundered down off the ridge intent on their annihilation. He asked, what had become of the one he'd named, 'the brawny limper?' They both laughed at how the Gwy horde had been put to flight and at the memory of the gloomy boatman. Comparing then and now seemed unreal, for the man was treating Erdi as an equal. As did young Prince Heddi, who glowing with respect and glad to have him as part of the upper echelon, put a congratulatory arm around his shoulder.

Of course, this was gratefully received, but Erdi felt a need to put things in perspective, reasoning, the grain soon to arrive, was of course better than nothing, but frugal use would have to be made and other food put by, for it alone would not guarantee survival.

Erdi accompanied Yanker part way home, taking the eastern route rather than over the two Habren crossings. This enabled his cousin to call in at his old home for what was in fact, the first time in many a moon. Erdi warned him of the change that had come over his father. He had of course already been informed of this by his own father, Dowid, but made no comment. Criticism of family, freely admitted by a close member, never sits easy when heard coming from one beyond the inner circle.

Mara was there to greet them, beaming with pride at what her son and nephew had achieved. Penda, on the other hand, took the attitude, that his son's latest honour was simply further proof, he had joined the invader's ranks.

Yanker didn't stay long, for of course he was rather keen to see Rhosyn and his daughter again, but was there long enough to receive congratulations from Inga and her daughter Talia.

On leaving, he muttered to Erdi, "That Talia's blossomed into a pretty young thing."

Then when told of her betrothal, he added. "I'm not surprised she's betrothed. I bet there were quite a few disappointed suitors. Strange thing is, when we were all growing up together, I hardly noticed her. She was more like a sister."

"I know it's weird, isn't it," said Erdi. "If she had been from across the far side of the valley, we'd have probably beaten a path to her door."

The exchange of a final wave, left Erdi feeling quite dispirited. The sight of his cousin's departing figure, brought a sickening empty feeling, but admonishing himself, he realised he couldn't afford to dwell on it. The adventure was over and there remained much to do. The grain needed collection and fair distribution, plus there was the small matter of the horses they'd borrowed and so with great reluctance, he dragged himself back towards his duties.

Following a discussion with tribal elders, it was decided, carts would be dispatched from each of the four sections of territory and at the Feasting Site, Erdi would be there, waiting to organise a fair division. How the loads were then redistributed, would be left up to the administrators he'd put in charge. The hoard did indeed look plentiful, but he knew when split down into family portions, it wouldn't amount to more than two moon's supply and frugality would be essential. In fact, the sheer trouble, gone to; the dangers encountered, probably bore more weight than the actual bounty provided and the act of helping all, his people and Y-Dewis alike, strengthened still further the growing bond between them, making the grain as symbolic as it was nourishing.

Then came the hauling of their boat down to the Habren. It would be more use there and he couldn't imagine the villagers at its present mooring simply letting it sit there without taking advantage, plus he doubted they'd have taken the same care as they would, had it been their own. It straddled the length of two carts and at barely walking pace, was carefully hauled south by a team of four oxen.

Gwenithen himself was there for the re-launching. He and his favoured circle, then sat waiting, looking as excited as would young boys, given a day off from chores. The chieftain's playful mood was infectious. Erdi joining them, shoved off and by instructing the warriors paddling, steered them safely up to Amwythig, where prior to a twilight return, they dined by a roaring fire on the river bank. Erdi hadn't seen such pleasure beaming from the chieftain's face, since witnessing his departure aboard the coach, setting out on that exuberant tour of the new territory.

Now on another matter, *said the Teller*; Brialla's brother Tawy, other than it giving a twinge when rain was due, declared his battle wound had fully healed. Strange thing was, however, there wasn't much rain for his new inbuilt oracle to predict. The glorious late summer weather that year seemed to blaze on without end. The people began to believe it was a gift from the spirits. A reward for ridding the earth of the old regime. It was as well they enjoyed it while they could.

One day when Mara was visiting Brialla, her brother approached and said, "I must thank you once again for tending to my injury."

It had been the first time Mara had closed a wound by use of stitching. The moment she'd caught sight of the initial crude attempt, she'd unpicked the three loops, carefully cleaned within and sewed the puckered edges together again as neatly as if repairing a garment. It would of course have been better done the day the sword had cut him, but she had still managed to lessen the inevitable scarring. Tawy drew her forward and gently kissed her.

Mara blinked, looking stunned and Brialla's mouth gaped in shock. "You silly old fool! What did you do that for?"

"It just felt right," Tawy replied. "It felt like Mara wanted me to."

"Wanted him to?" Mara said later, when relating the tale of the unexpected kiss to Inga.

"Well did you?"

"You promise you won't say anything?"

Inga nodded, eager to hear more.

"It made me feel quite tingly."

Back at Trader's, Erdi was relieved to see how well their son Tawy got along with his own son. Even though there was a huge age difference they seemed to enjoy games played together. It was just what Deri needed and the sound of his laughter ringing out like music, gladdened Erdi's heart. Also of course Vanya temporarily living there brought instant cheer to the place and she often dreamt up games and adventures for them.

Gwedyll, particularly loved having her there, for as mentioned before, on that afternoon they'd sat together beneath the oak at the Feasting Site, the two could have easily been mistaken for sisters. Not in looks and certainly not in age, but in understanding and humour.

Trader informed Erdi, the rest of their hoard was safely tucked away. With the newly cleared land being nowhere near ready for sowing, it would be needed for grain procurement the following year. They just had to hope the value of bronze didn't collapse in Erin as it had done in their own territory.

From here-on all attention turned to the autumn gathering at the Feasting Site. Tensions were expected. Not all the Y-Dewis had migrated east with Gwenithen and reports had come in that the Bleddi, taking advantage of the void left, were becoming quite persistent with their incursions. Stern words were needed when the tribes next met.

Erdi was now allowed on the council, but being newly admitted kept his contributions to nothing more than initial greetings and mumbled augmentation of assent or dissent. As time of the feast drew closer, he noticed talks becoming more animated, not helped by the news filtering in, the Gwy, emboldened by their seemingly endless supply of iron, were threatening from the south.

It was unanimously felt, that if the Bleddi's incursions didn't cease immediately, they should be threatened with severe retribution and before the raiding season was out, the Gwy needed a sharp lesson they wouldn't forget.

It was at his third meeting of the Grand Council that something of a contentious nature came to Erdi's mind. He'd remembered Vanya's dream. The dream in which Elsa had appeared as a Lynx. He tried to recall the words she had told him, those that had come floating through the dream. It was something involving wolves. Then as if by magic, the words popped out clear as sunshine, 'When storms blow up from the south, put your trust in wolves.'

"That's it!" said Erdi causing all to turn and stare. In cymry, bled meant wolf and the storms must have referred to the Gwy raids. He asked for permission to speak. It was his very first meaningful contribution. Turning to Gwenithen, he said, "Excuse me Sire, but would it help resolve both problems if the Bleddi were asked to administer your lands west of here, charged with the specific task of keeping the Gwy out?"

The initial stunned silence was followed by a discordant clamour and amid it all, Gwenithen glared at him without the slightest hint of a playful look. Knowing his words had landed like a fox amid a pack of dogs, Erdi said no more.

In fact, nothing had been resolved right up to the point of departure to the Feasting Site and other than throw in the initial idea that had given such cause for discord, Erdi had decided, it was best staying well out of it. Of course, that didn't lessen the feelings of hostility from certain quarters, with the two elder princes even warning that an unfortunate accident could befall a person not able to keep his mouth shut. It had made him very wary of journeying alone.

With Trader being delayed by the usual details, requiring attention before leaving on such a trip, their little party was late arriving at the Feasting Sight. None of the ladies accompanied them, having been put off by likelihood of tribal tensions. It was strange to not see his parents, Penda and Mara in their usual spot and even though trading was taking place it seemed muted and like no other fair Erdi had ever been to. The air almost crackled with friction.

Gwenithen, along with sons and tribal elders occupied the favoured area; the spot designated to those ruling the north Habren. In recognition of their rising status, the chieftain of Y-Pentwr and his retinue were allocated the location once taken by the Y-Dewis and as usual, the Bleddi arrived late.

Erdi, spotting his cousin, walked over to explain a notion that had come to mind. He told Yanker it might reduce tensions somewhat if he suggested his chieftain, Haraul took the trouble to walk across the divide to greet Gwenithen as a show of solidarity.

The man was having none of it, however and instead offered, to one he considered no more than an upstart ruler, the invitation to come and visit him.

Taking up this offer, Gwenithen, his three sons and elders set out on what was not a huge journey in physical terms, but represented a massive stride diplomatically. Erdi was told to attend as translator.

Gwenithen looked magnificent as he swept forward, blue cape billowing, gold arm-torques gleaming and bronze, gem-studded circlet constraining his locks. Haraul calmly awaited enrobed in grey linen, finely worked at the edges and the humble bronze torque, Erdi had gifted him, showing well against his simple white shirt. He looked relaxed, whereas Gwenithen gave the impression, if he'd have had two pairs of best boots, he'd have contrived a way of wearing all four at once.

On meeting, the chieftains touched knuckles in a wary show of friendship and Gwenithen's sons were nodded to out of courtesy. It was all very formal and smiles rather fixed.

Erdi, having lurked at the rear of the party, was suddenly summoned to the fore. Gwenithen hadn't understood a remark, his brother chieftain, Haraul, had made. On seeing who it was, the latter's face broke into a broad grin and grasping him by the shoulders, said, "I hear your mission went well, young rascal. Your cousin Dowin told me all about it. The felling of the feared Blood-Axe from Erin will be a tale told for many a year around winter fires."

Erdi felt certain he had been used like a political gaming piece. If the Y-Pentwr chieftain had intended a slight toward Gwenithen and the princes, he couldn't have managed better and it was time to calmly translate as requested, then shrink quietly into the background once more.

Suddenly a huge hound bounded in amongst them furiously wagging its tail. Up on hind legs, making excited whimpering noises, it started vigorously licking Erdi's face. At his command, it sat. He ruffled its huge head and ears and encouraged by this, its impulse to jump up again, required an admonishing finger to reduce the desire to a mere excited look of eye and ground-thumping tail wag. Erdi apologised to the two leaders and said, with their permission, he would return the dog to its owner.

All watched as the hound, loping waist high at each stride, gave Erdi the occasional upward glance, almost as if smiling.

The Bleddi had arrived and were waiting, watching with disbelief as a young stranger approached leading their tribal mascot, that was not only fawning, but actually nudging the man to ruffle its ears once again.

The chieftain, wolf-caped; a massive sword strapped viciously to his side, glowered with a look, that could not have been craggier, if carved from living rock. Then suddenly, something winging into his memory, softened all to a smile. He flung up his arms in greeting and roared, "It's you again! The twig-waver!" Erdi was grabbed and the uncompromising arm enfolding, left no choice, other than to be drawn into the tribal throng.

Groaning within he asked, 'Why do the spirits contrive to do such things to me?'

Gwenithen's little party, stood in stunned silence. The mighty man looked quite deflated, the two princes scowled with hatred, Prince Heddi looked awestruck and the Y-Pentwr chieftain wore a suppressed a smile.

Trader had also been a witness and shaking his head in disbelief, had muttered to himself, "He's such a quiet lad. How does he manage it?"

Erdi was welcomed by the four warriors, first met all that time ago at Trader's and could have stayed for the remainder of the day, feeling warmed and slightly exalted by the genuine welcome given. The whole tribe held respect for the man who had had the courage to approach a besieging army, unarmed and alone. They admired the way he had intervened and broken the deadlock. Erdi, in return warmed to these people. Admittedly, some were a bit rough and savage looking, to say the least, but there was a simple honesty about them he found refreshing. He couldn't imagine falling out with many of them. His position dictated, however, that once he'd reciprocated their welcome, he was obliged to return to normal duties.

On departure he spotted a woman of splendid girth sitting with an infant beside her and a baby at a breast. She raised her head and smiled. Erdi was shocked on realising it was Luda. He walked over and complimented her on looking so well.

"Pregnancy can have that effect, Erdi," came the reply, not from the girl he remembered, but from a confident, mature woman.

"What another?"

"Yes, and by the way it's kicking it's going to be a boy. If it is, I'll call him Dowin." (Yanker's real name)

As she plucked the baby off her breast, its little red face screwed into a look of puzzlement. "This one's Erdi," she said and nodding towards the small girl beside her, "and this is little Vanya." Luda's face absolutely radiated health and happiness. "I haven't forgotten you know," she said. "I owe it all to you and your family."

Erdi bent, planted the softest of kisses on her head and returned to where Gwenithen's retinue was camped. With nothing but cold stares and mutterings welcoming, he disappeared into the background to await events. His heart had been lifted by seeing Luda again and he'd felt warmed by her gratitude. It helped balance the fact, there are some who never forgive a person's offer of help or giving of sound advice. The princes were eying him meaningfully.

The sun was going down when the Bleddi chieftain and three fully armed woad-eyed warriors approached. Their camp fell silent. Gwenithen remained unmoved, enthroned, watching. At just beyond two sword's length, the visitors halted and their chieftain, with feet firmly planted and fists clenched, stood with chest rising and falling like a bull in human form. Finally, to the relief of all, he gave a perfunctory nod of head. Gwenithen, slowly unfurling himself, invited his guest to approach.

They disappeared within and the awning was drawn closed. Outside, relieved glances were exchanged, as all stood in silence

194

awaiting results. There came a roar for food and drink and large quantities were urgently bustled in. When more drink was called for, those leaning forward, ears cocked, attempting to ascertain the mood of the sonorous exchanges, were shocked bolt-upright, exchanging smiles of relief at the sudden boom of laughter.

The two finally emerged like brothers with Gwenithen grandly announcing, from that day forward, territories to west and south would be patrolled by their Bleddi brothers, who had generously offered their services to help keep the wild Gwy tribes in their place. This was greeted by cheers from most, dark mutterings from the two princes and a further shrinking into the background by Erdi.

When Prince Heddi rushed to congratulate him, he put a finger to lips and said quietly, "It's Vanya you need to thank. All this is a result of a dream she had."

What happened next, he should have been on the alert for. He should have known it was a trap, but he'd been too busy, beset by queries regarding land disputes, plus also tied up with the seeming endless jobs on his own little patch. Then to top all this, Trader had asked for his help and somehow, he'd not been thinking straight.

It was fortunate, Vanya happened to be there, for she asked him, "Where are you rushing off to now?"

"Gwenithen has summoned me."

He had mounted and was on the point of leaving when Vanya called, "Erdi you've been working too hard."

He reined in and asked her to explain. Obviously, something had been left unsaid.

Vanya pointed, "The settlement's that way."

"He apparently wants to see me down by the Offering Pool."

Thinking for a while, she asked, "Who brought the message exactly?"

"One of the warriors. Look Vanya, I'll have to go."

"Since when has Gwenithen sent his bidding by way of a mere warrior?"

Erdi dismounted and said, "You're right."

"If you ride to the settlement," said his sister, "No doubt you'll find Gwenithen, there in all his glory. If so, you can ask him directly why you have been summoned. I'd be very interested to hear his reply."

Madarch, who had become a bit of a fixture since the Erin enterprise, armed himself and rode along in support. They headed north towards the settlement.

I won't trouble you with the details, *said the Teller*, I'll take you straight to what awaited when they finally arrived at the Offering Pool. Yes you've guessed it, a small welcoming party led by the two princes.

The Teller paused. Now you're probably a bit puzzled, wondering, 'Having established foul play to be likely, why are they riding straight towards it?' Please have patience, the matter is about to be resolved.

The eldest brother called out, "Ah, I'm glad you were able to break off from such immense responsibilities. It's time you were taught a lesson."

Madarch tugging at Erdi's sleeve, pointed to the three riders closing in behind.

"I see you've brought the forest brownie along with you. That's good. He will benefit from similar treatment."

The look of self-satisfaction slowly changed, as would a smile when the unwrapping of a gift reveals it to contain excrement. Riders slowly emerging from three sides had him trapped, for flight behind was blocked by the lake. Erdi's little reception committee found itself completely surrounded. The old warrior Gregoth, the one who had offered his warm congratulations following Erdi's recent elevation in status, urged his mount forward.

His measured approach was watched by two pairs of widening eyes. He leant low, his words for royal ears only and following their impact, the two princes, obviously in dread of the coming meeting with their father, mounted to be led away. They of course were never likely to be the slightest bit comradely towards Erdi, but from that day on, thanks largely to Vanya's intuition and Gregoth's intervention on his chieftain's behalf, he had no further trouble from them.

Often in those golden days of late summer, Delt would ride the short distance up to Erdi's house and escort Gwendolin and Deri down to Trader's residence. Just as Mara, Inga and Brialla came alive in each other's company, so did Vanya, Gwedyll and Gwendolin in theirs, plus young Tywy was good company for Deri. The day's tasks were lightened when split three ways, they felt invigorated by sharing the same creative talents and of course, being women, they talked.

Don't sound so affronted, *said the Teller*. You know it's true. Ladies love to talk. And why not? Of course, there was the usual chatter about how best to fabricate certain things, where to find various plants in the forest and the relating of funny things children do and say. Well we all love that, don't we, provided it's kept within limits, but what these three ladies loved best to talk about, was other people. Not gossiping of course, well maybe a little, who amongst us can resist a tiny morsel of that? No, it was the funny traits some people had, they found endless pleasure in.

For instance, there was a certain woman who walked around, head in air, basking in all the attention, little realising most were aghast at what she'd decided to wear that day. Another woman who invited ridicule, was one who dressed as if she and her daughter were sisters.

"Old mare dressed as yearling, Lady Longtooth," Gwedyll had named her.

There was also a woman, with a particularly nasty side, who was referred to as, Pig in Leggings. Another who had had the misfortune of making a name for herself, came from over by Five Pools. She invariably said the same thing at least three different ways, to the point, she often lost complete track of the initial subject and even when relating the simplest of happenings, went all around, Y-Pentwr, as the saying went. Her name was Manda and so was of course known as Manda Muddle.

There were names for all of them. Not forgetting Lady, 'Whatever's best for you.' This woman was particularly infuriating, for no matter what was done for her, that was her stock reply. Vanya recalled the time, a friend had said to the woman in question, "I've a really busy day tomorrow, but rather than have you sit here alone, I'll stay and keep you company."

Vanya mimicked the woman's hooted reply, "Whatever's best for you."

It wasn't just certain women that received scathing appraisals. They also had names for some of the men. Pool Gazer, referred to one known for his self-adoration. There was a Mummies' Boy, an aunt flatterer, a leering man they called Cringe and one they loathed to the point of repulsion, called Filth-Eye. They knew of certain men who would argue day was night, rather than admit a woman's answer to a problem, was better than their own. They laughed at the fact certain men thought a sharp cough disguised what they'd really done. Either that or they blamed the dog. Sometimes the three ladies ended up crying with laughter.

"What about the guessers?" said Vanya. "You know the guessers, they ask for directions to somewhere and when you start explaining, they jump in with, 'you mean it's down by the lake.' No, I didn't mean that, if you'll listen it's-----'Ah, I know, it's that place up by Three Willows.' In the end I just say, sounds like you already know where it is. Best find it yourself."

"There's that other sort of guesser," said Gwendolin. "They try and guess what you're going to say and while you're telling them, they cudgel their brains, desperate for a clever reply."

"I know the sort," said Vanya, "They go 'Mm, Mm, Mm' as if they're listening, but the Mm's are all in the wrong place. More like interruptions."

"Trouble is, because they haven't really listened to a word said, their supposed clever remark, has nothing to do with what you'd just been trying to tell them."

"The ones I hate," said Gwedyll; "are those ones, you know the type, when you try to carefully explain something, they say very slowly, as if you'd had some veiled message in mind---------'Oh! I see. So, what you're really trying to say is---------'."

"NO, there's worse than that!" said Vanya, laughing. "What about those conversation snatchers?"

They all started laughing. "No listen," said Vanya, "You could be relating something massive, like----- like how you'd beaten off a pack of wolves with a broom, but before you can tell those hanging on your every word, what happened next,------ the snatcher, having heard the word, broom, jumps in saying, 'That reminds me. Back where I grew up as a little girl, we had a man who made his entire living, just from making brooms. Funny little chap. He had three dogs, Patch, Growler and--- I can't recall the third. It'll come to me in a moment."

They had been inside Trader's place, laughing and joking, sheltering from a downpour that had blown in. Vanya peering outside, said, "It's stopped now."

Gwendolin heaved up a large basket of washing they'd brought back from the stream. Now the sun was out, it needed to be hung to dry.

"You shouldn't do that in your condition," said Vanya. "Give it here, I'll do it."

"Whatever's best for you," Gwendolin quipped, setting them off laughing again.

The conversation and laughter they had was as good as any medicinal extract, concocted from plants they found in the forest. And yes, Gwendolin was expecting.

Now you might have wondered, said the Teller, why no mention has been made of Gwenithen's queen. The fact is, she had died whilst giving birth to Heddi. Poor lad had grown up never having known his mother. The fact Gwenithen didn't have a little lady permanently at his side didn't much trouble the old warrior, for after all there were ways a man in his position could act out any mood that took him, without having to talk to them afterwards.

His senior advisors, it seems had other views and thought they knew what suited their chieftain, better than Gwenithen knew himself. They in fact went to great lengths to put enticing options his way. It was on such day, when a young princess from the Salter tribe, was being feted, that a Bleddi warrior rode amongst the happy throng. Feasting stopped and all eyes turned to the battle-weary man, as he slid from his horse. He stumbled, nearly falling from exhaustion, causing two to rush to his aid. He had come with a warning; tribes from the Gwy valley were advancing north. The Bleddi had held them at the upper Habren, but urgent assistance was needed. It was only a matter of time before they broke through. With eyes staring wide the man said, "They've developed a new form of warfare."

The young Salter princess was showered with compliments, but in view of present circumstances, was hurried home. The following day a small cavalry unit was equipped and ordered south and after two days of gathering sufficient troops, food and armaments, the major force rumbled forth and crossed the Nwy river. The fighting men pressed on ahead, leaving those in the supply column to transfer cart contents to the boats, commandeered for the expedition. The good boat Gwendolin was queen of the fleet. Penda and Dommed were amongst the crews, made up of youths, plus those considered sufficiently senior to be held in reserve.

It took two days for the force to reach the battle zone, then following initial clashes, both sides pulled back to recover and plan further action. The men from the Gwy Valley, on seeing Gwenithen string his forces along a ridge, running across the flatlands between the Habren and eastern hills, must have realised what an opportunity they had missed. They would have been even more dispirited, had they known a small unit, as a precaution against outflanking manoeuvres, had been positioned in the woods, just west of the river.

Arth commanded the small squad. It was pointless sending more men as the narrow trail, cut deep by winter torrents, left no room for them. The planning and deployment, as if a practiced routine, had only been possible thanks to the relaying of vital information gleaned by the army scout. Erdi remembered the rather cold, enigmatic man well. He had been the one in unorthodox garb, who had pronounced his depressing verdict, the day Erdi had thought he'd seen Vanya for the last time. It had basically been,

'You have no choice, other than to turn back and follow the Habren's flow to the sea.'

On the present campaign Erdi at last came to realise why this unapproachable, in fact unappealing man was held in such high esteem. While the main force had been marching south, he had ventured ahead and completely alone had managed to remain undetected whilst seeking out their present vantage point for the stand to be made against the invaders.

Erdi, on the one hand, was keen to witness the new form of warfare spoken of, but on the other, was aware, it could be the last thing he'd ever witness. He'd received a garbled description and had been told in hushed tones of its devastating effect. He was in the most westerly force, commanded by Gregoth, the veteran officer who had recently come to his rescue, as he had done once before, not far south of where they now stood waiting to give battle. Below them, to their right, cutting into their defensive ridge, was a huge swirling loop of the Habren and arrayed immediately on their left, was the main body of troops commanded by Gwenithen. The Bleddi held the ground in the shadow of the forested eastern hills and youths placed amongst the trees stood ready to rasp on horns, if warning were needed of outflanking manoeuvres.

Gregoth, gave the command to wade the Habren and hack down timbers from the forest. These, when trimmed into stakes, were hammered into a line along their immediate front and the ends resharpened to wicked points. Then all waited, wondering, would such a show of force deter attack?

They heard them first; wailing war-horns followed by a loud howling from amongst the trees. Then pulses quickened at the first glint of weapons and there was a stirring amongst ranks at the sight of the whole dark battle line emerging from cover and advancing.

Swords thundered on shields; war-horns moaned once again. A rapid surge forward stopped dead and throats roared. The advance continued to the shield-beat with swords, before arrows sent steepling, fell on them like rain.

At a screeched order, ranks parted, allowing passage for small horse-drawn carts packed with warriors to rumble and bounce across the rough terrain towards them. The whipped ponies swept up the low ridge, cutting swathes through middle ranks, each impact bringing a roar as would the might of the ocean pounding coastal caverns.

On the western flank, it was a different story, for there awaited Gregoth's deterrent. The beasts, on sighting the bristling array, shied away, white-eyed in alarm, their retreat accompanied by a shower of missiles.

At the heart of the battle, warriors leapt from carts to hurl javelins and like maniacs, without the slightest regard for their own safety, swirled swords, wreaking havoc amongst Gwenithen's men. The empty carts rumbling back, had warriors leaping and scrambling aboard at such speed, they were snatched to safety before those, so savagely beleaguered, could comprehend what had hit them. All had been so swift and bloody, they simply stood looking stunned.

Although Gwenithen's army greatly outnumbered the enemy, the main force bearing the brunt, seemed to have no answer to the horse-borne threat and with so great an impact having been made by so few, a feeling of dread seeped through the ranks, for they had yet to face the massed body of troops chanting bloodlust, goading them to attack, down off their vantage point.

Although at the mercy of repeated battering attacks, that now included cavalry, all were ordered to stand, remain in line, resist the impulse to charge down off the ridge as each wave withdrew. The aggressive probing lasted beyond middle day and although in places defences were breached, desperate regrouping, quickly plugged gaps. Also, learning from the first onslaughts, a bristling array of spears was found to dampen the ardour of their attackers and limit damage caused.

There came a pause. Food, water and fresh weapons were supplied from the boats moored downstream. Arrows that had rained down were pulled from the ground and plucked from shields.

All attention then turned to the western slopes. A terrific din erupted from the woods. The small contingent led by Arth was under attack. There came a pause, then more clashing of steel and screams of pain. Another pause was followed by cursing and hacking and then echoing from amongst the trees, came the pitiful sounds of grown men dying. Erdi winced, hearing a stricken youth pleading for mercy, before crying out for his mother. Many a prayer was offered up and spirits beseeched, to give strength to those few valiant defenders. As long as the path was held, there was no danger of encirclement.

The main full-frontal attack, cavalry included, came late afternoon, and there was fighting on all fronts. Sheer impact forced their line back, but managing to hold shape and no longer fighting shadows, spirits were heightened, giving a collective resolve.

With the initial shock absorbed, a stand was made; all taking heart at the sight of Gwenithen's banner juddering and swaying as the bearer slowly edged forward; the elite guard, being urged on by the two impassioned princes. Adding to the fervour, war horns blared, 'advance,' and fighting for every step, all sensed the tide turning. With it came renewed strength and their lashing into the enemy with almost demented ferocity, sent the host reeling back, to teeter on the ridge-edge.

Once feeling the ground go beneath feet, panic set in and at the sight of comrades fleeing, even the bravest gave up the fight. What had surged up like a tidal wave, swept back down quelled, in tumbling disarray. Defying orders, a small contingent set off in chase, only to be recalled by a war-horn's sharp blast and a cavalry troop encircling, herding them back into line. Gwy warriors were known for the manoeuvre they excelled at, the fleeing-turn, all stopping suddenly to hack down disorderly ranks of pursuers. Their enemy had been badly bruised, but no-one was foolish enough to think them entirely beaten. Having said that, all knew, that on this particular day, they would not be back. Courage and discipline had brought a famous victory.

Gwenethin's men wandered the battlefield. Anything of value and of course weapons, were taken from the dead and two Gwy officers were dragged in to have their wounds tended to. They would be ransomed later.

Sign of rank was not usually an overt display, merely sufficient to be recognised by friend and foe alike. An officer didn't wish to render himself an obvious target, but there again was understandably anxious to avoid the death blow as administered to the less vaunted of those captured, once hostilities had ceased. The logic being, those dispatched would not be back to trouble them again.

A loud cheer rang out as Arth and his men emerged from the woods. The huge man had held the narrow gorge almost single handed. There had been no way for the enemy to advance other than straight through him. When attacks had ceased, the defenders had had to climb out over the slain to take the trail down to the valley floor. Arth, looking as cheerful as if returning from nothing more than a hunting trip, amazingly, didn't have a scratch on him.

Enemy horses were led in and those that lay dead or obviously beyond saving, were butchered for roasting later at the victory feast. The new wonder weapon was examined. Three had fallen into their hands. Each had been drawn by a pair of ponies. The shafts and frames were of ash, the floors were of interlaced leather straps, while bent hazel rods, interwoven with willow, formed the sides. All was bound by leather thongs. Wheels of solid oak, had rims of iron. These battle waggons had allowed a fairly modest force, to bludgeon a significantly larger one.

Then Erdi heard the news, Dommed was amongst the fallen. An axe blow to the back of the head. It seemed strange he should have met his end when so far behind the lines. There was too much death all around for there to be an enquiry, but one of the boat crew gave Erdi pause for thought later at the victory feast, "At least we won't have to listen to his moaning, all the way home." Had Dommed been felled by one of their own men?

Next morning, a small contingent of Gwy warriors appeared, approaching with caution, their mounts looking as wary as the riders. They had come with silver to ransom the two officers. Nothing was demanded for return of their dead, even though there was an accepted rate. They had had their ambitions severely dented and that was considered enough.

A funeral pyre saw the end of their own fallen. The Bleddi were left to spread the ashes across the battlefield and remain as a deterrent against further incursions. The rest of the force returned north.

Following victory celebrations, a meeting of the Grand Council was called. First a list of the dead was announced. This was the duty of the Caller. He was the one entrusted with the job of touring hamlets and villages shouting out the latest proclamations. It was a roll requiring a good memory, for just one word out of place could on occasions, be sufficient to alter the whole meaning of an edict. No huge memory was required that particular day, however, not by the Caller's standards anyway, for relatively speaking their forces had got off lightly. Even so, a plan was needed to ensure provisions would be available for widows and their children until a more permanent solution was found.

Then came the most important business of the day; Chieftain's commendations for bravery. Obviously Arth received first mention, but also well up on the honours list, were the two elder princes. Think what you may of them, when all around had been mayhem and disorder, they had actually acquitted themselves with distinction. Gregoth was commended for his leadership and initiative regarding the erection of stake defences, a ploy to be used by all in future and the Bleddi were praised in their absence, having fought as well as any of them.

The question of Dommed's strange departure from this world was briefly spoken of, but in order to move on to more pressing business, Gwenithen simply asked Erdi to look into the matter.

The terror weapon became the next, main issue of the day. The three captured vehicles had been dismantled and brought back most of the way by boat. Lessons had to be learnt. Their own version was needed and quickly. The iron master and master carpenter were there to give an opinion. A war-cart was rolled in for inspection. The use of leather thongs to form the floor was acknowledged as essential, for the way the carts bounced over rough ground, anything more solid would have flung the occupants out in all directions, like pots off a runaway trade wagon. The wheels, it was thought, could be improved upon. The massive things of solid oak weighed more than the rest of the cart put together. It was at this point Gregoth gave serious cause for thought, saying, "If these things had had finer wheels, the speed of them would have put us in serious trouble."

An idea for improvement of the sides was suggested. Cow hide as used on shields was given a muttering of appreciation, then the iron master spoke. "If the wheels were positioned further back from centre, I have a notion a good deal of the bounce would be taken out of her."

"What makes you think that?" Gwenithen asked.

"I can't say exactly my lord. It's just an instinct I have."

General murmuring met this reply, but Erdi had no doubt he was right. He had noticed the man was blessed with the same skill the Dwy boatbuilder had exhibited. He had no need for a measuring stick. His eye told him exactly. 'Part practice and part something you're born with,' the master craftsman had said.

Erdi of course, when welcomed home, had been asked about the battle, but kept his account brief and actually admitted, they had been taught a serious lesson. Perhaps a blessing in disguise. If they had come up against a larger force deploying such tactics, they would almost certainly have come off second best. He told Gwendolin of Dommed's mysterious death and the fact he'd been asked to look into it. His first job of course was to console the widow.

He found Inga red-eyed and still in a state of shock. Even though the man had been a brute of late, when suddenly such a person is taken, those grieving tend to only remember the good times shared. Erdi assured her that she would be provided for and managed to hold himself in check, not saying the, 'until,' word that had so nearly tumbled out. He could hardly start talking about her future partner with her man's ashes only recently scattered, but still, there was no doubt, it would not be long before ardent suitors would be wending their way to her door.

Erdi next sought his father. He knew his mother would not be home, she would be busy tending the wounded. Penda admitted that at times he would have gladly stabbed his neighbour in the guts, but assured he'd had no part in his murder. Erdi was taken aback. What he thought of as a possibility, his father was stating as fact.

"Well let's have no doubts. That's what it must have been. One moment he was there, next," he clapped hands together, "gone! And the Gwy savages nowhere near us. One of our lot must have clubbed him, but I haven't the vaguest idea why. Yes, he'd annoyed his whole crew, but hardly enough to get himself murdered.

Couldn't abide the man in the end, but I would never have felled him from behind."

Erdi, detecting some of his father's old spirit returning, asked if he could take note of those calling on Inga. He also asked him to try and remember those nearby at the time of Dommed's death. Most of the warriors had blood on their hands, they had even been known to kill one another when arguments broke out, but never from behind. This was quite a serious issue.

He next called at Trader's, giving him a more detailed account of the battle and also details of Dommed's demise.

"Won't be missed by many. How's Inga?"

Erdi told him and Trader continued, "She won't be alone long. They'll be lining up. She'll have to fight them off with a stick!"

When talk moved on to business, Trader told him, most of the new bronze artefacts had been traded on for meat and grain. "You've no idea how relieved I am. I've really had enough of those buckles and bits!"

Chapter Twelve

Now, said *the Teller.* We move a little forward in time. The winter feast was still held at the old time, on the shortest day, not brought forward to the point of celebration now. The belief, that each new year was heralded by a new sun, still held sway, but it was now generally acknowledged, sacrifice of bronze had nothing to do with it. Strange thing is though, you're not going to believe this, but people still dropped in small bronze offerings for luck when making wishes at the well. Strange how some ancient customs never die. You people wouldn't be superstitious enough to do anything as outdated, would you?

This was greeted by laughter.

The main talk between the chieftains that year was on the subject of iron and after attempting to find out how much rivals had access to, without revealing the dearth available on home territory, it became clear, actually none of them had enough of it. So where were the tribes of the Gwy valley acquiring their ample supply from? There was speculation, it could be coming in by sea or maybe from the eastern lands. Any of those trading down in their heartland and escaping with their lives had reported plenty of signs of iron working, but none of iron mining. So, it appears they were not sitting on a mountain of the stuff. The idea of a probing expedition was talked of, but there it ended and nothing definite was decided.

Erdi met up with Yanker again and told him of their punitive expedition and how they'd been shocked by the new battle wagons that had torn holes in their defences. Yanker said, he wished he'd been ordered to take part. He was back on administrative duties, hating every moment and said, if ever a trip were to be organised to explore for iron, he would welcome the chance to be included. He didn't shed a tear for Dommed, by the way and when told of Arth's heroic stand he'd quipped, "So Arth held the path."

Not for the first time and certainly not the last, Erdi shook his head and said, "Don't ever change will you, cousin."

They both made the short trip to the village where their boat, Gwendolin had begun her travels and were shown the latest construction. It was a clumsy, roller of a boat with a bull nose. Yanker stroking it lovingly asked with a smile, "How do you achieve such elegance? Just look at those fine lines." He gave Erdi a flick of a wink as the headman launched into his lyrical reply.

It was the first fair Madarch had ever attended and he'd wandered around as wide eyed as Luda had done, years before. He was there, courtesy of Erdi and when all were packing to leave, he noticed his swarthy friend slip a rather fine white shirt into the baggage.

"Where did you get this from?" he asked, withdrawing the garment and holding it up. "I've told you, while you're working with me, you keep your hands off other people's property."

Madarch looked truly hurt. "I not steal it, Erdi. The lady they call Mellinter give it me."

"Oh, you didn't, did you?"

"She want me to."

"First fair I bring you to and you-----." His voice trailed off and he shook his head in disbelief.

Melly Comfort, as Vanya had named her, had earned slight notoriety for aiding the trading of goods by offering her own feminine assets, to certain male customers as an inducement.

211

It was the first time Erdi had heard of her doing it without attempting to gain some sort of trade advantage, mind you. He looked at Madarch again and thought, 'Yes I suppose they might look upon you as a bit of a prospect; a hint of the wild; dark looks; proud wearer of the torque; slayer of Bloodaxe.'

He remembered the strange, almost inexplicable power that had attracted certain women even when in his decidedly stinky state and went on to reason, 'I expect there'll be no stopping you. Not now we've cleaned you up a bit.'

Some of the fairs were referred to and remembered by certain events that had occurred at them. There was the 'Ill-gotten ox fair', 'stone to gold fair' and this one became known as the 'foal for bowl fair'.

A man from the eastern hills had turned up with an item for Trader. It was a bowl fashioned from rock. Not ordinary rock, but the type you can almost see through and like gentle drifts of smoke, the rock had blues, purples and greys running through it, whose facets, even though encased, sent out faint sparks of light. It was finely wrought and beautiful to sight and touch. Trader negotiated for it and a buzz went round the fair, to the extent the transaction was brought to Gwenithen's attention, who on being shown the bowl, was extremely desirous to acquire it. After genial negotiations, it was agreed a foal out of one of his prized mares would be a fair trade.

Erdi asked Trader later, why had the man brought the bowl directly to him?

"He knew he'd get a fair deal, Erdi."

"But how did you know its value? You can't have seen one before, surely?"

"No and probably won't see another, but when you're handling stuff on a daily basis it sort-of gives you an instinct of how to value the odd rare thing that sometimes turns up. He knew I wouldn't try to rob him. You see, Erdi, half the art of dealing is knowing how to rate something. And before you say, 'That's obvious,' what I mean is, most people don't know what makes one thing infinitely better than something that looks roughly the same. Yes, any fool can see one horse is better than another, but they don't know if it's two horses better or a complete double handful better. The best horse traders know exactly, that's why they're successful and their rivals aren't. I'm not a bad judge of the things I trade in, so that's why he brought it to me."

"And the foal?"

"I've seen her. She's a little beauty. Some deals have that feeling of luck running through them, Erdi. It makes up for those------"

"That turn out a bit disappointing?" Erdi finished for him.

"Made a nice change from all those buckles and bits, I can tell you."

The following spring the people realised the beautiful weather of the year before had been but brief respite from the rains that had recently blighted. It even rained through blossom time and when the normal early summer rains were due, it poured down. That was what made Vanya's and Heddi's joining day so special, the sun shone radiating happiness throughout the valley, but before I tell you what happened that day, there are a few other things you need to know. Don't worry, I'm not going to dance the story round like I did the first night, but what do you think about this little morsel?

Brialla's brother Tawy at last plucked up the courage to tell Mara about the extent of his feelings for her. He knew that admitting it risked bringing their pleasurable meetings to an abrupt end, for certain women will tolerate a man being at their beck and call and don't mind admiration from afar, but as soon as that line is crossed and the one who's been a useful nuisance, declares undying love, then that's it! He gets the beggar's farewell. Tawy needn't have worried mind you, Mara was in love with him.

A woman in the audience, not realising how far her voice carried, said, "Well! Never you mind!" starting everyone laughing, including the Teller.

This put them in a tricky situation. No matter how much she loved him, she couldn't just pack up and leave as he'd suggested, for doing so would upset her children and grandchild beyond belief. Shouldn't think Penda would have been wildly delighted either. She told him, "We can't build our happiness on other people's hurt. It just won't work. It might for a while, but in the end, guilt will kill everything."

He tried his best to change her mind, but had no success. They had to content themselves with their few stolen moments. At least she was too old to become pregnant.

The Teller put a hand to an ear expecting further audience participation, but there was silence. Very wise, *he said,* rarely works the same twice. *This brought a laugh. He welcomed the odd interruption; within limits.*

I know that may have come as a bit of a shock, *he continued,* after all they weren't flighty young things, they were grandparents. Inside, however, they felt as young as they'd done in their prime. This also might come as a little surprise.

One day at Trader's, Erdi overheard Madarch and Gwedyll talking. He couldn't believe it; they were communicating in cymry. And here's something else I haven't told you. Didn't think I needed to because it wasn't that obvious, but now everyone could see beyond doubt, not just Gwendolin, but Gwedyll also gave swollen evidence of fairly recent activities.

Anyway, returning to Erdi. He went over to Madarch and asked, "When did you learn that?"

"He's been learning it for quite some time, haven't you Maddy?"

"But you can hardly speak my language properly, never mind cymry."

"I do know, enough to get by," Madarch replied.

Gwedyll, with an arched look, muttered to Erdi, almost singing the words, "Won't be long before he knows what his na—hame means."

Erdi thought, 'Yes, only a matter of time,' and looking at his strange friend came to the conclusion, 'Just goes to show----- people can be full of surprises.'

He continued to make it his business to see how Inga was faring following the loss of Dommed and on one visit, happened to interrupt a meeting between the widow and a male caller. The man was a good deal younger than Inga, in fact probably even younger than her eldest child and on Erdi's arrival his face took on the instant guilty look of someone caught in the act. Erdi took an instant dislike to the man.

On ascertaining that Inga had all she needed, Erdi walked across to his old home in the hope of finding his parents in. Mara was absent, no surprise there, but his father was home. Penda told him there had been a few male callers at the house opposite, but the present visitor had been the most persistent. He hadn't spoken to the man, but it seemed Inga found him agreeable for he had often heard her laughing in his company.

Erdi wondered why she didn't share his repugnance for the smug looking youth, but there again, she was probably still in shock. He had noticed, people often made strange choices following a break-up or a partner's death. A few enquiries needed to be made about the man.

Talia's joining ceremony was fast approaching and with her father dead, she'd asked Erdi to accompany her on the big day. He'd asked what she thought of her mother's admirer and the face pulled said it all. Erdi began to look into the man's background; who his family members were and how a young fit man managed to have so much spare time to go a-wooing?

The day of Talia's wedding was a bit dull and grey, but at least the rain held off. Everybody enjoyed themselves, but Erdi held himself in check. Gwendolin looked ready to give birth at any moment and he needed to stay sober. Talia of course moved out to live with her man and Mara came to stay at Erdi's house to be on hand to help with the birth.

One wet, late spring morning there came the lusty sound of a baby's cry and Deri was told he had a little sister. They called her Megan. It was a Y-Dewis name, but the tribes were now becoming that intermingled they shared names, ways of doing things and languages. Some of the words that were a bit of one and a bit of another sounded strange at first hearing, but when repeated by many, soon became the accepted term. The two tongues began to fuse into one.

Gwedyll also gave birth to a little girl and they named her Vanya. Well fancy that!

I have noticed a few tiny Vanya's have arrived on the scene since my last visit, *said the Teller.*

Erdi's enquiries regarding Inga's admirer had brought little to light other than he was known as workshy, had no visible assets and most men despised the relish he derived from flattering older ladies. The mere fact of coming down out of the hills seemed to have altered him. Gone to his head. He had a way of approaching the fairer sex, smiling, slightly crouched, with dance of step, his jerkin marginally back off the shoulders, that made male onlookers pray for, implore for something to send him sprawling, but many ladies delighted in it. What men saw as theatrical and creepy, sent mature women into raptures. Not all, I must add, for Mara and Brialla detested the man and couldn't imagine what Inga saw in him.

It was because of them being up in the market one day that the breakthrough came. Inga wasn't with them, for she no longer had Talia at home to look after the little ones. The fact Penda was there, Erdi thought remarkable and seeing his father laugh for the first time in months, he found more remarkable still.

They had been passing the stand where Melly Comfort had her wares hanging up for sale. Mara giving a furrowed look of disbelief, muttered to Brialla, "Is it me or is the one leg of those leggings much wider than the other?"

Brialla spluttered a laugh, "I think you're right, Mara." Then with her usual delight in devilment, she sidled up to the stand, scanned the rather specialised pair of men's leggings and with a wide-eyed look of glee, nodded vigorously. She returned, hand over mouth to stifle laughter and blurted, "It'll make her sore trying to get rid of that pair!"

At which all around, including Penda, burst out laughing. Inga's young admirer happened to be there and rushed over to give the affronted woman his support. Following close behind was a youth who, Erdi had found from his enquiries, happened to be the aunt flatterer's cousin.

Penda, nodding in their general direction, said, "That lad was with us the day Dommed got his head split."

Erdi decided to look into the matter further. He knew where the youth lived and a few days later, rode over there with Madarch.

He was guarded and surly on being questioned, "Why are you asking me? Your father was there. Go and ask him what happened."

"I already have and now would like your version."

"I can't remember. There was a lot going on. We were in the middle of a battle if you care to remember. We were back and forth with arrows, spears, water, wounded. I can't remember. It was back in the old year. Why are you dragging it all up now?"

Erdi could see it was obvious he was hiding something, but that wasn't enough to declare he'd committed murder. As they rode away, Madarch said, "I know how we get him talking."

He was allowed further use of the pony to visit his people in the forest and returned with a certain mysterious substance. It had been dried and stored since being picked in the late days of the previous year. Armed with this and a skin of cider, they returned to question the youth. Erdi had sampled the potent liquid. It had a few lumps, whiffed a bit, but other than that, was drinkable. Sort of.

At first, the lad wouldn't take his hornful, which was a bit troubling, but then, on seeing theirs being drained without any ill effect, he downed his in one go, belched and held out the vessel for a refill. He hadn't eaten and so within the space of one sun-span, the substance Madarch had sprinkled into the first dose he'd gulped, began to take effect. His speech became slurred and his eyes took on a wild glazed look.

"They're coming," said Erdi.

"Who are? Who's coming?" He looked terrified.

"Gwy warriors." They're pouring in over the Habren. "Dommed's leading them."

The youth looked ready to bolt. Huge beads of sweat had formed on his brow.

"Dommed's coming. He's coming to get you."

"Dommed's dead. I need drink. I'm parched. Burning up."

"Listen! Did you hear that? It's Dommed. Can you hear him creeping closer?"

"He can't be! I killed him!"

Erdi, nodding a thank you at Madarch, asked, "Tell me, why did you kill him?"

"Dern said to do it. He said we'd both get land. Dommed's land. I need more drink. Parched."

Erdi handed him water, which was guzzled that feverishly, half slopped down the front of him. He shook all over and his eyes stared wide with terror.

"Dern's your cousin, right?"

The youth nodded and pleaded, "More water. Need more water."

There was no use taking the lad with them in his present state. They settled him down and with knees drawn tight beneath chin and quivering all over, he closed his eyes.

Gwenithen had him and his cousin hauled in. Even though they were his own people he ordered the Seer to pronounce the dreaded living death and they were given just one day to quit the territory. Not only did it solve the mystery, it showed Gwenethin to be a just ruler.

Alright, *said the Teller laughing*, I rushed that a bit, but I wanted to get on with this next part.

After the guilty pair had stumbled off to a life as outcasts, the chieftain called for Erdi and Madarch to approach, intrigued to know how they had managed to get the youth to talk? Erdi, for reasons soon to become apparent, was reluctant to say the name of what had been used. Instead, he asked Madarch if he had any of the substance still on him?

Madarch, digging within folds of his garment, pulled out a small pouch and held up a portion of the contents.

"Ah madarch," said Gwenithen with a merry glint.

The man in question, taking on a troubled look, asked very slowly, in cwmry, "My Lord Gwenithen, is this in my hand, dried madarch?"

"Indeed it is."

Madarch turned to Erdi and demanded, "Why you call me mushroom?"

Erdi, hardly able to reply through laughter said, "It was what you had with you, first day I saw you."

Undaunted by such vaunted company, Madarch gave a maddened swipe, but Erdi was too quick for him and his look of mock trepidation, as if about take flight from the next attempt, sent the place into a rapturous uproar.

Now returning to Inga. Whilst Erdi had been going about all his land duties the previous year, he had met one man he'd instantly taken to. He was a Y-Dewis warrior who had lost his wife to the sweating sickness that sometimes flared up out of nowhere. You could leave for work in the fields early morning and return that evening to find your loved ones, stone-cold dead. The man was hard working, of pleasant demeanour and in need of a good woman. Erdi sought him out and in view of all those recently widowed and him being decidedly eligible, time was of the essence. He needed to introduce him to Inga, before one of the others snagged him and so suggested to the man, he best not stand on ceremony, but ride over immediately with a few supplies, for gifting to a certain lady and her family.

That's all it took. She had not been the least bit sorry on hearing her previous admirer had had his comeuppance, for she had begun to find the man odious long before the shock of realising he'd been the instigator of Dommed's murder. On watching the stranger dismount, she admitted to Mara later, that at first sight of him she'd said to herself, "If that man's available, then he's the one."

There was a modest gathering at their joining ceremony and Inga and family moved in with her new man. With Mara still at Erdi's house, Penda, apart from the slave still working there, was on his own.

Now at last we come to Vanya's wedding.

All the people were bubbling with excitement, warming to this occasion more than they would, had the day been the celebration of one of their own getting married. It went beyond the realms of simply the joining of two notable people. It captured the imagination of all. A handsome Y-Dewis prince, many young ladies secretly dreamt of, was marrying a young woman, most young men admitted to be way beyond their reach and not only was the lady beautiful; since her escape from the hands of slavers, she had also become a legend.

The marriage was like the first tentative step of a union between the peoples and was taken to actually symbolise the joining of the tribes. But what enchanted the ladies even further, sending them quite dewy eyed in fact, was it seeming to be an unbelievable tale of dreams come true. A girl from the valley had risen from humble beginnings to be celebrated as a true princess. All little girls dream of such, but the local people were ecstatic that one of their own had actually managed it. The women were anxious to see what she wore on the day and the children scoured the meadows for the legendary four-leaf clover. After all their searching, three were found and to bring luck, happiness and prosperity, were added to her bouquet.

All awaited her arrival at the Arrow field. The banks of the old fortress were hardly visible beneath the throng that had swarmed there to gain vantage points. Some had arrived first light to be sure of a spot commanding a view of the trail the couple would take on their way up to the wedding feast, being readied inside the fortress. All wore their best attire and from a distance the fort's banking looked like it had sprung an overnight covering of flowers.

As said earlier, the spirits had taken a hand and they were blessed with the promise of a beautiful day. At times, with it being in such contrast to the recent cold, wet spring, the sun felt almost unbearably hot, but mercifully, occasional cooling breezes brought relief, stirring trees, ruffling hair and towering up white fluffy clouds, that could be imagined as a realm of the Gods.

A murmuring went through the crowd and necks were craned. It was hard to see what had caused such flurry, but someone said at last, "There they are! I can see something moving!"

On the trail from the east a small group took shape, the detail sharpening, until a horse, rider and figures could be seen slowly emerging from the trees. As the column grew in length, it became clear it was the wedding party. Even from that distance they could see the foremost figure was Erdi. He was leading the horse, which with garlanded head held high, looked proud to be adorned by the bride, not sitting astride, but gracefully sideways on. Erdi occasionally looked up to give his sister a reassuring smile. Her long linen gown, the embroidering of which had excited so many fingers, oft billowed, causing Vanya and Talia, her maid of honour, to laugh, when hauling in the errant fabric to be stroked flat.

When closer still, the pretty colours of her floral headband became clear, reminding all it had seemed but yesterday, she had been that young girl they had voted Spring Queen.

Below there was movement. Things had started to happen. Prince Bonheddig accompanied by his eldest brother walked to where the Seer awaited. Gwenithen and his entire retinue followed, but halted, careful not to encroach into the magic space around the couple.

Vanya could now be seen quite clearly and women gasped and said almost with tears in their eyes, "Oh, she looks beautiful!"

Each time the light breeze wafted her hair, the sun caught the glint of gold from the large annular earrings, Lady Rhosyn had gifted for the great day.

"You must wear something borrowed, Vanya. It's tradition."

Around Vanya's neck, hidden but reassuring beneath her blouse, was the amulet her grandma Vana had always worn.

Immediately behind the bride and close attendants, were Penda and Mara followed by relatives and family friends. People craned necks in an effort to identify who had been thus honoured. Such details would be talked over at great length later.

As the Seer was approached, the joining song sent a shiver through those staring down off the hill. The sweet voices ringing, of the children's singing caused many a lady to dab an eye. The Seer's practiced voice, clearly carrying to all, gave notice that the ceremony had commenced. People half stood, weaving from side to side in the effort to peer through gaps. "Her father's giving her away," said one.

The Seer raised his arms and turning to all asked, did any have objection to his joining the couple? The wind stirring, to ruffle clothing, was all that broke the silence. Then the Prince's voice could be heard followed by the clear chime of Vanya's. When the singing re-commenced, all knew the couple had been joined. They made their way, slowly up the pathway to the fortress.

People rushed, frantic in their efforts to gain a closer look. Singing accompanied the couple's ascent and the petals strewn to dance on the breeze, floated down to bedeck the grass.

The image of Vanya laughing up at their gentle fall all around, was treasured, in many a memory. The crush on either side of the high banking intensified, everyone wanting to return home with having had at least one clear view of the royal couple. Just one brief glimpse of the handsome young Heddi and a moment's clear sighting of his happy young bride. Women later, vied with each other to give their account of how they'd seen Vanya and Heddi passing below almost close enough to touch. "They were garlanded together, draped with honeysuckle and blue ribbon. Joined for life. Vanya looked truly beautiful."

The evening's feasting could be heard by the few still lingering on the fortress banking. It went on long into the night. Not only had Prince Bonheddig and Vanya been joined, so had both tribes.

Erdi watching the couple depart next morning, felt satisfaction that all had gone well, but was also a little sad. His sister was leaving for a new life. They had been gifted a small plot of land above where he and Yanker had often walked in the hope of meeting Donda. It was a beautiful location with the beaver pool to look out onto.

It was a few days later that the warrior, only survivor of the massacre at the fortress, rode into Gwenithen's village. He was hauled into custody and Erdi was sent for. He explained to the man that banishment had been for life, not just for one year and asked him, why had he risked his life returning?

The old warrior told him, he had been living amongst a tribe, daily toiling over the construction of a massive bastion on the hills overlooking the spot where the Tamesa river flowed into the Habren. He went on to explain, he was returning to repay a massive favour. With Erdi having saved his life, out of gratitude he'd ridden back to give warning of what his former hosts had planned. Their aim was to control the Habren Gorge. They intended to gather tolls on all cargos in payment for allowing clear passage.

With that the Teller, thanking everyone, left the Grand Hall.

Part 4

Chapter Thirteen

With the third section of the tale having been relatively short, the Teller didn't feel in the limp state usually experienced and realised with relief, not only was he not completely drained of energy, but in actual fact, keen to be up and out in the fresh early morning air. He arose and found his way about in the dim murk that precedes the sun's first bent-pin glint from the east. He was thirsty.

"Oh please, not that water. The drinking water is in the other pot, the one with the lid on."

He was surprised his hostess was already up. She hurried to his assistance, ladling out water into a beaker. "This is from the trough out front. We just use the pool water for washing and cleaning. No telling what gets into it. Dogs use it and even old Eva's pig."

He thanked her and said he was walking down to the east gate, the sky looked clear of cloud and if he hurried, he would catch the sunrise.

The figure up on the palisade stood with back turned, gazing out to the east, but a skip of heartbeat told him, as sure as fate, it was Megan. She turned on hearing him climb the steps and smiled, almost as if expecting him.

Hello, *he said,* I was hoping to catch the sunrise.

"I often come up here for the same reason. It's peaceful."

They just talked generally for a while and then Megan mused, "I have often wondered what's out there. Out beyond our world. Well I think most of us do to some extent. Many folks here have never been beyond the Feasting Site or Habren river. Even I have only ventured beyond, what we call the bounds, a handful of times. Our only way of knowing what lies in those far off lands is from what we manage to glean from traders and from what Tellers such as yourself relate. But even that can be misleading. Many of those who have wended their way here have certainly entertained the majority, but their sagas tend to follow the same traditional exaggerations of heroism and endeavour, until personally, I find them quite meaningless.

Each Teller seems to feel the need to dwarf the exploits of the heroes of previous tales. Their sagas pile up the heaps of men slain in battle to the point, they outnumber those known to exist. One man standing alone against an army more numerous than trees in the forest. Are we meant to believe that? In the end they merely become tales fit for children or for minds of no greater maturity. You are the first to tell of true lives and people. It has helped me picture what is out there. I swear at one point, I could almost taste the salt of the sea, feel the motion of the waves and appreciate its vastness, but to tell you the truth, I've never once seen it."

Megan gave a reproachful look. "The trouble is, you've stirred up a desire to travel. To go and see what exactly is out there. I feel unsettled"

My life might seem romantic, *he answered,* but I envy something you people have, a sense of belonging, contentment. For some reason I was blessed with the gift I have, but sometimes it seems more like a curse, forcing me to wander ever onward.

"Have you never thought of simply staying with one people? Become their Teller."

Often, but it would be almost like breaking a pact with the spirit world. I would not be allowed a life of such contentment. They would probably devise an ailment, causing me to waste away, or at the very least, reclaim my gift. Snatch it from me. Maybe strike me dumb--- a stream of words leaving my mind, but strange unintelligible noises leaving my mouth.

"You joke."

I most certainly do not. I could end up like the flute player in that well known saga. Enchanting all with his beautiful melodies, until overheard mocking the spirits. Next day, no matter how hard he tried, he found himself condemned to produce nothing but ugly rasping sounds. Finally, being mocked by all as the scarecrow.

"Is it those same spirits that put such strange words in your head? I sort of know what they mean from where they appear in the telling. But it's not just me---- it puzzles most. They wonder where you get them from. Some whisper that you travel through time." *Megan gave him a teasing look.*

Can you remember which words exactly?

"I try to hang on to them, but during the course of the day they slip from the mind. There was one that sounded like racle or something similar."

Oracle?

"Oracle! That's it!"

And perhaps, desirous, effulgence, labyrinthine and ignominious?

Her eyes widened, "Yes! Those are the ones. Where do you get them from?"

The Teller explained their meaning and then said, Please, don't think of me as anything more than just a simple storyteller. If you imagine I bring wonders, they are but foothills compared to the mountainous mysteries that lie out there. I have heard of animals you could never conjure in your wildest dreams, of people with yellow skin, of milling multitudes of black people. Tales have filtered through of a faraway tribe who, having mastered the art of building temples with roofs supported on columns of wood, now build wonderous creations from glistening pure white stone. I understand your urge to travel. Compared to most I have seen plenty, but believe me it is nothing compared to what really lies out there. I hold a deep yearning to travel beyond our shores. Travel to see those distant stone temples with my own eyes.

"Where do they lie?"

In a land way beyond where the sun now hovers.

Megan laughed, "We've been talking that much we didn't notice sunrise." She gave him a searching look. "The way you described Erdi's method of putting his story together, sketching the outline before adding colour. Are you really describing what you actually do?"

Would you ask the iron master to reveal how he transforms dull rock into swords and ploughshares?

Not deterred she asked, "Is part of you Erdi?"

I would never equal his slingshot skills or powers of endeavour.

"I think you know what I mean."

I don't think it's possible to relate a tale without a little of yourself or people you have known, creeping in, but to answer your question, there is not a single character in the telling, based entirely on myself or others I have known. It's a story passed down through time and I do my best to stay true to it.

"What about some of the ladies. You must have drawn a little from experience, surely?"

The Teller smiled, You ask too many questions.

Their walk together, back between the houses, didn't go unnoticed.

A morning meal awaited by the hearth. He could hear the light ring of a hammer from inside the adjoining building. His host was obviously at work. The Teller decided to walk to the ramparts once more. He needed to frame the tale for the coming eve. It all needed rehearsal in his mind, not possible when accompanied by the tapping of a hammer. He headed towards the west gate.

Such was his concentration, the morning seemed to drift by as if comprising nothing more than a matter of moments. Many had observed him motionless up on the ramparts and had skirted around as they would a thing of wonder. It was whispered that he was there in body, but his spirit was away in a strange far-off land. Children were told not to approach, not to play noisy games. If that body were to be disturbed, the Teller's spirit might not find a way back in. He was left alone in his motionless state.

Even though his eyes had remained wide open, when the Teller finally stirred it felt like an awakening, as if from a dream. He turned to ascertain where exactly the thin clink of a hammer was ringing from.

'That one heard earlier,' he thought, 'surely it hasn't followed me.'

He stretched stiff limbs, walked towards the sound and entered the Iron Master's forge. The young man was putting the finishing touches to an iron shoe, the cutting edge of a wooden shovel.

Looking pleasantly surprised at the intrusion, he beckoned the Teller to enter and after general chat, complimented his guest on the knowledge he'd gained as regards the working of iron, adding, "Your description of how a spear head is fashioned was correct in every detail."

As he spoke the Teller realised, he had met the young man on his previous visit. He had been amongst the group of youths who had listened to the tale of Erdi's early years. It stood out as a rueful reminder; a reminder to never again relate two parts of the tale on the same day. It had been exhausting. The Iron Master's face now of course had the craggy jaw of maturity, but there was no mistaking it, he had been amongst those youths that day.

He pointed to the completed article on the anvil and said, "I can see that's a shoe for a shovel blade. Do you ever make the complete blade from iron?"

"It's possible, but we never do. It would use up far too much metal. It's too treasured to devote so much to a humble tool." He picked up the shoe, "All you really need is this I have in my hand. The wooden blade is then enough to actually lift what the shoe cuts, once you've got the stuff loose of course, but that's what the pick is for."

In my travels way down in the east of our island, I have seen complete shovel blades of iron. I wrongly assumed them to exist here.

"I think I know where you mean. I'm told they have more iron than they know what to do with."

The Teller thought for a while. When I told you the story of Erdi in his younger days, I made reference to a shovel blade, locally available, fashioned completely from iron. You were there that day. Why didn't you correct me?

The man smiled. "You're the Teller. You can't be expected to be right in every detail. I didn't want my interruption with the truth, spoiling a good story."

Not letting the truth spoil a good story could sum up quite a few people I know. *They both laughed. The Teller thanked the man and returned to his temporary abode.*

That evening the usual applause greeted his arrival. He said, Sorry I'm a little late, but I've been away gathering up details for the tale. The little sprites dropped me off in the wrong valley and it's taken all this time to travel back here.

A little girl piped up. "You're tricking us! I saw you earlier."

No you didn't.

"Yes I did. I saw you. First you were up on top of the wall and then I saw you walking about."

That wasn't me. It was just somebody that looked like me.

"You're making it up!"

What me make things up?

His audience laughed.

The Teller began; For the first time in years, Erdi felt the pressure of responsibilities lifting from him. He was now recognised as a valuable member of the council, seen as an asset, rather than a threat to the established regime. He was still required to intervene in land disputes, but was approached merely for his overall judgement and was not expected to become embroiled in the initial arguments. Also, now that Gwenithen had trust in his judgement, he tended to simply endorse his decisions. Truth be known, the chieftain had had his fill of land matters. Erdi certainly had, as well we know, but at least he was no longer bothered by petty day to day complaints and following a stroke of inspiration from Vanya, had started to interest Prince Heddi in territorial entanglements. With a little more encouragement, he hoped he would be relieving him of the entire role.

As regards his status on the council, he was known as a man of few words, but when he did speak others tended to listen. The chieftain's righthand man, the one who had once been so full of himself, had eventually rankled to such an extent, Gwenithen had deflated him somewhat by taking the pleasure of grandly bestowing a duty with title, but in fact, little substance. It had given the chieftain no end of merriment. And as regards the gloomy pair, Erdi himself was amused to discover, the very ones who had held his fate in their hands following the Erin venture, were in fact suffered, but secretly derided by all. What he had taken to be, when viewing as an outsider, a unified body of men, was in actual fact riven with discord and petty jealousies. He could see why Trader wanted nothing to do with the likes of them or anything they represented.

He always avoided taking sides on the minor points that seemed to entangle and enrage the same vociferous few, feeling it best to save his energies for when an injustice loomed or a wrong decision seemed imminent.

His own people, who had been so recently hostile, now looked upon his achievements and new status with pride. As his sister had done, Erdi had risen from virtually nothing. He had become a respected member of the council, to the point he was even at times, consulted by none other than Lord Gwenithen himself.

The trip for the year's shipment of grain was a duty that couldn't be avoided, but at least it gave respite from political wrangles, plus the demons of fear he'd experienced the previous year had been slain as sure as Madarch had slain Bloodaxe, to the point he was now looking forward to; relishing in fact, his next meeting with the Quiet Man, the chieftain of Baile Atha Cliath.

He had no part in organising the deployment of the mounted detachment sent to ensure the Habren gorge was kept open for trade. He did, however, make certain that the old warrior who had warned of the imminent threat was allowed freedom to leave, or stay, whichever he preferred. The man chose to stay and eventually took up with a Y-Dewis woman, one of the Habren Battle widows.

236

Erdi organised the hauling of their boat Gwendolin up to the Dwy and just he and Madarch set out for the settlement lying up near the river mouth. They had with them the last of Gardarm's hoard and the pair were welcomed like old friends, with Madarch even given the odd flirtatious cuddle. Erdi wondered what it was about the man. The attention he drew was only innocent fun, but it seemed to be a recurring mystery. Perhaps, gifting him the torque was a bad idea, for since its bestowal, the man had even taken a pride in his appearance, enhancing that innate hint of the wild.

One woman sampling the new fresh Madarch, as if the merest sniff would induce ecstasy, said, "Perhaps we ought to change your name to Rambler," which obviously hinted at his roots, but was also a local term for rose.

His response, an uncertain smile, sent all the women into raptures, as if witnessing an infant doing something comical.

'Perhaps that's it,' thought Erdi. 'Perhaps it's the man's innocence that attracts them. The fact, that even though a little on the wild side, he looks so harmless.'

Cronk was keen to join in their venture, but advised a brief pause, for it would not only allow wet weather to blow through, it also ensured departure coinciding with more favourable tides. Cronk explained, the timing was not only right for initial putting to sea, but more importantly, as long as the weather held, departure from Ynys Isal could be done on the same dawn's turn of a high tide, as had benefitted previously.

It is rare for two trips to be exactly the same and not only were they not blessed with the same luck of meeting with the copper traders, they also weren't favoured by the same conditions that had allowed a single day's crossing. A miserable night was spent holding station, waiting for sufficient light to navigate into the broad sweep of Baile Atha Cliath Bay.

Negotiation for the grain went fairly smoothly and a thing Erdi found enthralling was, compared to all other leaders he had met, Un-Farqune seemed to retain his sense of power and might, without ever losing the impression, he was entirely relaxed and approachable. There was something of a quiet steely core, however, that had his people ever enthusiastic to give their support and jump to it, whenever given an instruction. Erdi suspected, that even if ordered to run straight through a wooden palisade, his warriors would be only too glad to oblige. The man also had a quiet humour, which Erdi likened to, the pleasure of discovering water in what appeared to be a dried-up stream bed.

He and Erdi had been reminiscing over how the feared Bloodaxe had met his end, when the man had said with a merry twinkle, "Fancy being felled by nothing more than a paddle! You'd have thought Tua Fola had become tired of wiping his backside each morning."

Upon Cronk's translation, Erdi looked visibly stunned. "Excuse me sire, but how did you chance on that saying?"

"The man told me it might have some impact."

"We called him Wolf. Where is he? Is he here?"

"No, he's away back home, up by the great lake. He did leave a gift, however. It was on his second visit. I told him, those from 'across' would be back for grain and he arrived one day with what I'm about to show you. He told me it was for someone called Vanya. Come, it's just across the way."

Erdi was taken to a small hut. Un Farqune gave the briefest of whistles and an Erin hound unfolded itself and padded obediently forward. It looked to be no more than about nine moons old.

"I'll be sorry to see him go," said Un Farqune.

"What's his name?"

"Mac Tire," came the answer. "You're a little beauty aren't you Mac? A born hunter" Then turning to Erdi, he confided, "Those living up by the great lake---- they're terrible people for the hunting."

Erdi smiling, thought to himself, 'I could actually live here.'

He returned home with a pang in his heart not just for the place, but having been that close to his friend Wolf and yet in fact, completely missing him. The copper traders were again available to carry the grain back to the Dwy river and from there it was ferried, to be carted south for distribution.

Vanya, on seeing what Wolf had gifted her, hugged the hound and burst into tears.

At the winter fair that year, a plan was discussed regarding an attempt to discover the source of iron. The source their aggressive southern neighbours had been availing with such apparent ease. The army scout was the obvious choice to lead the party, but whoever joined him would need to be versed in the arts of survival and concealment. Someone jokingly suggested Madarch.

Another elder added, "Crazy as it sounds, he would be perfect, if only he'd also been blessed with his handler's vision and self-discipline."

"I'm not his handler," Erdi protested.

"So tell me, what are you then and what exactly is required here?" Gwenithen asked.

Erdi, having failed to detect the chieftain's playful mood lurking, rather artlessly explained, "Well sire, Madarch has merely been my assistant. We need someone with his skills, but also circumstances require a man capable of planning and spotting problems ahead."

"Well said! Just what we need. You can both go." Gwenithen said, slapping his thigh and roaring with laughter.

When the news reached Yanker over in the Y-Pentwr camp, that Erdi had somehow become embroiled in a dangerous venture, he asked permission to be included. With the promise of iron in the offing, this was granted.

So, on the first day of the new year up on the Feasting Site, the three, Erdi, Yanker and Madarch, were presented to the scout for his inspection. With his name being Bledunigol, he was of course instantly dubbed Blood Eagle, by the ever-impertinent Yanker. The man's look of disdain at first sight of them could have scorched a hole through a birchbark shield.

Erdi, staring back, muttered, "Don't look at me like that! I've worked alongside better than you!"

The man didn't actually hear what was said, but Erdi's meaningful glare wasn't missed. He sought an audience with Gwenithen, saying, that if these three civilians were to be forced upon him, then they needed to be rendered fit and capable.

Gwenithen didn't care for the man greatly, but couldn't help but admire his skills. The instruction was given; once Yanker turned up for duty, that coming spring, the three were to be put through rigorous sessions of survival, fitness and weapons training, under the watchful eye of Gregoth, the old warrior who had commanded the western contingent at the Battle of the Habren. Bledunigol, who amongst other things was known to speak his mind, had said to Gwenithen, 'he wasn't having his life put at risk, by two farm boys and a forest brownie.'

Gregoth, watching the arrival of his new charges one damp spring morning, could see, simply from the manner in which they approached, the two cousins considered themselves above needing his services. Keeping his thoughts to himself, he set the three their first task, a fast march up to Nant Crag stream and back. On returning, looking suitably fatigued, he had them run to the top of the old fortress mound and back. Not once, a number of times.

The next day it was Nant Crag again, only faster. The day following was the same, but weighed down by weaponry. A merciful break for training in the latter, allowed a few days for recovery.

Although Erdi and Yanker were entitled to bear a sword neither had been trained in the use of it and at last Gregoth sensed they were keen to learn. Madarch, not eligible to carry such a weapon, was given instruction in the finer arts of walloping adversaries by deployment of the broad-staff.

Following this it was three days of Nant Crag and back, only fully burdened and faster. When it came to spear and sling, Gregoth noticed the cousin's slightly rebellious air return, but even when witnessing their realisation, they were no longer quite as good as they thought they were, he kept thoughts to himself, the only visible response being, a slight raise of eyebrows.

When young they had practiced daily. Even when on foraging walks, they had always picked out something on the trail ahead to aim at and their competitive games hadn't seemed remotely like practice or training. They had become that skilled, it seemed like second nature, meaning they took their expertise for granted. Their recent lifestyles, however, had been a complete contrast and both soon realised, their lives spent tackling administrative problems, where the only sharp things required were mind and tongue, had led to a complete neglect of what they had once been so expert at.

Erdi was actually annoyed with himself. He'd expected to pick up from where he'd left off. Then the boat master's words had come back to him, "It's part practice and part something you're born with."

Their visible frustrations and faintly audible curses, as the truth sank in, was met as before, with no more than a raised eyebrow and smile from the old warrior and from that moment on he sensed their attitude change and in actual fact, they became two of the keenest recruits he had ever worked with.

He had never once raised his voice and the nearest he came to a reproach was, "It's up to you. What you're learning now could save your lives one day."

The harder they worked, the more mutual the respect.

Clothes were prepared for them in shades of green and brown. Of course, their own clothes weren't a great deal different, but these were purpose made of tough material and Gregoth knew such attention to detail brought with it a sense of privilege. A small elite force.

To illustrate the effectiveness of wearing what in fact concealed, he ordered all three to take up positions, part hidden near the edge of woodland. He said "A troop will pass close by. Don't move a muscle other than to look down. Your caps will block sight of your faces." The caps in question were of brown knotted wool.

The warriors hadn't been warned of their presence, they had merely been sent out on patrol. Even when looking directly towards the trees, they caught no sight of human form. The cousins were astounded. Madarch by contrast, couldn't believe they hadn't already known this.

When seeing the military garb gifted Erdi, Vanya asked for brief loan of the shirt. With its return, he felt something hard had been sewn around the neckline.

"What is it?" he asked.

"Elsa will be caring for you."

"Her rib-bone?"

Vanya nodded.

"That was to protect the whole family, not just me."

"Well! On safe return, we can hide it again in the thatch. It will reside wherever the need arises. Sickness--- a baby due. Your house---my house, wherever it's needed most."

With constant practice, Erdi's and Yanker's old skills with bow, sling and spear returned and to that was added proficiency with the sword, plus a few sharp tricks regarding the devilish deployment of dagger. On the seven days of what was termed 'losing themselves', no amount of searching by mounted warriors and hunting dogs could find trace of them. They turned up on the seventh evening as if emerging from out of the ground.

The use of hurdles to cross fenland had thrown dogs off their scent and caves in a sandstone outcrop east of Medle had kept them hidden. It was a place Madarch knew from his people's wanderings. Once there they had simply helped themselves to whatever bounty nearby woodlands provided and treated it as a welcome break from the ardour of the previous routine. Through the sixth night they force-marched back west and spent a pleasant day up in the old fortress. Erdi had reasoned, it would probably be the last place those charged with tracking them would look and he was right.

At the end of training, it was announced a slingshot competition would be held down on the arrow field. All warriors were invited to participate. You know the sort of invite soldiers receive. Amongst the throng watching from the fort's embankment were Gwenithen, Bledunigol and the old warrior Gregoth. When Erdi won the contest, with his cousin not far behind, Gregoth looked as pleased as if they had been his sons.

"Will that stop the moaning that has pained my ears of late?" he asked his scout.

The latter said nothing, simply giving a nod of thanks to his commanding officer.

The expedition set off travelling towards the Habren and then west towards the Nwy, where the boats had been tethered. The place brought back poignant memories to Erdi. As ever, a rope bridge had been slung across and it still had a crisp, fresh look, unlike the dark, bleak thing he had risked his life on the time before, but the shepherd's hut appeared to have been long abandoned. The boat Gwendolin and the two hide covered craft were loaded with provisions, the carts trundled back north and those assigned to the expedition spent the night camped on the river bank.

A ferocious band of rain lashing up from the southwest delayed departure the following morning, but come middle day they idled down the short stretch of the Nwy, before having to dig paddles deep to counter the swollen flow of the Habren. The boat Gwendolin was packed with warriors, as if out on a normal patrol, but the two hide covered craft, insignificant by comparison, followed as if hardly likely to be the whole reason for the little excursion. The scout and Yanker paddled the lead hide-boat, with Erdi and Madarch following close behind.

That evening they reached a location Erdi remembered well. Any sign of the original village was covered by willow, willowherb, meadowsweet and tall grasses, a magic island for children's games. From tunnels made in the foliage, curious faces peered. They had been drawn by the occasional drum of paddle against hull and watched as the three boats approached.

Suddenly, realising it was not traders, but warriors spearing their way towards them, all splashed across the recent inundation to the safety of the new village sprawled along a level stretch of banking. Barking dogs had already alerted the menfolk who emerged to crouch and peer, spears held ready.

Erdi, recognising the headman from previous visits, steered his craft to be first to scrunch onto the shingle. He stepped into the shallows, hauled himself up the bank and approached, arms raised, no sign of weapon, in a gesture of friendship. The man watching guardedly, stayed his ground, but on recognising the stranger, meaningfully buried his spear point and strode forward with a broad smile of welcome.

The scout, clearly infuriated at witnessing his junior being led in amongst the huts with the headman's arm around his shoulder, splashed ashore with a face that could have put a wolf to flight. As an afterthought, Erdi did introduce him, but too late, the damage had been done, to the extent the scout's sour glare remained fixed all evening. Although being leader of the boat patrol, he could hardly declare it, for the fact a man of such authority, rather than being serenely borne upriver, was instead paddling a pea-pod of a boat, would have raised suspicions and we all know how even the friendliest folk can talk. Such talk could jeopardize their mission; put their lives at risk and so consequently, he not only remained virtually ignored, but also had to endure Erdi being feted as the storyteller. It had him boiling with such fury, his occasional side-eyed flashes of resentment even caught the attention of the headman. "Yonder scout looks a little out of sorts," he said with a laugh, "I should watch your back if I were you." As is so often the case, body language had conveyed more than actual words.

It was not how Erdi would have planned it, it had just seemed to happen that way, for of course, all were keen to know what had befallen him since he and his brother had disappeared on, what many considered, a hopeless mission. Erdi's command of cymry was now such, little help was needed in translation for the benefit of the assembled throng. They cheered at his description of the incident in the gorge and gave an ecstatic roar when told how Sodron had met his end. There was great sadness and anger at hearing how Mardi had been unjustly put to death. They had loved the section where the sword had been reclaimed, and the headman later said, the two boatmen had returned with faces not just of gloom, but in fact of thunder. He'd probed, but had found them unwilling to disclose the reason why. So, it came as no surprise that the man should rub his hands together with such glee, when at last becoming party to the details.

On conclusion of the tale Erdi did his best to involve Bledunigal in the tight little gathering, but the scout would have nothing to do with it. He glowered in silence, resenting how the Erin saga had listeners leaning close, hanging on every word, relishing the detail.

The headman responded by recounting recent successes, combatting slavers raiding from the south. A permanent watch was now kept, with villages exchanging hilltop signals. Total vigilance was required at all times. On a lighter note, he went on to joke, with granny's knee-twinge warning of imminent storms, no longer at their service, they now had need to keep a closer watch on the weather. She had died that previous winter. The old lady wouldn't have resented such banter, having had a good, long life, spanning all of forty-five winters.

As well as they had been received, Erdi gave no clue as to their present mission. Their hosts had been left thinking they were all merely out on patrol.

The weather was cool, but fair, as they headed further upriver the following morning. The recent spate had flowed through leaving tranquil waters to aid their passage, but where bars of shingle channelled the flow into rapids, they were obliged to haul or log-roll the boats over. Erdi, looking back to the range of hills running north on the left bank, shouted across to Yanker, "Do you remember looking at those off Elsa's ridge? We were no more than children, but it seems like just yesterday."

They called in briefly at the village where Wolf had had his wound swathed in a beech leaf poultice. You remember, *said the Teller*, it was the village where on their return north, the headman, with his lively translation of Erdi's version of cymry into words all could

246

understand, had brought such entertainment. The people implored them to stay, but received a polite refusal and a promise of taking up the offer on the way back north. Erdi couldn't tell them he would probably not be returning on this stretch of the Habren and the warriors in the main party, under orders from Bledunigol, were told, "Avoid all contact when heading back downstream." He didn't entirely trust his men to keep a still tongue and success of their mission depended on complete secrecy. This and the previous village were to be swiftly passed, preferably under cover of dawn or dusk.

Late on the second evening, at a ford just beyond the Habren battlefield, a man Erdi had named Daresay watched as warriors, looking decidedly cautious, disembarked and busied setting up camp. He didn't miss the fact, that as the fire died down and those not on guard duty settled down for the night, two dim shapes had melted up into the woods. The strange profiles, with their dark canopies, resembling a pair of giant four-legged beetles, at first had him a little puzzled.

The following morning Daresay was witness to the elegant craft packed with warriors heading back downstream and understood the need for such armed presence in this dangerous border country, but was still mystified as to why two skin covered craft would have been taken up into the forest. You wouldn't accuse him of being a diligent, hard-working man, but there was something about what he had witnessed that appealed to his vengeful side and just for once, he was prepared to devote an inordinate amount of time into delving deeper.

It took three full days to reach the coast. They could have managed it in less time, but not without giving their presence away. At one point on high ground thin, lazy wisps of smoke could be seen drifting from the various shades of green far below, flatlands framed by a V in the hills.

A little further west, crossing rough scree country, they took care to skirt a small community busying themselves beside a bleak looking stream. From the sounds of dull thumping, ore was being crushed. Erdi knew the sound well.

Bledunigol crept in alone and returned with the news, the villagers weren't mining iron or copper, but the soft metal used when fashioning loom and fishing weights. Erdi was staggered by the lengths people were prepared to go to, seeking out a metal so dull in this area so desolate, merely to survive.

Their journey took them high into the western hills where, as if mocking their efforts, hauling two boats over such lofty terrain, a distant tarn glistened. There was no sign of habitation. They were in the realm of kites, fluttering, hovering, needing but one lazy swoop to be almost from sight. So far, so quickly while far beneath, four burdened souls crawled their way west.

At last, they began the descent and on a broad curve of the trail were greeted by the sight of coastal flatlands spread out like a map below and to the far north, beneath a light head-dress of clouds, jutted pale blue mountains. The path, following a stream's gentle wanderings through stunted woodland, brought them within striking distance of the coast. They did encounter the odd isolated farmhouse and found need to skirt a few larger settlements, but there was not much on these slopes to support large communities. Once on the coastal flatlands, the journey became almost sublime, as what had been such accursed burdens were launched on a generous flow, winding its merry way to the sea.

With the river opening out into a broad estuary, Bledunigol called back to Erdi, "Behold your realm." Pointing at the empty waters to the south, he shouted "Goll Deyrnas!" The man's laugh was as hollow as a cavern.

That night the boats were hauled up on to the broad coastal sands. The sight of smoke columns drifting above the trees inland had prompted the decision to investigate the following morning. They dined on fish they had caught and the last of their bread.

They were travelling light, needing to live off both the land and their wits.

The following morning Yanker and Madarch hid the boats and foraged for food. Erdi and Bledunigal took a trail leading inland. They found defended farmsteads and larger enclosures encircling two, maybe three huts, but it was a scattered population with nothing that could be termed an actual village. They had crept close enough to follow the movements of two herders. One was armed with a spear, the other had an axe strapped to his back. Both weapons had the dull-gold look of bronze. They saw no trace of iron. Finally, on realising, creeping about the country was no way of having questions clearly answered, they decided to break cover and approach one of the enclosures.

The scout knew enough of the local language to communicate the basics. The people, quiet and suspicious, listened with blank expressions as Bledunigol explained the reason for them being there. He said, he and his partner were simple traders.

This met with no response.

"We're trading down the coast. We spotted smoke and came inland to establish contact."

Still silence.

Finally, one man asked, "What are you trading exactly?"

"Hides and pelts," Bledunigol replied.

They might have been isolated communities, but these people hadn't survived in their remote coastal strip by being fools. It was obvious they didn't believe the trading story, but as the visitors didn't appear to pose any threat, they continued to communicate, if but guardedly.

The subject turned to what most men relish, hunting. From there it led to weaponry. With this they became more open, proudly producing weapons for inspection, bronze headed axes, bronze tipped spears and arrows, but no sign of iron. When asked about this they replied, 'Yes, the new metal was known to them, but they preferred to continue in the old ways. "In any case," they explained, "there was not enough iron lying about for it to make any difference to their lives."

"Doesn't it come in by sea?"

"No, copper comes down from the north and tin up from the south. Both by sea."

"Don't the eastern tribes bring iron in by sea?"

"You mean the Gwy?" The man's manner changed immediately. "Do you have dealings with those child stealers?"

"No certainly not. I was just--------"

"If you want iron in these parts, best you bring it with you! That also applies to finding a fool hereabouts! Do you think we didn't know you were here? The watchers see everything!"

That was it. Time to go. At least they had established the area was not a source of iron, either from underground or brought in by boat. Also, the fear that these coastal people could be affiliated to the wild tribes inland, had been allayed, meaning from now on they could approach directly without the worry of their presence being signalled up into the hills, as had obviously been done from the coast.

The night was spent camped in sand dunes and they set out next morning, first pulling their boats across shallow tidal pools, then launching them into the cold, dark waters beyond. The sun warmed their task, but an ominous bank of cloud, glowering in the west, was being drawn by the soaring range of hills that rendered this area so isolated. As the wind picked up, the boats began to buck and dive and with none having intimate knowledge of the sea, they decided it wise to head inshore.

Long stretches of sand, eventually gave way to a narrow estuary and they took shelter in its calmer waters, steering towards a small hut on the southern shore. It held nets, lines and fish traps, obviously a fisherman's hut, meaning a village probably lay some way upstream. It was decided, once the rain had passed, Erdi would again accompany Bledunigol exploring inland.

With the cloud and its frail trailing curtain, almost upon them, they sat hunched, cold in the gloom, watching all around ominously darken and as the wind picked up, the silken frond, so wispy at a distance, spiralled into a ferocious deluge, drenching all outside. No watchers would be flashing warning messages inshore in this weather.

The sun, a mere pale glow behind cloud, had passed its midway point by the time they dared venture out. Erdi and Bledunigol, up-righting their boat, set off upstream, paddling as far as a deep slow-water curve, where beyond the palisade on the northern bank, rooftops gently seeped smoke and the sound of children's laughter rang. The usual dog barking greeted their approach and armed men emerged from the gateway. Again, their weapons were bronze tipped, but this time faces looked more welcoming. With the river providing a route inland, they were obviously more used to visitors.

This time, Bledunigol tried a different story. He actually told the truth. It usually works out best in the end doesn't it. He was told there was no major source of iron ore locally and as far as they knew, none further upriver. They explained the course of the stream and what was traded up its valley. Copper, tin, fish, salt and occasionally slaves went inland; hides, furs, cured meat and livestock came back down. No mention was made of iron, either way.

The scout, aiming an unbridled look of derision at Erdi, imparted, he just happened to know of a certain man, who'd had the title, Lord of Goll Deyrnas, recently bestowed. However, like one diving, not realising the tide was out, he looked visibly irked at the flat impact and then had to listen, with rancour growing, as the headman enthusiastically explained, the old legend had a basis in fact, for to the north of them, occasionally visible at low water, black stumps of a drowned forest ghosted back from the past. Goll Deyrnas was not just the figment of some ancient's imagination, it had once existed.

On their return to the estuary, Bledunigol, now for some strange reason, in a rather unsettling genial mood, explained where the source of the stream lay. From that told, he had managed to fit its course into the map held in his head. Fed by waters tumbling from the north, it changed course to head due west and within fairly comfortable walking distance of its source, lay the mining village they had passed on their way to the coast.

"Easy to say," he added, "but walking is never that simple when crossing high moorland."

Erdi thanked him for the information, but showed no further interest. The genial side of the scout set off more of an inner warning, than did his usual flinty bitterness.

The night was spent in the fisherman's hut and the following morning brought the dismal sight of estuary mud. The tide was out, requiring the boats to be carried over the dunes and out across flat sands, for launching directly into the sea. With the weather mild, steady progress was made down the coast.

Plumes of smoke inland rose from scattered settlements, but they had discovered all they needed from that source. Inshore flashes off polished bronze accompanied their progress. The watchers had seen them. When clouds blocked the sun, warning horns were rasped. These were nervy people.

Middle day the scout recognised a landmark spoken of and with the tide running close to full, the boats were nosed into a slender estuary.

Fish had been caught and Yanker, who had assumed cooking duties, set about lighting a fire and cleaning the catch, while Madarch foraged for plants to brew. Apart from the weapons, their sheet-bronze cooking pot was their most prized possession.

Bledunigol and Erdi again explored upstream. The sound of women chattering and laughing echoed off the water. It was wash day. At the scout's beckoning, Erdi followed him up through the trees and they carefully worked a way round, to gain a clear view of the settlement. No contact was attempted. They returned to the river mouth, safe in the knowledge they had found peaceful farmers and fishermen, not a bastion for warriors.

Back at camp, they were greeted by a smile from Yanker and the aroma of food cooking.

"Where's Maddy?" Erdi asked.

"He's gone off again. You know what he's like, always sniffing out something."

Their scant meal was almost finished, when Bledunigol, looking upstream, began a slow shake of head in sheer disbelief. Madarch approached, triumphantly holding up a huge hare.

"How do you manage it, Maddy?" Yanker asked.

"Like I tell before. I just talk to them." He removed the twine from the animal's neck and knotted it back onto his belt of mysteries. From it also hung, a throwing dart, sling, dagger and pouches of things they never asked him about.

With appetites sated, Bledunigol said with a glower, "Don't make yourself too comfortable, I need to fix a map of this area."

A while back, Erdi had realised the scout carried various maps around in his head and what he'd just growled, hinted at the strong possibility, they'd now arrived at a completely blank section. He accompanied him to the settlement upstream and making the usual cautious approach, the scout signalled to emerging villagers, 'they had come in peace.' The reception was cool, but on being invited to enter, they were led to a massive hut, the like of which Erdi had never seen before. It sported a roof that impressive, the walls beneath were barely visible and the entrance, with its graceful overhanging curve, seemed as if only added to enhance the flow.

All settled themselves by the hearth and Erdi had now picked up enough local words to know Bledunigol was asking about iron. The headman's slow shake of head was an answer even a deaf man would have understood and his look of alarm at the mention of Gwy, told all. Then when the man pointed inland and scratched lines on the dirt floor with a stick, Erdi could see the scout was having new territory added to the picture held in his head.

Although, not on the verge of suggesting beer should now be quaffed, the mood did definitely mellow and the up-tone of the headman's words on their departure, meant he'd asked a meaningful question. The scout's answer brought a friendly gleam of teeth.

Heading back to camp, Erdi was of course keen to know what had transpired, but received nothing but a blank stare. You could admire Bledunigol, but you couldn't love him. He was a strange man.

Back at the river mouth, Yanker was told to doubt the fire and with a hint of viciousness, the scout began strapping their equipment back into the boats. Erdi helped and finally, with all complete, came the stark announcement, they were heading back inland.

"With the boats?" asked Yanker, astonished.

The scout nodded.

With a look of sheer disbelief, "Over more mountains? We've hardly had chance to get the things wet!" Staring inland and imagining the worst, he asked, "We're not going back up there, surely?"

A determined nod meant, 'Yes and don't ask again.'

Now at last, the scout revealed, all he'd discovered. Scratching a map in the dirt, he told them, no iron was ever brought inland up this particular river. Pointing his stick further south, where he'd scratched another valley curving up to the northeast, he added, "I've been told there's no point wasting time journeying to explore down there where the river enters the sea. If we head directly inland, we will strike its valley in any case. Exploring there tells us all we need to know. Plus, we'll be heading in the right direction.

Erdi pointed to the map and valley in question. "The right direction? Where does it lead?"

"Gwy territory."

The long ensuing silence was deafening----- finally broken by Yanker asking, "And we're hauling our boats all the way up there? Into the hills. Why are we doing that? To make presents of them?"

"Look," said Bledunigol. "You never go poking into a place of danger without planning a way out." Pointing to the line indicating the river running beyond the ridge to the east, his mood almost seemed genial as he continued, "I'm not certain, but I would gamble gold on the likelihood of the Gwy river running close to the head of that stream."

His stick scratched the map, but upstream this time, from the estuary south, up to its source and emphasising this, with a twist of stick, he added, "Enemy territory. From near that source, it should only be a short haul to the Gwy river. We hide the boats there. We'll be needing them, whether we accidently prod the hornet's nest or not. We must have a way out and the Gwy river is it."

Then, as if an afterthought, "Oh, you've one last night of comfort to look forward to. The headman knew we were camped here from the moment we pulled into the river. He's asked us to join them all this evening.

"What in these clothes?" said Yanker. "I'd have packed something a little better if I'd have known."

They part paddled and part hauled the boats upstream to the village. Yanker nudging Erdi as they slopped across a section of shallows, frowned and with an upward flick of head indicating the imagined eastern summits said, "And that Blood Eagle expects us to drag these up there?"

They were given a warm welcome, food and drink, but also something not so palatable---- dire warnings of what lay ahead. The stream they intended to follow, took its name from a war god. When it raged, the headman said, it protected them. When at peace winding its way to the sea, came time of danger. The god slept. It gave chance for the wild inland tribes to descend. They stole livestock, but worse, they stole people. If slavery weren't bad enough, horror lay ahead for any man of power, unfortunate enough to fall into their hands.

It was obvious the headman relished imparting this particular morsel, but strangely, Bledunigol's more measured tones in translation, without intending it, actually heightened their sense of foreboding. Apparently, a belief strongly held by the Gwy; was that the power drawn from a victim's body, held such magic, it benefitted the whole tribe.

It was similar to the Y-Dewis conviction, when revering the remains of Prince Aram and earth mother, Elsa, but mercifully, these two had been dead at the time. What the headman was so keen to impress upon them, was that the Gwy drew a man's power slowly, from out of the living body. Not surprisingly, Erdi and Yanker exchanged looks of serious trepidation.

The scout, clearly enjoying their discomfiture, sneered "Now I bet you're glad you came along."

"You mean we're still going ahead?" Erdi asked.

"Of course."

"Actually entering their territory?"

"It's what I do," was uttered with a look of complete disdain.

"The man's mad," muttered Yanker.

"It's like he's looking for a warrior's death," Erdi whispered, aghast. "A hero's meeting with his ancestors."

"Yes---- and taking us along with him. I don't even like Blood Eagle much, never mind his ancestors."

Erdi, tugging his cousin closer, muttered, "If we find no sign of iron being traded up that valley, then we should tell him---------- 'Enough! The job's done.' We'll say we're going back. We can use whatever river it happens to be and paddle the boat to the coast."

"Can't see that working. He'll claim dereliction of duty. We still haven't found what we came for. Where the Gwy get their iron."

"We've found out where it doesn't come from. That's half the battle. We already know it's not mined in the north, otherwise we'd be using it. We'll soon know if it's arriving from the west. I tend to think it isn't. According to reports, it's definitely not mined in their territory, which leaves just south or east. Why go straight through the middle of them? We can easily explore south and east, going back home and then safely using the Habren? It's asking for trouble. Yanker, I tell you, that man's looking for a warrior's death."

The scout, witnessing their mutterings and guessing at the content, simply wore a look of smug satisfaction.

They struggled with the boats upstream, blissfully afloat in places, but all too soon having to haul them across shoals and up small falls. They could have travelled at twice the pace unencumbered, but were ever mindful, one impatient rip could render a craft useless. Frustrations weren't helped by the stream's course taking them southeast, rather than towards their destination, northeast. They made progress, passing a tributary flowing up from the south and managed to cut out a few bends and curves by carrying the boats through woodland, but were then forced back to the water, by the valley's sudden constriction.

To their relief, once through this, they saw the stream's flow now came from a north-easterly direction, but half the day had gone and they had hardly laboured beyond the whiff of sea air.

After a further exhausting trek, with the boats now shoulder-borne, the scout, as if begrudging having to impart the words, half turned at the prow of the lead boat and rasped a message.

Yanker, relayed from the aft end, "Blood Eagle says we can rest."

Madarch, instantly alert, seized the chance to forage, while Bledunigol, wading off into foliage, reappeared on a nearby vantage point, to scan the way ahead. If not actually knowing the scout, one might imagine the crouching warrior, spear aslant, hair and cloak wind-ruffled, high on the ridge, to be a vision imbued with romance and yet Erdi was beginning to hate the man.

Returning with not the slightest attempt at eye contact, he dispassionately reasoned, if they covered the same distance as

258

achieved that morning, crossing the ridge directly east, ought to bring them to the valley he'd shown them on the map. How he'd managed to arrive at such exact reckoning, Erdi couldn't begin to imagine. As cold and unappealing as the man's manner happened to be, at least you couldn't hope for a better guide when hauling two boats through unknown territory.

Madarch suddenly re-appeared, bare chested, carrying his shirt like a tool bag. When lowered to the grass and opened, he proudly indicated numerous edible plants. Erdi recognised goose foot, goose grass and nettles, but the rest were a mystery. All were boiled in a brew, the wet mash briefly fooling empty stomachs, they had eaten something solid.

They continued up the watercourse, gently winding and falling towards them from the northeast, spending more time carrying and dragging the boats than sitting in them. At the two hamlets passed, people emerged to stare in wonder.

"They must think we're mad," said Erdi.

"Whatever gives you that idea?" replied Yanker, face streaming with sweat.

They encountered fallen trees and in places quite significant falls. All four, carefully lifted their craft in turn, around the hazards. Mercifully, by early evening, Bledunigol called for a rest and while he surveyed the surrounding country, they slumped to the floor with relief; not a word being spoken.

The sound of a bumblebee blundering amongst flowers and the stream's melody, was pleasantly mesmerizing, but a faint splash in a curve of backwater, prompted Madarch to sit bolt-upright and with the thought of food seeming to invigorate, he disappeared in search of a meal.

The scout returned, announcing they had travelled far enough up this particular valley and almost as an afterthought, imparted they would be heading over the eastern ridge on the morrow. Then looking around, asked, "Where's that brownie gone?"

"Fishing," said Erdi.

"Well he won't be able to wander off like this once we're over that ridge."

A fire was lit and the hare skinned and gutted to be skewered for roasting. Eventually Madarch returned, holding up a huge bunch of watercress, slimy brown roots dripping water down his leggings.

"Funny looking fish," said Yanker.

"Missed him. He too quick," Madarch replied, describing a rapid zig-zag motion with his hand.

They spent the night curled up in the boats.

"Now I know why we've lugged these all the way up here," said Yanker, voice slightly muffled.

"Get to sleep!" Bledunigol growled.

"If you're planning to get lost in the hills------ take a good boat with you."

"You heard!"

"Nothing quite beats a good **boat**!"

Hearing the cousins chuckling quietly beneath the stars, the scout gave a deep sigh. "Save your energy for the morning."

The following day was damp and misty with spider's webs arching white between the reeds. They were actually glad to be heading further inland away from the stream, for it had become more of a hindrance than a help. The boats were carried up between the stunted oaks, trunks black and twisted, leaves soaking them as they struggled to find a way through. It became that difficult, the scout told Maddy, as he now called him, to explore one direction and disappearing, he took a slightly different slant. On comparing what had been found, the line for the next ascent was chosen and by repeating the process, they edged stage by stage up seemingly impossible terrain. The cousins felt slightly demoted.

Middle day, to the relief of all, the ground now sloped down to the east. They had crested the ridge and a welcome rest was the reward. Seeing Madarch about to set off foraging, Bledunigal snapped a command, telling him to save his energy.

"Even if you find food, we can't cook it. No fires from now on."

The going was much easier with the slope now in their favour and in places they could even slide the boats over the grass. Plenty of game was spotted of course, almost as if deer and hare know men can't haul boats and hunt at the same time.

The sun was well over the western ridge by the time they at last spotted the dull silvered movement of the stream in the gloom below. Bledunigal instructed Madarch to go down to refill the water skins and looking fully absorbed, as the dim figure picked a way to the stream, gave the order in a strange faraway voice, to make ready for the night. Seeming almost human, he explained, they would maintain their vantage point and spy out the land at first light. With the return of Madarch, he asked, "See anything?"

Madarch shook his head.

"From now on, no foraging unless I say so!"

Madarch staring back, slowly opened the water bag to reveal a crayfish. The scout first gave an exasperated look to the night sky, then taking all by surprise, he ruffled Maddy's hair.

On a high inland ridge, beneath tall pines, chewing strands of dried meat rations enhanced by tiny scraps of raw crayfish, Yanker's voice arose, "This is the life. You can't beat a good boat."

In the cool mists of morning, the scout beckoned Madarch to join him in a scramble down towards the stream. Erdi and Yanker made as if to follow, but were told, "Not you two! Stay and guard the boats."

They began to feel as useless as would two of the Seer's devotees, if told to stay home on hunt day. The implication being, 'Stick to your studies, you're a liability'.

Seeing the scout re-appear at a half-bent lope up through the trees, Erdi could hardly begrudge him some degree of admiration. The man wasn't even short of breath. Madarch who had dogged his every stride looked equally fresh, leaving Erdi feeling slightly misplaced and inadequate in such a warrior's venture.

"What did you find?" he asked.

"Water!" snapped the scout.

When beyond the man's earshot, Madarch muttered, "They not use this valley for something heavy like iron. The trail's no more than deer make and the river's too lumpy."

Erdi smiling at Maddy's choice of words, approached Bledunigol and said, "So no iron comes in by way of this valley."

On receiving nothing more than a cold stare, he continued, "So there's no point in continuing up it."

Silence. Just the sound of items being meaningfully stowed.

"So, the iron must be coming into Gwy territory from east or south."

The scout returned a weary look of exasperation.

"Why are we putting our lives at risk when we've already discovered what we came for? Why go looking for danger? We can explore east and south from off the Habren. You know that better than anyone."

Bledunigol continued stowing all back aboard.

"You and Maddy can carry on, but Yanker and myself are returning south."

This at last brought a reply. Unsheathing his dagger to threaten the nearest hull, the scout sneered, "How exactly do you propose to do that? One more word and I'll leave you both stranded! Come on Maddy, help me pack these things. They could have done it themselves, but prefer to connive and run like women!"

The first hamlet they encountered was well up from the river. They watched from a distance, Bledunigol being in two minds, debating whether to silently work their way around or approach directly? A birdcall from off the ridge was answered by another near the village.

Madarch froze. "That not a bird," he hissed. "They not make that call this late in the year."

"Hide the boats in the bracken," ordered Bledunigol.

They watched and waited. A small troop of mounted warriors worked its way, not in a line but independently, melting through scrub and trees, closing in on the hamlet. Two men appeared from a hut, cowering, supplicating, looking absolutely terrified. Rasped questions were answered with barely audible replies and shaking of heads. The warrior's, urged their mounts forward and brushing the villagers aside, headed straight to where the four, crouching low, waited fearfully amid the trees.

Swords were silently drawn and hearts began to hammer. Even though carefully tracking movement of horses, watching as sinewy frames parted the foliage, Erdi almost jumped with shock, wondering how something so huge could have appeared so close, almost on top of him, out of nowhere. Then Gregoth's instructions came back, 'Remain perfectly still.'

The horse snorted, but didn't shy away and the warrior drifted by.

Once certain the danger had passed, Bledunigol ordered them, wait while he approached the huts alone. He was gone some time.

On returning he instructed in quite a blithe manner, "Haul the boats up to the settlement, we have a guide."

Erdi's mind was full of questions, but realising he'd receive no answers, kept a still tongue. Hopefully time would reveal all. They headed towards the small collection of huts, where thankfully, women with nervous smiles, offered pottage.

Frantic sign language indicated how terrified all had been. One poor thing, homing in on Erdi, explained with a pained expression and much wringing of hands, the reason for her particular distress. Her tale of lament streamed forth, and although listening hard, he failed to understand a single word.

The scout said, "She lost her boy up on the Habren. He'd hardly been old enough to shave, but the Gwy still took him and others to fight for them. Shall I tell her it was you who killed him?"

"There's something seriously wrong with you," Erdi snapped.

Bledunigol's reply was a callous laugh and Erdi felt completely helpless as the distraught woman, shocked by the sound and obviously feeling completely betrayed, fixed him with a glare of hatred. Swiping away his arm of comfort, she left the hut in tears.

Erdi's look of complete loathing only seemed to heighten the scout's mood of amused satisfaction.

Their guide, avoiding extensive wetlands glistening low to the west, led them along a track heading north. Apparently, the Gwy warriors just encountered were heading for a large settlement in a broad valley, immediately east, from which a stream fed into their own river.

Trees gave way to rough open fen and in places, dotted clumps of woodland stood where soil allowed.

Checking the strappings aboard and transferring various items for back-packing they swung the boats up to be head-borne. So much easier now they were in open country.

Left to their own devices they would have become bogged down in a maze of swamps, but were confidently led, as if their guide was simply on a trek, made daily. Pointing to a large mere splayed out like a sheet of steel, he explained it was the source of the river running down his own valley to the sea. They stopped to rest awhile. They had been toiling steadily uphill for well over a sun's span and were mighty relieved to lay their burdens down.

"Hang on to me," said Yanker. "Boat or no boat, I feel like I'm starting to float."

Seeing little more than their trudging feet, they crossed a small stream, following the windings of a path, up to yet another ridgetop, where a sudden breeze buffeting the boats, caused them to stagger and grimly hang on, fearful their burdens might suddenly take flight.

"Top of the mountain," their guide called back. "Should calm down in a while."

Crossing a small stream, boats still aloft, they could now at last feel the sloping ground was in their favour. It was dusk when the guide, pointing southeast, turned and in a wide-eyed whisper, divulged something of obvious import.

The scout translated, "In the depths of those valleys below;-----that's the Gwy heartland." Raising the prow slightly, he pointed into the gloom and with the hull adding resonance, said with authority, "Beyond that ridge, the Gwy river runs east."

From deep within the hull opposite, came Yanker's muffled, 'Aww, not boating again! I quite like it in here.'

Up at the prow, Erdi laughed, but he did have to give the scout credit where due. Not only had he been right in his prediction of where the river ran, in fairness, he'd given no hint of triumph at his supposition being correct.

They continued on, strange silhouettes, carefully feeling their way in the dark. Apparently, the night was their friend, their shield, as it was too dangerous to cross the skyline in daylight. The terrain now sloped sharply in their favour and all trace of their progress was swallowed up by the shelter of woodland. It seemed imagined at first, but no, senses hadn't been deceived; somewhere amongst the trees below, could be heard the flow of water.

Their pace down the snaking path, quickened, drawn by the sound and as if choosing that moment to glide fully into view, the moon bathed the Gwy river, chuckling and swirling from rocks down to pools, in its pale magic. The best sight and sound in days.

A freshening wind shivered leaves and tugged at their clothing. Their guide warned, rain was due, and added, whatever the weather, they couldn't afford to remain where they were. Come first light they must move downstream, for this was an extremely dangerous location. With that he slipped off into the night. Where to, Erdi couldn't imagine. No-one would attempt to cross those moors in the dark, yet as dangerous as the prospect seemed, the man obviously preferred that to risking a night in their company, beside the Gwy river.

As silently as possible, they cut enough branches to keep tired bodies off damp ground and taking turns keeping watch, they slept beneath the boats. As predicted, it rained.

It was still raining when they took to the water the following morning. Although drenched, they felt elated to be afloat once more, even if but briefly. Swollen by the night's rain, the tributary tumbling out from the western valleys, invigorated the main flow, slewing their boats into a surge downstream and being swept along, they could only stare wide eyed, when swirling past a small dock and nearby huts. They saw no-one and more importantly, no-one saw them.

Bledunigol swinging his boat across into calmer waters beneath the western bank, brought it about to face the flow. Erdi and Yanker did likewise. The pairings assigned to the boats had changed. It had just seemed to happen, about the time when hauling their burdens up over the first ridge. It was not a thing to worry about, but it did seem strange that Madarch, the man who had previously carried out Erdi's instructions, was now the righthand man of their moody leader.

Steering to the bank, the scout, stepping out, hauled the painter for Madarch to jump ashore. "I can manage this, Maddy" he muttered. "Help the other two get their boat hidden."

The riverside foliage, dense in places, was ideal for boat concealment and being mindful of upland streams' tendency to spate, lines were tied.

Squatting beneath the trees, they watched and waited, hoping activity around the huts, might give a clue as to the dock's usage. Foodstuffs, hides, timber or maybe even iron? The rain had stopped, but heavy drops still plopped drearily all around and a thin mist maintained a leaf sheen, ready to drench at the slightest touch.

Suddenly alert, Madarch hissed, "Listen! What that noise?"

From downstream, came the ominous sound of deep voices chanting.

The scout beckoned and they followed, darting from one drenching clump to the next, in a crouched run. When close to the dock, they halted, kneeling in the sodden grass. Peering through foliage, Erdi watched a laden craft approaching and although obviously fearful, was intrigued by the intensity of the crew's battle against the waters.

As paddles worked against the torrent, the bow wave surged and those aboard, bracing against the spray, fought to make headway. With a sudden yaw shore-wards, he could have actually reached out and yanked the hair of the sternmost warrior, but with a loud guttural growl accompanying each stroke, the crew working as one, gained against the flow, taking the lank red mop, jerking from sight as the boat closed in on the docking area.

Men emerging from the huts, waited and a line was thrown. The boat swinging round into the lee of the dock was tethered, allowing crew members to scramble ashore. Those still aboard began passing up the cargo, bars of something dark brown and heavy; iron.

Bledunigol whispered, "Maddy, we've found it. Come night-time we can head downstream."

On hearing the words, Erdi breathed a sigh of relief, but then feeling a needle-sharp prod in his back, looked round to see a lance. Following the line of the shaft, his heart sank, for there at the end was a mounted warrior and ranked alongside, his smiling companions.

Chapter Fourteen

Now, *said the Teller*. I bet you're dying to know what's been happening in home territory.

There was a groan from the audience accompanied by, "He's always doing this!"

Mara now spent most of her time at Vanya's house. It was merely to help set up home of course, with the fact that her friend Brialla and brother just happening to be a short walk away, being no more than one of life's happy coincidences. When the three were out together, however, ladies noticing Mara's radiance, would give a wistful sigh. They knew what was really going on.

She did of course return home from time to time and found it unrecognisable. With land being at such a premium, it was only natural Y-Dewis families would be instructed to move in and farm the two vacant plots. Penda now had hordes of children to growl at. He was surrounded by people he couldn't understand and didn't feel the least bit compensated by the fact, his warnings regarding fish had been vindicated. The local pools were all but fished out. He still had the slave for company and not being able to get his tongue around the man's name, called him Tam. There many Tams but only one Slave Tam.

One day, when Mara called in, wanting to share her concern at Erdi having been absent for so long, she at first thought the house to be empty, but then sensed Tam eying her from the depths. There was an enticing aroma from something cooking and she was mildly surprised at how tidy the place looked. Normally she'd found, men left to their own devices being happy for an abode to have a faded, more lived in feel, than most women would find comfortable, but looking around, everything seemed quite fresh. On turning to leave, she spotted a cloth had been dropped near the fire and instinctively bent to pick it up and hang it on a peg, but was stopped by the words, "It doesn't go there."

She folded it, placed it on a stool and her slight frown on leaving, indicated deep ruminations churning.

Out in the fields, Penda, greeting with a smile, seemed calmer than of late. Mara voiced her fears regarding their son, to which he replied, 'no-one had been informed as to where exactly Erdi's mission would be taking him, but not to worry as it was generally accepted, the venture would require at least one moon to accomplish.'

Mara had the strange feeling, she was conversing with a kind friend, not her husband and father of their children. A silence followed.

"Tam keeps the place very tidy," she said at last. "Seems as if he's quite a good cook as well."

"In view of what Erdi's doing for us all, I've been told I can keep him."

"What? Gwenithen said?"

"I suppose so. The decision must have come from the highest level."

"I hope he doesn't change his mind. You know how the moods take him."

Another silence.

"Look I'm sorry-------"

"That's alright, Mara. Vanya needs you at the moment."

270

Walking away, she had the distinct feeling of being hopelessly adrift from what had so recently bound all close together. Whatever the reasons, or wherever the fault lay, the land of her memories seemed lost forever and she couldn't prevent the tears that blurred her vision.

Penda's assurance that their son was in all probability safe, initially helped allay fears, but she was unable to stop nagging doubts creeping back and Vanya accompanied her on a visit to the Seer, asking for a divination. Call it female intuition if you like, but she felt Erdi was in deep trouble and the worry of it was beginning to make her feel physically sick.

The Holy Man, when at last emerging from his trance, was confronted by two very anxious faces, with looks pleading for reassurance. In view of this, he reversed the order of events seen in his vision.

"I perceive a far distant patch of blue sky-----------"

'And? What else?' was conveyed by worried looks.

"Preceded by, dark rolling clouds of thunder."

Looking terrified, they returned home with dread in their hearts.

Back at the Gwy river, *said the Teller,* the little band of four was marched along its tributary, deep into the valleys they had circumvented the night before.

Peering into the audience, he found the one in particular he was looking for and asked, Or should I have said, the valleys walked **around,** the night before?

A lady's eyes shone as she smiled up at him.

Their arrival in the main encampment was met by a howling din of triumph. War carts rumbled, with occupants shouting to the sky, delirious at their capture. Young boys with maddening shrieks, wheeled their ponies in thundering circles, delivering the occasional stinging whiplash, to those roped together, enraged in silence, having to stand and take it. Other youths, galloping off into the adjoining valleys to spread the news, soon had the crowd swollen to one of feast day proportions, all eager for a look at those foolish enough to wander into their territory.

Amongst the tribal elders there was one able to speak cymry, but probably learnt way back in his youth, for the style of delivery seemed somewhat antiquated. He called for calm and asked, 'why the strangers had had the temerity to enter their territory?'

"We heard gold could be found in western streams," Bledunigol answered.

"My chieftain wishes to know, from where do you originate?"

"A settlement in the flatlands, north of the Dwy river," he lied.

"You have come far? By what means did you get here?"

"A boat took us down the coast and from there we walked inland."

"And what quantities of gold did you chance upon?"

"Not enough to match a single grain of sand."

When translated, the words were met with laughter, jeering and shouts of mockery. Given the slightest excuse, it would not have been hard to imagine all control lost and the captives being ripped apart, as if by a pack of starving wolves.

The chieftain, easing himself off the royal bench, approached the roped string of lost souls and jerking each clasped head one way, then the other, scrutinised, muttering to himself. When Erdi's unruly mop was then pushed back to gain a closer look, the stench from the man's breath caused such a violent recoil, if Yanker hadn't taken the strain, he'd have been sent sprawling. Further sickened, as screaming laughter assaulting from all sides, he did his best to hold his breath, having never before smelt vapours of such revulsion, exuding from a fellow being.

"Our lord is deciding which of your heads is to grace a vacant spot above his door," said the elder. Fortunately, with beards unchecked since leaving home, Erdi and Bledunigal were fairly unrecognisable as having been two of the protagonists up on the Habren. Impending death was bad enough without the thought of being singled out for special treatment. Small comfort. They were herded towards a pen reserved for slaves, or shudder the thought, for those about to be sacrificed. Bindings were removed and at spear point, they were forced through the entry on all fours.

Once inside, with the hovel having no room to stand, there was no option, other than squat or sit. The roof was thatched, the back and sides were solid wattle and the front, wooden bars. The entry hatch was held shut by an iron rod. The whole place stank of urine and in one corner was an odious pot, around which flies buzzed with furious intent, the sound at times swelling to a sonorous drone.

"There must be a way out of here." Erdi examined the roof, but the thatch had been laid on wattle and all the cage bars were firm and unyielding. Two cross members either side of the hatch and one running the full length above, held everything rigid. All the yew wood withies had knots sealed with birch bark pitch and the door's locking bar was held by some device they couldn't reach, let alone see. Boarding had been nailed to conceal it.

"They're surely not going to kill us?" Yanker asked Bledunigol sitting to his left.

"With any luck we'll be too highly prized for that and traded on as slaves. As far as they know we are simply idiots on the hunt for gold. Don't do anything that might cause them to think differently."

"What about the head over the door business?"

"His little joke, I'm hoping. If none of us attempts heroics, we might just get shipped downriver in chains." The scout then added, "And no-one's holding me in chains for long."

"That man's breath alone, could kill," said Erdi.

"Pity it didn't," sneered Bledunigol.

"I smell something like that before," said Madarch. "We had to cut complete leg off. What started small, began eating its way up the body."

"Yes, I've smelt it before," said the scout. "Gangrene."

Children came first. They taunted and poked sticks through the bars, snatching them back before having them seized, yelling hysterically at the game. An older youth, attempting to jab Yanker, using a particularly vicious fire-hardened prong, became just a touch too reckless and Yanker, biding his time, snatched, to haul his tormentor to the bars for a lusty bite into fingers. It drew the salty taste of blood and the resulting scream brought warriors running.

They cursed, threatened with swords, but shouting something like, "Well what did you expect?" drove the boys off.

Yanker buried the seized stick in the dust at the back of the cage and an outburst of wailing brought the comment, "He's probably getting a good thrashing for playing with tonight's food."

"I said, no heroes!" growled the scout.

"I only bit him. He got what he deserved."

Women were next on the scene. Gummy old crones with not enough teeth for a set of dentures between them, growling bitter curses, followed by young mothers with tiny children, some even with babes in arms, coming to point and laugh.

A serious brown drift of tribal elders approached, calmer, as if assessing the worth of their captives. Erdi felt a sudden gut-jabbing jolt that had him bending low, attempting to hide his face, for amongst them was a man he knew only too well. Time hadn't been kind, but there was no mistaking who it was. As faces peered and comments were muttered, he agonised, not daring to look up. Finally the group drifted off again.

"That was Daresay!" said Erdi.

"**Whaat?**"

How could one word contain so much derision? Erdi explained to their leader who Daresay was and where he'd first met the man, adding, "But I can't understand what he's doing here?"

"Have you no idea at all? Not one clue about territory travelled through?-------- That ford on the Habren, where I first saw your sorry hide; I would wager it's no more than half a day's walk from where we camped last night on the Gwy river."

"He's coming back," Yanker warned.

Daresay approaching with a warrior in tow, gave the instruction for a sword probe and Erdi's head was forced up, enabling the squatting Daresay to peer directly into his face. A sickly smile of triumph spread, so very slowly.

"You wouldn't listen, would you? I told you not to risk venturing into these parts again." His laugh of congratulatory triumph, was made all the more nauseating by the avowal, it was the spirits that had favoured him.

275

With eyes glinting he added, "Something told me it was you back on the Habren. I daresay you thought carrying the boats that way would keep you hidden, but I still knew." Wagging a finger, "I still knew it had to be you." Slapping a thigh, he chuckled at his own ingenuity.

Erdi was too disgusted by the man to explain, they'd only carried the boats that way out of convenience.

Daresay continued his gloating. "All that way, over the hills and back again, just to end up in a cage. You could have saved yourself all the time and effort and walked straight here like I did. Look at you! All locked in like rock doves. With just a few words from me, my friends would have provided a much, much better cage than this."

Grabbing the warrior's sword and prodding within, he taunted, "Guess what these wild beauties do to the likes of you? Go on, guess. Guess! You thought yourself so clever that day, discovering the sword. Well how do you like the feel of this one! Eh? Eh?" His prodding actually drew blood. "I often thought to myself, if I'm patient, bide my time, daresay the spirits will bring just reward. I know it's taken years, but here you are, all crammed in, ready for treatment. Oh what wonderful treatment." Handing back the sword, he disappeared at pace, anxious to impart the news.

"We're not that crammed in," said Yanker. "If we all budge up a bit, we could easy squeeze another one in."

The scout, absolutely seething, gripped and rattled their cage bars, entreating through clenched teeth, "Ancestors! Give me strength!"

Erdi saw his cousin's look of mock trepidation suddenly freeze and a horrified voice said, "Erdi, he's back and I don't like the look of it."

"Dear mother! He's got the whole war council with him."

"Sorry, shouldn't have joked earlier."

"Don't worry. A touch of madness in this nightmare might just keep us sane."

The purposeful return with chieftain and Seer, was closely followed by a huddle of elders, wearing troubled looks, as if burdened by the immense duty, circumstances had now forced upon them. A serious discussion followed, with the chieftain nodding as would a man receiving sound advice from those, never imagined to be wrong. Finally, his loud clap of hands suggested a decision had been made and all turned and left.

Shortly after, came the ominous chink of iron biting stony ground. Flinching at each impact, four worried faces, stared out in dread.

"Sounds like they're digging our graves," said Erdi.

"I doubt we'll be that lucky," Yanker mumbled.

The scout, kicking the bars, yelled "How can you joke at a time like this? Now they do mean to kill us! He recognised that cocky cousin of yours. Thanks to him we're finished!" He yelled down the cage at Erdi, "It's that face of yours! Damn thing's about to get us killed!"

"Now just one moment!" said Yanker protesting. "I'm afraid I must stop you there! You can hardly blame his face. He was born like it."

Fortunately, the scout's attempt to rain blows to emphasise expletives, was constrained by limits of their confinement and then finally by Madarch reaching across Yanker to grab his assailant's wrists.

Bledunigol stared, surprised. Considering how slight his frame, Madarch could exert a surprisingly painful grip.

"Maddy," was all Bledunigol said, in a soft admonishing tone.

Erdi realised his last moments would probably be shared with a man, who for some reason had detested him at first sight, in the same way as Daresay and Prince Gardarm had done previously and there was absolutely no contrivance on his part that could have altered the fact. Like Trader had once told him, "You can't please everyone."

That evening, when dragged out, they were led to where a huge fire blazed. Each was forced atop a mound of loose earth, dug from the four pits holding the stakes. Hands bound rear of uprights only loosely shackled, it was the tight neck-ropes that left no possible room for movement. Then the singing started.

Women swaying and weaving in a strange dance, taunted with earthenware pots, then swung them up to be head-borne, before waving them low, to taunt once again. The singing stopped and accompanied by incantations, the pots were filled with water. Now their significance began to dawn, for carrying them head-borne once again, the ladies approached, four abreast, each smiling sweetly, before swilling the contents around the captives' feet. A resounding roar greeted each libation and as the ground gradually eroded, the neck-ropes tightened.

This continued until a tribal elder, noticing all four were on tips of toes gasping for air, approached and casting an experienced eye, decided the ground below needed firming up. He was actually quite diligent, taking great pains to extend the ritual, thus not only facilitating full extraction of essential essences from dying bodies, but also of course, enhancing enjoyment for all.

There was an excited stir, as the Seer, enrobed head to toe in ceremonial black approached, his crouching dance sending cloak-hem boar tusks jerking to life. His brandished torch, flames whirring and flickering, lit up each face in turn. The sight of reddened features, fearful white of eye, evoked low moans, as going from one to the next, his howling incantations to the spirit world, were echoed by all in unison. His swaying and chanting, evoked such passion, the tribal throng was soon worked up to a frenzy.

A sudden, swift arm-flap, then predatory glare, brought instant silence.

A terrifying silence, broken only by the crackling fire. Then a lone gravelled voice arose, as if notes needed forcing through rust and dust before able to unite and assault the ears as a rasping melody. It was spine chilling and when lustily joined by every man, woman and child, the dance resumed, urged on at pace by rhythmic clapping.

Erdi could feel all about him darkening and starting to swim. As the ground gradually ebbed below, he felt his life force slipping away. He prayed for his wife, his children, his parents, to Elsa's spirit.

The scout managed to growl through strangulation. "I don't wish to die like this. Give me a sword. For the love of the spirits give me a sword. I'll fight the lot of you!"

The dancing stopped for the earth beneath to be firmed again and the chieftain approaching, snarled curses in such a venomous screech full into each face, the stench assaulted like blasts from a death pit.

Madarch grimaced, blinked and gasped "Paaw, stinky!"

"Smells worse than you used to," Yanker managed to growl.

Erdi, feeling a surge of love for his two companions, gave a wry chuckle, thinking, 'Even at the point of death, what amazing spirit.' Grimacing, he sucked in enough air to laugh, properly this time. What was there to lose?

The shocked look and burning rage from their tormentor, although only a minor victory, bestowed enough strength to summon a further effort. Somewhat strangulated, but a laugh no less.

The man's glare, like furnaced-rivets menacing closer, killed any further attempt in his throat, but seeing the slow spread of puzzlement that an item of sacrifice should have dared to mock, furnished enough strength to growl, "You stinking reptile!"

On demand of translation, his official although reluctant, obliged and for his trouble was struck to the ground. Then screaming mad as a witch, the chieftain ran, leapt and swinging his mace of authority, delivered a resounding thwack across Erdi's face.

It was that stunning, the pain that sickening, it knocked him into a world where he could have sworn, his mother was floating, looking down with a face of grave concern.

Into the delerious swoon, drifted Yanker's voice. "That's done it! Now they're really going to kill us."

To their amazement, an abrupt order had them cut free to be forced back into the cage. Necks were badly bruised, Erdi's throbbing face partly blocked his vision, but although shambling wrecks from fear and hunger, amazingly, they were still alive.

Slumped and drifting in and out of sleep, all looked up at the sound of the bolt being drawn. A young girl crawled through the entry and whispered in cymry, "I was told to bring you this." It was water. She gave a hesitant smile in Maddy's direction and crawled back out again. The hatch was relocked by the guard and they passed the night sleeping fitfully, too exhausted to discuss their temporary reprieve.

The following morning the girl brought bread and water.

"This doesn't make sense," said Erdi through the good side of his mouth. "What do they intend to do with us?"

With shake of head and a finger to lips, she pointed to the guard beyond the bars. The poor girl looked terrified. Her nervous smile, drew a warm look from Madarch and she crawled back out. Their cage was relocked.

That evening food was brought in a pot, but the following evening nothing. On the next visit, the girl whispered, "You only get what is left over." She was an undernourished little thing herself and Erdi wondered whether she was for trading south, like Vanya had been.

Later, asking no-one in particular, he said "How is it, those women could smile, when what they were doing was actually killing us?"

The scout almost sounded genial, when explaining "They don't see it like that. Once they realised who we were, we became too valuable to be traded as slaves. We're more valuable as captured spirits, harnessed to give strength to the tribe. Your skull will be kept for the same purpose. As for the rest of your miserable carcass, it will be discarded--- no further use to them."

"Well that's alright then," said Yanker. "I feel so much better, now it's been explained so clearly."

He was flashed a look of unbridled hatred.

"I realise why they fight the way they do," said Erdi. "Ambush. Striking then fleeing----- there's simply not enough of them to engage in all-out battle."

"You know nothing," growled the scout. "Didn't you notice something different about one of the contingents fighting us on the Habren?"

Erdi's silence implied he hadn't.

"They weren't from this tribe. Don't know exactly who they were, but they weren't from this tribe."

On the girl's following visit, she described in a whisper, something strange was being constructed. Two wicker-work columns, as tall as a man. An order barked, brought a look of terror and she scrambled back outside.

Madarch flinched at the sound of a resounding slap and thin cry of pain.

Their limbs now cried out from the time spent cramped, unable to stand. They longed to stretch out, but there was hardly room to even squeeze past to use the disgusting pot in the corner. It was easier to pass it to whoever had need. What had brought such initial revulsion now became a necessity. It was the poor girl's job to empty it.

Erdi's mind wandered back to the time Mardi had interrupted his Big Hendi story, asking about such bodily requirements and he said to himself, 'Not long now, Mardi. I'll soon be joining you.'

Each morning they had bread and water but at night, if there happened to be food left over, they survived on scraps. One cold dawn they were told in a terrified whisper, 'The wicker thing is starting to take shape. It's a giant.'

"They mean to burn us," said Bledunigol. "We're to be sacrificed to the spirits inside the wicker man."

"Dear mother! Anything but that," said Yanker, now beyond any thoughts of humour.

"You can thank your cousin. The know-all. His remark obviously riled that much, dragon breath thought strangulation too good for us."

From the beyond the bars, came a growl for silence.

Madarch, in his position close to the hatch, chose this moment, of all moments, to playfully blow on the girl's neck. Turning in shock, her puzzled look with a hint of a smile, was the only glimpse of humanity in the nightmare they were living through. Shuffling through the low hatch, she took their only morsal of light relief, out with her.

"What a time to do a thing like that!" yelled Bledunigol, clearly incensed. "Here we are waiting to be cooked alive and you start flirting with that------that scrawn-bag!"

"She not mind," said Madarch.

"Not mind? That's not the point------------!"

"Oh, leave him," said Erdi. "Any small comfort is all we can hope for now."

"Small comfort? What, with a thing like that?"

"I only did it because she friendly," Madarch reasoned.

"Friend? How can she be a friend? Probably doesn't even know what day it is let alone anything else."

"He said, friendly, not friend," Erdi returned with a sigh. "Here we are, on the verge of being burnt alive and you carp at something that amounts to nothing."

"Nothing!" he yelled back. "I don't consider it nothing and think yourself lucky I can't reach your scrawny neck!" The scout's face was as dark as his mood. "Real friendship, real understanding can only be achieved between two men. True meeting of minds. Understanding between men hardened by battle and life's labours. It's women who talk endlessly about nothing!"

At this, the others decided to drop the subject. The ensuing silence grew ever more burdensome and like days before, this one dragged as if never ending, with yet again sleep's blessing being denied by cramped conditions and irritating flies.

283

They were not short of visitors, mind you, *said the Teller*. Children arrived to pull faces and savage any attempt to stretch limbs beyond the bars. Taunting youths waving firebrands as a reminder of what lay ahead, were particularly sickening, as were the perfectly decent looking women, who without the slightest hint of compassion, daily debated their fate. Warriors were strangely absent, possibly having sneaking regard for their bravery.

Although obviously disarmed, Madarch for some strange reason had not been relieved of his belt of mysteries. Dagger, dart and sling had been seized, but he still had other items, including the twine that had snared the hare. With nothing better to do, he splayed its loop beyond the cage bars and said, "The guard, he always stand in the same place."

"Yes Maddy. Ready to remove the head of anyone foolish enough to give him the opportunity," said the scout.

"I could trap his leg."

"Whatever good would that do?"

"Then I could jab him with that stick I grabbed," said Yanker with enthusiasm.

"Oh that's a good idea," said Bledunigol. "That will really do some good. I've been told, if sufficiently riled, they take great delight in feeding starving victims their own private parts. I want to arrive in the next world as a man, thank you."

On her next visit the girl reported, the arms of the edifice had been completed. She looked at Madarch, gently pushed his hair from brow, gave a sad smile and left. That night she brought the last scrapings of the tribal meal in a pot.

Yanker examining, passed it on to Bledunigal, who taking his first and only scoop grumbled, "Hardly enough to feed a child."

284

"No, we certainly won't grow up to be big boys on that." Seeing the food pot raised, Yanker winced, but the expected blow never arrived.

Later, came the din of singing and raucous laughter. Bleary faces peered through the bars. Then came the urine. Streams of it, accompanied by more laughter.

The condemned, did have the satisfaction of hearing Yanker's defiant yell, "You're nothing but a bunch of stinking budducks!" but there was little else to lift the feeling of despair and humiliation.

Erdi asked the girl the following morning, what had got them into such a state?

"The cherry wine is ready," she whispered.

Erdi, translating for Yanker's benefit, added, "She said they all got drunk."

"Really!"

Then came the devastating news. She whispered, 'It had been a celebration. The wicker man was complete and its limbs had been stuffed with straw.'

It was exactly at this point, possibly aided by spirit of Elsa or maybe even by the spirits themselves, a plan that had been churning suddenly popped up, complete as a possibility inside Erdi's head. But they needed to act quickly. On his muttered instruction, Madarch undid the largest pouch from his belt of mysteries and handed it to the girl with whispered instructions. She tucked it inside her blouse. It was only a slim hope, but better than nothing. It depended entirely on the girl being brave enough to do as asked and to then return that night with the guard. Even if there was no leftover food for them, she had to pretend there was.

The day dragged endlessly. Each time on hearing footsteps, all four heads jerked up in alarm. With the expectation of being hauled out at any moment, to be forced into the belly of the wicker man, it was impossible to stop the trembling. Not just the hands, the whole body. Time and again they thought their end had come. They prayed to the spirit world for help, like they had never prayed before. They prayed for evening and their one slim hope of escape.

Even with their limited view, everything confirmed this was to be the night. Joyous sounds of greeting rang as the tribes assembled. The fire's glow was greater than any preceding, throwing waves of light into the highest branches. The intensity increased as more were lit, one for each village on a night to remember.

Aroma of roasting meat, induced mind-numbing panic, instant limpness of limbs and urgent need of the pot in the corner. A fearful reminder, their own bodies would soon be enhancing the mix of cooked flesh.

Four petrified faces, as if cast in bronze, stared out beyond the bars. Children and youths, racing to peer, ran excitedly back to give the latest report.

"Do they think we might have flown away?" asked Yanker. None mocked his quavering voice.

"Where's that girl?" Erdi muttered through gritted teeth. All four, even the scout, were clinging on to the bars, trying to summon a scrap of resolve and stop hands from shaking.

The sound of singing was raucous, almost demented.

"Dear mother!" said Yanker. "Please let it work."

"I hope she do it," came a worried plea from Madarch.

"Here she is!" said Erdi.

With a struggle, the two swapped places, with Yanker and Madarch now at one end and Erdi crouched next to Bledunigol.

The swinging rhythm of tribal singing, as if from a marching throng, suddenly changed, as if all had suddenly met the end wall of a quarry and at the sound of babbled confusion, the approaching guard, realising something strange must have happened, paused as if about to return.

"Don't go back. Please don't go back." muttered Erdi, willing the warrior to approach the cage.

"He's coming," said Yanker. There was a rasp as the bolt was drawn and a squeak as the hatch opened. The girl crouched and shuffled in.

"Sounds like you did it," Erdi whispered.

The girl gave a grim nod and handed him the food pot. For the first time it was full.

"They said it's your last meal," she whispered.

On a hushed instruction she removed her top. It was pale grey.

"Wait!" hissed Madarch. "He not stand in right place."

"Where's the water you budduck?" Yanker shouted. That brought no results, so he yelled, "Hey! You with the stinking feet, we've got no water!"

At last, the guard, not needing translation to recognise derision, moved to give the cage a good slap with his sword. One foot alighted where the snare awaited.

"Got him," said Madarch, pulling tight. When the hardened stick pierced his trapped leg, the man let out a shriek of pain and anger. The next stab, straight through his boot drove him into such a thrashing frenzy you'd have thought a small dog was worrying his foot.

Erdi with the girl's blouse barely covering, edged through the hatch. On straightening, he gasped, not expecting the pain that shot up his body. They had been cramped for that long, he felt almost crippled.

The warrior, even in his addled state, now realised it wasn't the girl who had emerged and withdrawing his sword from the attempted thrust at his tormentor, screeched at yet another stab, before swinging the steel down hard on Erdi's neck. He stared, first in disbelief at the blade, then at the prisoner, swaying like an apparition. As he made to swing again, Erdi smashed the food pot in his face. An incensed charge, tumbled him backwards over the roof of the prison, where pinned struggling and bellowing, he had the sword wrestled free by Yanker. There came one last hoarse call for help, before Bledunigol snapped his neck.

They were all now free of the cage, but weak from confinement and felt helpless as if anchored to the spot as groaning wide-eyed figures stumbled towards them. Their advance was slow, but determined, like avenging monsters from another world.

Bledunigol relieving Yanker of the sword, advanced and waited. On deftly slicing down one, then another, he shouted, "Get the message back, Maddy!" The last they saw was his sword flashing, scything down ghouls in succession as the dark surge groped relentlessly towards him.

Once in motion, their limbs began to free up and they followed the tributary down to the main river, praying their boats had not been discovered. The dockside huts gaped empty; all occupants drawn to the grand burning.

A frantic search through riverside growth finally revealed their craft, just as they'd left them and with shaking limbs, they clambered aboard and shoved off into the night.

Using the paddles to steer clear of rocks and branches, they let the current do the work. Erdi, realising they'd entered a clear stretch, turned to hand back the garment that had offered brief disguise. The poor girl had been warm enough whilst running, but now sat with arms clasped tight across pale ribs and either through fear or the cold, was unable to stop her teeth from chattering. He helped her don the garment and then, un-battening a cloak from the hull's side, draped it around her. Drawing its warmth tight, her dark-eyed look said thank you. He returned to steering duties.

Erdi felt the collar of his own shirt and the tender spot beneath. Elsa's rib-bone had been cleaved in two, but it had saved his life. 'Thank you, Vanya----- thank you, Elsa,' he mouthed silently.

For fear of having hulls ripped on the rocks, they didn't venture further into the night. Erdi felt fairly safe in the knowledge, the effect of Madarch's little potion would last until morning. The secret of the pouch's contents had been divulged a few days earlier, dried wavy cap mushrooms, those most powerful, picked late in the year. The girl had chopped and ground them fine, before stirring the lot into the cherry wine. Her name was Milda.

Early the following morning, not yet light, Milda shook them awake. She was terrified. As stiff limbs were slowly stretched, she berated, saying they should move. Apparently, most of the previous night's gathering would not have been drugged by the wine. Only those close to the chieftain had had the honour of sharing it. Lesser mortals and those from outlying valleys had blurred their wits with beer and cider and fortunately, that, plus lack of leadership had rendered them impotent. This morning, however, was another matter.

"They'll assume we've headed north for home," said Yanker.

"I think we'd better assume they'll search all directions. It's not as if they lack manpower to do it," Erdi replied.

They were cold, weak and hungry, but had no choice other than to force themselves back into the boats and take to the chill waters. On their insistence, Milda, their little heroine, was told to remain aboard as the boats were eased over lesser shoals and fish weirs. Isolated huts were passed, but even in the pre-dawn gloom, silent travellers heading downstream didn't go unnoticed. It's always the dogs that draw people outside to stare. The temptation to relieve the sullen watchers of their morning meal, did cross Erdi's mind, they were starving, but falling to the temptation would almost certainly have cost them their lives. Not only were they still very much in enemy territory, they were also, almost certainly being hunted. Every moment spent on the water was vital.

The river looped its way lazily through woodland and they couldn't help but feel a sense of freedom growing with each stroke of the paddle, but when negotiating tight gorges, the torrent over rocks became that strong, it forced all into the water, guiding the boats through the shallows for fear of them being ripped to pieces. It was then, the sense of terror returned.

Shaking with cold and hunger, splashing and in places wading waist deep, fearful looks upstream and into dark flanking woods, reminded freedom was in actual fact, still a very distant prospect.

Late morning, passing a tributary feeding the Gwy from the west, they drifted into sight of a sizeable settlement straddling both banks. A prominent wooded hill, standing off to the south, would have probably meant something to Bledunigol, but other than knowing the river was taking them in the right direction, they had not the slightest idea where they were.

Erdi knew it eventually linked with the Habren and maybe along the way, might come the answer to their quest, the mysterious source of iron, but for the present, with the current drifting them inexorably towards the large riverside community, this was the least of his concerns.

As if drawn by some hidden force, more people emerged to watch in eery silence from both banks. The cousins urgently debated their next move. Would these be friend or foe? Sheer audacity was decided upon. Waving acknowledgement at the shouts and gestures, now urging them ashore, they hardened smiles to grimaces and skimming past, braced themselves for the expected shower of arrows.

The community watched in silence, as the boats disappeared around the bend.

"I think we're clear of Gwy territory," Yanker called. "We probably missed the chance of a good meal."

"And it could have been our last," Erdi called back. "I doubt we're out of danger yet."

"I can still smell that roast pork----crackling done to a crisp, flesh within---tender and succulent." His voice echoed across the water.

"Keep dreaming," Erdi said with a wry laugh and then asked, "Did you notice their weapons?"

"Yes, bronze."

"Which means the iron mines must still lie ahead. Oh no! More rocks!"

The river ran fast through the narrows and as before, they headed for the bank. In the gloom of overhanging trees, jumping from pebble shoals to dark glistening rocks, they guided their craft through the freezing torrent, but where small pools swirled, they were forced to lunge across, pulling the boats behind.

It was in these stretches they felt most vulnerable. The roaring water blocked out all other sounds--- sounds warning of impending danger. In their state of fatigue, it was not hard to imagine, mounted warriors streaking between trees, plunging into the flow to impale their fragile craft with lances.

By early evening, a quiet section was reached and pulling the boats up into hiding, they rested in silent exhaustion on the riverbank. It was a pleasant green expanse, suggesting a farm or settlement would not be too far distant. Their overnight needs were carried over to the shelter of trees and with a westerly breeze blowing, Erdi decided to risk a fire. The others went foraging.

They returned with nettles, dandelions, sorrel, goose foot, thistles and goose grass. Using river water, all was boiled to a broth. It was their first food since a morsel of bread two mornings previous. That pot-full of scraps, brought the evening before had been sacrificed to the cause, but at least by way of exchange, they'd relieved the corpse of its dagger.

Once the fire had done its job, embers were spread, then covered with earth and they all huddled together, naked but for their cloaks, fitfully sleeping through the swirl of nightmares.

In dank mists of morning, dithering with cold, they forced themselves, back into the icy grip of damp clothing. When hung on branches, water had dripped, but nothing was remotely dry. Their boots oozed dark shiny patches as they pulled them on.

Erdi, first to the riverbank, scanned upstream. Seeing all was clear he beckoned. The boats were slid into the water and all clambered aboard. The going was much easier now and mercifully the sun shone like a soothing balm. Leggings were removed and spread to dry and their shirts steamed on their backs. A sense of freedom grew, but they knew better than to relax or allow the slightest notion of a celebratory glint------- the spirits delighted in dashing low those that did.

The Gwy's flow slowed and they entered sections with expansive loops and more open countryside, with the sun's location indicating, they were now heading northeast, towards steep wooded hills rising up from the south.

At a large settlement, friendly folk, pouring out beyond the palisade, beckoned them shoreward. Some even entered the water. Their smiles, plus the enticing aroma of food drifting across the water, almost broke their resolve, but they dared not stop. Yes, they would have been fed and in all probability even been told of the mysterious source of iron, but translations would have been long and protracted, exposing them to the likelihood of recapture. Milda, still naked as clothes dried, grabbed her cloak to huddle beneath, as with wistful looks, her companions waved to the throng as they paddled past.

"Oh, I can smell that roast pork again," wailed Yanker.

"In your dreams," said Erdi.

Middle day, they reached the northern limit of a ridge soaring dark to their right, where the river's course altered, taking them due east. Their clothes were now not only completely dry, but no longer reeked from the libation of urine.

Although, by now starving, to the point of actually shaking from want of sustenance, they managed to somehow, force themselves on, comforted by the knowledge they had escaped an horrific death. Beauty surrounded, but being weak and exhausted, they were hardly aware of it, paddling on trancelike towards evening. Enough light remained to steer by, but following advice from Madarch, Erdi called a halt and they scrunched up onto a small pebble beach on the western shore. There was a spread of grass and the boats were again hidden amongst bank-side foliage.

Madarch had argued, they needed the remaining light to search for food, vital if they hoped to continue next day.

Checking the wind was again favourable, a fire was lit. Yanker and Milda foraged for plants and Madarch kept watch upriver.

Not being one to let an opportunity slip, he also scanned for signs of trout. Three were tickled from under the banking and he returned, offering up his gains in the usual manner. His basking in acclaim, however, was soured slightly by a pang of jealousy. Milda had asked Yanker, who had possession of their only dagger, to accompany her to dig up roots she'd found. It was rough stony ground and tugging had left her with nothing but leaves. They returned with burdock to add to the feast.

"Tell me, Kairios," said Yanker. "How did you know where to dig for them?"

Erdi translated.

"By the leaves of course, but why does he call me Kairios?" asked Milda frowning.

"Because of what you did to that cherry wine," said Yanker laughing.

On being told what he'd said, she gave him a playful slap.

Madarch, now clearly put out asked, "How you know what kairios means? You never learnt cymry."

"Maddy, even I am capable of picking up the odd word."

To make matters worse, whenever Yanker came up with a nickname it tended to stick and from that day forward Milda was known as Kairios (Cherry). Madarch, deeply brooding, wished he'd have thought of it.

The trout, stuffed with chopped sorrel and goose grass, were covered in clay and baked. The remaining food they'd foraged was brewed in their pot and for safety, the fire was then immediately snuffed. At last they had had a proper meal and slept all the better for it. None stood guard. Exhaustion overtook before such a sensible notion had come to mind.

Madarch was first awake. The previous night he had noticed the trail of a hare-run between shrubs and long grass and went to inspect the snare he'd fashioned from fishing line. As so often the case, it was empty. He was then amazed to see a column of smoke burgeoning into a massive plume, just upstream from where they'd camped and he walked towards it, hoping to beg some bread. A nice surprise to gift Kairios, as she arose from slumber.

Closer, he heard the actual crackle of burning timber and was surprised at such a large blaze that early in the morning. The wind veered, blowing smoke to billow around him and snatches of laughter rang out amongst cheery conversation. No hint of chiming female voices. They were all male.

He froze; the thought suddenly hitting him-----he couldn't recall having seen any sign of habitation this close to where they had camped. 'Maybe hunters.' He strained to listen, but unable discern actual words, he crept closer. Then on a strong gusting breeze, heard, not only words, but also their rhythm. A chill shot through him. It was the exact same tempo, heard whilst imprisoned in the cage.

He cursed himself. With his mind so taken up by the girl, he had completely forgotten all his training, ignored all his instincts and had so nearly blundered in amongst them. Looking about, trying not to panic, he realised, the ease with which he'd so blithely wandered unnoticed into the open, would not be quite so simple when attempting retreat. These were indeed hunters and given the chance would probably roast him on the spot.

With heart hammering, he ducked, crept and then running low, gained the cover of trees, standing a slingshot distance back from the river. His chest heaved as he gulped for air and his legs had no more strength than melting wax. Their time in the cage had taken its toll. Looking back towards the fire, he saw no-one emerging. He'd not been spotted.

In a stumbling run through cover of bushes and trees he reached where the others still slept. A glance back towards the billowing smoke told him the way was still clear. No-one had emerged out onto the small pasture. He shook each in turn signalling silence as eyes blinked open. They gathered their things, ran down to the water and slid the boats into the flow. Their paddles that had been so carefully, so silently dipped on first leaving, were pulled with such determination it verged on anger, once safely round the bend. They would not be recaptured!

At the end of each long reach, they dared check behind, to sigh with relief, at seeing low sunlight shafting through motes of dust and flies, lighting up, not thrashing paddles, but calm, peaceful water. Then came the flurry to be beyond the next bend. At any other time, they might have appreciated the beauty of the river with its exaggerated loops, teeming bird-life and alert-eyed game, daring to lap from the shallows, but their minds were clogged by mists of fear, to the point they dared not even pause to dangle a fishing line.

A large settlement was passed on the southern bank, but as before, they could not risk stopping. By middle day they had entered steep wooded country and with the sun shining from the left, right, then left again, realised they were negotiating huge loops the river had cut through the terrain.

"I think we're going round in circles," Yanker called.

"Rivers don't have circles," said Erdi.

"Ahh, you say that, but how do you know? This one might."

Smoke drifting from a settlement on a promontory to the east, was the last sign of humanity, before a forest, darker than anything ever experienced before, enshrouded as they drifted into its vast maw. Being slowly absorbed into eerie silence, they dared gaze in fear and wonder, expecting two headed serpents, dragons and wide-eyed demons to slop forth, intent on devouring them.

As they skimmed steadily on, with fearful looks ahead, then suddenly behind ---- anticipating paddles madly churning, thrashing towards them through the gloom, they continued trancelike, to the next pale sun shafts, casting dim pools of light on flat murky waters.

Then suddenly, with the dark veil lifting, they entered a widening cheerful flow, where the last light of day bathed sheer crags of a gorge. Feeling as if released from evil, all smiled and slumping with relief, let the current take them. Where a strange pinnacle of rock protruded from the forest, a halt was called and the boats pulled ashore.

Again, they were exhausted and shaking with hunger, but this time there seemed little chance of succour. The surrounding forest was seemingly barren of edible plant life. As they'd paddled downstream, it of course hadn't gone unnoticed, in places the woods were teeming with game, but no hunt would be successful in the state they were in. One look told Madarch, absolutely no chance of fishing, for the banks were too sheer to tickle trout and patiently offering a fishing line, would invite re-capture. Searching amongst the trees, he and Kairios did eventually discover mushrooms.

While Yanker kept watch upriver, a fire was lit in a hidden dip and once the pot had been brought to the boil and hot-stone inserted to keep it simmering, flames were immediately extinguished. The resulting broth was all that sustained them on that particular day.

The following morning, climbing from concealment and having stretched stiffness from limbs, they crept towards the river. At Erdi's signal, all halted, and peering through the foliage, watched as three boats packed with Gwy warriors went gliding past.

The mere sight brought the horror flooding back and with the enemy now ahead, it made use of the river a liability, leading to almost certain ambush and horrific death. Erdi reasoned, the broad width of flow and the time spent journeying, meant they must surely be close to its joining with the Habren and he suggested they continue on foot. To add to their woes a thin misty rain enveloped, insidious rain that works its way into everything.

Gathering possessions, they ensured the boats were securely hidden. Two slings, plus the two spears, unstrapped from hull sides, were their only weapons, plus of course, the dagger they had liberated. All others had been taken on their day of capture.

Erdi, handing one spear to his cousin, kept the other for himself.

"Why you got the spears?" Madarch asked, sounding clearly put out.

"What d'you need a spear for, Maddy?" Yanker countered. "Why need a spear when a good paddle will do?"

Erdi explained to Kairios, who now noticed even her nickname had been shortened to Kairi, the peculiar use Maddy had once made of a paddle. Her mouth fell open and his chest swelled with justifiable pride, when out of admiration, she gave his arm a squeeze.

They clawed their way up steep soggy ground and eased down the far slope, being mindful not to add to discomfort, by slipping and adding broad muddy smears to the terrain. On the edge of a steep drop, they stared in complete puzzlement, for directly below, flowed a broad river, a twin to the one just left, except what had flowed away from them, now flowed directly towards them.

"Told you this river went round in circles," Yanker whispered.

At the sound of rhythmic splashing, they scrambled for cover and watched frozen in terror, as the same three boats, packed with warriors, drifted below. They were thankful for the fact, generally, people tend not to look up, unless sudden noise or movement prompts them to.

With the sun lost behind cloud they took the trees for guidance. The mossed side indicated north, enabling them to plot a course east, hopefully towards the Habren.

They worked their way through dense undergrowth, hissing curses at briars and other impediments and when finally chancing upon a path, gratefully took it. In a small clearing was evidence of digging, plus mounds of cold ashes and amongst the burgeoning undergrowth were a number of smashed clay tubular structures. Erdi, recognising them from his stay down on the Lefels, said, "We've found iron."

"How do you know?" asked Yanker.

His cousin, picking up a lump of slag from a pile of debris, brandished it and said, "This is what's left when you smelt the ore."

They chanced on a path following the course of a stream. It was slimy with rain and treacherous under foot, but at least they were free from the wet tangle. Thankfully, by middle morning, the rain stopped and spirits were lifted by dazzle of sunlight flickering through the foliage.

Voices echoing through the trees, brought an abrupt halt. There was the dull thumping of a hammer and smoke drifted. Creeping to the edge of a large clearing, two men could be seen, smashing rock. Others were huddled down by the stream, all looking in a desperate state; wild men in filthy rags and the shelters built were of the crudest form. A distinct smell of horse sweat drifting, was traced to where trees lined the stream and standing quietly in their shade, adding a touch of nobility, was a string of ponies.

A small dog, ceasing its zealous scratching of an angry bald patch, cocked an ear and its sudden bounding across the clearing to yap and leap from side to side in front of them, left no choice other than to break cover and approach the centre of the chaotic scene.

Slimy grins, whitened grimed faces and they were made welcome in a most unsettling way. Scoops of a dreadful concoction were slopped into a bowl, but although ravenous, they managed to resist with an uneasy, 'No thank you,' smile and shake of head.

Every man in the place was now walking slowly towards them, drawn towards Kairi in the same way young bulls persist in surrounding a small dog. They wanted to touch her, feel her hair as if never having seen a woman before.

Yanker's meaningful spear prod, prompted one, who was obviously the leader, into action and heeding the order barked, they all backed off. He spoke a version of cymry that made it just about possible for Erdi to understand and he quizzed the man.

They were smelting iron and with a surge of relief, Erdi relayed to his companions, the Habren was less than a day's walk away. Any elation, however, was halted by the headman suddenly reaching across to deliver a slap. The hand, that had slyly wandered to probe the ragged opening left by the sword-cut in Kairi's blouse, was instantly withdrawn, but a lunatic grin warned, it would not be the last time its owner would venture an attempt and a lustful look indicated, not even the cloak now suddenly pulled so tight, would stop him.

The headman, if you could call him that, led to where ore was mined. He said, initially they had found it, lying ready to be picked from the surface, but for consistent quantities they now needed to excavate. It was smashed, washed and smelted in the forest and pure iron traded down on the Habren.

Erdi asked about dealings with the Gwy tribesmen. The man shuddered and said no, they didn't deal with them directly, but felt certain, that was where much of it ended up, taken in boats and barges up the river Gwy.

A further in-sweep of rain forced all to seek shelter. The headman, grandly ushering them into one of the hovels, forcefully repelled all efforts of those desperate to gain close proximity to the woman. The odd resentful backward glance from those ejected, skulking off like beaten curs, warned they would not be held in check forever. It hardened Erdi's resolve to be out of there as soon as weather allowed.

Barring the way to yet another ragged brute, manically attempting to gain entry, the headman gave him a conspiratorial grin. It wasn't returned.

The wind-blown spray from rain lashing in, forced them into an unwanted huddle away from the door and Erdi, noticing Kairi's growing unease at the headman's pressing interest, eased himself between them. With it helping pass the time, he asked what commodities they traded iron for?

Rather begrudgingly, following a baleful look at Madarch, who had a protective arm around Kairi, the man divulged, food and fodder were obvious priorities, then there were the forged implements they could trade on, but most prized of all, were forest ponies. They were used for transporting iron down to the Habren and once winter made working in the forest virtually impossible, for riding back home. Two were retained for the following season, the rest traded on for quite a tidy return. The iron was traded, roughly once every moon.

Late afternoon, the rain having stopped, Erdi thanked his host, saying they must away. The man looking absolutely shocked to the point of outrage, insisted they stay the night.

"You're in luck. We just happen to be taking iron down to the Habren in the morning."

His over earnest expression didn't come close to masking innate slyness and Erdi's feeling of unease and disgust at seeing leering miners closing in, swelled to such a degree, he began to wonder what gave these creatures a right to life?

Yet without such savage breeds, would the coveted iron still be available? In years to come, by some miracle bestowed by the spirits, would the like of his sister Vanya eventually emerge from their bestial couplings? He shuddered to think what creatures they coupled with.

Erdi watched as the earnest face, almost frothing, spouted, "You can join us. Believe me it's safer that way. These woods are dangerous, confusing. There's something about them that swallows you up. Countless people have become lost here. We've stumbled across skeletons."

Erdi, of course wondered, 'Why hadn't the trip been mentioned earlier?' His inner alarm now rang that vigorously, he stopped the man's streaming entreaty of, "It will be dark soon. The forest will swallow you. Untold dangers await. You can't leave now," with a firm, "No! We're leaving."

Just then, there came a cacophony of squealing from up in the forest.

"Quick! Bring your spears," the headman urged.

Yanker's eyes lit up. He, like all, knew exactly what it was. Madarch grabbing Kairi close, joined the general surge and Erdi was left with little choice, but to follow. As they ran towards the deafening screams of panic and unable to bear the sound, Kairi clamped hands to ears. It raged from the bowels of a large pit. Covering branches had been breached and leaning to peer through the ragged hole, Erdi saw a huge boar writhing in agony on the stake it had impaled itself upon. Even though an experienced hunter, he found the noise heart rending and yet none seemed

302

willing to dispatch the beast. Almost as if revelling in the death throes, a mute, erect line of sweat stained creatures, leering across at Kairi, slowly rubbed filthy, tumid regions, as if entranced.

Madarch enfolded her with a protective arm.

Erdi, taking matters into his own hands, pulled back branches and now having a clear aim, Yanker put the creature out of its misery. Three slid in to shove from beneath and others heaved on a rope from above, hauling it from the pit.

Fate seemed to have determined events. They were starving and this was their first real chance of red meat, since Madarch had trapped the hare. It would be Yanker's dream come true, crispy on the outside, succulent within. Against his better judgement Erdi said they would stay, but unheard he murmured, 'for the meal at least.'

They helped prepare the carcass for roasting and Kairi sent Madarch foraging for something suitable to be chopped and added to the faggots she was making. The mood in the camp jangled with an unsettling mood of expectation and good cheer. The two joints selected by Erdi for their exclusive use had the bristles singed, skin scraped and scored and Yanker guarding with the ferocity of a dog, warned off all interested wretches at spearpoint. What they did with the rest of the beast was up to them and it wasn't pleasant to witness.

Their stomachs had grown that used to near starvation, the rich diet of the feast made it hard to avoid vomiting and one sniff of the brew the miners were guzzling almost brought the impulse to instant fruition. Recoiling from the stench, severe gritting of teeth was required to keep the food down.

"Paaw! I swear one of the dirty devils has farted in it," Yanker said.

"What d'you mean one of them? Smells like they all gave it a go," Erdi added, with eyes watering.

The mood became rowdier and leers towards Kairi made it obvious, attention was turning to the next morsel in the offing. Emboldened by the potent brew they were almost at the point of unashamedly fighting, like rampant juveniles, desperate to be close to her.

Erdi standing, thanked all and said quite truthfully, they were worn out and in need of sleep. As they headed towards the allotted shelter, all eyes were on them and as talk around the fire intensified, almost bristling with urgency, they heard one word recurring.

Amongst the many languages and dialects there were a few words most held in common. The words for mother, father, moon, sun and river were fairly universal, but also the word for woman. That, accompanied by lustful laughter, was the word repeated, around the campfire.

Kairi was petrified.

Erdi hissed, "Quick! Grab our things!"

They slipped off into the night, which direction, they cared not. They were simply desperate to put the nightmare place behind them. Once into the cover of trees, all paused as howls of anger echoed up from the camp, then rang from all directions through the woods. Even the dog started yelping, reaching a cracked hysterical frenzy, as if being staked out as bear-bait.

As men crashed this way and that, stumbling through the undergrowth, driven to madness by alcohol and lust, Kairi clung to Madarch in sheer terror. Calmly, checking all directions, he pointed the way uphill. Forests being his domain, they all filed after him. A loud yelp, then silence, indicated the dog may have been trodden on, or more likely, booted into the bushes, for being utterly useless.

Guessing it was not tracking them, they picked their way more carefully, easing through the tangle to what was considered a safe distance. Reaching a clear section where boar had been rooting, they sank down with relief, to make preparations for a miserable night in the musty damp of the forest. Kairi gave each of her saviours a hug of gratitude.

The next day was as drab as that just endured and with no sun to assist, they again used mossed trees for guidance. Chancing upon a trail, they followed it. This gave out in a wild tangle, which despite Madarch's instincts telling him they were walking in a huge circle, they worked around to stumble across another path. It led along a cliff edge, leaving no choice but to follow. A track slanting over sloping ground led to a copious stream, where water ran a filthy brown.

Voices were heard. To their horror, they realised Madarch had been right, they had ended up back at the very camp, escaped from the previous night and just upstream the same wild creatures were washing ore.

As the headman had said, this forest was confusing. It could swallow people up, but at least they'd not been spotted. In their condition, in the tangle known only to those hunting them and denied the screen of darkness, they gave little for their chance of escaping a second time.

Slowly, silently, they backtracked and this time, bowing to Madarch's judgement, followed the stream's windings and chuckling descents, to what he insisted was east.

Late morning, they again heard voices and spirits were lifted by the unmistakable sound of women in conversation. With them present, surely their men would be of calmer disposition. The camp had a low palisaded defence and a ragged individual standing guard. Spotting the woman in their company, his face lightened and he motioned all to enter.

A man, obviously the leader of the enterprise approached to make them welcome. He confirmed they were mining and smelting iron and they were taken to view an unwelcoming looking hole in banking, outside of which, men were smashing dull brown rocks. The nearby stream ran from clear chuckle to choked turbid from waste washed away.

Back in the enclosure, with much pumping of bellows, furnaces belched smoke and as at the previous camp, ponies stood tethered. The two women they had overheard, busied themselves supposedly with something of import, but their looks were drawn towards Kairi. In rags no better than those hanging off the men, they pulled themselves erect, giving such a haughty flick of head, you'd have thought they considered themselves royalty. They had not a single wholesome hint and glowering looks showed unbridled hostility. Hatred at first sight. For such a tiny young thing, Kairi had drawn quite a surprising amount of attention in the wilds of this particular forest.

The headman pointing east said, if they topped a ridge just south, a stream would lead them to a small settlement on the Habren's western shore. At this point, a commotion at the gate had him marching over to where an altercation was boiling into curses and insults.

"Two more of them," he said on return. "Two, hoping to share our spoils." With a sly look, he added, "and our women. **You're** all welcome to stay if you like."

Kairi, knowing exactly where he'd be gazing, avoided eye contact.

Gladly leaving them to their spoils and women, they thanked the man and headed up over the ridge in search of the stream mentioned. This was followed to near end of day, until at last, swollen with the tide, middle distance below, spread the mighty Habren.

The sight gave renewed energy and they wound their way down the long, steep descent almost at a run. Not only was their goal within sight, they were starving. Apart from a scrap of bread given at the previous encampment, they'd had nothing all day.

They were relieved to find a normal community awaited. These good people survived and did very well I might add, fishing, farming and from dealing in horses and iron. The metal was brought out from of the forest and they traded it on to those living west of the Gwy river. The forest ponies they trapped, were kept for breeding and the offspring went in lucrative deals, to be used largely as pack animals.

Their visitors were made instantly welcome. Pointing back to indicate the route just taken, Erdi received looks of complete incredulity, the shaking of heads implying it had been madness. Many had been known to enter their forest, never to be seen again.

This was fairly easily conveyed by sign language, but with there being such a communication barrier, it took the whole evening before they could fully understand the intricacies of all the information imparted. Gradually, over the course of the meal, with much pointing, arm waving and the aid of scratched details on the solid earth floor, it was possible to discern, this was not the only village dealing in iron. The new metal had drawn men from far and wide and many hauled it to locations on the river Gwy itself. It seemed that the people doing the trading were not Gwy tribesmen, "Impossible people," the headman had added with a shudder, but a tribe living due west of the forest. These controlled most of the trade and the Gwy, bringing them mountain ponies and slaves, were their main clients.

He also added, that that particular tribe, living west of the forest, were not a people to be taken lightly. Beneath a calm demeanour lurked a ferocious spirit and if riled, were a fright to behold.

You will know of them as the Siluriks, meaning rich in grain, *said the Teller. There was a murmur of understanding from amongst his audience.*

Yanker and Madarch had helped in the gleaning of all this, which is often the case when those not under the same pressure as the one being directly spoken to, seem to have a greater understanding of what is being said.

Of course, all were eager to know what had caused these strangers to risk their lives by walking unguided through the heart of the forest, but Erdi managed to duck their questions with the vaguest of replies. It brought a pang of guilt, for the people could not have been more hospitable and had even been at great pains to press upon him, details of a trail that would shorten their journey on the morrow.

Any plan regarding future trade for iron, however, was best kept to themselves. They had achieved what they'd set out to do, had found a bountiful source and their Lord Gwenithen would not be one to reward loose talk, no matter what mood he happened to be in.

They spent a comfortable and mercifully, peaceful night, thanked their hosts and set out next day towards a location on the Gwy; that same village where Erdi had had the luck of chancing upon Padlor.

"I thought you said the village was near the sea," said Madarch.

"It is," Erdi replied.

"Well the sea must be that way. We're going the wrong way."

"Trust me, Maddy, the village is this way," he said pointing southwest.

"Then this river's going backwards." He stood scratching his head as a log bobbed past, heading upstream.

"It's the tide, Maddy. The tide's coming in. It happens on all coastal rivers, but for some reason is more pronounced on this one."

In view of that fact, they were ever watchful for craft making use of the natural occurrence. To be caught now, when within sight of freedom, like a death arrow on the last day of the war, would be a tragedy beyond comprehension.

It was just as they headed inland, danger was spotted. They had reached the trail, the short-cut they had been so kindly informed of the night before and fast approaching, were two hide covered craft paddled by Gwy warriors.

To their relief, there was no cry to halt, no sudden increase of pace in desperation to reach them; fortune had smiled and they'd not been spotted. The trail they now followed, with of course some degree of urgency, kept them well-hidden from the river, but each was mindful to suppress any note of triumph. They might have eluded their hunters yet again, but to celebrate now would almost certainly invite disaster. As we know all too well, those spirits, *said the Teller*, are ever out for devilment.

As Trader had impressed on Erdi, years before, luck, good or bad, ran in patches and on this occasion their luck held, even to the point of the ferry being moored on the southern shore, almost as if waiting for them and the ferryman, on remembering Erdi, poled them across the Gwy for nothing.

At first sight of the wild wanderers entering the village, the headman looked visibly stunned and grasping an arm, hurried Erdi into a nearby hut. Even with the passage of time and being decidedly hairier than when they'd last met, he'd still been recognised. The others followed. There was a trader within, in command of the cymry tongue, who told them, Gwy tribesmen had been asking after them. Two boats had gone to block passage up the Habren and another crew were lying in wait on the Gwy river itself.

Erdi enquired after boats trading down the coast, but was told they were too late, three had left just days before. There could of course be others, autumn was still not fully upon them, but it was too risky to remain simply on the off-chance. Besides, their presence endangered all.

Thinking this over, Erdi told his companions, it left but one safe option. There was a place he knew, but it now involved a river crossing and yet more walking.

He explained to the headman where their boats lay hidden. With it being one of the most memorable spots on the river, the man knew it well and laughed at their tale of safely watching their pursuers glide by, only to so nearly blunder into their clutches, moments later. They had apparently walked across the neck of a huge, well-known loop in the river. He assured them, their boats would be collected on the next trading venture up the Gwy and kept safely stored. Erdi enquired what reward would be needed, but the man waved the notion away, saying all could be settled on eventual collection of the boats. Thanking him, Erdi added, 'If for some reason they failed to return the following spring, he should consider them his.'

They were instructed to remain hidden; food would be brought and they'd be called early the following morning to be led to the ferry. Shelter would be offered for one night, but no longer.

With this the Teller thanked all and left the grand hall.

Part 5

Chapter Fifteen

The following morning the Teller was sitting hunched close to the hearth. A wild storm had blown through during the night leaving a damp chill in the air. He heard a knock on the sounding board and looking up, was pleasantly surprised at seeing the Seer's unmistakable figure duck in through the opening. As he straightened, the Teller rose to greet his approach. He had arrived with the notion of them taking a stroll around the palisade, posing the question, What is his motive this time?

He donned his cloak and *they walked in silence, avoiding the soggiest areas, down to the east gate. Early risers gave the holy man humble greetings and reverential nods. They mounted the palisaded walls and on surveying the latest development of the grand works, the Seer said,* "I was wondering,---from all the tales handed down, were you ever told exactly when this fortress was reoccupied?"

No not exactly, *said the Teller.* All I know is, it must have been quite some time after Erdi's era, for I was told, when need came to refortify, the original hut circles had become grassed over. The only sign of former habitation, were shallow bowls dotted here and there like ghostly reminders of a lost age. I have no idea of the numbers living in the valley at the time, only that the population was probably at least twice that dwelling here in Erdi's time.

What is often forgotten, was the fact more moved in from the west, driven down from the hills by the worsening weather. Amongst them was a small tribe from beyond the far mountains. They had a tradition of building in stone and I suppose that is why some of the houses here have walls of stone, rather than wattle. Their descendants carried on with that same tradition.

"The heart of the ramparts is packed with stone," *added the Seer.* "I just took it for granted, never thinking who might have inspired that method of construction."

Yes, the stumps of the old palisade were dug out and those first two ring defences constructed. The weather had improved of course, don't know when exactly, but I presume it was a gradual thing. It was probably rather like the rain stopping. You can rarely say exactly when it did, only that it must have done, because the sun's out.

"I suppose it was the raiding we have become so accustomed to-----even in the early days, it must have been what forced them to go to such lengths."

Yes. With increase of population and pressure on resources it almost became a way of life. They raided in the summer and sang about it through the winter.

"Nothing much changes, does it." *said the Seer with a chuckle.*

No. Things do in fact change, but basic human nature doesn't seem to. As the annual game of war intensified it added a fair deal of urgency to the notion of walling themselves in. A feud can be started in the blink of the eye, but it can take numerous lifetimes for peace to be regained. It was relatively easy to launch lightning attacks on neighbours, but incredibly difficult to hold the ground encroached on, so just as now, the main gauge of success was livestock stolen and then of course, a place was needed to retreat to, safe from retribution.

The Seer nodded understanding, but his eyes showed the meaning of the final word, yet another from the Teller's strange compendium, hadn't quite penetrated.

A place safe from a neighbour's revenge.

"Ah." *The light of understanding now shone.*

They strolled on in silence for a while. A comfortable silence, finally broken by the holy man asking, "Tell me, did Mardi's genius ever show in other members of the family?"

The Teller smiled. I must ask you to be patient. Let's see what the spirits bring forth in tonight's telling. This will be the final part by the way. Sorry to say, I'll be leaving you on the morrow.

"Really. So the tale has almost run its course. I was hoping you could have stayed longer. I hope you don't mind, but what I really wanted to ask you was-----.

'So this the reason for our little stroll,' *thought the Teller.*

"Have you ever considered remaining in one place, become the Teller for one community?"

Believe me, I have, many times, but sadly, what I have been gifted won't allow it.

The Seer giving a resigned shake of head, accompanied him back to his place of stay. They parted at the doorway and on entering, the Teller felt an immediate quickening of heartbeat, for Megan was standing beside the hearth. Her grandchild was having her first shoes fitted and didn't look too happy about it.

"Manda prefers running about barefoot," *said Megan with a smile.*

"You'd have thought we were bridling a wild pony," *chortled the shoemaker's wife, ruffling the little girl's hair.*

"They too big!" *was said with arms tightly folded and a scowl.*

"That's so you can grow into them, petal," *explained the lady of the house.*

"You don't have to wear them all the time," *Megan added.*

"You're lucky to have shoes," *said the cobbler.* "Most folks can't afford them for sprigs like you. I never had a pair at your age."

They all looked up. A sharp knock on the sounding board heralded another visitor.

"It's getting busier than Y-Pentwr," *said the cobbler's wife.*

Ryth's ruddy face appeared and close behind trailed a woman. Even though the man had not had the good grace to usher the lady in before him, the Teller assumed her to be his wife.

"Ah, I have them ready for the fitting," *said the shoemaker, giving a suggestion of a bow before hurrying to collect the footwear from the workroom.*

The little girl was momentarily forgotten and the lady, when offered a stool, slipped her feet into the shoes and stood to test for comfort.

"Well? What do you think?" *asked her husband.*

"Well I must admit, I had hoped they would turn out a little less weighty," *was said in quite a hesitant voice.*

"They're not quite finished, I could make slight adjustments," *said the shoemaker.*

"Nonsense! Are they comfortable?"

With slight twist of foot she replied, "Well ye-es, I suppose so."

"Good. Make her two pairs," *boomed Ryth. His wife, hurriedly redonning her old shoes, stamped down hard into a heel, doing her best to catch up with him.*

There was a stunned silence. "Well!" *said Megan, finally.*

The Teller would have had no problem passing judgement and it would not have been flattering, but his personal pact prevented such direct intervention in their lives.

Megan gave him a smile as they left and the little girl, giving her grandmother's hand a tug said, "Grandma, that man likes you."

Megan turned and blushing slightly, said, "I'm sorry. What things children say!"

Please, don't apologise. *Then musing aloud, he added,* On occasions children can be quite perceptive.

The cobbler's wife bustling about, tidying, tending the fire and stirring the pot, hummed to herself as if not having heard a thing.

In the Grand Hall that night the Teller informed all, spirits willing, it was to be the conclusion of the tale. There were a few groans, for although keen to know the ending, it also meant he'd soon be leaving.

He began; Dawn hadn't yet broken, when Erdi and his fellow travellers were roused from sleep. They were instructed to leave immediately. Two Gwy warriors had ridden through late the previous evening and in all likelihood would return before morning's end. As you can imagine, this scrap of news put a little urgency into their step, *said the Teller with a grin,* plus, in view of latest developments, they were led through the woods. Not to the main dock on the Gwy river where the large boarded ferry was moored, but to another on the Habren itself.

They were going by boat. The tide was ebbing and would aid their crossing. As the dawn light crept, clouds portended a dull day, but away to the west, as had appeared in the Seer's vision, a thin, pale-blue band on the horizon, offered hope.

They'd had no time for food or to even offer thanks to the village headman. As mooring ropes were stowed, Erdie called to their guide, "Please get word upriver. Tell Gwenithen's people we're safe. Make sure he knows, we survived, thanks to Bledunigol. He died a hero."

"Bled what?" came a cry from the riverbank.

Erdi cupped hands to mouth for the words to carry, "Bledunigol. Lone Wolf; he was our leader."

A wave from the distant figure, acknowledged he'd understood and the boat was soon a mere speck heading for the opposite shore. Arriving far side, they were helped on to the small dock and handed their meagre belongings.

"I feel ashamed, I have nothing to reward you with," Erdi said to the ferryman.

"As I told you before, getting you to safety is reward enough."

Thanking the man and his son, the latter obviously proud in his role as young helmsman, they headed inland.

For the very first time, now feeling confident they had finally escaped the horror, they spoke of the man who had given his life for them. No matter what personal feelings they might have harboured, none could dispute his bravery.

"Why didn't he run like we did?" Madarch asked.

"He knew, if one of us didn't make a stand; hold up those savages, there was little chance for the rest of us," said Yanker.

"But they all drugged, probably only seeing ghosts and phantoms."

"And we were half crippled," said Erdi. "Believe me, I have no doubt at all. If he hadn't done what he did, we wouldn't be here talking about it now."

"He got the warrior's death, you predicted," said Yanker. "But why do that for us? Doesn't make sense. The man hated us." Then turning to his cousin, "Well I might have ruffled him a bit, but you! Talk about spears of hatred!"

"I think he did it for Maddy," said Erdi.

This shaft of insight stopped Madarch in his tracks.

They turned. "What's the matter Maddy," Yanker asked.

"Am I different?" he asked with a troubled look.

"Totally different from when I first met you," said Erdi.

"And all the better for it," added Yanker.

"But am I still a man?" He still wore the worried look.

"Of course. What a thing to ask." Erdi, turning to Kairi, asked in cymry, "Is Maddy still a man?"

She didn't answer as such, but walked to where he was still rooted and enfolded an arm in a squeeze.

"What made you ask that?" said Erdi.

"When me and that Blood Eagle were alone, he talked to me different. It gave me a creeply feeling. He talked to me, not like to a man, but like I was a girl he was caring for. I wondered if I was changing into one."

"Not a bit," said Erdi.

"It gave me worries. That time I blew on Kairi's neck. I did it because I liked her. But inside me was another reason. I knew it would anger him. I wanted him know my real feelings."

His worried expression, plus their weakness from hunger, had the cousins laughing, more helpless with relief at feeling normal again, than him being hilariously funny. Kairi found it infectious and Yanker finally said, "Come on creeply. Time we were moving."

Mid-morning, their cheer was heightened further, when chancing on a wild tangle, where the first of the season's blackberries had ripened and those they didn't eat were put in their pot for later.

"They not normally out this time of year," said Madarch.

"We're much further south," Erdi replied. "It's far warmer down here."

At midday, no longer in a rush, they rested beside a seeping brook. The cloud cover had rolled away, with only the last vestiges still clinging to the range of hills rearing up to the east and that distant dawn blue patch, heralding earlier like a slither of hope, they now at last dared bask in the full expanse of it, lolling in the sunshine, dark lipped from devouring the remaining blackberries. At last, thoughts turned to home.

The cousins had missed their families desperately, but with the scout ever ready to sneer and with the horror of the nightmare they had lived through, this was the first time they had openly discussed it. The hollow ache they shared was made all the worse, almost to the point of nausea, by the fact their every step was now taking them further away. At middle day they were stunned by a sight that briefly took their minds off it.

All stopped, for directly below them yawned a huge chasm. Madarch dared to edge towards the lip, only to be pulled back by Kairi, clamping a hand to heart and scolding him. They did eventually peer into the depths, but not standing, lying on their fronts. Along the ravine floor, a thread of water ran between muddy banks and gulls labouring their way to the coast, looked no more than mere specks.

"How are we meant to cross that?" asked Yanker.

"There has to be a way over," said Erdi. He realised that the Tinners must have been confronted by the same problem when travelling west with Vanya and had obviously known a way round. "We'll follow it inland. Every river can be crossed in the end."

As hoped, the waters entered the gorge from flatter lands and walking down through the trees, they came to a large settlement, straddling both banks. Warmed by friendly greetings, they continued along a main path between the houses down to the river. Boats lay atilt on the muddy bank, each tethered to a mooring post as were the craft on the opposite shore. Walking to the edge, to peer beyond the glistening ooze, they saw flowing at a steady rate in the gully below, quite uninviting silt-laden waters.

Recognising this to be a serious obstacle, Erdi signed to a boatman the question, 'How do we cross?'

'You wait for the water,' came the answer.

Thinking he'd misunderstood the reply, he put the same question to another. The answer came back as before, "Wait for the water."

Following a discussion regarding this peculiarity, it was decided they had better offer their services in exchange for food and do as the natives did, wait for the water.

With harvesting still ongoing, extra hands were welcome, food was offered and by early evening came the message, 'the water has arrived'. On returning to the afon, the word most tribes used for river, they saw it now brimmed full and all the boats that had seemed to slumber earlier, were now afloat looking pert for action.

The first boatman, they'd chanced on earlier, was that tickled by their looks of incredulity, he ferried them over for the sheer pleasure of it, where far side a small crowd began to gather. Of course, they'd been objects of interest on the northern shore, but here they were soon enveloped, causing quite a stir in fact, to the point, any doubts they might have had regarding accommodation, were soon banished.

As you know people from these islands have long been known for the pride taken in their appearance and so, having chanced upon something untamed, exotic, as if from another world, all wanted the distinction of housing them. It was only when the adventurers took stock, seeing themselves as others saw them; desperate looking wild-haired wanderers, cheery of countenance, in near identical clothing, they realised it wouldn't be a thing these people would have chanced upon every day of their lives. Also, it hadn't gone unnoticed, their lank haired, skinny female companion, although rather hollow eyed, had in fact the makings of quite a pretty face. They all four began to feel human again. What a contrast to that so recently endured.

Later that evening they were invited to take another look at the river. The ebbing waters had stranded the boats once again. Erdi had of course witnessed various tidal rivers, but even his first view of the Habren estuary hadn't been quite this dramatic. To Kairi, it was a whole new experience. She looked upon her escorts with wonder.

The following morning, fussed over and fed by hosts sad to see them go, they set out for the lefels. They had been told, keeping western hills to their right and maintaining a steady pace, should have them there by evening. This proved correct, but with the sun now just an orange glow in the west they were confronted by a tricky problem. They had left higher ground behind and before them was their objective, a sea of grass stretching away to the southwestern hills, but how were they to enter without a boat?

Smoke rising, two, maybe three slingshots distance from dry land, meant the likelihood of some form of dwelling crowning a habitable hump, but they had no way of reaching it.

Shouts and shrill whistles did no good and so Maddy's notion was tried. A signal fire, as used when drawing up the plan of home territory. Smoke rose dark-columned through the still evening air and by use of a cloak, distinct, individual clouds were sent curling up into what they hoped would be taken as a call for help.

It worked. A man appeared, barely afloat, his reed boat looking comically inadequate, with view ahead almost blocked by his knees, but steering towards them, he actually looked as confident as any marsh duck. Besides it was better than anything they had. As the ripples from a deft back-paddle settled, he eyed them suspiciously from a safe distance, swaying slightly above his own reflection.

Erdi signed, they were friends and called out the name Padlor. The man returned a completely blank look. The message was altered, 'We look for friend,' and then called the name, Padlor. Pointing to himself he shouted, "Erdi."

The man, flicking his boat around, disappeared back into the reeds. They sat down and waited. Light was fading fast and plans had been made to bed down, when the sudden clatter of ducks taking flight caused them to sit up. Heard coming from the depths of the tangle, was the unmistakeable sound of paddling. The prow of a wooden boat swished into view, and aboard with cheery faces, were Padlor and his son, Darew. Their boat reared up on meeting the bank and both jumped out.

"I can hardly believe it!" said Padlor. "Thought the man had been on the grog, but fair play, Goose said I'd find you here."

"Goose?"

"Yes," said Padlor laughing. "It's a name the ladies gave him. His arrival was as strange as his looks. They saw him suddenly loom from the reeds one day and one mumbled darkly, 'He wants following!' But he's harmless enough and at least he's out there each day, giving it his best. You have to respect a man for that."

They all laughed; Erdi was given a warm hug of greeting and he introduced his travelling companions. Easing themselves aboard, they were paddled along the threads of water, but at times their course boldly rasped through dense, dark barriers to gain open water far side. Then when gliding across a reed-girded mere, with ripples glinting fractured gold, Erdi felt Yanker give him a nudge.

Tucked small in the stern seat, Kairi, with a hand on Maddy's shoulder, stared up dreamily at the night sky, while her saviour, swaying gently with the motion of the boat, fought against sleep, jolting, blinking, to the point of awakening, only for heavy-lidded swaying to triumph once again.

With the moon now enshrouded, their destination appeared as a low hooded gathering; murky huts conspiring, until through gilt rags of cloud, cool pallid beams lit shimmering reflections; walkways; boats and beyond steeled glints, low drifting turf smoke.

Other than the villagers, of course wanting to know the fate of Mardi, (why hadn't he returned?) they were spared the usual barrage of questions on arrival and as food was ladled, Erdi broke the sad news. Seeing its effect, he placed his bowl down and arose to embrace Padlor's wife. She stood rigid, fists clenched, tears streaming down her face.

Make-do places to sleep were arranged and they were told more permanent arrangements would be made on the morrow. A frog chorus sang them into dreamland.

Of course, all wanted to know what had happened to Erdi since their last meeting, but I shan't trouble you with the details, *said the Teller*, other than say it took a number of sessions, for which he was grateful Blood Eagle was no longer there to sneer at. But before moving swiftly on, there are two things you'd better have knowledge of and both happened on the first morning of their stay. After wild locks had been trimmed, I hasten to add.

Firstly, with thoughts constantly of home, Erdi and Yanker were keen to discuss with Padlor how their objective could be achieved. They would of course need to be patient. Allow time for their pursuers to tire of their daily watch on the Habren and hopefully return home themselves. This would leave the river open as a way north, but by then they'd be struggling against swollen waters.

No need to wrestle with the problem further, however, for Padlor, telling them he had no trip planned until following spring, closed off that little trail of debate. So, as much as their hearts yearned for home, they decided the best plan was to winter in the lefels and take Padlor's offer of a boat to the mouth of the river Gwy early the following year. It was just well, as it happens, but I'll tell you all the details after this next little snippet of interest that happened on that first morning.

Fynon came visiting. She held an infant close and her face told all. She had been given the news regarding Mardi's sad parting. Her cheeks were tearstained and with eyes glistening at the attempt to smile, she offered up the child for Erdi to hold. He was puzzled, but none the less, cradled the little mite in the confident way experienced fathers manage and looking down was stunned to see a tiny version of his late brother smiling up at him.

"Mardi!" he said in shock.

"Yes, that is his name," replied Fynon.

"But it can't be. My brother was so shy. He couldn't have------"

"He most certainly did," she said with a smile, a little brighter this time.

Erdi shaking his head slowly in wonder and disbelief, held the young lad close and kissed his forehead. When lowered to the floor, the child was obviously keen to toddle back to his mother, but giving Erdi a backward glance, the scrutinising frown from the little lad could have been from his brother in miniature form.

Bet you didn't expect that did you? *Said the Teller*. It certainly shocked me, I can tell you.

His audience laughed.

But now I'll whisk you past all the settling in stuff, straight to what came to pass when Erdi next met up with Bastinas.

It was after the first fishing trip where they'd returned with trout and pike and had laughed at each other, faces covered in red ochre, daubed to repel the flies. Padlor told them the dye came from caves in the forest they'd just struggled through. Of course, he'd also heard tell, miners tunnelled there for iron, but with such information being jealously guarded, he'd never probed further. He knew for definite a rare purple dye was occasionally chanced upon in the depths, but that was for the exclusive use of those holding firm grip of the territory immediately west of the forest, the mighty Siluriks. But anyway, I digress.

When Erdi visited the hump of dry ground where Bastinas had his forge, the iron master happened to be working on a wheel rim, which as you can imagine, was a rare item in the middle of the fens. Padlor said, the pair of completed wheels would be delivered back to a smallholder on the mainland. This led Erdi to remark, "Those battle wagons I spoke of. They had similar wheels. If the carts had been of a much lighter, more mobile construction, I have to admit, they would have had us in severe difficulties."

They watched as Basty, tapping the rim into place, quickly quenched it, before it set the whole wheel alight. Amid the drifting steam, he listened to Padlor's translation of what Erdi had told him and as the air cleared, his face clouded slightly.

Now this translation business, *said the Teller*. From now on please assume translations have taken place, otherwise the whole thing becomes rather tedious.

Pausing, narrow-eyed and grinning, he added, I suppose you're thinking, 'Why didn't you tell us that back at the beginning?'

The abrupt outburst of laughter would have been heard way out beyond the palisade.

Returning to Bastinas; the man at last replied, such vehicles shouldn't have had hefty things like those just worked on. They should have been spoked. On seeing exchange of puzzled looks, he used a piece of charcoal, to draw a diagram on the board he used for calculations. He then drew separate components of the wheel and explained how all fitted together. Of course, it was unlikely he could have built such a thing, but he knew enough of the basics to be able to explain to a man who could and there was just such a person on the mainland, a man skilled in turning and joining.

So, this is how the whole venture started. On delivering the completed wheels inland, they did as planned, journeying on to a community where the master craftsman had his workshop. Transporting the wheels had been no easy matter by the way. The things strapped flat, had certainly put an empty boat to sit and on having been towed to solid ground, the customer had then to be sought, to haul them home by cart.

Making a spoked wheel was no easy matter either. It took three attempts before they got it right and four visits before they finally had a pair to take home. Just because a person knows what a thing should look like doesn't mean to say they actually know how to make it.

Hands up, *said the Teller.* How many here could say in all honesty, they know how to make a wheel?

There was much looking, one to another, but only two actually raised a hand.

Now I hope you two will be patient and allow me to explain to the others here, where exactly, their attempts went wrong.

They made the hub easily enough, cutting a block of oak, trimming its corners and turning it on a pole lathe. This was driven by a treadle hooked up to a whippy sapling outside the workshop window. The first problem came in estimating the number of spokes needed. It took Bastinas to dream up the solution, travelling a small wooden wheel around the outer surface of the hub, counting the number of turns, then rolling out the same distance on a plank of wood. This was sawn into equal widths and of course much longer lengths, (not easy when sawing down the grain) and when laid out around the hub, they fitted exactly. The spokes had equal male sections, fashioned either end and the hub had the female half of the joints chiselled to receive them. Each spoke was shaved to remove sharp corners, tapped home into the hub and Erdi was amazed to see a wheel taking shape. But this is where the fun started. The attempt to cut the outer sections, I think you call them fellies locally, were that bad they looked comical. It took a return home and two days of Basty knuckling his genius brain before the answer came.

A broad sheet of cowhide was the answer. As they returned armed with this, Erdi resisted the temptation to enquire how a wheel could be fashioned from such material. Better to watch and wait.

Basty, taking a line, measured the exact distance from hub centre to spoke end. When I say end, I mean the end prior to the tenon standing proud. From a central pin tapped through the cowhide he arced a line in a perfect circle, marking with charcoal as he went. An outer circle, about two fingers width, was described in the same fashion. The resulting circular shape, cut from the hide, was marked out into equal sections, which in turn were cut, giving them a number of near identical arced pieces of leather. These formed the patterns for the resulting fellies that were sawn from a length of ash boarding. Holes were drilled in their undersides to take the spoke ends and they watched expectantly as the craftsman tapped all the pieces into place. Erdi looked in wonder. The first time he'd seen such a wheel. "Give it a roll," he said.

It was given the gentlest of pushes. They all watched it roll, buckle and fall to bits.

"It just needs the iron rim," said Erdi, "Then it should hold together."

Basty shook his head. Somehow each felly needed cutting to be as one with its neighbour. As careful as they had been, the butting together had left wedge shaped gaps and somehow all the fellies needed jointing together. This was fine in theory, but they puzzled over how to joint in, the very last piece. It was back to the fens again, hoping Basty would come up with the answer.

He said the solution woke him in the night and was up early the following morning, keen to return and put it to the test.

This time, his genius brain had moved the process on further. Three original fellies were drilled for nailing together and when trimmed, created an arced shape he called a former. A complete set of new fellies, sawn from straight lengths of oak were steamed for each to be bent in turn around the wooden former and under tension, left to dry. The following day, alternate fellies, trimmed to length and drilled to receive spoke ends were tapped into place on the spokes and the remainder were left untrimmed, a little longer than necessary. When these were offered up against those already fitted, they were scribed exactly for the trimming, with the excess wood being whittled to form pegs. The fellies to receive these were removed for joint-holes to be drilled and the tenons on the spoke ends were each given a thin saw cut from top to bottom. All the fellies had been drilled clear through to take spoke tenons and the whole thing was eased together for wedges to be tapped into the spoke-end saw cuts, locking all together. With the new fellies being less likely to split across the grain as was feared regarding the earlier version and the hub finally drilled to take an axle, they at last had strong spoked wheel.

On the next visit, two identical wheels were collected. The joiner had refined their finish, rounding the spokes to a greater degree and chamfering the underside of the fellies. They now not only felt kinder to the touch, they were also kinder on the eye. They weren't large enough for a war cart, more suited to a dog cart in fact, but that wasn't the point. The whole point of course being, they now had the secret of how to make them.

Then came Basty's expertise. Using the same tool as the one made to travel around the hub, he measured the distance around the outer limits of the wheel and rolled out the identical distance on a flat iron bar. This was trimmed to length, then heated and hammered into a circle on the horn of his anvil. The ends were then heat-welded together. I make this sound simple. It wasn't. It takes incredible skill to achieve something that looks so simple and it also took much time and effort.

When the iron circlet was offered to the prone wheel, Erdi, having been in the company of enough skilled men to know when to hold his tongue, refrained from blurting, "It's not big enough." The ring of iron was buried deep in the furnace and when retrieved with tongs and tapped into place, it fitted perfectly. As the steam billowed, you could almost feel the quenching, pulling the whole construction tight. Nails were then driven through the holes in what you people now refer to as the tyre, to ensure, even after the inevitable shrinkage of the wood it encircled, it would remain secure. Basty, cloth in hand, not risking burns, lifted it upright and rolled it sweet as music out into the sunlight.

While all this had been going on, Madarch and Yanker had helped with turf cutting. Enough needed to be stacked to dry before onset of winter. They also assisted with reed cutting, the loaded boats being completely hidden beneath the stacks they towed home.

A number of houses and stores were re-roofed. Kairi helped with this and chores, such as wheat grinding, hide scraping, clothes washing and smoking of fish. If it weren't for the biting flies, life in the lefels would have seemed idyllic.

Other duties included, maintenance of the wooden walkways, clearing of reeds newly sprouting in the duck runs and of course fishing. They not only fished the freshwaters, but with weather permitting, ventured out onto the waves.

The duck runs were funnelling channels along which ducks were lured towards dry ground for netting. They used a number of these in rotation, being mindful not to wipe out the whole duck population.

Although initially, it might seem as if their world was just a few raised patches of dry land amid a sea of reeds and water, there was in fact quite a significant range of higher ground that made inroads from the east and also actual rivers, idling to the sea. It was in the latter that the best fishing was done. Trout caught in still waters don't always taste of mud, but they can do. I won't list all they caught and trapped, but the catch mainly consisted of trout, eel, chub, perch, pike and occasionally beaver. What they didn't consume and process themselves was traded for that not available in the marshes; wood, wool, hides, furs, certain edible plants and of course grain.

Also traded, were fish caught at sea especially mackerel. Even Kairi accompanied them on occasions, which she found a wonder, as she had never before, even seen the sea, let alone fished it. When as always, late in the year, mackerel no longer make themselves available, they ventured into deeper waters, angling for a large tasty fish, that as yet, Erdi had only seen the salted version.

Padlor's weighted line, had a marker tied and only when it had plummeted the full length, did they commence fishing. This particular species, apparently nosed around for prey in the cold depths of a trench running along the sea floor. They jigged their bait as if alive and were occasionally rewarded with a fish equal in length to an arm's span, from elbow to fingertip. Padlor had occasionally caught fish twice the size, but none of the like were hooked in Erdi's time there.

If you think Padlor showed marvellous skills of survival, for one not even native to this watery world, it was as if nothing compared to his skills at trading. It was a pleasure to see the relish with which he went to work when tackling a tricky deal. Erdi just wished he could somehow arrange a meeting between him and the man's boyhood companion, Trader.

Negotiations were conducted in the home village, but also on the mainland. Wherever they occurred, a noticeable change came over Padlor. He somehow seemed to emerge from his placid manner, to become more brisk and alert, confidence shining out of him. By comparison, those on the receiving end almost resembled stumbling dance partners. Although obviously keen to negotiate to his advantage, he instinctively knew how far to push a deal without leaving scars. After all it's not advisable to dominate to the extent the other party never wishes to repeat the experience. Some deals could be like banter between old friends, but witnessing others, Erdi actually felt sorry for those clearly out of their depth. He could sympathise, for it brought back memories of his first stumbling deal in Erin.

When eventually, a point of balance seemed to have been reached, Padlor would stare, giving the hand offered to seal matters, deep consideration, leaving Erdi almost squirming with embarrassment, feeling quite sorry for the genial owner of the proffered hand. With pause lengthening, he'd think, 'Surely you've reached a fair enough outcome, now Padlor.' But his friend would smile and commence the last little squeeze with words such as, "What if we just eased a few more of those into the proceedings? Or, "What would you say if we just throw in those others for luck?" The ensuing silence, when absorbing the shock of that final blow, would almost inevitably bring a sigh of resignation and hand-slap of capitulation, followed by a drink in celebration of such a mutually beneficial conclusion having been reached. With a tiny luck-token, handed back by Padlor and clink of ale mugs, one would have thought, they'd both had been battling on the same side.

Obviously there was the occasional show of indignation during proceedings, but nothing like the antics Erdi had witnessed from the Bleddi. These were altogether quieter, calmer folk.

Occasionally Padlor's bartering was done, not directly with the final customer, but by negotiating with a middle man, such as himself and these could be quite brisk affairs and not guaranteed to reach a successful conclusion. One time, on seeing Padlor slap a fellow trader on the back and declare, "You'll do very well with those," Erdi, having now learnt a little about the bartering arts, realised his friend had just settled an old score. How he wished he could somehow get Padlor and Trader together again.

As winter closed in, there came the long nights huddled around the turf fire, where stories were told, also legends of old and of course tales of what had befallen them during their own lifetimes. Details of certain escapades were requested time and again, favoured for their exciting or amusing content, but of utmost importance was the person's particular skill in the telling. A potentially engaging tale told in a dull manner never had a second hearing. Erdi became a regular contributor and also, with his mysterious tales from the east, Bastinas was constantly called upon.

You can imagine the scene can't you, *said the Teller leaning towards his audience in mock dramatic fashion. A hint of a smile accompanied;* With the mists in the marshes chilling the bones, transported to a world beyond wildest dreams, beyond frigid shores where the north wind moans to a land of wine, spices and mighty triremes. Wide sailed ships being hauled from shore, serried blades as one, dip the pallid azure. Men straining on oars, in banks of three, towards islands dotting that sparkling sea.

The Teller, eying a certain lady in the audience, continued, Thus, the people became lost in Basty's tales, fascinated by details of a world of warmth; a world of perfumes and succulent fruits; a world where worship was conducted, not in woodland groves, but within temples columned and roofed with timber, forerunners of what they now tell me, are wondrous buildings of columned stone. The sea was as warm as a midsummer pool and tides never rose or fell more than the height of a man. There was wine squeezed from grapes, oil pressed from olives; there were figs, pears, walnuts-----Yes they had heard it all before, but never tired of the detail.

Often his narrations were preceded by the urgent beseeching, "Basty? Tell us again, the one about the lion;" or, "Tell us about that battle at sea. Tell us about Troy." Bastinas was like a window into another world.

As the days grew shorter, talk turned to the fire feast, celebrating the dawning of the new year's sun. The meeting of the multitude was at the foot of the hill Erdi had seen on his first visit, rising so prominently from the fens. With dawn imminent, the chanting huddle of Seers wound its way up the spiralling terraces to herald the new sun.

Its first glow, ready to bulge from the horizon brought gasps of relief from those gathered below and in an orderly fashion all mounted the hill passing those descending, smiling serenely as if having received a blessing, dreamlike, almost in a state of grace.

Obviously some years were cloudy, but in that particular year they had the good fortune of a clear frosty morning. And incidentally, not one scrap of bronze was involved in the ceremony.

Now we turn to a few details of home. News had reached them, that apart from Bledunigol, the other three adventurers had survived, but no-one had the slightest idea where or how they would battle through the depths of winter.

Gwendolin, once again sheltered with her children at Trader's abode and being a woman temporarily alone drew unwanted attention from a certain male visitor. He of course always had an excuse for his visits, but both she and Gwedyll knew the real reason for his continual pestering and found him the most obtuse of blockheads, for each time, when seemingly on the point of leaving, rather than sense their blessed relief, he would always dream up something else to blather. Hints were dropped, but to no avail; the man was stubbornly persistent. It was when he said, "I am only thinking of you. You know you can rely on me if the worst happens," that the response became a little more decisive. Gwedyll had been that incensed, she'd flung a pot at his head.

Gathering the broken pieces, she said, "It's not that we've got pots to waste, Gwen, but I can't believe the cheek of the man." Her fury had been heightened by the fact he was a warrior from her own tribe.

Gwendolin, still clutching her baby daughter tight, had been quite taken aback. Then smiling to herself thought, 'There's no doubting she's the chieftain's sister.'

When news of Bledunigol's courageous last stand was delivered to Gwenethin, he stared unseeing, absorbing the fact he was a good man down, quite unaware that the messenger, already fearful of how the news would be taken, quivered before him, looking absolutely petrified. As said, the chieftain had never much cared for his lone wolf guide, but nobody else came close to matching his skills. With a certain amount of satisfaction, he thought, 'At least the man died a hero.' Then at last, on noticing the messenger's fearful white of eye and being baffled as to why he should still be hovering, he frowned and flicked dismissal as if to an annoying fly.

One morning, moving dark against an overnight's dusting of snow, a troop of Bleddi warriors rode in. They reported success at thwarting recent hostile incursions and were generously rewarded for their efforts. Having such a mobile force as a shield was now acknowledged as a stroke of genius. Also, being perfectly placed to glean news filtering up from the south, they had managed to discover the origin of the force that had swelled the ranks of the army arrayed against them that day on the Habren. They had been Silurik warriors.

Their chieftain, having been lured by promises of great pillage and plunder, had, against his better judgement, offered them as mercenaries. But as often happens when not defending home and family, with hearts not in the fight, they had not only returned in sad disarray, but depleted in number, leaving their disenchanted leader with not the remotest notion of repeating the arrangement. Good men had been lost for no gain whatsoever.

Another little gem of interest, oh you'll like this, *said the Teller*. The Bleddi felt certain their southern neighbour's ardour for raiding could well have been blunted. Temporarily that is, on account of their chieftain having passed on to the land of his ancestors. Apparently, he'd died in screaming agony as the stinking, gum abscess ate away his jaw and spread to his brain.

Early one morning, approaching her old home, Mara heard the sound of the most melodious choral singing rising from a neighbouring hut. She said to Penda on entering, "Those Y-Dewis might have some strange ways, but there's no denying they have brought some beautiful songs with them."

"Forever singing of the valleys of home," he grumbled. "If they miss them that much, why don't they do us a favour and go back there?" Well, that's the polite version of what he said.

Mara had called to see how her husband now fared. She obviously felt a fair degree of guilt at what was, let's be fair, abandonment. She didn't actually live with her admirer, but they were often seen together. Even though always ensuring her friend Brialla accompanied them, as said before, people knew what was really going on.

Much to Tam's annoyance, she set to, tidying up a few things.

"Leave it, I can do that."

Ignoring him, she proceeded to make Penda's bed. Straightening and looking around in case of anything else needing doing, her eyes alighted on the section allotted to the slave. Everything was tidily in its place and bed neatly made. To a woman's eye, it looked unslept in.

Turning meaningfully towards her husband, she waited and when his tremulous look did at last meet her gaze, she retorted, "Well! I'm sure the two of you have lots you need to talk about!"

The silence left behind hung like a pall, only broken when a pot boiling over required immediate attention.

Back in the lefels, winter had touched everything with its magic wand and frost sparkled white on every surface. The ice had frozen that thick it could be skated on. They all three tried the bone skates and once having learnt the art of staying upright, went skimming in exploration through the white wonderworld. They were joined by the young men of the village and Darew, Padlor's son, warned, 'stay well clear of the white plumed reeds bordering the iced broadways, as the surface within was often treacherous.'

They raced one another down the longest stretches and like boys once again, competed, clattering icicle shards at distant targets. Thin columns of smoke rose to the pale blue heights and villagers, whether on scattered islands or up in stilt-houses plied them with food and drink. In dark places beneath those lofty dwellings, steady melting of night's frost plopped onto sheer ice, thin enough to lacerate. The food offered to those awaiting, safe on sturdier ice, was lowered in baskets from a walkway. Occasionally, when cheerily returning home from such forays, healthy glow heightened by the sinking sun, in the hope of softening criticism regarding dereliction of duties, their catch of fish or duck would be held up.

The glint of excitement with which Kairi welcomed the homecoming, didn't go unnoticed and women's faces softened when watching, whose arm she always clung to.

As night closed in, the evening star, bright to the west, also peered down as if taking an interest. Basty knew it as Hesperus.

Now I will take you forward, a little, into early spring, *said the Teller*. All was being made ready for the trip up the coast. They would be going home at last. It was intended that Fynon would accompany them, taking her son to meet his grandparents and to pay their respects at his father's grave.

That was before a trader came calling. He was first of the year and bore the news, the way up the Habren had finally been blocked. All those now travelling through the gorge were relieved of a portion of cargo for the privilege of continuing. The problem this posed, would be far greater than suffering what amounted to robbery, for they would have their new secret aboard, a pair of spoked wheels. These in all certainty, would not only be taken from them, but copied for fitting to battle wagons, for use against Erdi's own people. For this reason, they would not be returning by way of the Habren gorge. They would be forced to leave the main river and negotiate a tributary, the Tamesa. It led the way to a well-worn ridgeway track heading north. This was too arduous and hazardous a route for an infant. Erdi had already lost his brother, he didn't dare risk losing another, who had so recently found a way into his heart, his brother's son.

Erdi told Fynon, once the Bethegol tribesmen had been driven from the gorge, he would return for them. On seeing her pained look of disappointment, with a hug, he said, "I promise." Reaching down to tickle his nephew, a move guaranteed to send him into a fit of giggles, he repeated, "I promise."

A little face looking up said, "Again." Watching the fingers poised, ready to dive under his armpit, the little lad, shaking with laughter and a shoulder raised against cheek, braced himself.

Seeing Fynon's wistful look, Erdi pointing to the burgeoning shape of the young lady in their company, added, "The trip will be hard enough as it is.". There was no hiding it, Kairi was quite visibly pregnant.

338

Now I know you're probably thinking, 'What a fuss over a pair of wheels,' said the Teller. To you they are commonplace, but what you have to remember is; at the time we're talking about, nothing like them had ever been seen before. Well not on these shores anyway. Added to their burden, was a short axle with collars and split-pins, gifted by Bastinas, essential for furnishing the wheels to a cart, once the opportunity arose. The old genius had a glint of tears when handing these to Erdi.

It was a prelude to the much weeping and sadness as they finally departed, early one morning, to catch the tide that eased them out over the sandbar to the sea beyond. It's always harder for those left behind. Aboard the boat, however, three held a hidden thrill. They were going home.

The first night was spent camped on the sands of the Habren estuary and next day Padlor dropped them off on the western shore while he continued up the river Gwy to ensure all was safe for them to approach the small port. A rider was sent to give the all-clear and they completed the journey late morning. They received warm greetings from the headman and were reunited with their old friends the two boats. He would take nothing for their retrieval, nor for their storage.

The altered shape of Kairi drew a few glances and folk now noticed the once skinny girl with the haunted look had blossomed into quite a pretty young lady. She had a healthy tan, her hair shone and something sparkled in her eyes, as it did in those of the swarthy young man, who tended to her needs.

They dined that night in the clifftop hut, overlooking the river and not only did Padlor part with the wherewithal in exchange for the food, he also gifted them a pair of beaver pelts on the dockside the following morning.

Erdi, feeling a little overwhelmed and embarrassed, said, "Padlor, I can't accept these. They're far too valuable. We already have salt-fish to trade. You know these pelts are like gold."

But, unwilling to take no for an answer, he insisted, saying they could well be in need of them. They were light to carry, instantly tradeable and there was no telling what difficulties might lie ahead. There followed, fond farewells and messages called across the water,

"Tell Fynon I'll be back. I won't let her down."

"I will."

"Thank you Padlor."

"Keep those well-hidden," meaning the wheels.

It was a dull morning, but to them it seemed beautiful. As they caught the surge up the Habren there came the thrill, at last they were on their way home.

Chapter Sixteen

Erdi and Yanker paddled the one boat as it now seemed only natural that Madarch and Kairi should share the other. They were working against the current, but up the broadest stretch and around the most southerly lazy loops, they had the tide with them. In the latter part of the day and into early evening it was slower work against the current, but there had been no recent rain to add zest to the flow and the thought of home drove them on.

They tied up at the dock Erdi remembered well. It sat below the settlement where he had won the flitch of bacon. This time there was no sign of the man he'd defeated, as Pegger, like many that had gathered there that evening, was not a member of this particular community. The headman remembered Erdi, but not being amongst those resenting his victory at the time, made them all welcome. They offered a trade of salted fish for their food, but it was waved away.

The following morning, stiff from their exertions of the previous day and knowing that apart from a little help on the first stretch, there would be no tidal pull, they decided on being slightly less ambitious. Middle day, where a large river flowed into the Habren from the east, they paused to haul in fish and then late afternoon, beneath the shadow of hills ranging to the immediate west, Erdi called a halt.

He gathered fuel, Madarch helped Kairi scour amongst the plant life and while Yanker cleaned the trout they'd managed to hook, Erdi coaxed a fire to life.

Their mood might not have been so relaxed had they known they were camped beneath the main Bethegol settlement, the very tribe now controlling the Habren gorge. They saw a fire's glow that night, pulsating on the western heights, but had no idea of the significance of those adding fuel to it. As is often the case, sheer ignorance brought them the luck of the nonchalant. Had they known what threat hovered so close, fate would almost certainly have punished such audacity.

They continued north and by late morning on the following day, blithely steered into the Tamesa river. Loops and shoals slowed them, but spirits were lifted by birdsong echoing through the woods and by the vast carpets of bluebells, almost glorying, as patches in turn, were soft-bathed in sunlight. Although narrow, the river allowed steady progress and they spent the night at the point where it alters course, flowing from the north. They had passed isolated farmsteads, but apart from searching stares, had felt no hint of hostility.

They struggled through the following morning, hauling their boats over rapids, shingle and fallen trees and at middle day, reached the point where the Tamesa now flowed from the west. The work was almost a pleasure through the rest of the day. Every stroke of the paddle, every drag of the boats over shoals, was taking them home.

Along a peaceful reach of the Tamesa, with the warm gold of evening flickering between branches, they called a halt and peering beyond dappled shallows, could see on the eastern bank, an ancient barrow, at peace beneath the trees.

Efforts to set up camp were halted by the sound of children's laughter and a dog barking and reboarding, they eased the boats across the stream. A well-worn path threading through a wood cleared of tangle by foraging animals, led to a small settlement and on nearing they heard the clear music of cymry being spoken.

Kairi's face instantly lit up. They were made welcome and at last dared believe, home was within reach. The villagers offered food and shelter, plus local knowledge regarding the territory to the north.

Late morning the following day, just as described, the Tamesa altered course flowing from the north and they followed it as far as a small palisaded settlement perched on a hill amid a pretty valley. Information given the night before, told them, this was the place where both boats and river, needed bidding farewell. The route they sought, leading towards the ridge-way, went directly north, whereas, continuing up the Tamesa, would take them in the wrong direction, west.

They'd discussed with the headman, the previous evening, their notion of stocking up at the next settlement, before continuing north and the glint of mirth accompanying his reply, implied there was something he was not telling them. Then his chuckle, as he added, "I wish you luck," had a definite ominous ring.

The boats were nosed in alongside various craft, tugged aslant by the current and although all were perfectly serviceable, none had that blend of practicality and pertness, engendered in their own. Madarch and Kairi remained on watch, while the cousins took the steep ascent towards the hilltop settlement

If the locals of this particular community wished to be understood, there wasn't really a problem, but when talking amongst themselves in their own version of cymry, it was almost impossible to understand a thing said. Holding court, centre village, was a man whose build suggested he'd not encountered problems in life obtaining food and from the moment Erdi caught sight of his haughty manner, he knew him to be the man they'd need to be dealing with. He sensed it was not going to be easy.

In fact, the initial meeting said it all. When told of the hospitality received downstream, the look returned said, 'Well don't expect that here.'

Erdi's attempt to interest him in a trade for their boats was dismissed out of hand and turning to his cousin, he said out of earshot, "Can you believe it? That smug, bloated, lard-bag, says they have boats enough."

Yanker, amused by the reminder of healthy disdain for the pompous so common in their youth, responded breezily. "Oh no, cousin. Please convey to His Lardiness, one can never really have enough boats. That's what I always say."

"We can't just abandon them here, Yanker. What sort of idiot dismisses a deal, without even looking at it?"

"The one standing right in front of you, but we've beaten better than him, Erdi. And he better not think he's getting them for nothing. I'd rather torch the things."

On these borderlands, many quite happily switched from one tongue to another, sometimes not even realising they were doing it and like most, could also read body language. The one they assumed to be the headman, had not actually overheard the little exchange, but definitely caught the whiff of derision and eyeing them meaningfully, had every intention of making their stay as difficult as possible. In view of which, no matter how a trade for their boats might be dressed, he was determined to show no interest and felt certain, his proud stance with chest out and look of eminence, would be taken as an embodiment of strong resolve.

This is where, absolutely delighting in such displays of grandeur, those wicked little spirits come into play, for as luck would have it, one of the villagers having got drift of the deal, dared to voice an interest and the headman, although peeved at having had his authority undermined, loitered, interested in the outcome.

If one were to be unkind, *said the Teller*, he could be likened to a child, only wanting a toy when another's playing with it, but let's give him benefit of the doubt and say, he possibly relished interfering, or more likely, was angling for a slice of risk-free gain. For whatever reason, that strong resolve was fast dissolving.

They all walked down to the river and on approaching the craft, the man's vexation, at a suitable scathing comment not springing to mind, was heightened by seeing his kinsman's obvious delight, once catching first sight of them.

Yanker, not taking his eyes off the headman and considering what they had been through, feeling understandably protective towards the boats, muttered, "Erdi. One word. Just let him say one word. -------I swear, he'll be in that water."

On a closer look at the craft and knowing criticism would now only show as ignorance, the headman, wisely holding disparaging instincts in check asked, "So what's that you've got covered up? What's in the boats?"

"Just things we need. Nothing of importance. It's only the boats themselves we're interested in trading."

"Pity they're not of wood."

"No Yanker!" Erdi, physically restraining his cousin, flashed a calm-down look.

"What were you hoping for them?" was asked, not realising how close he'd come to a ducking.

"A small pony."

"Now I know they're mad!" Grabbing his companion, he added, "Come on, these idiots are wasting our time."

"I have a small pony I'm willing to trade," came the fragmented entreaty from one being so unwillingly dragged.

The headman, now absolutely incensed, manhandled the startled villager to pin him tall on his toes up against a tree and was just about to give him a blasting, when Yanker's admonishing, "Now steady on. There's no need for all **that!**" pierced like a sharp pin.

Although deflation was instant, embodied by his captive sliding to a more comfortable posture, it didn't prevent the glare and raised fist indicating what lay in store if he dared join in the laughter. Following a muttered exchange and token attempt at pulling the man's collar straight, the headman span round to ask, "Right, that's that sorted. Now what have **you** to offer, if I should happen to allow this deal to go ahead?"

"What a way to carry on," chided Yanker with merry contempt, followed by, "Haven't you forgotten something? We've not seen the horse yet."

Just as Yanker had commented, it all seemed very strange, but many things encountered when travelling don't appear to make sense.

While the cousins were taken back up the hill to the settlement, Madarch and Kairi remained to guard the boats, instincts telling them there was a fair chance of the headman returning to snoop amongst their belongings if left unguarded.

The pony, although a little long in the tooth, turned out to be exactly what was needed and after its owner had returned for a thorough inspection of the boats there came the hand slap, confirming the deal. Erdi, realising on occasions, for the greater good, pride needed swallowing, had sacrificed two of their salted fish to placate the headman for it all to go ahead.

Offering the same to the new boat owner, brought food and lodgings, but of utmost importance, it also gained his full co-operation. Not only was bad weather brewing, prompting him to say, 'stay as long as you like,' he was also more than willing to introduce Erdi to a man versed in the art of shaping and assembling various wooden components into a thing of immense benefit and not only that, keep his mouth shut. He, like most, harboured deep contempt for their conceited townsman, who had assumed such authority.

All was explained to the craftsman and after three days, during which it absolutely lashed it down, word was sent that the job was complete. He had also hafted them, two bronze axe-heads. They'd had to sacrifice their two perfectly good spears for the trade, but Erdi sensed axes rather than spears would serve them better on the remainder of the journey.

Departing north down the broad sweep of trail, the following morning, leading their pony and small cart, all were in a particularly light-hearted mood. The gifted artisan, who had dropped everything to construct the vehicle, was now the proud owner of a beaver pelt. All their things were aboard and smiling up at Kairi, atop the small load, Yanker suggested she give the headman a wave.

He was standing by the palisade gate, chop-fallen, looking truly stunned as if witnessing a contrivance from another world. Not only that, they'd had the affrontery to conjure it up, in his own village, right under his nose.

How those local spirits must have chortled as Kairi called, "Enjoy the fish!"

The cousins exchanged surprised looks. The girl was beginning to show true spirit. Maddy of course, had seen her worth from the start.

The trail was muddy and the going slow, but at least they were unburdened. What their boats had carried was now on the cart, or in fact was part of the cart.

The grey sky had given way to a pleasant day by the time they bid the Tamesa farewell. Its flow was unrecognisable and even had

347

they required it, the turbid, tumbling waters after so much rain would have made immediate progress up it impossible.

The trail now followed a tributary flowing from the north. Seeing a scanty, one-horse settlement on the western bank, they eased the small cart over a log bridge, to pause for refreshment and directions. Both were freely given and with some enthusiasm I have to add, for the wheels on their vehicle couldn't have brought more open-mouthed wonder, had they dropped from the sky.

They were advised to keep to the stream flowing first from the north and then west, until sighting a trail on the opposite bank. This would take them up to the ancient ridgeway. They did exactly as advised and with the sun going down beyond dark north-ranging hills, rested the night.

Their pony seemed totally at ease in their company, even though it now had a new name, Boats. Feeling utterly torn at bidding their faithful craft farewell, the name they'd dubbed the item of exchange, seemed only apt and fitting.

By morning the waters had calmed sufficiently to allow them over the ford and they began the gradual climb up onto the ridge, clearing with axes where necessary. The track was well defined running between dense bracken, gorse and stunted trees. In places wild ponies grazed and high above, buzzards and eagles soared.

Giving a low spread of encroaching gorse a swipe with his axe, Erdi said, "When I think of the lengths we went to, to rid ourselves of axe-heads and here we are trading a fine pair of steel spears, to get two of the things back again."

Middle day, the track edged a narrow valley to the west. A small defended farmstead, neatly perched on a natural terrace, stood directly across on the far side and a little further, protruding clear above the expanse of a deep wooded valley, stood the prominent humps of two hills in line, the nearest having smudges of smoke drifting off the summit. Brave souls still obviously clung to life up there, despite recent years of poor weather.

Much further north rising from the flat plain, standing out from the sea of green as if awaiting arrival of the other nearby protrusions, resembling two massive beasts from a former age slowly plodding towards it, was Y-Pentwr, Yanker's home.

They rested awhile. It was a beautiful day and all reclined atop springy blueberry bushes, abounding in the clearer patches. There were only two huts encountered up there in the wilds and those emerging spoke a strange incomprehensible dialect.

The ridgeway followed, actually straddled what was called a mynd and to distinguish it from all the other mynds dotted around that part of the world, in view of its significant length, it was not surprisingly called, the Long Mynd.

From off its northern promontory, they could actually see the flatlands of home and the impulse was of course to press on, but having chanced upon a drover's hut they decided to waste a little daylight and take advantage of its shelter for the night. Their water supply was replenished from a nearby brook and as if not wanting to be left out, Boats, breaking off from grazing, plodded over to stir up mud and noisily partake.

In a small upstream pool, Kairi gave their last piece of salted fish a good swill. It wasn't ideal, it could have done with a day's soaking, but it was all they had and dining off it once boiled, drained, then simmered again, and with home territory finally in sight, it tasted delicious. Still a bit too salty, but delicious.

The following day, they came down off the heights and keeping a wary eye on the weather, managed to reach Habren ford before the deluge arrived. The river had calmed enough to allow a ferry crossing, but with what was billowing from the southwest, it would soon be raging again. The ferry crossed once for them, once for the cart and Boats as they do, made his own way across.

"I don't suppose there's any danger of payment this time?" said the ferryman. "Or is it to be, Gwenithen's seal again?"

Erdi, making a pretence of fumbling amongst clothing, said, "I've forgotten it." He'd in fact purposely left it behind. Not a good thing to be in possession of considering the territory they had ventured through.

All laughed, then rushed inside to avoid the deluge. Food was provided, they were warm, they were safe, but as the rain drummed down and the river swirled wildly below, they had the frustration of knowing they were so tantalizingly close to home and yet unable to continue.

The ferryman of course, was eager to know what adventures had befallen them, but in view of their iron ore discovery, Erdi didn't dare tell him. He trusted the man, but even so, it wouldn't look good if word did happen to leak out before Gwenithen had knowledge of the details.

The two axes were more than enough reward for all they'd been given and to deflect the man's gentle probing, Erdi imparted details regarding the cart's construction. As said before, no wheels such as these had ever been witnessed in the area before.

Leaving bright and early next morning, they reached home, middle day. Well that's not strictly true, first stop was Trader's place and what he thought about their horse, was best kept to himself. Surprisingly, from unpromising beginnings, having had Delt's help, he'd turned into quite a fair judge. He was, however, itching to ask about the cart, but held back, wisely waiting until the flood of emotion had subsided.

I'll leave you to imagine the tears of joy and rapturous welcome, *said the Teller.* The searching questions; the imploring of not to leave home again; the astonishment that they all looked so thin. Well, all except one.

Gwedyll, pointing to a certain stomach, asked, "So, which one of you did that?"

Madarch, slightly bashful, admitted it was he who, spirits willing, was about to be the father.

There followed congratulations, plus a certain amount of relief at his answer and the tale was told of how their lives were saved by Kairi's brave actions and the scout's extraordinary sacrifice.

Trader, his head full of questions, was at last able to ask about the cart, but it was all extremely rushed, for the prime duty was to report all to Gwenithen. Word would have leaked out they were back and he was not one to take kindly to the fact, he'd been kept waiting.

As they rode from Trader's place, they could still hear Gwedyll and Kairi chattering away excitedly in their native tongue, the latter sounding as happy as a bird set free. Hurrying on their way to their meeting with Gwenithen, the trail took them past Erdi's abode, causing him to shudder at how quickly a house standing empty loses that glow, that hidden essence that engenders home.

On being ushered into the hall, Erdi had hoped to gauge the man's mood. It was difficult. There was no hint of displeasure, but there again there seemed no glimmer of a smile.

They all three, bowed.

"So, the wanderers return."

A long silence ensued.

"So, tell me. What did you find?"

Erdi, stepping forward, gave a detailed report of where they had travelled, what they had discovered regarding iron and how

Bledunigol had met his end. By this time, Gregoth, their training officer, having been sent word, slipped in to join them. He had of course noticed the wheels on the cart outside, but bided his time in silence. His patience was rewarded. Erdi apologising for their delayed return, explained the reason and then said it had actually turned out to be a blessing in disguise. Rather than go into lengthy descriptions, he asked, would his lord and master permit him to actually show what a man's ingenuity had created?

The sight of the little cart with its wheels almost begging to be raced across the terrain, altered the mood entirely. Gwenithen clapped his hands and absolutely beamed. There was just about room to comfortably seat one of such generous girth, for apart from their capes and one other small item of interest, all had been left at Trader's.

As the chieftain clambered aboard and plonked himself down, the cart rocked and Boats stirred, but apart from that, all held firm and on his insistence, Erdi ran the pony at a trot to the end of the village and back. The strange sight of their mighty leader, lashing an invisible whip and grinning gleefully, as if having stolen a child's toy, drew people out to stand and stare. Erdi just hoped, none thought it had been his idea. It felt quite unseemly.

Yanker's brooding look in judgement, indicated he obviously shared similar feelings. He couldn't imagine his own chieftain, Haraul doing such a thing, not even if worse the wear from drink.

Once all were back inside, composure supposedly restored, Gwenithen leant down from his royal seat and said, "Let me see if I have this right. First you journeyed on the Habren heading south."

Erdi said, "Yes sire."

"Then you crossed the mountains to the sea."

Erdi nodded.

"Following that, your travels took you down the coast, am I right?"

"Yes sire."

"You then took the boats inland, up over the mountains to receive the benefit of the Gwy's attentions, before taking a jaunt down the Gwy river."

"It wasn't-------"

"It was there you discovered the source of iron, but rather than return home directly with the information, you took the notion to winter in western fenlands."

"We had no choice, my lord."

"Quite a journey by any standards." His face suddenly broke into a playful grin, "So where is it?"

"Where is what, my lord?"

"My present."

Gregoth stifled a laugh. Yanker hadn't understood the request, the exchanges having been in cymry, but had grasped enough from Gwenithen's energised manner and his cousin's reaction, that the man in power was exerting it for his own entertainment. Madarch had caught the gist, but remained expressionless. He had long ago absorbed the lesson; it wasn't wise for forest folk to draw attention to themselves. It rarely worked to their advantage.

"I'm sorry I don't understand." Erdi replied, truly at a loss. "We have returned with an adaptation of the wheel----"

"Yes, very good, but that's military stuff. That's for Gregoth here." Thumping his knee with a fist and almost bouncing in his chair, he demanded, "I want my present!"

"I'm sorry my lord, it never crossed my mind-----"

"You mean to say you've been all that way and you've not brought me back something in tribute?"

For a while Erdi stood there stunned, wearing an expression of sheer disbelief, but then sighing at the fact he'd been left little choice, said, "One moment my lord. If you'll excuse me." He'd intended to surprise Gwen with it later when alone, but needs must and he returned with the beaver pelt.

Gwenithen beamed, "Now that's more like it." He was of course in one of his playful moods. Yanker who had grown to admire Gregoth, watched the old warrior's downward glance and slow shake of head. From what he knew of the man, he guessed the reaction to have been, partly out of disbelief, but mainly out of embarrassment.

On later being informed all their military equipment had been lost in the recent venture and having been badgered by both Gregoth and Prince Heddi, the chieftain gave the matter serious consideration. Three days later all troops were summoned to form a guard of honour along the length of the arrow field. Erdi, Yanker and Madarch were instructed to lead the pony and cart between the lines to where Gwenithen, Gregoth and other notables awaited. Recognising a number of faces of his own people amongst the ranks, Erdi was mildly surprised by the extent to which the two tribes had merged.

They were ordered to kneel and then rise and approach in turn.

Gwenithen pulled himself up to full regal height, "For extraordinary valour and initiative, I present to Erdikun-----"

It was one of the finest swords Erdi had ever seen. Yanker was awarded the same. The sword presented to Madarch was not of the same quality, but a sword no less and whether he liked it or not, Maddy was now considered a warrior.

Thinking back to his feeling of repellence when first seeking his friend out in that wild woodland camp, it simply staggered Erdi, that he had managed to stumble across a character that gifted, he likened it to being as rare as chancing upon a gemstone in a dung-heap and he reasoned, just as had happened through his own winding trails through life, it doesn't matter where a person starts, it's what is made of the opportunities that counts.

Gwenithen, standing proud, with chest out, called to all, "I cannot praise these men more highly. They are a credit to us all." On his repeated upsweep of arms, cheers erupted. He was not an easy man to gauge. One day like a child, on another, like a statesman.

At least his two eldest sons were consistent. They had murder in their hearts, but would bide their time, for their father would not live for ever.

Yanker was of course keen to return home to Y-Pentwr, but before given leave to do so, was summoned once more. Gwenithen had one last task for him. His chieftain, Haraul, was formally invited to attend a council of war, the enemy being the Bethegol. Reward for sharing in such an enterprise would be the regaining of free passage down the Habren. As an extra inducement, the possibility of a trade mission for iron, was dangled.

Things now became feverish; attention being focussed on war cart construction. An elite needed to master the art of driving them and horses required training to pull them. Each cart had a whip-man and an armed warrior. They were light and incredibly mobile, making those they had encountered on the Habren seem ridiculously cumbersome by comparison.

Erdi was summoned one day for a meeting with Gregoth. The old warrior needed a clear idea of where the Gwy and Habren rivers ran and also a rough notion as to the extent of the forest holding the iron ore. Erdi did his best, but then suggested, a clearer picture might be gained if Madarch added his contribution. He was sent for and without seeming to have to think about it, using charcoal on a tally board, drew a map showing the course of the two rivers. He hazarded an inspired guess at the portion of the Habren he'd never travelled on and by adding a large three-sided blob at the Habren-Gwy confluence, did the same as regards the forest where iron had been found.

"Sorry it so rough," he said, handing over the tally board with a smile.

Gregoth, looking at Erdi said, "I think we have found our new scout."

Madarch was rewarded with a horse and the promise of his own house on the edge of the growing settlement. His first assignment took him to the Habren gorge. He was gone a number of days and reported back with details of the small force occupying a well defended site on the eastern heights. From this stronghold they commanded control of the river. He had done well and Erdi was proud of him.

Just briefly, there are some other details you should know, *said the Teller*. Prince Heddi was coping well with the administrative duties, Erdi had been so keen to relinquish. He didn't know it at the time of course, but it would stand him in good stead for what lay ahead. Vanya was thrilled to hear there was now a new little Mardi in the world, as of course was Mara. Even Penda's face broke into a smile when told.

Once the Y-Pentwr chieftain, Haraul arrived, battle tactics were discussed. The two elder princes were keen to lead a small force, to immediately sweep the enemy from their redoubt on the Habren. Old Gregoth, however, advised caution and time to assemble a strong fighting force, an essential portion of which, he advised, should be comprised of cavalry and the devastating new weapon, war carts. He explained at length, the battle plan he had in mind, but his words, 'caution and planning' didn't fit in with Gwenithen's mood of the day. Even his final phrase, 'Guile then impact,' failed to register. Haraul gave it his full backing, but the princes' dash and enthusiasm suited their father's mood that day and the wiser plan was not considered. It should have been. The elder brother was brought back tied across his horse, a corpse, by which time Haraul had returned to Y-Pentwr in disgust, even declining to attend as guest of honour at the funeral.

Now at last, in the wake of such a disaster, Gregoth found himself listened to. Not least by Gwenithen. First, however, he requested permission to deploy the new scout on a little trip south of Habren gorge. Madarch returned three days later with the details and a meeting with Gwenithen was requested. Erdi was also asked to attend.

Gregoth began, "You remember Sire, when living up in the mountains, we hunted bear?"

Gwenithen nodded, "What of it?"

"Did we ever enter the arth's cave."

"Of course not. Never. The bear came out when hungry and we were waiting."

"This is how the force on the Habren ought to be handled. Rather than risk more lives attacking directly, we stop supplies reaching them. Starve them out and we'll be waiting."

"Then we smite them."

"No Sire. We let one pass through our lines and drive the rest back into their lair."

"But that defeats the object."

"Indeed not, Sire. They will then be working for us. They will be our bait."

"Yes, go on."

"Well Sire, incensed on hearing their men are trapped and dying, the Bethegol will swarm out like angry wasps. We'll be there waiting for them. The scout has returned with details of open ground south of the gorge, perfect for deploying the new weapon."

"Why wasn't all this mentioned before? I've lost a hot-headed fool of a son because of it."

"I am truly sorry Sire. Did I not mention, guile and then impact, earlier?"

Erdi supressed a smile. He was later entrusted with the task of gaining support for the plan from the Y-Pentwr chieftain. Haraul was not keen, to say the least, but with Erdi's assurance, all would be meticulously organised this time and Yanker averring his full trust in the old warrior, Gregoth, the chieftain finally acquiesced.

Once sufficient war carts had been constructed, the first stage of the plan was rolled into action. The trap around the gorge had already been set and the main force was assembled to advance to the Habren. They forded low waters and advanced south, to take cover in the forest awaiting further orders.

Madarch roving ahead, returned with details of two hamlets lying between them and the intended battlefield. The occupants were taken in, unharmed, but prisoners none the less. They could not allow word of their presence to leak out.

On being told, rather than one, two of the beleaguered Habren force had been allowed to escape, all moved up to the forest edge and waited. Madarch, now constantly roving ahead of the army, returned with news of latest enemy movements. Just as predicted a huge force of Bethegol warriors had left the hills and was advancing north.

At this point Gregoth gave the order to advance beyond the forest and behind a defensive line of stakes, all set up camp in the open. A number of strategic gaps had been left in the stake wall.

Later that day a Bethegol scouting party emerging from the trees far side of open ground, pulled up short at the sight confronting them and whipping their mounts around, returned to report. That night the two armies camped no more than five slingshots apart.

The following morning, blaring war horns signalled the advance and seemingly, without any notion of a battle plan, the enemy swarmed towards them. There had probably been a few wise words of caution, but as often happens, bravado had beaten reason and the Bethegol cavalry thundered towards them ahead of the main force. When greeted by spears and stakes, attacking horses reared in terror, reeling back to collide with the onrush of foot-soldiers. Adding to this mayhem, home ranks parted to unleash the war carts, horse-manes flying, wheels whirring and gleaming steel axle blades quivering deadly menace. They swept amongst the disorganised mob hither and thither like demonic scythes through wheat, causing complete havoc. Warriors aboard, flighting arrows and javelins, chose the moment to leap and wreak carnage on foot, before being whisked away in the carts to safety.

Above the clash of battle, wailing horns announced general advance and like a spring tide surging up the Habren, their main force was thrown into the fray. In complete disarray, the enemy was driven back, stumbling over their own dead until finally, knowing the day was lost, they fled the field in wild panic. Mounted troops cantered in pursuit deftly lopping off heads or impaling the least fleet of foot. It turned into a complete rout.

Captured officers and the half-starved Habren garrison were ransomed in return for acknowledgement of free use of the Habren river. The Bethogol chieftain, receiving the ultimate humiliation, was forced to grovel on his belly in tribute to Gwenithen and his brother chieftain, Haraul. Hero of the day was the next in line to Gwenithen's crown. His actions, creating mayhem in his war cart that day, would be related in battle poems recited around winter fires for years to come.

So, at last the way was now clear for Erdi to keep his promise to Fynon. Permission was granted, supplies were loaded and paddled by four men at arms, the boat Gwendolin was steered by Erdi serenely down the Habren. They were hampered by two days of bad weather, but other than that made it in good time down to the lefels, where thanks to knowledge gained on those numerous fishing trips, Erdi had no problem finding entry or negotiating the waterways.

Whilst away on his mission, three things of significance happened. Maybe it was the flush of victory or maybe the truth sinking in at last, Gwenithen decided the fish pools needed proper management and Penda was put back in charge. He and Tam went about the business of restocking and Penda looked the happiest he'd done in years. He and Tam worked well together and at last there seemed to be a purpose to his life.

The second piece of significance was Trader's change of fortune. I have already mentioned, that having recovered from that unpromising start regarding horse flesh, he had now become a recognised judge of it, but that was only the beginning, for with war carts coming to such prominence and realising swift mountain ponies were ideal for pulling them, he was not slow in procuring an exclusive deal with the Bleddi. From being a highly respected trader, he was soon to be raised to an eminence, even he didn't expect.

The third thing started out as nothing more significant than a wildcat kitten. Heddi mentioned to Vanya one day that his brother had taken possession of one, supposedly as a pet. Vanya, of course was incensed and asked Heddi to accompany her with the intention of having serious words regarding the matter. The kitten was almost certainly descended from her childhood friend Minchy and Vanya was determined to see it set free.

Marching in to where the royal personage, next in line to the crown reclined, she tore into him with a ferocity of such splendour, it could not have been bettered by the mother of the wild thing she was determined to save.

He actually looked quite taken aback, replying rather lamely, that the small creature amused him.

"Aren't you aware of how dangerous they can be? You'll never tame it. It would rather die than be tamed."

Recovering a little composure, he replied, "You dare tell me, one who has vanquished multitudes in battle, that a tiny thing such as this, is dangerous?"

Glaring, he ventured a hand inside the cage to haul out the small bundle of fur. It was immediately jerked back. Sucking a finger, he said, "It bit me through to the bone." They all watched as the kitten scampered to freedom.

By the time Erdi had returned with Fynon and his nephew, the prince was dead. His refusal to contemplate amputation of his sword arm, had allowed the poison to spread and kill him. Prince Heddi was now first in line to Gwenithen's crown and the latter treated Vanya like the daughter he'd never had.

Mara of course treated her daughter in law similarly and tears of joy flooded at first sight of her grandson. At the family gathering later, Fynon, although puzzled by decidedly unconventional living arrangements; such as, the small, strange man constantly shadowing her father-in-law, while another, referred to as uncle, attended to Mara as would a husband; once realising no-one seemed perturbed and in fact, treated it as being perfectly normal, she simply shrugged and went along with it, allowing herself and young Mardi to be drawn into the loving embrace of the family.

On a sudden suggestion from Vanya, a wooden ladder was produced and climbing it, to root in the thatch, she descended holding two wrapped bundles. From the first, young Mardi was handed the severed rib bone and with a piece in each hand, he didn't drum as most children would, but examined them as if deep in thought. On first sight of the object unwrapped from the second bundle, the revered remains of Elsa were gently laid down and his face glowed with wonder, as the rings of bronze were pulled up to form the shape of the Seer's hat. The very one his father had worn. It was as if the spirits had contrived everything to come full circle.

So, *said the Teller*. My story is complete. Obviously there are more threads to their lives left to unravel, but isn't that just the same as with all our lives, ever changing, interweaving? I give hearty thanks to you all, for listening to my tale, which spirits willing, will be continued on my next visit.

There was a roar of appreciation as he left the hall.

The following morning, thanking his hosts, he bid them farewell. As the cobbler's wife straightened his collar as done many times for her sons, he lightly kissed her forehead.

In the house opposite, a ruddy faced man ducked through into the gloom to inform the lady within, she had been summoned.

Megan returned him a look of dismay and then almost at a run, took the shortest route to the grand hall. Behind, she could hear the murmur from the crowd gathering down at the east gate. Ahead, the hall had that deserted feel. She knocked the sounding board. Impatiently knocked again. Finally, a worried face appeared. It was a maid, left to keep the fire tended. Megan was told, 'Yes there was a court gown that needed alteration, but she was not party to the details.' Then as if addressing one who should have known better, added, "Everyone's down at the east gate."

The Teller, acknowledging all the well-wishers, nudged his horse forward through the crowd. He scanned all the faces, but the one who meant the most, was not there. He had been handsomely rewarded for his efforts, but could hardly remember what he had said to the chieftain or in fact to the Seer who had clasped him as if unwilling to let him go. He had felt numb and none of it had seemed to matter because the one person who did matter, for some reason had not appeared to bid him farewell.

The children following his departure down the palisaded entryway, seemed almost annoying. He took the path leading south knowing all eyes would still be on him. Something made him turn and looking up, he saw her. Megan was standing on the highest section of palisade. Her wave, sent a jolt shivering up his body and he waved back.

'I hope you find your stone temples,' *came a silent cry from the heart. Megan watched through tears as the Teller rode from sight.*

As his horse plodded on, his thoughts churned and he reined in. 'Will the spirits allow me? Should I return for Megan?'

Epilogue and sketch maps

Having finished the tale, I felt quite weary and was actually wondering myself, 'So what happened next? Did the Teller give in to that compulsion to return?' Probably the same as you, I was hoping he would.

Well, I'll tell you what, I subsequently found out and it's nowhere near as simple as that. In fact, I was quite surprised. So much so, I wrote about it in the third volume.

The author.

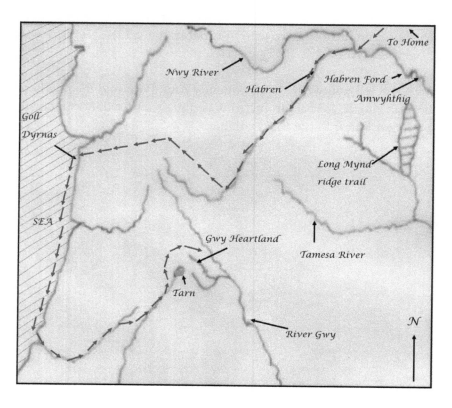

Rough sketch map showing route taken to Gwy territory

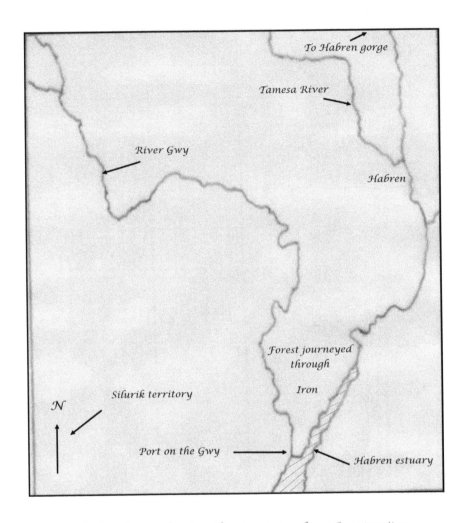

Rough sketch map showing the river route from Gwy territory to Habren estuary

Ingram Content Group UK Ltd.
Milton Keynes UK
UKHW010929070623
423006UK00001B/18